BURY MY HEART WITH A KEYBOARD

Also Available From Jacy Morris

1000 Pieces of Sweet (Coming Soon)
The Abbey
The Drop
Killing the Cult
The Lady That Stayed
One-Shot (Coming 2025)
The Pied Piper of Hamelin
The Taxidermied Man
An Unorthodox Cure

One Night Stand at the End of the World Series
One Night Stand at the End of the World
One Night Stand in the Wastes
One Night Stand in Ike
One Night Stand in a Place with No Name
One Night Stand in the Box
One Night Stand in Beaver… Utah

The Enemies of Our Ancestors Series
The Enemies of Our Ancestors
The Cult of the Skull
Broken Spirits

This Rotten World Series
This Rotten World
This Rotten World: Let It Burn
This Rotten World: No More Heroes
This Rotten World: Winter of Blood
This Rotten World: Choking on the Ashes
This Rotten World: Rally and Rot
This: Rotten World: Tempered in Blood
This Rotten World: Up in Flames
This Rotten World: A Plague of Locusts

BURY MY HEART WITH A KEYBOARD

A COLLECTION
BY
JACY MORRIS

Editing by Erin Al-Mehairi
Exterior formatting and illustrations by Don Noble
Interior formatting by Katherine Silva

ISBN (Paperback): 979-8-9868455-7-9
ISBN (Digital online): 979-8-9868455-6-2
First paperback edition September 2024
Published by Third Estate Books
https://www.thirdestatebooks.com

TABLE OF CONTENTS

FOREWORD

I write a lot. This isn't a brag so much as it is a confession, like when someone goes to an AA meeting and declares they are an alcoholic. Every day, I wake up, and I'm thinking about what I'm going to write. Sometimes, I dream about writing. I am consumed by it.

That being said, I am not a patient person. When an idea pops into my head, I am ready to attack it, to see if I can transform the ephemeral into words on a page, literary alchemy, conjuring my nightmarish visions in the reader's mind. As far as I'm concerned, writing, in all its forms, is the only form of magic humanity possesses. To envision the downfall of the world and make it feel real, as if you can smell the smoke and rot… well, that's one hell of a trick.

As a result of the combination of my prolific writing and impatience, I am not the best at submitting stories and waiting for responses. I don't have the time for that; I'm always onto the next thing. Time is the one thing none of us have enough of, and to wait for good editors to read these good pieces is something I can't afford. Most of these stories were submitted once. After their regrettable rejections (It's hard to get published in this world.), I shuffled them off to the dark corners of my mind. At the end of 2023, I looked at this pile of work, and decided I should probably do something with these things, as I love all these stories in their own way.

Included within are three novellas and eleven short stories. This is my 2023 in writing, minus the stories I published or which were accepted by publishers. The novellas are fever dreams of destruction. I hope you enjoy these crazy rides. The short stories come in two forms. Five of them were written for specific submission calls, and the remaining six I wrote for my first public reading on Black Friday 2023 at Rose City Book Pub in Portland, Oregon, an event I dubbed "Not Thankful: A Night of Indigenous Horror." These stories are all my brand of Indigenous horror, sharp cuts slashed by a knife whose handle is crafted of outrage, its blade forged of concentrated pain.

While some readers might not consider all the stories in this collection to be Indigenous, I propose that they all are, whether they feature Indigenous characters or not, because that is a part of who I am, no matter what time of year it is, or what color my skin is at the time. The characters may not specifically be Indigenous, but the ideas behind the stories are. I exist in two worlds, and these stories reflect this duality. In the winter, as my skin pales, much like Daniel in Sieg Hair, I can pass for white, because I am indeed half-white. In the summer, as my skin tans, I can only pass for Indigenous, and I drive slower and prepare to have eyes upon me when I enter a store. So don't be fooled by the non-Indigenous characters because you never know what's on the inside.

These stories are my babies, my bastards, unloved, unfed, withering away in their mass grave. Bear witness to them, so that they might head onto the next world able to say they lived, if for but a moment, in your mind. Thanks for attending their wake. Sorry about the smell.

SONGS OF SORROW

Acknowledgement of Your Land Acknowledgement

Thank you very much for your acknowledgement. I hope it had the desired effect. I hope your life has been made better by this statement. I hope all vestiges of white guilt have been purged from your soul as the language of my people was purged from their mouths with beatings and isolation. This is a fair trade.

I hope your virtue-signaling gains you the appropriate status among your peers, of which we do not seem to be considered as such. I hope they call you an ally and a champion of people of color. I hope people mention "how powerful that was."

Again, I acknowledge your acknowledgement.

Now, I will acknowledge what your self-serving, unctuous acknowledgment does for me, as I can't help but see what it does for you. I thought you'd want this gift. Another fair trade.

I sit in a staff meeting, rolling my eyes, wishing I could be anywhere but here as people who believe even less in a land acknowledgement than myself are forced to repeat the drivel set forth by someone who was probably well-meaning, but totally ignorant, as the well-meaning frequently are. I grit my teeth as the people around me chant with all the fervor of an Indigenous child being forced to read the Pledge of Allegiance.

In this way, I am transported. Your words conjure a portal through which I step, whole-heartedly, the screams of the suffering pulling me away. Names of people broken, obliterated, slaughtered, and shuttled off to the nether-regions of America parade through my head. My mind conjures visions of the dead rotting in fields, visions of men defending their homes, women, children, and elders running for safety as red holes spring forth from their backs and blood pours from their wounds. Green grass is painted red, in the name of land. This we can all acknowledge.

Thank you for this hell. Thank you for this vision. It's good to be reminded of what was done. Not good like, "Oh good, my favorite TV show is on," but "Oh good, I had almost forgotten why I am the way I am, why I stand up and say what I say, why I write what I write."

Your land acknowledgement is my own personal version of the Necronomicon. Together you chant the words and transport me to a place where the rules don't make sense, didn't make sense, and will never make sense. Where the dead wander, asking, "Why?" I have no answer for them. I just hope they won't swallow my soul.

Thank you for speaking about us in the past tense, for transforming me into a living ghost who walks the lands of a people presumed dead and gone. Thank you for the monument you built to our people, whom you honored with a concrete and asphalt mausoleum poured over their bones. Thank you for the tombstones marking the spot where their spirits left their bodies—high-rise apartment buildings, acres of black asphalt, sidewalks to damnation.

I acknowledge your acknowledgement, but I also kinda sorta can't wait for this trend to end and for the next thing to come along.

WHATEVER DIES, STAYS

The shovel rested against the staircase, the blade gleaming, apart from one spot where a stubborn clod of dirt had bonded to it. Normally, Jason wouldn't have brought the shovel inside. He tried to keep a physically clean house, as there was no hope of him ever having a spiritually clean one. But today was a different day, a day when he could stop caring.

It felt good to let it all go, to deny the routines he clung to, insidious addictions forcing him to keep himself alive and healthy. A part of him worried someone would show up, find him living in his own squalor and filth. But no one he knew would show up. He was the last one alive.

He sighed, exhaling the weight of the world and its expectations.

The evening sun shone through the curtains, orange and warm.

The sunset. Could be my last one.

Jason relished the daytime, relished the quiet in the house. At night, things were different.

He opened the front door and stepped out onto the porch. The railing was new, white, hand-painted by himself. He didn't know why he bothered. No one else would have. Hell, no one would have bought the house in the first place, not with its morbid history. But that was a nighttime thought. It was day now, his last one on Earth… maybe.

On the porch, he eased himself into a rocking chair, pulled a rectangular package from his pocket and slapped it on his wrist a few times. He opened it as a child opens a Christmas present, relishing the tearing of the cellophane, the plucking of the foil.

He eyed the cotton filters. With grit-stained fingernails, he plucked a cigarette from the package on the verge of giddiness. His wife Patty had made him give them up years ago. Said he'd have a stroke, and then she'd have to wheel him around in a wheelchair and wipe his ass for him, and she wasn't going to do it. So, he'd given them up for her, given up lots for her. He wasn't bitter about it, but if he knew now what he knew then, he would have smoked the whole time. Maybe then he wouldn't have had to watch her wither away to nothing.

No. No negative thoughts. Not today.

He lit the cigarette with a match, had plenty of those around, as at night he could only partially rely on the house's electricity.

A woman walked by the house pushing a stroller, and he nodded at her, smiling and waving. Nothing could ruin this day.

Through a cloud of smoke, he watched the sun descend, setting into the west, the orange light bathing his face in its radiance.

When the gloom of twilight overtook him, he moved inside. The summer had been bad for mosquitos, and despite all the homespun remedies his wife had taught him over the years, he found the best way to avoid being eaten alive was to flee inside when the sun disappeared.

A pall of quiet clung to the walls. It would only last so long. He headed to the kitchen and readied his candles, replacing the stubs with fresh ones. He had candles scattered about the house, and his pockets always bulged with matchbooks. He didn't even try the lights. The harsh glow of light bulbs seemed to make them angry, and he didn't want anything to ruin his plans.

He flipped open the lid of a cardboard box, exposing a dozen painfully sweet pastries, cream-filled and iced to within an inch of being more frosting than doughnut. He plucked out a chocolate eclair, stuffed it in his mouth, and chewed. The sweetness hurt his teeth. He hadn't been to the dentist in a while, not since Patty died. Didn't see the point of it. Teeth were for others. There was no one here to care what his teeth looked like, whether his smile was yellow or white.

The bruised world outside darkened, and he lit his candles, breathing in the acrid stench of sulfur and reveling in it. *Can the dead smell?*

From the cupboard he pulled a tumbler, fished in the icebox for a handful of cubes. He unscrewed the top of a bottle, dumped the potent contents in, swirled it around so the ice cubes tinkled like the wind chimes Patty had loved. He took a sip. The shit was bad for the heart, but that didn't matter anymore either. Hell, it might be easier if his heart did explode tonight. He took another sip, savored the burn. *All the good stuff hurts.*

He took his drink to the kitchen table, sat down, and flipped open a photo album. She was there, looking back at him, healthy, her eyes glowing. He was there too, brown-skinned, full head of hair, less of a gut and more of a paunch. They were happy then. He hoped Patty was happy wherever she was.

A great sigh escaped his lips.

From the foyer, he heard another sigh, wondered which one it was. There were several options. He flipped the page, watching his life flit by, him and Patty, Patty and him—no one else. They had been each other's worlds. They didn't need anything else. But then, along came Marzipan, and suddenly, there were less pictures of them, and more of their orange cat, fluffy and pillow-like because Patty couldn't stop feeding the guy. To be honest, neither could he.

When Patty died, from the cancer, Marzy had comforted him like no one else. Then Marzy had gotten sick—nothing to do about it. That's just what happened to cats when they got older.

A shape walked by in the hallway, growling, its cold, blue feet slapping against the wooden floors. Jason looked up once, just to make sure it was one he recognized and not something new. The little girl—she was going upstairs, just like always. Somehow, she always started downstairs. A scratched record, the needle stuck in a groove.

He'd tried not to pay attention to the history of the Holgate House, but the realtor who had sold him the place had insisted on transparency, almost seemed to revel in it. No one understood why he wanted to buy the place. Before he'd come along, most people assumed the house would be torn down, some bank would buy it, smooth over the history of the place with wrecking balls and bulldozers.

The town knew about the Holgate House. Everyone knew about it, though few people believed it. The house had sat on the market for almost a decade, collecting dust and falling into disrepair. Until Jason came along, carrying a cat who was dying of cancer under his arm.

Despite his prognosis, Marzy remained upbeat and happy, even as he learned a new house. He liked the backyard the best, never strayed too far.

A bang came from the hallway, loud and violent. Jason jumped, as he always did. How could you not? Wasn't no way to get used to something that shouldn't be making sounds in the first place.

Ronnie Holgate stomped through the house, pushing open doors with his hollow hands, banging them against the rubber stops Jason had installed after he'd plastered over the holes created by the doorknobs.

The ghost poked his head in the kitchen doorway, sneered at Jason sitting at the kitchen table. He growled, his teeth pulled back from those ghostly choppers, and then he rushed at Jason. He'd seen it all before.

Just as Ronnie reached him, he vanished in a puff of smoke. Jason breathed outward, his breath coalescing in the frigid air. The candle flames wavered on the table but stayed lit, even as Jason reached for a book of matches from his pocket. Didn't matter how many times it happened, he always expected Ronnie Holgate to crash into him and knock him to the ground. One time he wouldn't be a puff of smoke, but cold hard flesh. Another thing he didn't need to worry about any longer.

Upstairs, ghostly boots clomped across the floors. He took a sip of whiskey from the tumbler.

Not too much longer now.

In the corner of his eye, the wife appeared. Marnie Holgate, complete with flour-stained apron. She puttered around at the stove as if something was actually cooking on it. Jason hadn't used the stove in a long time, figured it belonged to Marnie, the way the stove at his old house had belonged to Patty.

A scream upstairs. Though no one standing outside the house could hear it, inside the house, it set his teeth on edge, could send a man running to help or to hide. The house's walls prevented the noise and the violence from escaping to the outside world. A house was an absorbent thing. Energies were like that. His wife had taught him this.

Fill a place with smiles and happiness and that feeling can seep into the walls like cigarette smoke. Only difference was you could paint over nicotine-stained walls. The type of energy that had been unleashed in this house wasn't anything you could cover up. Maybe someday Miller would make a paint that could paint over spiritual energy, but that day would come long after he was gone.

Marnie heard the scream, dropped an invisible pan of something on the floor. It landed with an audible clang, though he couldn't see the pan or its contents. Jason liked to think it was something simple, something that wouldn't have taken up too much of her last moments, maybe eggs, something like that.

She rushed from the room as Jason took another sip of bourbon. He knew the rest of the tale, had read the police reports, heard the whispers from his neighbors.

He'd watched it all go down a few times, tried to figure out if this was the place he wanted to be. When Marzy was still alive, he'd cling to Jason during these hours. In Jason's head, he thought of this part of the evening as Bang Time. All sorts of bangs going on upstairs. Doors, knees on hardwood floors, fists on skin. Screams were a sort of bang too, could set your heart racing just like a shotgun blast.

Jason flipped the page in the photo album. There'd be plenty of time for what was going on upstairs. Today, he was downstairs, looking at pictures of his wife, his cat, both.

He wished Patty could be here with him. Even though she had been all sorts of non-traditional spiritual—crystals, tarot cards, spells—in the end, she went the way of her parents, burial in a cemetery, the same one as her parents though in a different corner. That's the way cemetery plots went. Get 'em while they're hot, or else you'll be across the yard.

He didn't blame her for it. Lots of fear to be had when one is staring down the barrel of the end. All sorts of doubts and musing about the afterlife crept in. For Patty, she'd become a believer in her last days, wanted to be buried like her parents had. Millions of people couldn't be wrong, could they? Hundreds of millions? A billion?

Jason didn't know. All he knew was what he could see, and what he saw in this place, well, it had given him some ideas.

Upstairs, the sound of the shotgun went off. One bang. The daughter. He took another sip, pulled his lips back from his teeth in a pained smile.

Two. The mother.

He flipped the page—him and Patty in their wedding get-ups, back when all their friends had still been alive, and before the loving couple figured out they couldn't have kids, had been forced to settle for pets instead. There had been cats before Marzy, but none like him.

Kind as a kiss, Marzy loved his people more than any pet he'd ever shared his life with. Some people claimed dogs were more loyal, loving pets, and Jason guessed they were for the most part, but he'd take the best cat over the best dog—and Marzy was the best.

In the end, when hospice had come in and hooked up Patty's wasted body to tubes in preparation for the end, Marzy had stayed by her side, his tail curled around her, his cheek pressed to Patty's. Marzy knew what time it was, wasn't no doubt, and while Jason felt as sad as he'd ever felt in his life, he swore the cat felt it more.

He moved houses more for the cat than for himself. Couldn't stand looking in their bedroom and seeing old Marzy curled up on the bed where Patty had slept. He thought the change of scenery had done them both good, even with the… goings-ons.

The sobbing began, and for once, Jason joined in, reveling in the sadness of lost life. Only difference was, unlike Ronnie Holgate, he hadn't killed his people. Marzy had passed away in his lap in the middle of the day. He was glad of that. He knew the specters in the night scared him with their loud noises.

But it was all for the best, all for the energy.

The house had been infused with something awful, the spirits of those cut short had been splattered against the walls. And then the coup de grace.

The third bang. There it was. Old Ronnie Holgate, overcome with his rage and sadness, turned the shotgun upon himself, put it up under his chin like a camp counselor telling ghost stories with a flashlight. He'd launched his brains through the top of his head, sent his soul crashing into the ceiling along with 'em. Now he was part of the house.

The house was paid in full, in more ways than one. He'd gotten a hell of a deal on the place… you know, because no one wanted to buy the fucking thing. He'd bought it in cash with the money from selling his old house, had made plans with his accountant to keep the house unlived in for a while—told him he was going on vacation, to see the world. The accountant had all the money he'd need to pay the property taxes even after he was gone. Wasn't no one to leave his money to, and dammit, he didn't know how any of this worked. Just theories really. But he thought maybe a house needed to be left alone for a while for it to take. It was like a stain on a shirt. Throw it in the wash immediately, and you got a chance to get it out, but throw it in the hamper and let it sit for a while, and the fucking thing is done for.

Just in case time was the key, he'd provided for such. At the end of ten years, it would be put up for sale when the money ran out. Someone else would buy it. By then, it'd be a nice fixer-upper, a good starter project for someone who needed the equity. They wouldn't stay long, not with the Holgates running about, but equity was king. Get out what you spent plus more when you decided to move. He just hoped no one else had an idea like he had—didn't want the place to get too crowded.

When Patty died, his head had cleared, sort of. Marzy kept him on his toes, kept him going to the store, kept him showering and taking care of himself. Though he never seemed to mind how filthy Jason got, he knew how sensitive his little nose was, tried to smell nice and be presentable for him.

He'd started thinking about the afterlife, had read a story in the paper about the anniversary of the Holgate Massacre, and his wheels had started turning.

Now he was here, listening to the sobs of Ronnie Holgate as he floated through the house—his blue, bare toes trailing three inches off the wooden floors, his arms slack, black blood dripping from the gruesome hole in the top of his head.

Marnie was there as well, her apron painted with the red stuff, on her knees, smearing invisible blood around the floor with a sponge. The kid would be upstairs, rocking back and forth in mid-air on a small rocking horse only she could see.

Most people would have fled, but him and Marzy weren't most people. *Marzy's a fuckin' cat!* He smiled and drained the last of his bourbon. The Holgate's sobbing would continue for hours, until midnight when they would fade away and content themselves with causing chaos around the house. Knocking over dishes, making the taps drip, slamming doors.

That shit didn't bother him. Comforted him really. Made him feel like maybe his plan was going to work after all.

It was about time, so he poured himself another bourbon, threw in another couple of pieces of ice. Before he went out back, he stuffed a cruller in his mouth, squeezing all the air out with his jaw and compressing it into one sweet ball of dough. He chewed with his mouth open. It seemed the closer he got to the end, the more like a kid he became.

It blossomed in his chest now, pushing the sadness out like an unwanted guest. Hope.

Out back, the darkness of his secluded yard spread away into shadows. As he closed the door, the incessant wailing of the Holgates disappeared completely, and he worried once more that his plan wouldn't work, that the yard wasn't technically a part of the house. But a house wasn't a vault, couldn't block all the energy contained within. It had to seep out, right?

His theory ran through his head once more in the gloom. The ice cubes tinkled against the glass as he tipped it back once more. *Whatever dies, stays.*

In the dark, he moved to a shadow on the ground, four-feet-wide, six-feet-long, six-feet-deep. His blistered hands proved he'd dug it himself. He lowered himself inside, stood looking up out of the hole at the moon above. A full moon. Patty would have been proud.

He closed his eyes, ignored the thought he might be crazy and that nothing in the house was real and had all been in his head the whole time. He wrinkled his brow and concentrated on the night. It was quiet now. The crickets, bewitched by the moon, held their chirps, kept their legs frozen in place as they too appreciated the cosmic eye above.

Jason's ears opened wider, and he allowed his senses to fill his mind. The wind, soft and rustling as it flowed through the treetops. The furtive sound of something moving through the grass. He smiled, knew that sound.

Marzy.

He lay down in the bottom of his grave, wrapped the end of a rope around his forearm.

Not too much longer, sweet one.

From the earthy hole, he tugged on the rope. A contraption above, metal and hanging, dumped one-hundred-and-forty-four cubic feet of dirt onto Jason, and before he could change his mind, he was suffocating. His body strained against the earth, fought for life despite the wishes of his brain and his heart.

It was a while before the struggling stopped. A while still before he grew cold. A while longer before he could leave his tomb. When he did, the moon was absent, and he stood on a patch of bare earth showing the first signs of green growth. He felt something brushing against his ankle, followed by a soft, ghostly purring. When he looked down tears came to his eyes.

A CHEMAWA THANKSGIVING

Victor didn't have a lot to be thankful for. Huddled in the cafeteria, a draft blowing through the doors, cold air pouring off the single-pane windows, Victor tried not to focus on the things he missed, tried to focus on the good things, but the bad things were so much more… bad.

He felt guilty still being here, still surviving while his family lay in the ground outside, chilly November rain seeping into the soil and wetting their bodies. It had been splashing down for some time now, the type of rain that got into your bones if it managed to touch your skin. He hoped it would stop by the time Monday rolled around.

On Monday, Old Thompson would take them out into the fields, have them start digging, tearing up the ground in preparation for the spring planting. He much preferred the cobbling lessons he'd first been given when he went from being his mom's son to being an orphan and a ward of the Chemawa Indian Training School. But he'd butchered a few too many pieces of leather for the headmaster's taste, and in turn, had been relegated to "farmer" in their eyes.

He hated farming. If he ever got out of here, something for which he prayed every day, he would never farm a day in his life. He'd go to live in the cities he'd heard about, where there wasn't a tree for miles, and the ground was layered in concrete like a cake covered in frosting.

As he pictured this cake in his mind, perfect and wonderful and round, and covered in so much frosting your teeth hurt just looking at it, his belly grumbled. It had been a long time since breakfast. There were only two meals on holidays. They didn't want Indians getting fat at the training school. What type of message would that send the parents if their children came back pudgy and soft, if they came back at all? The government men who stopped in periodically to check on them would throw a fit if they saw a bunch of plump Indians running around, but they didn't seem to bat an eye whenever they noticed a fresh mound of grassless dirt in the cemetery.

He squeezed his eyes shut. You're doing it again.

But he couldn't help it. Couldn't stop thinking about them. People had been walking on eggshells around him all month, ever since his brother died, followed by his sister, his mother, and then his little sister, Minnie. After Dad left, Mom had taken a job as a housekeeper at the school, because she said she wanted to be close to her children as they received their education. He was the last one left now, an orphan, gone from running and playing and being one of the few Indian kids allowed to roam as he wished, to being a prisoner, one of the sullen-faced little boys and girls who sat with their heads down, trying to conjure images of better times.

A male soldier in uniform, who demanded everyone call him Lieutenant Gunderson, stood up, all pomp and circumstance, straightened his uniform as a good soldier should, and then ran a metal rod around the innards of a triangle. The conversation ceased immediately. The Lieutenant always received the respect he was due, one way or another.

Blinking tears from his eyes, ignoring the concerned looks from his schoolmates, Victor lifted his head, locked in on the Lieutenant's words.

"It has been a trying time this last month. I know that, but for today, at least, we can be thankful, for the Lord above, for the bounty He has provided. Eat well, rest tomorrow, know that God above loves you all, loves the ones we have buried, loves the ones who are still here."

It was a remarkably soft speech from the Lieutenant, a man quick with the rod when a boy didn't seem to understand his role at the school. He treated them like soldiers, expected them to walk upright, say "Yes, sir" and "No, sir" when spoken to. He expected perfection in all areas, from work to play. If you didn't live up to his standards, a quick cuff to the back of the head or a visit to the Lieutenant's house would learn you.

The Lieutenant lifted his hands, and everyone rose at the same time, their conversations forgotten and ignored for the time being. Prompt execution of instructions was another of the Lieutenant's demands. While he wouldn't deign to walk across the cafeteria and hit a kid who might have risen slowly, many of the students here had been summoned to the Lieutenant's house afterward. When the offender showed up later, hobbling and laying on their stomachs in bed when the lights went out, everyone knew why.

Victor had been to the Lieutenant's house several times over the last few weeks. As he'd begun to train with the other students, he had discovered a tendency to wander in his mind. There he'd be, shaping a piece of leather with a pair of heavy-duty scissors, and then his mind would meander off on its own, wander back to the time when he still had a brother and two sisters, and a mother, but not further back than that, not to the time when he'd had a father, a man not unlike the Lieutenant, but perhaps a little drunker, but just as prone to teaching lessons with the back of his hand. Off he'd be, remembering their time in Siletz, when they lived in a small, two-bedroom house, piled on top of each other, when they'd go to the local schoolhouse, a small one-room affair, where the teacher actually liked you, didn't look at you like you might be something they'd tracked in on the bottom of their shoe.

In the midst of these memories, the handful of happy years of his life, he'd awaken, as if out of a dream, to find Mr. Lattimore standing there, a cross look on his face, as he began yelling about the ruined leather in his hands. "Report to the headmaster, Davis."

Oh, that walk. In some ways, the walk was even worse than the beating, the anticipation of pain somehow worse than the pain itself. Across the campus he'd plod, past the girl's dormitory, past the fields lying fallow after harvest, past the main building where they gathered for church (blech) and dinner, and onto the Lieutenant's hut, perhaps the nicest building on the property, certainly the nicest Victor had ever been inside. The Lieutenant's house was twice the size of the home Victor had shared with his family, the furniture rich and shiny, lacquered so you could see a shadowy reflection of yourself in the wood grains as you bent over to take your punishment. But before that, before the pain, came the anticipation, each grudging step bringing you closer to suffering.

And somewhere in the back of your mind, you were also aware that Lieutenant Gunderson could kill you, had probably killed dozens of Indians in his time. He'd fought wars against tribes, done his duty as he liked to say, had the medals hanging on his wall to prove it. In church, they say it's a sin to kill people, but then, outside those uncomfortable pews, in the real world, here's a man wearing treasure for doing it. It didn't add up in his mind, but that's the way a lot of things worked.

Victor's biggest fear was that the Lieutenant would snap, paddle him into a puddle, and dump him in the cemetery with his family. The first strike of the paddle was almost a relief, a distraction from the worry of the whole affair.

"Davis!" an adult snapped at him. He'd done it again, drifted away.

The kid to his left, Larry, shoved him, propelling him forward. He walked between the rows of long cafeteria tables, headed to the food line, speeding up to fill in the gap he'd left when he'd lost track of the real world and journeyed to one of the painful places.

At the end of the food line, he waited, craning his head to see what they were going to eat. Most of the time they were served cheap meals, stuff that could be ladled into bowls, stuff you could cook all at once in a pot. These meals included all the nutrition they'd need to grow big and strong, but not fat, never fat. Stews and soups dominated the menu, so today was a special day. Actual food you could chew, a gift, a reminder that somewhere inside, the administrators of this school were human.

Victor didn't know if he wanted them to be. It was almost more depressing to realize they had emotions and hearts, were capable of showing kindness to students, when so often they showed nothing but coldness, as cold as the brick walls around them. What's worse? A monster? Or a human who acts like a monster? A monster is what it is, can't control its nature… a human who acts like a beast… well, that had to be worse, right?

"Come on, come on," the cantankerous cook compelled, urging the kids to hurry their lazy butts through the line. Victor picked up his tray, turned sideways, and shuffled along the line. *Actual turkey, stuffing, mashed potatoes.* Steam rose from the food, and for the first time, in a long time, he thought about something else, was present in the here and now, not being pulled away by the ghosts of his family.

The cook dumped a spoonful of peas and carrots on his plate, perhaps the only part of the meal he wasn't excited for. He'd had enough of those in the twenty different variations of soup he'd eaten over the last month.

He cycled through the line and returned to his seat, holding his tray with trembling hands. If you spilled your food, that was it, tough break, kid—there were no seconds, not even for an accident.

At his seat, he stared at the food, refusing to eat it. For now, it was good enough to look at it, let the smell crawl up his nose and curl up there, settle in like a dog making its bed. He studied the turkey, prodded it with a fork to lift it up and study the browned skin on the outside. That was the best part. He followed the grain of the meat, tracing it with his eyes like the mazes the students sometimes drew for each other on the back pages of the Bibles in church. The mashed potatoes seemed a little lumpy, bits of brown skin hidden throughout the cream-colored clouds. The stuffing sat rough and clumped, bits of greenery hiding in there, the slick shine of onions reflecting the light from the bare bulbs above.

Off to his left, Larry Flathead reached over, almost got his dirty fork into his turkey before he slapped him away.

"What?" Larry asked. "If you're not gonna eat it, give it to me."

"I am gonna eat it."

Larry was an alright guy, but always hungry. He'd grown several inches over the course of the last few months, couldn't seem to stop growing. At night, in the bunkhouse, Victor fell asleep to the sounds of Larry's stomach grumbling, trying to eat itself to make Larry grow even taller. Sometimes, Victor gave him the last of his soup, but today's meal was off-limits.

Larry shrugged, decided to eat his own meal slower. No one was dismissed until everyone was done. Those who rushed through their meals had to wait until everyone else finished.

Victor picked up his fork, scooped a mouthful of potatoes onto the tines, and placed them in his mouth. His eyes closed on their own, hid the world away so he could better taste this fluffy concoction, buttery and creamy, hot enough to take some of the chill of the day from his bones. Once he got that first taste, he couldn't resist, couldn't slow himself down, and forkful after forkful entered his mouth against his own will.

"Jeez, you musta been starving," Larry said.

Starving. Like his sister out in the cemetery. Living among the worms. His appetite evaporated. His food had stopped steaming, and he remembered a time when his sister had first tasted turkey, back when they'd lived with "him," before they'd come to this place. It was a memory he'd carry with him forever, the shocked look on her face, the widening of her eyes, the dimples in her cheeks as she couldn't help but smile. He poked at the turkey on his plate. The skin had been her favorite part as well.

With the side of his fork, he pressed down around the edge of the turkey, separated the skin. He looked side to side, made sure none of the staff were walking between the rows, and then he plucked the severed string of turkey skin from his plate and stuffed it into his pocket, glancing around once more to make sure no one had seen.

He raised his hand in the air, waiting for someone to come by.

He heard the click of boots behind him, looked back to see Lieutenant Gunderson standing there, a smile on his face for once. "What is it, Davis?"

"May I be excused to go to the restroom, sir?" Never 'Can I be excused?' Always 'May I.' A month ago, he'd seen a new kid piss his pants in confusion because of this fateful word choice.

"You may be excused, Davis."

Victor rose from his seat, headed to the end of the cafeteria, turned left, and stepped into the gloomy hallway leading to the restrooms. He walked calmly, only glanced over his shoulder once, and then he sprinted for the main door. Once outside, he ducked low so no one would spy him through the windows, sprinted away from the building, the cold rain pelting him. He dodged the puddles as best as he could, knew he would be in for it if he came back with sodden shoes and wet pants.

Onward he rushed, down the path, angling toward the trees in the distance where his family spent their days. The cemetery felt different in the dark, scared him in a way it shouldn't have.

In the gloom, it took him a moment to find their graves. He found his sister. Above her grave stood the wooden cross he'd been forced to make, already fading, the incessant rain draining the wood of its strength and color. He ran his fingers across the bronze plaque, small like Minnie, set in rough, pitted concrete so it wouldn't blow away in the wind.

He didn't mean to, but he sank to his knees and had to resist laying across her grave. "I brought you something, Minnie."

He fished the turkey skin out of his pocket, dangled it in the air like a hypnotist's pocket watch.

The ground pushed upward, pulsed underneath him as the rain intensified. He scooted backward, gave her room to grow. Her hands appeared first, pressing up out of the earth, her brown skin pale, mud pouring off her arms where the rain washed it away. The arms bent at the elbows, like grasshopper legs, her palms resting against the muddy ground. She pushed, and her head appeared, the skin pocked and marked by decomposition. Worms tumbled from one of her eye sockets, and her hair hung black and long, weighed down by clumps of mud.

"Minnie," he sighed.

Her mouth opened as if to speak, and more clumps of dirt, and other, whiter, wriggling things fell out instead.

"I brought you something."

She smiled, her teeth showing through a hole in the side of her cheek. Victor leaned forward, slid the chunk of prized turkey skin between her teeth, and then waited patiently for her to close her mouth. Her jaw ground up and down, and he sat back on his heels, smiling at her, talking to her as he'd done so many times, big brother taking responsibility for little sister.

"When I get out of here, I'm gonna take you with me, you, mom, everyone. We'll move back home, next to the river. It's quieter there, you'll see. You'll like it."

He talked more and more, telling her about what was going on, letting her know she wasn't really missing anything, but that he missed her and loved her. When he was too cold to feel his fingers, he stood, regarded his wet pants, and knew he'd be visiting the Lieutenant. But he didn't care. Minnie was happy. That's all that mattered.

As she descended into her grave, and he patted the mud down so no one would know about her, he said, "I'll see you soon."

With that, he turned to go back to the cafeteria, ready to take his medicine. His chest constricted with a booming cough that made his head swim. He spat a wad of phlegm onto the ground, and continued onward, wrapping his freezing arms around himself, not even bothering to dodge the puddles anymore.

THE PRETENDIANS

Sometimes it seems the more people are around you, the lonelier you are. On the reservation in Idaho, he had felt lonely, longed to see the world outside, longed to escape the grasses and hills and tumbledown huts, to instead be surrounded by people going places and doing things. But now, in the suburbs of Portland, he had re-discovered the old loneliness, found himself even more isolated than on the reservation. At least there, he had family. Loneliness swells and festers much like the bite of a snake upon the ass. You need someone else to suck the poison out, and even then, you're still going to die—probably.

That's sort of why Ben Lovesee was here, sitting on a bench in a gloomy tunnel, lit by LED lights, their glare supposedly softened by waffled grids overhead. He held out his hand, young and strong, the fingers defined from hours of coding. The concrete tunnel stretched away into the distance, miles of darkness on either end. If he wanted to, he could walk to the end of the Max platform, ride an elevator up twenty-six stories, and step out into the cold November daylight, continue walking, and maybe take a tour around the zoo.

Holidays were the worst of times for him. He didn't give a shit about Thanksgiving, or all the food, but damn if he didn't just want to be around people like himself.

Funny, they tell you to go to college, that this is the way to improve yourself, to help your family, to make a life. No one tells you when you're done, you have skills that are only worth money in certain places.

Coding… no one needs coding on the Fort Hall rez.

The same way no one needed a guide, so Sacajawea, a distant relative he supposed, had been forced to leave her people, dying in her twenties in someplace named Saint Louis—nothing saintly about it from the things he'd read online. If he could have gone back and redone his education, he would have been a teacher or a doctor—there was always need for those on the reservation.

But that's the thing about college, once you choose that path, there's no going back. A college degree is a straitjacket. The government locks you in with loans, interest, falsehoods like the ticking seconds of a clock. Pay me back or pay the price. But what would the price be? Going broke? Going back home? Sometimes, sitting in his shitty, cost-controlled apartment, he considered giving up. Considered quitting and living and breathing free until someone came to kick him out.

Oh, he knew people, got along well with everyone—just didn't connect with anyone. In his office, a square-honeycombed hive of business-basic, chest-high cubicle walls, he toiled alongside a bunch of Indians, not like the type you'd find on a reservation, but the type you'd find in actual India. They buzzed with chatter amongst themselves, smelled the same, ate the same type of food, went to see movies produced in the language of home. They'd invited him out a few times—they weren't mean—but he'd failed to connect nonetheless, didn't know how to bridge the cultural gap between himself and the "real" Indians.

Sitting at home, over the Thanksgiving holiday, he had found himself reclining in his sparse living room, staring at the TV, knowing nothing on the screen could cure the lonesomeness coursing through his veins. He'd reached into his pocket for his phone, tried to figure out what he was going to do about it, typed a string of letters into the search field.

The number came up immediately, and he studied it—just had to click the link to get someone on the other end of the line—someone from the Suicide Prevention Hotline. Ben shook his head, pressed the back button on his phone to navigate away from the incriminating page. He wasn't there yet. In his chair, one of a handful of pieces of furniture he'd bought for his apartment, he said, "Three million people in the Portland area, and I'm all alone."

An idea crossed his mind then, images of a basic-looking woman and a basic-looking man in flannel shirts finding true love. He'd seen it on the TV a few nights ago. *What was that site called? Farmers Only?* He switched the words up, typed *Natives* instead of *Farmers*, and then scrolled through the results. The first website he came to was literally called NativesOnly. com, and it was—much to his disappointment—a website about plants and what regions they were native to. Not quite what he was looking for, although, if things continued like this, he might have to go out and buy himself a plant.

His apartment didn't allow pets, or he would have gotten a dog, maybe a cat. He worked long hours, so a cat might have been more appropriate. The company he worked for didn't give two shits about how many hours they worked you, just wanted to squeeze every last drop of work out of you before your contract was up, so when the time came, and you realized how shitty the job was, there would be no hard feelings when your contract wasn't renewed. But yeah, a cat would have been nice. *But a plant? Eh, let's consider it a last resort.*

A site caught his attention… *NativeBuddies.com.* With a thirsty finger, he clicked on the link, a smile dawning on his lips. It took him a few moments to input his data, a few more moments as he decided if inputting his debit card number was a wise move, which he decided it was. Loneliness makes you do dumb things sometimes, but hey, if he got a friend out of it, then that would be fine.

Once he was in the site, it was like any other dating app—pictures, profile details, strange, attention-seeking catch phrases. He wasn't totally comfortable making his own. His magic came in the form of coding, not in self-promotion. He scrolled through his photos to find something that would make him not seem like a lonely loser. He'd taken one picture in his living room, but the emptiness of his apartment made him look like a hostage in a third-world country, begging someone to give the kidnappers what they wanted so he could go home.

Finally, when he was ready, he hit the "save changes" button, leaned back in his chair, and waited for the invites to pour in. After fifteen minutes, he gave up on that, pulled up the NativeBuddies app—there's always an app—and began proactively scrolling through the people on display. Some of them were obviously fake; you had to read through a lot of scammy profiles to find the real ones. Most of the fake ones seemed to be low-level escort scams filled with typos and all sorts of suggestive emojis. He scrolled past these until he settled on a black and white picture of a man.

He read through "Dave's" profile, eyes scanning, mind keying in on phrases and words that were important to him—"technology," "video games," "friends." His heart racing in his chest, Ben Lovesee sat in his chair agonizing over the message he would send "Dave." Ten minutes later he regarded his first draft… with utter disbelief. The words that had escaped him, been tapped out by his traitorous fingers, sounded… well, they sounded like he was looking to hook up, not hang out.

He closed the app, leaned over with his head between his knees, and bashed his inert phone against his head. "Stupid, stupid, stupid." If only he had a friend to help him out, but all his friends were back at home, doing reservation things, or off in other cities, trying to get out from underneath the mountain of debt that marked their "better lives." And, if he had a friend with him, he wouldn't be doing this in the first place, right?

He went to his favorite AI program, typed in a string of key words, hit enter, and smiled as it spit out something totally generic, but at least not… pervert sounding? After a quick copy and paste, he tapped so hard on the send button, he was surprised he didn't crack the screen.

Then he sat back in his chair, his heart hammering, wondering if he'd made a mistake. *What if the dude responded? What if he was some psychopath who collected Indigenous skin and wore it around his house?* "I guess you're never alone if someone is wearing you," he laughed.

A small scream escaped his lips as his phone buzzed in his palm. Sweat beaded on his upper lip as he opened his phone with trembling hands, found the multi-feathered app icon, and tapped on it.

He'd almost cried reading the response. It was so… friendly, so thoughtful. "Of course, I'd love to meet you. Us Natives gotta stick together. The city can be a crazy place sometimes, right?" From there, they'd traded messages back and forth, decided to meet each other halfway since neither of them had a car, then they'd get to know each other on the Max while they traveled into the city. More to do down there, don't ya know.

So now, here he sat, a heartbeat away from bolting to the elevator and riding it to the surface to go and look at the penguins in the zoo. He always liked the penguins, even if their pen smelled like bird shit and bacteria-filled water. Their rounded bodies, stubby legs, and sleek feathers always put a smile on his face. *But no. I have to stick it out.*

Another train squealed to a stop in front of him, and he tried not to stare at the people as they departed. At this time of night, only a handful exited, and they did so with the stoney faces of people just trying to get home after a long day of work. The doors on the Max slid shut, and it took off, squealing along the rails.

Maybe he won't even show. Would that make me happy or sad?

As the people left the platform, crowding into the elevator, only one person remained—a Trimet cop who swaggered down the platform as if he owned the damn thing. His pudgy face screamed "total bastard" to Ben. When he spun on his heel and began walking in Ben's direction, he couldn't help but feel the flush of fear. His stomach dropped as the cop stopped in front of him.

He'd been sitting here too long, was too brown to loiter.

"Noticed you didn't get on the train."

Ben tried to look the man in the eyes, but found an emptiness glaring back at him, almost as if the man was talking to the bench upon which Ben sat instead of Ben himself. He tore his eyes away from the void and said, "I'm waiting for someone."

"Uh-huh."

"He should be here soon."

"If he's not here by the next train, I'm going to have to ask you to leave. This isn't a homeless camp."

"Uh, sure," said Ben, anything to get this heartless symbol of authority out of the area.

The cop turned and began whistling as he walked away, didn't even bother to turn back around and see what Ben was up to. He wore his authority like armor, had bludgeoned Ben into subservience with his uniform.

Ben leaned back, opened the app on his phone to see if there were any new messages. He spotted a red dot underneath the feathers on the app's icon, tapped on the image, and then read greedily, "I'm here."

"What? Where?" He scanned the platform, looked across the tracks at the curved wall arching overhead, its tiles painted with shadows of wildlife and native plants in sunset tones.

From the west end of the tunnel, a man appeared, rail thin, his head skinny and balding, thick glasses perched on his nose. The hair on the top of his head was combed over to the side, and a thick, bushy mustache hid the upper half of his lip. The man somewhat resembled the picture from the app, but something was off. His skin was… paler than he'd expected. Maybe that's why the photo was in black and white in the first place.

Nervous sweat sprouted from Ben's palms, and sensing a handshake or some sort of greeting, he wiped them on his jeans as he stood up.

As the man approached, plodding softly across the concrete platform in his generic white tennis shoes, he stopped a foot away, held his hand palm up, and said in a deep voice, "How," in mock greeting.

Something about the whole interaction revolted Ben. Alarms blared in his skull, but he forged onward, driven by the whip of isolation. "Dave?" he asked, hoping this was some sort of mistake.

"Dave is my reservation name. Now I go by Proud Chief. I'm Cherokee."

"Oh, ok. I'm Ben Lovesee, Shoshone, Lemhi band."

"A pleasure to meet you. I'd like you to meet the others."

Then they appeared, one by one, materializing from darkness at the ends of the tunnels, dressed in Pendleton patterns, feathers and jingle bells dangling from their clothing, dreamcatcher earrings hanging from their pale ears.

"What is this?" Ben asked.

"The Tribe of Portland," Dave assured him, a smug smile upon his face. "You'll never be alone again."

A blonde-haired, blue-eyed woman approached Ben, said, "Hello," and introduced herself as Sacheen Morning Fire, also Cherokee, on her great-great-great grandmother's side.

Another man, freckled and wearing a leather jacket complete with movie-style fringe, introduced himself as Warrior Two-Foot. "According to my Ancestry.com report, I'm two-percent Navajo."

Ben backed against the wall as they crowded around him, hitting him with tribal names, Cherokee, Navajo, Apache, Sioux, tribe after tribe, claim after claim.

What have I done?

"You're one of us now," said Proud Chief, aka Dave, producing a small bundle of sage, lighting it on fire with a lighter, and wafting pungent, tangy smoke over himself with stiff, reverential hand movements. One by one, the Portland Tribe followed suit, producing their own smudge sticks and smoke until Ben could barely breathe.

"Where is your sage?" Charley Kills-the-Man asked. He was part Apache.

"I… I don't have any."

"What are you? A Pretendian?" asked Proud Chief.

"No, I uh, just don't "

They regarded him coolly, their faces grim and emotionless. "He's not one of us," said Charley as the others crowded around him, bells jingling, smoke wafting in cloudy drifts.

"Not one of us."

"What a waste of beautiful brown skin."

"Not one of us."

"I'd trade anything for your hair. Scalp it right off."

"Not one of us."

They pressed against him, reeking of sage and fry bread oil, pressing into him, hungry.

Ben began to choke, began shoving them away, men and women, and even little children, carrying their Ancestry reports in their hands, with pale, pudgy fingers, but it was no use. They pressed and surged, packed in so tight, his chest could no longer rise and fall to draw breath. With his last lungful of air, he forced out a primal, vocal-cord shredding scream for help—from anyone, from the police, from the children-killing government, anyone! But the voices of the Tribe of Portland, dozens and dozens of them, drowned out his cry. They smushed against him until his skin split, until his eyes bulged out of his head, the left one eventually popping out and resting upon his cheek.

"Such a beautiful shade of brown."

They kneaded him like dough, his juices squirting out, dripping onto the cold platform. The children dropped to their knees to lap up his essence.

"Am I three-percent now, Daddy Proud Chief?" one child asked.

"Yes, yes, you are."

As the time dragged on, and Ben Lovesee could feel pain no longer, the Tribe of Portland drifted away, their greedy mutilations obscured by a cloud of sage smoke. A Max train zoomed by, scattering the pungent mist of sage, leaving behind only an empty platform, twenty-six-stories underneath the ground.

THE OMEGA WOMAN

The last Native American sits in a rocking chair amidst waving grasses, a cat twining about her legs, dodging the chair's rockers as they come perilously close to crushing her tail. Smoke curls up from a cigarette clamped between fingers the color of tea.

She rocks back and forth, remembering the days when there were others of her kind out there, brown people with fire in their hearts, constantly nursing the wound of having a continent severed from their soul so many generations ago. It's a lonely time, a time to die, a slow death with alcohol, cigarettes, processed foods her body immediately turns into fat.

She sits outside, because inside, there is nothing, not in her house, not in her body. Coldness lives there, a frigid emptiness begging for the end of time.

Her elbow contracts, has lifted things heavier than this cigarette in her lifetime, the chilled hands of parents on their deathbeds, the handle of a small coffin paraded across cold autumn grass and settled over an open hole in the ground, a finger extended to those who would use her for their own gain.

Funny thing about being the last of your kind. People want to see you, touch you, the way they came to see Geronimo when he was a prisoner of war, and they cut him loose like a falcon for a day so people could see how he killed. He took down a buffalo for their entertainment, and they went away happy. On his deathbed, he reportedly told his nephew he never should have surrendered, stating what everyone already knew.

Nancy Douglas, not a particularly Native American name, but the one she was given, handed down through marriages and broken lineages, takes a drag off her cigarette, tries to feel the spirits around her, as she has done from time to time throughout the entirety of her life, thinks maybe she feels something, someone calling her, telling her it's time to go, the people are waiting for her on the other side.

But then it's gone. The gates have opened, and she can feel the eyes on the other side of the glass. She is protected, partly from herself, but more from people who want to touch her almond skin, run their hands through her silver-black hair, braided to keep it out of the way as opposed to any sort of tribal homage.

Her breath rattles in her chest, and the silence of her world hits her once more.

They wander by her cell. She is their fish, not the salmon who leaped out of the water to feed her people, but a goldfish, tamed and shiny, fun to look at for a few minutes. They come in a steady parade to see the last Native American. Her tribe doesn't matter anymore, never mattered to the gawkers, and there's no one left to appreciate the difference between a member of the Nez Perce and a member of the Confederated Tribes of Siletz.

They wave at her. The children press their faces to the glass and blow on it, their cheeks puffing out like puffer fish, and she smiles for them, her eyes squinting shut. The children never did nothin'; she can spare them a smile.

Then onward they move, checking out all the other, non-living exhibits, stuffed buffalo, the salmon itself, mounted on the wall, its tail in mid-flap, the shiny plastic water fashioned to look like it had just leaped from its surface. All the other extinctions of man, line the walls like trophies in a lodge as the world bakes outside.

The cat rubs against her ankle, and Nancy bends down and picks her up, marvels at the survival skills of the creature, imagines cats will be here long after she's gone. The cat meows and turns a lazy circle before settling in her lap. The cat has a name, but she's never shared it, likes to keep her secrets. Nancy stubs out her cigarette on the arm of the rocking chair, pets the cat with her hand, reveling in the sensation of soft fur upon skin. *At least they brought these things with them.*

A pain strikes her chest, and she throws her head back, finds it hard to breathe, tries even though she doesn't want to any longer. Her arm goes numb, her mouth dry, cold sweat blossoms all over her skin. She reaches to her chest, kneads it with one hand, her other stroking the cat in her lap. If she can take the sensation of fur with her before she goes, if she can hold onto that as her last memory before oblivion, she thinks that will be just fine.

Above, the sky drifts by lazily, the screens above on a never-ending day-night cycle. She longs to see the real sky above, the gray smudgy thing they've turned it into, even if for just a moment.

Her eyes squeeze shut, and the sensation of cat fur fades away, as she does, lifting into the air, gazing down upon her sad body. The last of her kind. Fuck it.

She floats upward, bumps against the screens and their fake sky, presses into the cloud that looks like a dragon, a cloud she has marked a thousand times over a thousand days. And, she can't get through, can't find her way out. She presses against the cold glass, but it refuses to let her through. She doesn't belong to herself, never did. She's trapped.

Below, the cat on her lap glances up, watches her float around. She licks an orange paw, marbled with white, like an ice cream float made with orange soda. She hops off the chair, looks over her shoulder and carries herself over to the door, sauntering in that "I-know-it-all-and-expect-it-all" sort of way cats have.

She stares upward, pointing the only way she knows how—with her eyes—at a vent among the ceiling screens. Nancy rolls, a nebulous energy, somehow able to contort herself across the clouded ceiling. At the vent, she thins her essence, tapers her new being into a spear, slips through one of the square holes, and journeys through darkness, deep and dark and fearful. After an infinity, she spots a light, and glides toward it, hoping to meet all those who have gone before.

SEE ME

Huh, her bed hasn't been slept in.

Fiona Hauser's first instinct was to be pissed. If her daughter Mel was going to live under her roof, then she'd better for sure live by the damn rules, and one of those rules was you didn't stay out all night, not without letting her know.

She rushed through her house, perpetually covered in a layer of pet dander and fur from the strays her daughter always brought home. Though Fiona had found homes for most of the strays, a few of the animals Mel brought managed to find their way into her heart. Such is the way with strays.

One of the strays, a permanent member of the family, looked up at her with blinking eyes, meowed, as if to say, "Where is Mel?"

"I don't know, kitty. I don't know."

Fiona strode through her house, steaming, and then the steam went cold, condensed in her heart, and turned into the fear all parents feel when they're not sure of their children's whereabouts.

Mel was her only child, and she'd never wanted another. Raising her on her own was a trial, one with its ups and downs, but she wouldn't have given it up for the world, even if this unplanned miracle had locked her into poverty, working for slave wages at two, sometimes three, different jobs. But you had to do what you had to do. While the child she'd raised wasn't perfect, hadn't seemed to find her footing in this world yet, that's the way it is for most people.

The world wasn't made for success anymore. It was made to keep you down, one foot on your throat while the other kicked you in the ribs.

Mel hadn't fallen that far, still had dreams of going to college at some point, but for now, she was living free, the only price for her room and board the following of Fiona's rules, which sometimes led to arguments, but most times led to love, the appreciation of each other's presence, because life didn't go on forever… didn't go on for all that long at all in the grand scheme of things.

Fiona glanced at her phone. No messages, nothing to tell her mother what Mel had gotten up to. "Spoiled little brat," she muttered under her breath, not feeling the words, just wishing that's all this was.

Her fingers flew as she fired off a message. "Where are you?" Send.

Wait, suffer, wait some more, get pissed, get worried, start panicking.

Four hours later, after multiple texts, Fiona reached out to some of her daughter's friends—didn't just text them, actually pulled up the keypad on her phone and dialed them like a prayer.

"You seen Mel?"

"No."

"Uh-uh."

"Not since yesterday."

The hours rolled by, and she thought of Winona Ryder in Stranger Things, started wondering if she should pull out the Christmas lights from the overstuffed closet containing all her holiday decorations.

Day became night, and after a quick drive through town—small, rundown, no place to hide if you were planning on that—she went back home, hoping to find Mel sitting in the kitchen, staring at her phone while shoving slices of buttered toast into her face, that damn cat sitting on the table, even though Fiona had told her not to let it sit there a thousand times. A fight would ensue, a glorious fight, not a fight to make one storm from the house, not one they would even remember a week down the road, but the type of fight that lets you know someone cares, that they didn't not give a fuck about you. A good fight. A love fight.

When she pulled into her driveway, the gravel crunching under her wheels, the house sat dark, and tears fell from her eyes.

I'm being stupid. She leaned against the steering wheel, her forehead pressed against its rubbered, contoured hardness. *She's an adult. She can handle herself.*

But can she? Can she? What if she picked up another stray, another animal, but not of the four-legged variety?

No. No. No.

She ran inside, plugged her phone into the kitchen outlet and stewed there, her phone in her hands, waiting for it to ring, buzz, explode into a thousand fragments, waiting for Mel to let her know she went to the quarry with her friends and their car broke down, or they got a wild hare up their ass and decided to go to Vegas. The coffee dripped in time to her tears, and she gripped her phone in her hands, firing off messages more and more frantic in nature, their tone shifting with each silence.

Mel, you better get your ass back here. I'm so pissed at you right now.

Text me, please. I just want to know you're alright.

Did I do something?

I know you're an adult, but your ass is grounded when you get back home.

And so on and so on, until the coffee in the pot was gone, and the sun came up, and then she knew. Something was wrong. Mel wasn't coming home. The certainty settled into her chest like Oreo, the way-too-overweight black and white cat who sometimes slept on her breast in the middle of the night, constricting her breathing, making her sit up gasping and sweating. Oreo didn't know any better. Neither did Mel. She'd always been too trusting, always been one to follow her heart instead of her mind.

But Fiona knew, had learned that lesson a long time ago when it came to Fiona's father. She should have done something when she was younger, whipped the trust right out of her, but she couldn't. In her daughter, Fiona saw what she had used to be, what she could have been, and selfishly, she allowed Mel to continue as she was, perfect, joyful… but she shouldn't have. She shouldn't have.

In the car outside the police station, she sat in the parking lot, fearful, wondering what they would do to her. Would they turn this on her? Was she going to get Mel in trouble? What if Mel was up to no good, and the police found her, ruined her perfect record, gave her a black mark she could never leave off her résumé?

Better that than to never know.

She stepped out of the car, moved aside as a white man rumbled up the sidewalk, no apology, no nothing.

Shaking her head, she continued to the police precinct, pulled the door open, and stepped inside. It wasn't like the movies, a bullpen with dozens of cops all walking to and fro, toiling away on paperwork. There were only a handful of people here—a matronly woman behind the desk, a uniformed man sitting off to her left, a couple of weary citizens waiting on a bench running along the wall.

Fiona took a deep breath, though everything she felt told her to run from this place, that this was the place people went to die, to be assigned a slow death in cells, and later be released to an even slower death, the stigma of their sickness preventing them from living normal, pain-free lives. But still she went… for Mel.

She stood in front of the matronly lady, her lips painted garish red, her round head bedecked with poorly colored curls. The lady's head stayed down, those unnatural curls frozen in place, the stench of excessive hair spray stinging Fiona's nose, the flavor of it crawling in the back of her throat.

Fiona cleared her throat. Nothing.

"Excuse me," she said.

Nothing.

Now she was really in a pickle. Thinking maybe the woman wasn't the person to talk to, she moved over to stand in front of the cop. He was older, his hair gray and short, his face lean, the cheeks drawn inward as if he was sucking in his breath at all times, as if something inside was trying to slurp his skin inside his skull.

"Pardon me," she said.

The cop lifted his head, looked right through her, reached for a stamp, clamped it down on a paper with a satisfying k-chunk, and shuffled it off to the side. He reached for another stack of papers, important things, the records of lives ruined, his head drooping down to focus on the paperwork.

"I need help."

K-chunk.

"Can't someone please help me?"

A man in a suit, a badge hanging from his waist, pushed through the half door at the end of the desk, and Fiona moved to step in front of him, confront him. It was all she could think to do. The man didn't seem to see her, steamrolled her right to the ground without so much as an apology.

She sat sobbing on the floor, her legs bent underneath her.

"They can't see you," a woman said from the bench.

When Fiona looked at her, she saw things she had missed when she walked in. Initially, she had assumed the woman was old, due to the gray in her hair, but upon closer inspection, she saw the cobwebs there, growing down from her hair and hanging to her shoulders. Ancient mummy dust make-up darkened her face, and her clothes were coming apart at the seams. The rubber of her shoes had melted into the floor, not just puddling, but becoming a part of it. Her brown arms were wrapped around a little boy, his face slack, his eyes empty.

Fiona didn't understand.

Unable to swallow this information, she responded the only way she knew how. "I need someone to help find my daughter."

"I need someone to help find my son," the woman said.

"How long have you been waiting?"

The woman shrugged. The fingertips resting on her son's arm were splayed, spread out as if her brown skin was sinking into his.

"I'm not like you," Fiona said.

The woman shrugged, a bit of dust fluttering from her hair and onto the floor.

Pushing herself off the ground, Fiona mustered all the outrage she could find. What did it matter if it landed her in jail? With her daughter gone, the world had already become a prison, barless, yes, but a prison, nonetheless.

"Fucking see me!" she shouted. Her voice echoed throughout the precinct, loud, proud, ignored.

She strode up to the desk, snatched the k-chunking stamp out of the uniformed policeman's hands. He continued the motion however, stamping the papers with air, before shuffling them from one pile to the next.

In frustration, she flipped the stamp around in her hand, pressed it to the man's forehead.

K-chunk.

More shuffling, more stamping.

"What the fuck is this?"

She strode over to the doughty woman with the abysmal curls, slapped her across the face, snatched the papers out of her hand. Still the woman continued her robotic gestures, going through the motions, the slow grind of the law's bureaucracy.

"I'm going to fucking kill you!" she screamed and threw the papers in the woman's face. They drifted to the ground like autumn leaves, spreading about her and settling to the floor.

As Fiona was about to climb over the counter, her phone buzzed in her pocket. Frantic, she reached into her jeans, pulled the phone out, fumbling it before unlocking it with her thumbprint.

"Amber alert? A fucking Amber alert?"

She didn't even read the description.

Around her, the officers went into a frenzy, hopping out of their chairs, running out to the motor pool with their keys in hand. The woman at the counter picked up a phone, dialed a number, and began talking to someone on the other end. "Missing child, blonde hair, blue eyes, age twelve, last seen at the Gas and Sip."

Fiona spun, bewildered by the action as the police precinct cleared out, but for the droning woman on the phone.

"It always happens like that," the woman on the bench said. "Some white kid goes missing, it's all hands on deck."

Fiona understood now, got the gist of it all, let her phone drop to her side, moved to the bench against the wall, sat down. It was comfortable at least.

SCUZZPISH

"Scuzzpish." Angus said the word aloud the first time they saw it, the mirth of pronouncing the word apparent in his voice.

Brian had seen the word as well, had been playing with it in his mind as soon as he spotted it emblazoned in bright orange spray-paint on the facial stones of a short tunnel.

"What the fuck is a Scuzzpish?" Angus asked.

"Beats me."

They lapsed into silence, two men out on an adventure, on a quest to bring home fish and stories to tell their wives who were probably happy to have them out of the house. The two men were longtime friends, ever since the confused wilds of middle school. As adults, they'd made it a practice to get away from the world and fish every few months or so.

This time, they were headed to Hills Creek Lake, 389 square miles of lake filled with three types of trout and one type of crappie. It was a new lake as far as things went, formed in 1961 when the Army Corps of Engineers had built a dam for electricity. Their home base would be the sleepy town of Oakridge, a small blip on the map, population 3,201, so insignificant you couldn't even drop the little yellow guy on the google map to take a look around.

As they neared the town, they hurtled by a large boulder on the side of the road, the words "Beware Scuzzpish," in the same frantic, orange spray-paint. This time, they both said the word, laughing at their timing.

As the sun set on Oregon, they pulled up to the Airbnb, scoped out a place to eat, and headed over after securing their important goods in their rooms: fishing rods, bait, a cooler full of ice and beer. Their twelve-foot fishing boat would take care of itself, and from their spot in the bar, they could keep an eye on it through the front windows if anyone started fucking around with it.

They crossed the street and entered a dingy dive dubbed The Corner, a smalltown joy, serving up burgers and chicken strips with a homey baseness only those who had grown up in a small town could enjoy. There was no aioli, no fucking truffle oil, none of that fancy Portland shit the hipsters put on the burgers and fries to ruin them. Just beef, and oil, and potatoes, and cheese... all the basic food groups.

The bar's beer selection left a little to be desired though. For as much as Brian disdained gourmet food trends, he had a different outlook when it came to beer. Dejected, he ordered a Coors Light and bellied up to the bar. Angus elbowed him in the ribs and said, "Get a load of that guy. He looks just like Sam Elliott."

Brian pretended like he had something on his chin, wiped it on his sleeve so he could peek at the man in question. Angus was right. He looked a little bit like Sam Elliott, only a little skinnier, more "old timey prospector" looking. On his upper lip, a bushy gray and black mustache bloomed.

When Brian turned back to stare at his brown face in the mirror behind the bar, he said, "Don't."

"Don't what?" Angus asked.

Angus knew damn well what Brian meant by the simple warning. Everywhere they traveled, Angus had the annoying habit of striking up a conversation with the local folk. It was his way, and Brian hated it. He just wanted to drink his beer and eat his burger in peace, but Angus was always one for adventure.

Brian looked down at his brown hands, wondered if he'd encounter any redneck racists out here. A guy resembling Sam Elliott... who knew what a guy who looked like that believed?

To his relief, Angus swiveled his bar stool and stared straight ahead. He was a good guy, but too trusting. Of course, he could afford to be. He was one of them, had the right skin tone for the sticks. As far as Brian could tell, he was the only brown person in the town, not that he had seen much of it, or that there was much to see. A few restaurants, a couple motels, a gas station-slash-grocery store.

They passed the evening easily as the sun vanished. He could breathe out here, though he knew there was always the potential for racism to rear its ugly head, but it happened a lot less than one would suppose. Though, all it took was one time for you to worry about it forever.

He was thinking about a time in Clatskanie where he and Angus had basically been chased to their truck when some drunk rednecks had gotten it in their head that Brian wasn't white enough to drink in "their" bar. But that wouldn't happen here. Everyone was too happy. In his circumspect studying of the mirror, he'd spotted no one with that sneer on their face, the one that festers in the lips and eyebrows when one human is revolted by another human's very existence. The people who thought this way were all too stupid to hide the look on their face. It was an easy tell, and one he'd noticed before. In those situations, he'd finish his beer, tell Angus they should turn in for the night, and off they'd go.

But tonight was different. Tonight was a happy night. Oldies played on the bar's speakers, and the Coors Light, despite being slightly warmer than he preferred, went down easy. He was contemplating ordering another when a man clutching a pool cue leaned up against the bar to Angus' right, a mustache like the end of a broom.

He waited patiently, tapping his foot to *Jack and Diane*, or Sucking on a Chili Dog Outside the Tasty Freeze as Brian liked to think of it. The waitress was too busy making yet another vodka and Red Bull to take Sam Elliott's order.

"Fuck," Brian muttered under his breath as he felt more than saw Angus turn on his barstool.

"Anyone ever tell you that you look like Sam Elliott?" his friend asked.

The mustachioed man turned then, his yellow teeth peeking through under his bristles. "Why yes, I have heard that a few times." The man's voice was high-pitched, squeaky, and tinged with madness.

Angus, you fucking idiot.

But Angus was undeterred, and he struck up a conversation with the man, whereupon he learned all about his son who ate three pounds of beef a day and refused to get a job. They learned about his no-good wife, and how he was going to leave them all one day. Then they learned his name.

"Kip," he said as he shook Angus' hand. Brian waved hello at him from the other side of Angus, wondering how long it would be until Kip went away.

The waitress took his order and delivered the man a Bud Light. "Say," Kip said. "How much you wanna bet I can beat you at pool with one arm?"

Fuck again. Angus wouldn't be able to resist a bet like that.

They staked five bucks on it, and Brian turned to watch as Kip, holding his beer in one hand and his pool cue in the other, proceeded to wipe the floor with Angus. Despite his misgivings, Brian was impressed. Kip played pool better with one hand than either he or Angus could with two.

When the eight-ball finally rolled home, and Kip had revealed himself as nothing more than a harmless drunk with strange familial problems, Brian couldn't resist. He asked the question that had been on his mind all evening. "Hey, Kip, what the hell is a Scuzzpish?"

The wiry man's mouth dropped open, and his eyes darted around in their sockets as if they were trying to escape his head. He leaned his head down, dunked his mustache into his pint before he spoke. "Uh, oh, uh… that's what you might call a local legend," he screeched.

"But what is it?" Angus pressed.

Kip walked over to a rack and slid home his pool cue, which he hadn't let go of for the entire evening. Then he turned, picked up his beer, and walked back to the bar, leaning forward so he could make eye contact with both Brian and Angus as he spoke.

"Well, y'all are going up to the lake, right? I saw the boat when you come in, figured you was up to some fishing out there at Hills Creek. It's a new lake, you know. They put up the dam about 1960 or thereabouts, but do you know the reason they put up the dam in the first place?"

"Electricity?" Brian ventured.

Kip shook his head and took another sip of beer. "Nope. That's what they told people, and maybe it's part of the reason, but the real reason is because of the Scuzzpish. The Scuzzpish is like a local legend around here, but back then it was more of a local reality. Hard to find, easy to fear, you know what I mean?"

Brian nodded his head, eager to hear the story. He loved local legends, though Oregon was historically new enough to not have many to call its own, other than the Native American ones he'd heard as a youngster.

"Well, the Scuzzpish is what you'd call… territorial. Ain't no one seen it because in order to see it, you'd have to go into its territory. And its territory is like one of those old roach motel commercials. You remember those?"

"You can check in, but you can't check out!" Angus said.

"Precise-a-mundo!" Kip hooted. "Anyway, this one's territory, lord knows if there are others, is right smack dab in the middle of that lake. Rather than just having people disappearing all the time, they put up the dam, flooded the land and so forth. Now no one dies. Although, every year or two, some good folks like yourself say they saw him out there."

"What's it look like?" asked Brian, intrigued.

"How the fuck should I know? Do I look like a fish? Anyway. Don't worry about it. Scuzzpish ain't nothing you need to worry about."

Kip spun away then, pulled his pool cue free from the rack, and plunked a couple of quarters into the slots on the table, driving the tray home. "Want a rematch?" he asked Angus after he'd racked the balls.

"No thanks."

"Suit yourself. I can use my left hand this time."

"That's a sucker's bet," said Brian, and Kip flashed his yellow teeth at him.

"Sucker's born every day," he said. He broke the rack then with his left hand, the cue ball smacking heavily into the balls, sending several into the corner pockets.

In the morning, feeling rested and ready, they loaded up their gear and headed out to the lake, the memory of the night's entertainment bouncing around in their heads.

As they pulled up to the boat launch, Angus said, "We still don't know what a Scuzzpish is."

"It's bullshit," Brian said. "Just some local gobbledygook rustled up to freak out out-of-towners."

"Yeah, but they could tell us what it looked like at least."

"Why would they do that? The unknown is more terrifying than the known."

"I think it's like an underwater bigfoot."

"Ok," said Brian as he climbed into his boat.

"What do you think it is?"

"I think it looks like a pyramid, all swirly at the top, and it's brown and smells like something that comes from a bull's rear-end."

"Ha ha!" laughed Angus as he climbed into the boat. Brian cranked the outboard, and they muddled away from the shore, pulling their baseball hats low on their scalps. It was midday, and the noontime sun shone down bright and hot, the wind whisking away some of the summer heat, but not enough to keep them from sweating.

They settled into a space in the middle of the lake, far from the houses and docks that existed near the boat launch, where kids played in the water. *Scuzzpish couldn't be all that real if people let their kids swim in the water.*

His line dangled in the lake. On the small radio they'd brought along, they caught a staticky signal coming from Eugene some fifty minutes to the northwest. The music sounded tinny and foreign, even when it was a song he recognized.

Angus was busy reeling in his line. He could never let it sit, didn't trust that something hadn't come along and nibbled off the worm he'd impaled on his hook. Somewhere down the line, Brian would grow annoyed with his constant reeling and casting, but he wasn't there yet.

Angus hauled his line over the side of the boat, pulled out a bottle of spray juice, spritzed his worm, and then cast the thing into the lake once more. Brian shrugged and took a sip from his beer, a nice cream ale with a picture of a pelican on the side of the can.

They sat in silence, boats gliding around them as the sun traveled overhead.

"Nothing's biting here, man," Angus complained.

"It's not about the fish; it's about the getting away."

"Yeah, well, when my Judy sees me coming home with nothing in the cooler, you know how she gets." He did his best impression of his wife. "So, who is she? Where's she live?"

Brian smiled, feeling for Angus because he knew it was true. "Good old Moody Judy."

"Don't let her hear you say that," Angus said.

"I won't."

The time passed, the sun swirling overhead. The beer cans emptied, seemingly on their own. As the sun turned orange and began to dip down behind the pointed fir trees dotting the hills to the west, they knew they were going to go home without a single bite.

"Welp, I guess that's it," Brian said.

"Sometimes they bite, and sometimes they don't," Angus said. It was what they said whenever they came home emptyhanded. Saying the words made it feel better, reminded them that this whole trip wasn't about the fish. It was about spending time together, appreciating their friendship, watering it so it continued to grow.

Brian reeled in his line. He'd checked it a few times that day but found the same worm clinging to it each time. He usually replaced the worm when that happened. If you put the little guy out there in the middle of the water, dangling them as bait for a massive fish, and they made it through, the least you could do was throw them back in the water so they could crawl around on their own, live their life for a bit.

Just as he was about to pull his line into the boat, he felt a small tug. He whipped his wrists, set the hook, and then let the line play out. Whatever he'd hooked took off like a shot.

"You got one?" Angus asked. "You son of a bitch." Seeing the look of pure joy on his friend's face, Angus rebaited his own hook and flung it out into the water in the hopes he could join in on the fun.

Brian called for the net, and Angus scrambled across the bottom of the boat, rocking them back and forth. "Holy jumpin'!" Angus said as he scooped the fish out with a green, nylon net. "It's at least a foot, man."

"Foot my ass," Brian said. "That's sixteen inches or I'm your mother."

They unhooked the beast, weighed it, and tossed it in the cooler. Just as Brian sat down, Angus tossed his line into the water.

"Hey, what're you doin'?" he asked.

"I'm not letting you have all the glory," Angus said.

Brian shrugged, fished in a Styrofoam container of earth with his fingers, questing for another worm to put on his hook. Once baited, he cast the wriggling offering into the water.

"Night feeders," Angus said.

"Yuh," Brian answered.

For the rest of the evening, they pulled fish after fish into their boat. First Angus caught one, then Brian, then Angus. It was unlike anything they had ever experienced in their lives. By the time Brian realized how late it was, he had swapped out his fish in the cooler several times. The law said they were only allowed to keep two.

"Makes you wonder," Angus said.

"Wonder what?"

"If the fishing's so good out here, why no one else is around."

Brian studied the glassy surface of the lake, noting their solitude. No one else was on the water. But that was ok. The lake was out in the sticks. It was the end of summer. People were getting back to their everyday lives as their vacation days ran out.

With a sudden clarity, Brian realized he hadn't pissed all day. His beers finally caught up to him and he stood in the stern of the boat, hanging worm over the water. He trickled away. From behind him, Angus said, "Good idea." More trickling.

In the dark of the night, with the stars twinkling overhead and the water lapping gently against the side of the boat, they both experienced the pure pleasure of relief at the same time. And then something strange happened.

"You hear that?"

"Hear what?" Angus asked.

The sound came again, as if air bubbles were breaking the surface of the water. Brian looked down, his urine crawling back inside. At the stern of the boat, near the outboard motor, he spotted a commotion, a disturbance, as if the motor's propellers were churning the water. He placed his hand on the outboard to see if it thrummed, but there was nothing.

Tilting the outboard out of the water, his stomach sank. The motor's gearbox and propeller had been ripped clean off.

"What is it? Angus asked. "I can't see. It's too dark."

Brian fished in his pocket for his phone. Turned on the flashlight so he could get a better look. As he studied the motor, something struck the side of the boat with a dull, hollow thud. The force and the sound startled him, and his fingers spasmed, launching his phone into the lake.

"Let's get out of here," Angus said.

"We can't."

"What the fuck do you mean we can't?"

"See for yourself."

They did the boat dance, sidling around each other while trying to maintain their balance and avoid tripping over all the gear in the bottom of the boat.

The flashlight on Angus' phone blinked on, and he beheld the damage. "What the hell?"

"Looks like we're paddling home," Brian said.

Angus stiffened up. "Uh, about that."

"About what?" Brian asked.

"I didn't pack the paddles."

"You what?"

"We never needed 'em before!"

"That's stupid as hell. Just because you've never needed something doesn't mean you won't ever need it. That's why they invented shit like insurance!" Brian said. "You should know that; you sell the shit!"

Their voices echoed over the lake as they argued back and forth.

The echoes spread out and away from the boat, but they reached down into the water as well. Below the surface of the lake, the yelling of the men transformed into vibratory ripples that startled the fish, sent them scattering in the depths… or maybe it was the other being they were reacting to… the thing that lived beneath them, had lived beneath them for as long as their piscine history stretched back.

From the depths, a massive ball of air floated to the surface. It broke the water, surrounding the boat like a shining soap bubble. The reflection of the stars above twinkled upon its surface.

"What the fuck is this?" Brian asked. He picked up his fishing rod and poked at the bubble. It stretched but did not break.

"Smell's awful," Angus said.

And it did, like fish rotting in the sun. Their throats spasmed, searching for magic words that would make this all go away, but they remained silent.

With an aquatic roar, water jetted up into the bubble, stream after stream of water, as if the boat perched over some sort of fountain. The churning lake water rose, soaking their shoes, then their pants legs.

What is this? This can't be happening.

While Brian tried to make sense of everything, Angus sprang into action, began bailing the water out of the boat with his hat. But it didn't matter, the water rose faster than he could bail, even when Brian joined in. As the boat flooded, they became sure the lake was going to fill the bubble, and they were going to drown.

But then the water stopped. Their ragged breathing echoed within the bubble's confines. "Call the police," Brian said.

Angus fumbled in his pocket, pulled out his phone, drenched in water. He tried to turn it on, and then tossed it in the bottom of the boat with a splash when it wouldn't respond. His eyes grew round enough to reflect the moon above. Brian had never seen fear like that on his friend's face, and it made his heart flutter in his chest.

"We're sinking," Angus said.

"Fuck you," Brian said. But it was true. Their boat, filled with water, was disappearing under the surface of the lake. The twinkling bubble around them held strong, keeping the rest of the lake from washing over them, even though Brian wished it would burst, because then he could swim for it, try and make it to the shore.

Down and down they went, and Brian pulled a flashlight from his gear, clicked it on. All around the bubble, fish watched them with bulging eyes, their mouths set in toothy frowns, hundreds of them.

"This can't be happening," Brian muttered. Angus said nothing, just hunched into a ball, his hands clenched into fists and his eyes squeezed shut.

The flashlight played across hundreds of fish, and then their scaled bodies parted as the boat thunked into the bottom of the lake. The light was swallowed by a dark form, and Brian chased it with the light as it darted around them. At first, he thought maybe the boat had kicked up a cloud of mud, but upon closer inspection… it was… human-ish. Dripping flesh coalesced into a bare upper torso, a hundred bulging eyes peered out of its murk, and below its waist, its body flowed into the lakebed. The creature smiled at him, jagged teeth appearing in his wide, featureless head. It held out a hand, plain, not dissimilar from Brian's own but for the webbing between its fingers. It placed a lone fingertip against the bubble. It burst with an eardrum-splitting pop, and water crashed over the two fishermen… followed by teeth, thousands of teeth.

Kip went out early that morning, while the sun was still down. He walked the perimeter of the lake, looking for any leavings of the Scuzzppish. It was good business. When he came upon the boat, he shook his head. He'd liked those two guys. He shrugged his shoulders and giggled a bit. "I can beat you with no hands as well, apparently."

He dragged the boat from the water and went to get his no-good, beef-eating son to help him drag it back home. It'd take 'em a while to scrub it clean, rip off all the identifying marks, but it ought to be worth something to someone somewhere.

SONGS OF REVOLT

hAIck

Oh, God. I'm fucking killing it tonight. The audience swayed like a
kelp forest in the ocean current, dyed hair and glowing tattoos reflecting
the multicolored-stage lights. The music thumped hard. Squirt Gun
Nelly guided the songs from place to place, his head cocked to the side,
earphones clamped between his skull and his bare, bony shoulder.

His hands flew, faster than even he could see, his body bopping along
to the music.

He leaned forward, opened his mouth, matched it to the words.

You're never real.
Not as real as me.
Not as real as the hate
You and I can breathe.

The crowd swelled now, rough seas, the fawning public reaching
out for him, like that picture in the church… the one with the naked
motherfucker reaching for God. Only, now they weren't reaching out for
God, they were reaching out for Squirt Gun Nelly.

He took a second, his hands flying over the presets as he studied the
crowd, looking for prizes, kid in a candy shop style. He didn't know what
a candy shop was, but he'd heard the phrase in one of his songs, one he'd
thrown away before it could be released, before it could hit the streamers,

the commercial-makers, the product-sphere. Bad tunes could kill a man, and his place in the world was already so precarious.

*There—her. She's the one. Oh, and him. Him too. I'd like to see him suck him when she takes it in the mouth then I'll be all—*the bass dropped, a thick line no one would have thought to mix in with the bready synth reels he'd been spinning all night. But that's why they loved him. He was the Creator. His hands flew, queueing up the next valley, the next peak.

He turned his head, beckoned toward his manager, got his attention. On the screen behind him, he caught sight of himself. As tall as a football field and decorated with logos for the latest soft drink, a mirror image stood there, smiling back. He was a skeletal man, his arms junkie skinny, decorated with tattoos that looked like maybe they'd been drawn by a five-year-old. *Hell, one of 'em was.* His hair poofed, shaggy and blond, and he couldn't help but smile at himself. He was a fucking genius. Some people think they're geniuses, but he actually was one.

He winked at his manager, the synapses in his brain firing a message across to him, a message containing the faces of his three would-be lovers for the night. A stack of NDAs, some black-market Tranq of white-market quality, and he'd be in for a good night.

His manager nodded at him, gave him the thumbs up, and Squirt Gun Nelly knew, behind-the-scenes, his bodyguards were moving now to intercept the trio and bring them backstage—a gift. The music rose, electronic sounds no one could ever think of designing. They reverberated through the stadium, the language of God himself. Behind his podium, Squirt Gun Nelly grew hard, couldn't stop thinking about the lucky fucks he'd picked from the audience.

The song came to an end, and the crowd roared, screamed in appreciation. Some artists didn't even allow their songs to end. They just wanted some stream of consciousness bullshit to keep the party going. But not Squirt Gun. He needed the pause, the applause, the adulation. It's honestly the only reason he did this—well, that and the money, and the genitals. He loved genitals of all kinds. He needed his songs to stop though, needed to hear the applause of his fans, their screams. If he didn't have them, then he didn't have anything.

SGN cued up the next song, his arms flying like hummingbird wings, though he really wasn't doing fuck all of anything. The gestures, the bopping, were merely magician's tricks meant to mislead, to draw the eye away from the fact he wasn't really doing shit. The sound of drums kicked in, machine-gun fast, rattling the crowd, hitting them with one-hundred decibels of body shock.

Their hands went into the air as if surrendering, even as their feet continued to pound the dance floor. He nodded his head, knowing he had made it.

Back home, a thirty-room mansion in the hills of Los Angeles, he had more cars and more toys than anyone could ever want. And still he had money to burn.

It hadn't always been this way.

He'd struggled for years as an artist. He'd tried every avenue to become rich and famous. He'd tried painting, and even though his work looked exactly like what he saw in the world, no one seemed interested. He'd tried writing, cobbling together stories about his life on the streets, which were all fabricated and designed to make him look tough. That's when he'd started getting the tattoos, to document the life and times of Squirt Gun Nelly on the skin, a made-up past, a fabrication of hubris and pride he'd been lying about for so long he'd actually come to believe it.

His books had failed miserably. "Writing by numbers," one reviewer had typed before plopping down a shit emoji. He'd contacted the person, found out who they were and threatened a lawsuit to get it taken down. Unfortunately, they weren't the only one, and soon he gave up his litigious attacks, abandoning his writing persona and burying it deep, lest it ruin his future success. M.A. Drexel died with thirty book sales to his name the day Squirt Gun Nelly took the book down from online retailers. Thank God he'd never actually put his picture on the back cover.

Though not exactly handsome, he was good looking enough to pull what he wanted. It hadn't always been that way. When he was younger, most women of good sense ignored him, saw right through his desperate need to be more than who he was, just a suburban douche from Palo Alto. Nothing particularly special about him.

But goddammit, that wasn't fair! He was special! Why couldn't anyone else see it?

Then came the music. His last-ditch effort to appear relevant to society, to be someone, to become famous. He'd picked up a guitar because everyone who was anyone could play guitar. He'd taken some lessons, watched some YouTube videos, thought maybe he could play some punk rock, but when his fingertips started turning bloody from practicing so much, he put the guitar down. Bleeding for fame was not part of his plan.

Then, miracle of miracles, he discovered something even less difficult than punk rock. Techno… hidden under the guise of many names, this collection of digital arrangements appealed to him in a way he couldn't describe. His fingers no longer bled, and designing simple beats became his jam. Start with the beat, bring in some other instruments, all queued up and ready to go. You don't need to know how to play music when computers can do it all for you.

He was proud of his first album, thought it sounded pretty bangin'. Unfortunately, no one else agreed. One record company asked him if he was Kevin Federline in disguise. They didn't even officially reject him. They just sincerely wanted to know if he was trying to pull a fast one on them.

That stung. He'd stood on the edge of a bridge, studying the road far below, the cars zipping past underneath. One step, that's how far away he'd been from ending his life. But then he got to thinking about how much it would hurt, about how hitting the ground would obliterate his body, crack bones, splatter organs, drive the shit from his guts, and then he thought about the fall, about how he'd be thinking about the pain the whole way down, and how, maybe, at the halfway point, he might decide he wanted to live, but then it would be too late, and then what the fuck would he do? He'd scream like a little bitch, and that would be his last sound on this earth. He'd be dead and gone, and no one would know… except for the thirty people who'd bought his book, Pimp Love: How to Bang the Best.

And wouldn't that be a shame? No one would know his genius, his greatness. He could do things, man! Anything he set his mind too, all he'd needed were the tools, and then he'd found it—TWAT GPT! Thanks to the assistance of this simple tool, the entire world had opened up to him. All it took for immortality was thirty seconds in front of a screen. All he'd had to do was type in a string of words and requests, and out came a song, better than anything he could have ever done himself.

At first, he'd felt like an impostor, a huge douchebag pretending to be talented, but then he'd started justifying it, saying things like, "Well, it's just a shortcut. It's just a way to even the playing field. Right? Given all the thousands of hours a musician might spend training, absorbing music, learning theory, practicing, experimenting, anyone could do what the kings of music could do. That's all it is. The brain is nothing more than a computer, fed scraps of information like the way those two dudes in *Weird Science* fed a computer all the information needed to produce the perfect girl. With TWAT GPT, someone else had done all the feeding. He was just strolling into the house party like Robert Downey Jr. and asking Gary and Wyatt for a favor. And the best thing about it? He didn't have to wear a bra on his head.

One month. That's all it had taken. While other artists spent decades honing their craft, he'd produced a number one album in one month, and the fucking public loved it. He was a stream king, hitting the top of the charts on all the major platforms. Hell, he'd already been featured in an ad for Brown Showers—AI-run coffee makers that sensed when you needed coffee and made it for you.

The public—God bless 'em—loved his tattoos and his music—and the music was his—he'd typed the queries into the damn program himself. No one could come up with queries like him. To wit: "banging thumping techno song with love in the lyrics and the voice of an angel." *Oh shit! No one can think up shit like that!*

A woman in the audience flashed him, and he smiled at her, gave her a wink, peered over his shoulder at his manager and gave him a nod. There was plenty of Squirt Gun Nelly to go around.

His first album, *Reverse Puking*, went gold, which wasn't like as good as platinum, but no one really went platinum anymore. If you could sell five-hundred-thousand albums these days, that was like being Michael Jackson—or even better—Justin Bieber. No one did a half-mil in the industry anymore. It was all about streaming. His songs were streamed a hundred million times a day, meaning, he made two-thousand dollars every day just for existing.

But it was the tours where he really cleaned up, where he really leveraged the songs into profits. Floor seats at ten-k a pop. Nose bleeds at two-grand. A one-hour long performance would net him a cool milly in no time at all, and all he had to do was bounce around on stage and act like he was playing music.

He looked over his shoulder, his jaw dropping, just as his manager tripped over *THE* cord, the one that kept everything powered on stage. The lights cut out, the music stopped, and Squirt Gun Nelly stood nonplussed on the stage.

In all the confusion, he missed the shadowy figure darting to the hard drive at the back of the stage. He didn't notice as it bent down and slotted something into the machinery. The manager, nervous about being electrocuted to death, waited for the stage engineers to appear and plug in *THE* cord. By then, the shadowy figure had darted away, left a surprise for Squirt Gun Nelly in his equipment.

When the plug went back in, everything began to reboot. Nelly stood awkwardly behind his console, wondering if he should say something, soothe the crowd in some way.

He glanced down at his playlist, read off the song titles.

Slice Like a Poor Golfer, Cut Like a Serrated Knife
Straight Genius
I Could Be Yours
Mansion Blues
Songs is My Gift
Buncha Drrrumz

And… ah, yes. *Jigglin' Bits* was up next. When the screen behind him booted up, he had his head down. He was about to press the button that would drop *Jigglin' Bits* and its elephantechno beat, when a collective gasp went up from the crowd.

A quick glance over his shoulder, and his jaw dropped. The screen was no longer dominated by the current version of himself, but rather by a younger, hungrier version. The massive skyscraper screen shook with the grainy cell-phone footage, a vertigo inducing image that made the entire arena feel like it was spinning.

"What are you doing?" a woman's jet-engine-loud voice asked over the speaker stacks, a voice he knew.

"I'm making an album."

"What?" the woman asked, the amusement apparent in her voice. "Since when did you become a musician?"

"Check it out. I just type something in here," the sound of keys clacking on hundred-foot-tall stacks of Bose speakers assaulted the crowd. "And boom! Out comes a song."

"That's not music," the woman said.

Squirt Gun Nelly knew the voice, had loved it once, back before he was famous. Had fallen out of love with the voice when perfect-tens started looking his way, when celebrities said he was hot, when people told him he was the next coming of Jayzuz.

The young man in the video, wide-eyed and innocent, clicked a button and began bopping to his own music. In a startling coincidence, the song was *Jigglin' Bits*. *"I love your bits, they pleasin' me, I love it when you're on your knees."*

"That sucks," the woman on the video laughed.

"What do you know?" his past self said, his face screwing up with pain. He hated to see it. It hurt him almost more than the booing, but not quite as much as the half-full water bottle that bounced off the back of his skull.

"You better turn that shit off. You gotta get up early to work tomorrow," the woman on the screen said.

"Man, fuck Taco Bell. This is my future."

The camera feed cut off then, and when Squirt Gun Nelly turned back to the crowd, his jaw dropped even wider. The audience surged up and over the railing, a wall of flesh steamrolling the security guards, who, to be honest, weren't putting up much resistance. They slid across the coliseum floor, oozing like a landslide comprised of arms and legs and torsos, crushing each other, pinning each other to the ground and using each other to propel themselves toward the stage, a roiling mass of pissed-off, betrayed humanity.

Squirt Gun Nelly had a gold record to his name, so he didn't think too much of it. Someone would step up for him, block off these simps, and usher him away to safety. But that's not how it went. When he turned to find his manager, he'd vanished, the security guards with him.

That one glance cost him the time he needed to escape. When he turned back around, he beheld a freak of nature rising up on the back of humanity—a lone, hungry-looking dude, his skin dark as night. He ran across bent backs in shoes worn beyond practicality and months beyond the date when they should have been thrown away, the muscles in his stick legs bunching. He strode across the massive, writhing ball of humanity. Every eye glared at Squirt Gun Nelly, hate etched in their irises... he had betrayed them. Where before they had lived vicariously through him, had wanted to be him, now they hated him with every music-loving cell in their bodies.

The skinny man, ribs sticking out of his shirtless sides, worked harder than everyone else to achieve his goal. When the wriggling mass of arms, legs, and heads shifted underneath him and threatened to pull him down into obscurity, he rose, working for every last inch, clawing and scraping. Then he took the leap, his body lacquered in a sheen of sweat reflecting the twenty-story glare of young Squirt Gun Kelly back at him. He leaped, soaring through the air, attaining perfection and an artistry that SGN could never hope to emulate. He landed on stage, his right shoe obliterated by the impact, the bare skin of his foot squeaking across the polished stage.

Squirt Gun Nelly, aka Brad Harris, stood rooted to the spot. "That was awesome," he said to the man. Even he, the great denier of work and toil, knew true talent when he saw it.

Behind the man, more people inspired by the man's acrobatics ascended from the roiling mass of humanity and joined him on stage. SGN stood alone, facing down this group of former fans.

"You're a joke," said the dark man, and SGN could see the anger in his eyes, understood it only fractionally.

They swarmed around him, their hands mean and greedy. He spotted the woman who had flashed her tits at him, the man who had flashed his cock, but they weren't interested in that anymore.

One man squeezed his arm so hard the bones shifted, the skin splitting. He fell to the ground, trying to cover up, but they pressed their violence and outrage into him, not pummeling him the way he had expected, but squeezing and pinching and pulling.

"Don't beat him," the dark man said. SGN knew it was him without being able to see the man, knew the voice because it was filled with the ache of experience, the pain of struggle. If SGN was at home, he would have described the voice to Twat GPT, made it the new voice of his next album.

In their outrage, they pinched him, fingernails plucking small, Chiclet-sized chunks of flesh from his body. They plucked his hairs out one by one, and he screamed in pain, his hands slapping at the arms around him.

The crowd filled the stage now, breaking whatever they could get their hands on. Speaker stacks tumbled like felled trees, their rectangular trunks breaking apart in sections. They ripped and shredded SGN's console, tossing the pieces in the crowd where they wrestled over who would be the first to eat a piece, shit it out, and flush it down the toilet, because that's where they all agreed Squirt Gun Nelly belonged.

"More like Shart Gun Nelly!" one person yelled.

Still, they pinched and prodded, and SGN began to cry, until someone pinched his tear ducts shut, ripped them free. From then on, only blood ran down his cheeks.

The dark man appeared, a strange gun held in his hands. He leaned down, pressed a loving palm to SGN's face and smoothed the blood off his forehead. "Your cries are the real music," said the man, and then the gun in his hand buzzed to life.

The angry crowd cheered his attacker on, even as they fish-nibbled swatches of skin from his arms, legs, and back with their fingernails.

His forehead stung as the buzzing gun stitched his flesh. The dark man's tongue stuck out the side of his mouth, bubblegum pink, as he concentrated. Finally, the man stepped back, admired his work. "This is the real art," the man said.

They left then, departing as quickly as they had come, but for the people still trying to bring down the screen.

Laying on the stage, Squirt Gun Nelly looked upward as the screen switched, from young him to current him. He would have cried if he could have, but that ability had been taken away when they ripped the tear ducts from his eyes. On the screen, Squirt Gun Nelly lay on stage like a baby who hadn't yet learned to crawl. His body bled from a thousand wounds, a thousand cuts, a thousand rejections. He lifted his head to the sky… the word "hAIck" tattooed across his forehead.

Sieg Hair

Chapter 1
In The Chair

"You watch the Blazers last night?"

"I got no idea what you're talking about. I don't watch monkeyball."

The racism was thick today, as it was every day. Daniel listened to it and nodded his head though it broke his heart inside, shattered it into a thousand grief-laced pieces. But that was ok. He was used to having a broken heart. It had been broken for years.

"Do me up, Daniel. Gotta look good for the show tonight." The man who spoke was a goon, a Cro-Magnon specimen who should be lying on a metal table in a lab somewhere having his brain imaged, his DNA scanned, his testicles removed. Everyone called him Clint. Daniel didn't know his last name—didn't care. It was better not to know.

Daniel had his part to play, but he didn't want to play it too deep, didn't want to get too close. It was already killing him inside, all those broken heart pieces whisking around in his chest, a tornado of pain which he had to keep hidden. He was so close now.

"Man, Torque Wrench is the best."

They weren't. Take the worst band you ever heard, shave their heads, and plaster them in Nazi tattoos, force them all to have strokes to limit their musical ability, and what you'd have left over would be a close approximation of Torque Wrench. The only reason they had ever sold an album was because they were racist dogs, cavemen spouting off master-race bullshit with every distorted, rhythmless song. Well, almost every song. They had a handful of ditties about getting drunk and fucking, which the apes went nuts for. But the skinheads came for the racism, the chance to run in a circle and bust each other in the chops in the name of good fun. They lived and breathed violence, this group of shaved-headed Fourth-reichers, dreaming of the day when they, the lowly, the disenfranchised, would rise up and regain their rightful place at the top of the ladder. They couldn't see how pathetic they were, how even if such a day did come, they'd still be at the bottom because they were neither intelligent nor talented. They were nothing, and that's why they were here on the compound in the first place.

It was tough to be nothing alone. Even if you had to be a fulltime racist to have some friends, that was better than the alternative in some people's minds. The world was big and hard, spent every second of every day trying to pound you into hamburger, returning you to the ground from whence we had all come. The violence of the world was much easier to face with someone by your side. Daniel had someone like that once.

"Earth to fucking Daniel," Clint said.

"Oh, sorry."

"Man, are you sure you're not on the monkey grass? I swear, you spend more time in the clouds than the moon."

Daniel didn't have it in him to tell Clint the moon wasn't in the clouds. Motherfucker probably still thought the Earth was flat.

Daniel reached for a set of clippers, old and ancient by clipper standards. According to the original owner, those clippers—black and silver with a cracked black cord snaking from its end like a rat tail—had given two-thousand-three-hundred-and-thirty-one haircuts. They would give an untold number of cuts today, all buzzes.

The clippers clanked to life with the twist of a button, so small and so deadly. The buzz of the clippers like a yellow jacket hovering in next to an ear, and for a brief second, Daniel thought he saw a small distortion around the buzzing razors as they slid back and forth, faster than the eye could see.

"What do you want?" Daniel asked.

"A little off the top."

It was an old joke, one Clint made every time he was in the chair. To be honest, there wasn't much on top to take off. Clint, a real genetic loser, was starting to go bald at the tender age of twenty-five. The remnants of hair still clinging to his scalp reminded Daniel of the initial sprouting of a Chia pet. Still, the clippers managed to cut his hair even closer.

As Daniel dragged the vibrating blades across Clint's scalp, his ever-present right-hand-man Aidan sat in a rickety chair engaging in small talk, only this talk was so small it might as well be called infinitesimal talk. Aidan prattled on and on about girls he wanted to bang, how much ass he was gonna kick tonight, how much he couldn't wait to get wasted. He was the only person on the compound stupider than Clint and listening to him ramble drove Daniel crazy.

Instead of Aidan's dimwit words, Daniel focused on the humming of the clippers, on the feel of stubble on his palm as he swept Clint's hair to the ground. The ground… the ground…

SIEG HAIR

CHAPTER 2
BIG D'S LAST DANCE

The concrete floor of the dancehall had grown slick, layered in a combination of spit, spilled beer, and condensation from the heat of so many bodies crammed into such a small space. There must be a hundred and fifty people inside the club. It was made for fifty. The club's promoters didn't care. They packed Grants Passers into the dancehall like cattle while counting their money in the dim light of a back room somewhere.

The lights onstage whirred and flashed. If Daniel had been epileptic, he would be lying on the ground and jittering about by now. Instead, it was his brother doing the dance. He tried desperately to reach his brother, pushing through bodies packed tighter than cigarettes in a newly opened pack. He moved as if in a nightmare, an inch at a time, despite the hammering of his heart. It seemed he would never make it to his brother's side. The people, shocked and terrified, stood like statues.

If he had the size of his brother Dwayne, it would have been easy to push through the crowd. Everyone in the family referred to Dwayne as Big D. Daniel, by way of his brother's size, had been given the nickname Lil' D, though he wasn't all that small. But standing next to his big brother, both in age and size, he always felt little. Now, seeing him lying on the ground, the heels of his Doc Martin's hammering against the concrete floor, foam dripping from the corner of his mouth, and blood oozing from his split scalp, his big brother seemed small for the first time in Lil' D's life.

The crowd of strangers stood observing Big D on the ground, but no one did anything. Lil' D's voice erupted from his throat, a volcanic thing.

His screams carried fear, primal, enough to get people to move out of the way. As they parted, Daniel rushed to his brother's side, squatting on the slippery concrete, and pressing his hands to his brother's skin, warm and full of life. He spoke soothing words to his brother, but he couldn't calm Big D, couldn't keep him from shaking.

The band on stage, American Circus, stopped playing when they noticed something wasn't quite right in the pit.

With the music stopped, Daniel's ears rang like an alarm. The crowd around him fell into a hush, while the people further back who couldn't see what was going on yelled things like, "Play the fucking music!"

"Call an ambulance!" someone called.

Security showed up, fat men masquerading as tough guys, their only power being that there were several of them in the club. Out on the street, Big D could have taken any of these lumps of shit in a fight.

"What happened?" one of the security guards asked.

"He fell." That wasn't the whole story, but in the shock of seeing his brother, massive and full of life, dropped to the ground, Lil' D couldn't think of anything else to say. Big D's legs stopped kicking, and his eyes closed.

By the time the ambulance appeared, he was gone. Though his chest rose and fell, his brain had swollen so badly in his skull he would never recover.

As Lil' D rode in the ambulance, tears falling from his eyes, he tried to think of what he would tell his father. He tried to think of what he would tell the police. He tried to think of anything other than his brother's death. When he closed his eyes, he saw their faces as if they had been tattooed on the interior of his eyelids—the swastikas on their arms, the gleam of their shaved heads under the multicolored, flaring concert lights.

After Big D was gone, everyone just called him Daniel.

SIEG HAIR

CHAPTER 3
REPARATIONS

With Clint's head buzzed bowling ball smooth, Aidan hopped into the chair. His peanut-shaped dome was the type of skull that begged for hair, but rules were rules. The only person who got away with having a full head of cabbage was Carl Trotter, the benefactor for this particular gang of degenerates. Carl Trotter was a pig of a man—a bigot, a lech, the sort of dude who would get a girl drunk so he could have his way with her, turn her into nothing more than a set of holes for his own gratification. Carl seemed to hate women only slightly less than he hated anyone who wasn't white.

His army of goons had no name. This was by design. Hard to label someone a gang or a terrorist group when they didn't have a name. They were quite simply the dregs of Grants Pass and all the surrounding towns. Trotter's band was comprised of broken, lonely people without the braincells to figure out a way to belong to a different, more wholesome clique. If it wasn't for Carl Trotter, half these people would have killed themselves or gone on their own killing sprees a long time ago. Carl liked the skinhead look. In his own words, "Skinheads look dangerous as fuck, even if half of them have never actually been in a real fight in their life."

"A little off the top," Aidan said.

Offended, Clint said, "Hey, that's my line."

"Fuck you," Aidan laughed.

Daniel turned his back to the two arguing simpletons. They were the type of people who went through life unseen and unappreciated… and rightfully so. Daniel tried not to hate people, not to belittle them for their failings, but these two were awful, abysmal examples of humanity. Daniel had seen dogs scooting their asses across carpets with more nobility. Clint and Aidan were walking cocks with fists dangling at the ends of their arms. He supposed the haircuts were fitting for them in that respect.

The barber shop sat plopped in the middle of a compound on the outskirts of Grants Pass, Oregon. It was a wild scrap of land, which had been cleared some years ago by Carl Trotter. The pig had inherited it from his father, who, before him, had inherited it from his father, who had killed the tribes who still "squatted" on the land in the early 1900s. Taken by blood and conquest, Daniel felt the presence on the land of these skinheads, these beasts, as an affront, like a graffiti mustache drawn on a missing child's poster or the words "Rest in Piss" scrawled in sharpie on a memorial plaque.

Daniel was a registered member of the Confederated Tribes of Grande Ronde, though he didn't look it. Of mixed heritage, his white blood ran strong. Most of the time, his skin was pale. Though, if left in the sun for too long, he would brown up nicely. Of course, if he let that happen, the people who considered him a friend now wouldn't hesitate to kick his ass, stomp him into a puddle for tricking them, which had been about as difficult as tricking a three-year-old with the old, severed thumb trick.

He knew he was playing a dangerous game, but that wasn't going to stop him. He would have his revenge. Though, if he really thought about it, he guessed it wasn't his to have. It was his brother's, Big D. Sometimes, at night, he would talk to Big D as if he were still alive, talk to him the way he had when they were kids trying to fall asleep in a couple of broken bunk beds in their father's trailer, Big D on top and Lil' D down below. He missed those conversations, but having them now still helped in some ways.

"Do you want me to kill them?" he'd ask at night.

"Kill 'em dead. Make 'em pay," Big D always said.

"They have families too, you know."

"Then they should have acted like it."

"Isn't it wrong to kill?"

"Killing is life. In order to live, your body has to kill germs, bacteria, plants, animals. Killing is our nature. Besides, these people are amoebas. You gonna cry next time you get a cold, and your body fights it off?"

"No."

"Then don't cry for them. Life's not special."

"It was when you were around."

"Yeah. I get that."

Daniel finished shaving Aidan's head. The soles of Daniel's boots slipped and skidded on the bits of hair on the ground. With a broom in hand, he swept the hair into a dustpan as the next person sat in the chair. The entire crew had mustered for today. Tonight's concert was going to be big, huge even.

Some of the other skinhead bastards from neighboring cities were coming just to see Torque Wrench. It was a meeting of the clans, a chance to get fucked up, crack each other across the jaw, and fuck the poor, broken meat puppets who clung to the men. Animal shit, the type of shit his ancestors might have engaged in back in the day, back when the land was still theirs, and no one gave a shit what color your skin was. He couldn't blame them. Music, dancing, fighting, loving, these things bound the entire world together, though the people he had surrounded himself with couldn't see it.

Michael was the next person in the chair. He worked as a ranger in the forests, the chaparrals that were once home to Daniel's people. He liked him for that. Oh, he'd still have his revenge on him, but for Michael, he might feel bad about it, might see his face—the way he saw his brother's—on those nights he couldn't sleep.

"Danny Boy!"

"What's up, Michael?"

"Just lookin' to look sharp."

"I don't think a haircut's gonna make that happen."

"Psshh," said Michael, a toothy grin splitting his face.

"How were the trees this week?"

"You mean the shrubs? They were fine, all still there. Hot as hell though."

Daniel could believe it. It was the middle of summer, the part where even people who like summer started to get sick of it, started to hate the heat. It was the type of heat that sometimes made you feel like you were going to burst into flames just from walking through the dry air.

"Spent most of my week watching redskins pluck pine cones from the trees for some sort of conservation experiment. Those fucking people, man.

Isn't it enough they get all that casino money? Now they got to own the whole damn forest."

Enough indeed. "Buncha bullshit," Daniel parroted, though he felt no such way. As far as getting rich off casino money, Daniel's own tribe sent him a check every summer, which just about allowed him to pay off accumulated credit card debt every year… just about. Wasn't no getting rich from it. Daniel could have set Michael straight, could have played devil's advocate, maybe turned his mind around a bit, but that wasn't what he was here for. Instead, he let the ranger go on and on, regurgitating all the stereotypes and bullshit Daniel had been hearing about his people since he was little.

As he pondered his own self-hate, he dragged the clippers across Michael's scalp, watching as bits of hair jumped off his head, flying through the air like spiky missiles, leaving behind a perfectly shaped scalp, but for one strange mole on the apex of Michael's skull. He wondered if Michael even knew it was there.

"What the fuck are you talking about? We can be whatever we want."

"Ha!" Big D spat. "If you're dumb enough to believe that, you're probably dumb enough to believe voting matters."

Lil' D spat into the dirt. Everyone knew voting was bullshit. Didn't matter which rich white fucker you voted for, they were all going to fuck you over in the end. Dig under your home, find some oil, then plunk a fucking pipeline right in the middle of it. You and your friends, and all the fake Indian white folks who wanted to be anything but white could sit around, playing drums and chaining themselves to machinery all they wanted. In the end, that fucking pipeline would be built, and your home would be ruined. It's just the way it was.

"Of course," Big D continued, "maybe you could be whatever you want. You could pass."

His big brother referred to his skin. Though they shared the same father, Lil' D's mother had been white, some lady who fell for his father's bullshit Indian mysticism. For a while, she had made her home with them, and their trailer was bursting at the seams with four people inside. But when reality had hit, and her dad had become who he actually was instead of who he pretended to be, she had stopped playing Indian-lover and gone back to wherever she came from, somewhere in Portland. He'd seen her twice since, decided she didn't really care for him, was embarrassed by him and his father. But she had given him one gift at least, his skin. Fairer than anyone in his family or anyone in their little community of oppressed minorities living in Grants Pass, a community which consisted of several hard-working Latino families, some Native Americans, and even a Black family, who everyone agreed resented having to live among the Mexicans and the Indians.

Once, he had told his teachers in middle school, in the dead of winter, he was Native American, and the teacher—one of those old-school white teachers who taught to keep from getting bored because her husband was rich and always away on business trips—had the nerve to tell him, but "I don't think of you as Indian. I don't see color."

It was supposed to be a compliment. *I think of you as white.* But it wasn't a compliment; it denied everything he was; it denied the history of his life, the pain and suffering of his ancestors. White people had a hard time understanding that, thought minorities were too thin-skinned and oughta get over it. Lil' D was of the opinion that shit like that, the destruction of your culture, the denigration of an entire people, seeped into your DNA. Somewhere on the tip of the twentieth chromosome, the pain and hurt of humanity lingered there, a dominant allele that wouldn't be cowed by mixing with white DNA. He could have leaned into his whiteness, denied he was anything but another country-ass white boy, but this was not what he wanted. Plus, even though Big D gave him a hard time for his skin, if he ever did start acting like a peckerwood, his brother would stomp his ass until he came to his senses. Big D was good like that. And when his brother was done, his father, who was something of a huckster about town, would do the same. Didn't matter what his skin color was to his family, they knew underneath his pale skin, he was of them, one and the same—blood.

"Maybe you could be president," Big D said. "You could get up in that white house and pass off some reparations for us."

"Oh, yeah? And what sort of reparations would you want?"

"Nothin' much. Just a place on the beach, somewhere away from this goddamn heat." Big D tilted a half-full forty of Olde E up to his lips. Lil' D hadn't yet gained the knack of actually enjoying beer, so he always thought his bro was pretending when he would smack his lips after taking a big swig of the piss-looking stuff. Of course, if he ever did get a taste for beer, he doubted he would drink forties of Olde E. He'd seen the people who bought that shit at Dale's. They were never good people. That his brother might be one of those "not very good people" never crossed his mind.

"A place on the beach? What the fuck would you do with that?"

"I'd sell it. Move back here, be king of this place for a year or two, until my money was gone."

"Then what?"

"I'd call my bro in The White House. Tell him to get us some more of those reparations."

The flow of it. The back and forth was perfect. Even as the wind swept across the chaparral, sending the scrubby fir trees into their ridiculous dance and kicking up a blanket of gritty dust, they couldn't help but laugh at the silliness of it all… and the truth of it. It was just like something Big D would do. *Go big or go home.* That was his motto, though the "go big" part of his mantra never seemed to work out. Somehow, he kept finding his way back home. Sometimes he'd disappear on a random job, just peacing out randomly. Wasn't long before he was back, a couple of weeks at most, broke and penniless, his eyes sunken deeper and deeper into his head. His brother was how he knew not all men were meant to work. Some were meant to drift. But the country wouldn't let an Indian drift. It blew him back to his home, like a leaf trapped in a courtyard and plastered up against a corner. Sometimes it might escape when the wind gusted right, would swirl around for a bit, but it always wound up back in the corner, and a little bit of itself gone, dragged against concrete. Then the cycle would continue, until the leaf was ground to nothing.

"I wouldn't do it."

"The hell you wouldn't."

"I wouldn't."

"Why the fuck not?"

"You'd just drink it all away."

"Pssh. You ever stop to think why I drink, Lil' D?"

"Not really."

"Well, stop and think about it sometime."

"Why don't you tell me?"

"Cuz I'm drunk, stupid."

That's the way Big D was. Sometimes, Lil' D thought he was a genius, other times he thought he was just another common trickster, like their father, the type of dude who could make you think he might be a medicine man for a day or two, but who, when it turned out he didn't have any money and lived in a low-rent trailer and ate food stamp dinners, would have no answers at all. He'd just spread his hands wide and shrug his shoulders, smiling at you as if to say, "What are you? Blind? Don't blame this on me. You should have known." His family was a bunch of scorpions, willing to trick the nearest frog, and then gaslight their ass when someone complained they weren't who they said they were.

But maybe Big D was a genius. He'd made it this far.

"Maybe you drink to trick people," Lil' D said.

Big D winked at him, tipped the beer back.

"People want to be tricked. It's not really a trick if you give 'em what they want," Big D said.

"No. I don't think that's it."

"Yeah?"

"I think you like to trick people into thinking you're dumb, into thinking you're just another drunk Indian, that way they have no expectations for you. Then you can't fail, can't let people down."

Big D harrumphed, his head sagging. He looked exhausted, broken, as if Lil' D's words had been the equivalent of a hundred body blows. He looked like that picture, the one of the broken Indian, all slumped over, a spear hanging limp under his arm, sitting astride a horse. Instead of a spear, Big D held a forty of Olde E. Instead of a horse, he sat on the rusty tailgate of his father's old Ford, not the one he currently drove, but the one which had broken down a few years ago, which would sit outside their trailer until the end of time came.

At school, Lil' D, always curious, always fascinated by history and the raw deal his people had received, had looked up the photo, found out it was made by a white man who had imagined what it would look like when Indians were pushed clear across the country to the Pacific Ocean. The most iconic image of his culture… made by a white man. Ironic… he guessed. Irony was hard.

His brother sat up then, straightened his spine, and his small smile returned to his face. He never let his smile get too big, as if doing so would let his soul escape. "See, I told you you'd make a great President. You got me sad already."

His brother drained his beer, chucked the empty bottle into the dry soil, and walked inside to watch Judge Judy. Lil' D didn't know why, but he stayed outside, gave his brother time to cool off. Half an hour later, when he walked into the living room, Big D was yelling at the TV. "Hang the bastard! He's guilty as fuck!" The bastard in question was a black man, and Lil' D wondered if this was irony again or just coincidence. Sometimes it was hard to tell.

Ranger Michael left the barber's chair, ranting and grumbling about his job, about the unfairness of the world, about how the white man was being shunted off to the side. But they'd take it back one day—this according to Michael. He snapped a smart salute at the flag on the wall, black and white and red—a perfect representation of hate—and then he shook Daniel's hand. The lost man walked out of the barber shop as a dusty Jeep pulled up. A woman climbed out, a green shock of hair hanging off the front of her otherwise bald scalp. Curves in all the right places. Through the dusty glass door, he watched Michael talk to her, smile at her, flash a grin that said he wanted to be more than friends. But no one was more than friends with that girl. No one.

SIEG HAIR

CHAPTER 4
THE ROMANI

Sage Jensen stepped into the barber shop, and for a moment they were alone. In his head, Daniel went through a conversation he'd held with Sage a thousand times in his mind.

"You don't belong here," he'd start.

"What're you talking about?" she'd ask.

"You're not one of them. You're better than that."

She'd look deep into his eyes, see the truth of who he was, know she was wrong. Then she'd take his hand, and they would hop into her Jeep and leave town, head out east, away from the ocean, away from the place where Native Americans stood, looking behind them and wondering how they'd lost it all, an entire continent. She would see him for who he was, realize she had been a fool and loved him all the same, even though his blood wasn't a hundred percent white, and he'd tan up like a Thanksgiving turkey in the summer if he left himself in the sun for too long.

Pipe dreams, his dead brother whispered in his mind. *Pipe dreams. The type of dreams the old chiefs had when they smoked their pipes and tried to listen to the spirits, see into the future, and guide their people. The type of dreams that would never come to be. Turns out they were just catching a cheap buzz and then bossing people around.*

"Hey, Danny," she sighed as she plopped into the barber's chair, an ancient thing salvaged from a barber shop that had gone under. Its white vinyl was lined with thousands of infinitesimal cracks, like an old man's face. He knew a face that looked like that, a little darker, a little less white.

"You gonna go full baldy?" Daniel asked.

"Pshh. I do that and everyone starts mistaking me for a dude."

Daniel laughed. There was no chance of that, not with those full, almond-shaped eyes, as green as the shock of hair on her forehead. One look at her hips and the curves of her chest, and no one would be mistaking Sage for a dude, even if she had a mustache.

Daniel turned his back to Sage, even as another car bounced into the driveway. The big man—Carl Trotter—pulled up in his gas-guzzling Humvee. You could feed and clothe a family of five for what he spent on gas driving that relic around. It wasn't one of the newer ones, but one of the originals, built to last in the desert, where gas was plentiful because your country wrestled it away from other tribesman thousands of miles away, just another of the horrors of colonialism. Daniel got the impression Carl Trotter drove the thing because of what it represented. It was the one lasting symbol of the only war America had won on its own since they'd stopped beating up on people wielding bows and arrows. Sad, really.

Daniel unplugged the ancient clippers and pulled a set of scissors from the counter.

"No clippers?" Sage asked.

"They're overheating. Gotta tinker with 'em later. Gonna give 'em a rest." That wasn't true, but he couldn't tell Sage the real reason why he wasn't using the clippers on her. Didn't have it in him. What he did have in him still surprised him.

With his thumb and index finger shoved through the sterling silver loops of the scissors, and a plain black comb in his hand, Daniel went to work, dragging the comb across her scalp, pressing it tight to her skin, and snipping off any bits of hair that dared stand up.

"How was work?"

"Oh, you know. Just a bunch of sad drunks, sitting at a bar for hours and bitching about taxes and laws and democrats."

Daniel knew the type. They were always in Sage's bar, old fucks who made their money off the labor of others. They'd sit at the bar paying for beers with money some poor migrant worker had conjured from thin air via the magic ritual of the bent back and the snatching arms. With that money, the money they hadn't earned but for their station in the hierarchy of society, they would sit at the bar and complain about everything that

prevented them from profiting even more off the labor of the brown man.
Taxes, democrats, laws… the bane of the lazy white man.

At Sage's bar, which really wasn't hers, but one of Carl Trotter's many
nefarious outfits, you'd find these types there at all times of the day. Turns
out when you got nothing to do, you just sit around drinking. He supposed
that's one thing all Americans had in common, didn't matter what your
race was.

Dad had been out of work for a week. He had been unintelligible for
about as long. Fired from his job at the ranch, he had taken his last week's
pay and bought up all the Natty Ice he could lay his hands on. Every
fifteen minutes, he would step outside and say he was going to listen to the
spirits. What he was really doing was taking a piss in the dry dust. It was
cheaper that way, used less water than flushing the toilet. Didn't matter
to his dad that everyone in the trailer park saw him pissing up against the
wooden fence, the slats the color of dried whale bones. A man with no job
had no shame, couldn't get any lower. A man with no job was free.

Big D was gone, somewhere out in the world, on some adventure
he thought would make him rich, maybe even famous, but which would
eventually leave him even more broken when he returned. It was just Lil'
D and Dad, or what was left of him. He'd be like this for another week
or two, until his money ran out, and he had to sober up and go looking
for another job. Seemed like every farmer in and around Grants Pass had
hired Jericho Greene at one point or another, and while none would offer
him a permanent position, whenever they needed someone for a shit job at
poor rates, Jericho Greene would inevitably fit the bill.

Need a latrine dug for your migrant workers outside the barracks?
Jericho's your man. Need an old outhouse filled in? Give old Jericho a call.
Dad wasn't picky, in his beer or in his work.

On this particular day, his father had decided he was a medicine man
again, always told Lil' D and Big D about how, if it was the old days, he
would have been big shit.

His father stumbled into the trailer, his ancient boots clomping on
the carpeted floor. He collapsed in a chair, upholstered in a hideous
burnt sienna cloth. To the right of the chair sat a twelve-pack of Natty
Ice upended on its side. His father's brown hand reached inside, pulled

another can free and popped the top, slurping up the liquid as if it were life itself, which to many people it was.

"Whatchu doin' here?" his father asked him.

Lil' D hated when his father got like this. Most times, when his father got drunk, Lil' D would make himself scarce. But right then, he was fifteen and had nowhere to go, nothing to do, so all he could think of was to sit in the chair and let the basketball game on the TV play on and on, millionaires sliding across the lacquered court in shoes that cost enough money to feed him for a month if he was careful. "Whaddya mean?" Lil' D asked hesitantly. Dad was dangerous now. He had that edge to his voice, the type of edge all children of alcoholics know. It was gonna go one of two ways, insane laughter or slurring outrage. Lil' D felt as if he were standing on the edge of a knife, waiting to find out what he was in store for. Neither option was good. His father's drunken hilarity was obnoxious and only interesting to himself. His fury at least was quick and understandable.

"Why you still here? Why ain't you tryin' ta get out, like Big D?"

"I'm fifteen. What am I supposed to do?"

"There's things," his dad said.

"You want me to go?"

His father's open mouth snapped shut, his lower lip covering his upper. His head weaved from side to side, and his eyes, red-rimmed and blurry, blinked once or twice. "No," he said, and Lil' D thought he was going to start bawling. "But you should. Ain't no point in you sticking around here."

Lil' D kept his mouth closed. On the TV, a giant man threw a basketball through the hoop as if it were nothing.

"You stick 'round here, yer gonna be jus' like me. You want that?"

"Don't want anything."

His father, drunk and gone, and speaking like a lizard said, "That's the problem. Man's gotta want something. Man's gotta strive. Like me!" At this he thumped his chest, swelled up with pride. "I work hard."

"And what do you want?"" Lil' D asked.

At this his father stood up, stumbled over to him, leaning down and bathing Lil' D's face in Natty Ice breath. "I want you… to be… better than me." His father thumped him in the shoulder with his fist. "Ya gotta be better. You're the best of us."

Lil' D didn't know what to say, felt his face flush red. He knew the words coming out of his father's mouth were just drunk talk, the type of nonsense he'd heard a thousand times over. But he couldn't leave, wouldn't think of it. What if he missed his brother when he came back? What if his dad got drunk, dropped one of his cigarettes on the carpet, and burned himself up.

"I want you to leave."

"What?" Lil' D asked.

"Get out!" his father yelled. "You're too good for this."

He wasn't though. He was just like them; he was family. He knew which way he was headed. "Too good for what?"

His father wrapped his fists in Lil' D's Blazers T-shirt and pulled him to his feet. "Get out!" he yelled. "You're free!" He shoved him through the screen door, the metal frame smacking against the wall of the trailer. Trailer dogs tied to ropes barked and yelped at the violence. The other denizens of the trailer park momentarily looked in their direction and then averted their gazes, minding their own business as good residents of a trailer park did.

"You're like a bird, a baby bird, all fluffy and special, but you can't sit in the nest forever, Daniel. Can't sit in it forever." His father began to sob as he spoke, and Lil' D turned and walked.

"Go on, baby bird! Get!"

His father yelled this over and over until Daniel was out of sight. He walked all night, tears in his eyes, and when he began to shake, he returned home, found his father passed out, crushed cans on the floor and a cigarette hole burned into the carpet. His father had pissed himself.

The next day, Dad would wake up, wouldn't remember what he'd said. Drunks never did. Only the sober remembered the drunk's words, etched them into their hearts where they stayed hidden and hurtful.

The pointed tips of Sage's hair pressed into his palm, the heat from her scalp warming his own skin. He loved her, hated who she had allowed herself to become, but loved her just the same. Maybe he was being stupid. Maybe he just needed to "get his dick wet" as his older brother had been fond of saying from time to time.

"You going to the show?" Sage asked.

"Gotta do some clean-up here, but yeah, I'll be there." This was a lie, but it was all he could manage at the moment.

"I don't even like this band, but like, what else is there to do. Right?"

"You could sit out back and look up at the stars."

"Would you look with me?"

"Doesn't take two people to look at the stars."

"It's a big sky, Daniel. I wouldn't want to miss anything."

"You got me there." Daniel took one last pass over Sage's scalp, got down low, and scanned for any outliers. Her eyes followed him in the mirror, but he tried not to notice those green orbs, the shine and the slickness of them, the perfect whites, the plump red lips quirked into a smile. *God, she's hot.*

She don't like you. It's just how she lives, how she gets by, Big D said in his head. We all got gifts to get us by. I could fight. Dad can drink. You can get lost in that beautiful brain of yours. Sage flirts to make men think they got a chance. Keeps her safe.

Daniel held a mirror out to Sage. When she grabbed the handle, their fingers brushed, and he held that moment tight, squeezed it so it wouldn't escape.

"Looks good, Daniel." Sage stood, and Daniel resisted the urge to let his eyes slide across her body. "I'll see you at the show, yeah?"

"You got it."

"If it's boring, maybe we can go look at those stars together." She dropped him a wink, and his brother's voice said, *It's just how she lives, man.* Still, a guy could fantasize, right? At the door, she had to turn sideways and edge past Carl Trotter, who didn't hesitate to press against her with a wolfish grin on his face as he stepped inside. Carl's belly was round, an alcoholic belly, perfectly spherical like a basketball. Meanwhile, his arms and legs hung skinny. He looked like he was sick, like he was full of parasites, and at any moment his belly was going to burst open and spew hundred-legged, hundred-eyed monstrosities all over the floor.

Daniel hated Carl Trotter. There were many dangerous people at the compound, but Trotter was the only one who could make dangerous people, the only one who could transform a perfectly ordinary human being into a weapon of hate and bigotry. Daniel gave him his biggest grin. Trotter liked his people happy… and stupid.

When the door swung closed, and he finished watching Sage bounce away, Trotter turned and let out a redneck, "Oooh-weee." He swiped a hand across his sweaty forehead, exposing the ever-present pit stains underneath his arms. No one sweated more than Carl Trotter. It didn't matter what he was doing. In his back pocket, he carried a rag he used to dab at his face and his upper lip when he was trying to look the part.

A disease. That's what Carl Trotter was. He was sick, unhealthy, so much so he could never die on his own. While some people were only slightly sick, or slightly unhealthy, eventually death would catch up to them. Carl Trotter had leaned into his excesses so hard he'd basically pickled his insides, hit his arteries so fast and so hard with cholesterol that he'd galvanized the fuckers and his heart in the process. Carl Trotter would not go quietly in the night. But he would go. Of that, Daniel would be sure.

"You hit that yet?" Trotter asked him.

"Go fuck yourself." That's what Daniel wanted to say, wanted to take the scissors in his hand and shove the tip into one of Trotter's eyes, twist it around a bit, feel the man die. "Has anyone?"

"By that age, a girl like that? Someone has, whether she wanted to or not." The look on his face told Daniel that Trotter didn't care if the latter were the case. His cavalier attitude about rape was another in a long list of reasons to hate the man.

As he sauntered over to the barber chair, Daniel took the time to sweep up Sage's hairs and dump them in the garbage bin. With a fresh floor to catch Trotter's hair, he plugged in the electric clippers.

"You excited for the show?" Trotter asked.

To be honest, I'm kind of sick of talking about the show. "Oh yeah. Can't wait."

Trotter's entire face was bulbous and red, inflamed with evenings of alcohol and other drugs. He didn't care, didn't hide it. None of the good-ol'-boy cops in Grants Pass bothered him. He was the right color after all. Walk around with a face like that and brown skin and you'd have every cop in town following you whenever you dragged your ass up to the corner store for a pack of smokes.

"Lots of people coming to this one," Trotter said.

To Daniel, it sounded like he was basically talking to himself. Some people were like that. They talked just to hear their own voice, to work out the jumbled string of thoughts all knotted up in their minds. Trotter was one of those. Unlike his face and his body, Trotter had an attractive voice, a rich, deep timbre that reminded Daniel of a humidor stocked with expensive cigars. There used to be a store like that in the mall, and when he'd turned eighteen and fancied himself a pipe smoker, he would go to the tobacco shop and step inside the walk-in humidor and breathe in the rich, full scent of dried tobacco. That smell was how Trotter's voice sounded. It's one of the reasons he couldn't fully blame someone for falling under his hateful spell. For a fucking racist, he had some sort of peculiar charisma. If Daniel wanted to cut ties with his entire family and live in Trotter's compound fulltime, he might be happy to do it. But then he would be a traitor, and his brother's killers would go unpunished, and in the afterlife, his family would beat his ass, and half of 'em wouldn't even be able to speak English, so there would be no way to apologize. But still, sometimes he dreamed of giving in, living on the compound, having Sage at his side.

"Didja hear me?" Trotter asked.

"Oh, sorry. I spaced out for a bit."

Trotter laughed. He was good-natured with white folk. But brown up someone's skin a bit, and he could be a terror, the type of guy who would be the bad guy in a movie, the type of guy who would get a half-inch from your face and tell you he was going to kill your whole damn family. Daniel had seen it once when a Mexican delivery driver came onto the property. From the window of the barber shop, he'd seen old Trotter come running out of the clubhouse with an AR-15 in his hand, a look on his face that made Daniel's heart skip a beat. He hadn't aimed it at the delivery driver, but the unspoken threat of violence had slowed the driver's footsteps. When Trotter told him to leave the package on the ground and get the fuck off his property, the driver was only too happy. The tone Trotter had delivered his words with was nothing short of murderous... the type of tone that made a man's blood run cold in the night. In his nightmares, Daniel still heard that voice from time to time.

"Well, don't fucking space out when you're cutting my hair. That cabbage is my moneymaker."

Daniel didn't think that was the case. Trotter's true moneymakers were all the "tools of oppression" variety. Like a parasite, he fed off hard work, off the stoopbacks of all races, calloused-hand motherfuckers with no power to change their lot in life. Without lifting a finger, Trotter added to his bank account every day. *Must be nice.* But Daniel had to admit, the man had a damn fine head of hair. It was criminal. Thick locks, flowing, professional looking, some people had all the luck. Daniel himself was thinning up top. At the age of twenty-one no less! Maybe there was no god.

"What do you want me to do with it?" Daniel asked.

"Just a trim."

"You got it." The antique buzzers clicked to life in his hand, jittering around like a live snake in the grip of his palm.

"Jesus," Trotter said. "We gotta get you some new clippers."

Daniel smiled. "No need. These'll get the job done."

"Sounds like a goddamn trash compactor crushing up bunnies."

"There are many ways to compact a bunny."

Revenge is hot. He'd once heard how it was a dish best served cold, but Daniel wasn't serving no dish. He was gonna deliver it hot and fast so he could get on with the process of grieving.

Inside, his father lay in a puddle of his own vomit. When he'd come home and learned of Big D's death, he'd started drinking and hadn't stopped since. It was tough. Here he was, the child consoling the parent. Who was there for him? Who would come and make sure he was feeling alright? No one. That's who. He dragged his father from his vomit puddle, pulled an ancient, smoke-stinking Afghan off the back of the couch, draped his father in it, and then went into his father's room. Empty beer cans lined the headboard of his dad's empty water bed. The water bladder had burst some time when Big D and Lil' D were 9 and 7-years-old. They'd been jumping up and down on the bed. After their father whupped their ass, he'd dragged the bladder out into the dust, and had slept on the plywood boards underneath ever since.

When they were older, he'd asked his father why he never bought a new bed. "Sleep hard and your day starts out like shit. From there, your day can only get better."

Lil' D didn't think that was the whole truth, but he was never quite able to pry the actual truth from his old man. When Jericho Greene didn't want to talk, he wouldn't, and there was nothing you could do about it. On the headboard, crushed, empty cans of Natty Ice lay like dead cockroaches. Lil' D bent down and dropped to his knees on the dingy carpet. Reaching his forearms underneath the bed, he pulled out a box made of ancient cardboard that appeared to be disintegrating before Lil' D's very eyes. Inside the box lay a rifle, bolt-action, deadly. Lil' D didn't know much about guns, but he'd once seen his father take a coyote's jaw off with the fucker after a farmer had paid him to thin out the coyote population around his farm. "Hundred bucks a carcass," his dad had bragged. "Can't beat that. Get to go hunting for a living. You find a permanent job like that, then sign me up."

But Lil' D didn't agree. He'd seen what the bullet did to the coyote, how it had been living its life one minute and then tumbled to the dust with a horrid yelp that now lived in his nightmares. The bullet obliterated its jaw, turned it into bits of blood, bone, and fur in the blink of an eye, and his father, lying on a piece of cardboard with a beer close at hand, had needed to put another round in the suffering beast. When Lil' D had gone to collect the corpse, while his dad finished off his beer, the red on the dust made him feel uncomfortable. Blood in the dirt was just plain wrong on some level.

Back in his father's room, he dug around in the box, found his fingers brushing against cold metal. He pulled the ammunition free and stuffed the bullets in his pocket. Standing, he slung the rifle's strap over his head, left his father's room, and stepped over his father's unconscious body on his way out the front door.

He was halfway to the pickup truck before he heard the voice.

"I heard about your brother," the voice called.

When Lil' D turned, the rifle was in his hands, and the look was in his eyes. There was no doubt about it. If anyone had seen him, they would have known. This ancient, elderly man, the type of guy a person Lil' D's age would see and forget about as soon as he took his eyes off him, he knew Lil' D's mind just by looking at him. He must have seen the man a hundred times, but never bothered to speak to him. To the young, the old were invisible, until they spoke.

"Yeah? Watchu hear?" Lil' D asked, offended. In his mind, he had imagined himself as a boulder dislodged from the edge of a cliff—

unstoppable. Instead of rolling and tumbling and proceeding down a path that had been inevitable to him, his momentum had been halted. Despite his error, despite his intrusion, this old man was still an elder, still contained more knowledge than three Lil' D's, all in wrinkled, ancient packaging.

"I heard about your brother." Lil' D's jaw clenched. "He was a good man."

"What do you know about it?"

"I know much about it," the man said. "Come inside, and I'll tell you."

With his impetuous hurtle toward suicide thwarted, he considered the man's words, and realized he didn't want to die that night. He slung the rifle over his shoulder and stepped up the small, covered porch leading to the interior of the old man's trailer.

"I didn't know you knew my brother," Lil' D said.

The old man walked hunched and limping, his pace agonizingly slow. His shoulders sagged, and he gripped the handle of a small cane in one arthritic palm.

"Everyone knew Dwayne."

Lil' D had his doubts. Wadn't no one that called Big D "Dwayne" anymore, except for the newspaper. He had almost crumpled up the small obituary upon finding out they had referred to his brother as Dwayne Greene instead of Big D Greene. They had made his brother small, and he hated that.

"Please. Have a seat," the man said, gesturing to a small loveseat in the middle of the trailer's living room. It was wide enough for the short man to lay on, but Lil' D's legs would stick off the edge if he tried to do the same. The little man continued into the kitchen, shambling, slow and sick. In Lil' D's mind, he figured it wouldn't be long until this man joined his brother in the grave.

The old man bustled about in the small kitchen, which, if it was anything like the one in his own trailer, would be mostly broken but for one burner and an oven that had never been used because that's where all the pots and pans were stored. As the little man clinked and clanked about, Lil' D studied a flag hanging over a chair. Blue on the top half, and green on the bottom half, a red wagon wheel sat in the center.

The man returned, pushing a small, metal cart, polished to a high sheen. It was the type of cart you'd find in a fancy restaurant, some waiter pushing around steaming pots of coffee and tea. "Tea?" the old man asked, and Lil' D noticed the man's accent for the first time. It wasn't pronounced, but it was definitely there. He couldn't quite place it, but he liked the sound of that accent, felt a certain musical quality he couldn't quite identify.

Lil' D nodded his head and accepted the man's offer. While it wasn't a beer like he'd shared with his father, it wasn't water, and he was thirsty. Lil' D hated the water that came out of the tap in their kitchen. It tasted of sulfur.

The man set a cup on a coffee table and poured the tea for Lil' D with shaking hands, steam wreathing his gnarled knuckles. Lil' D could barely contain his need to reach out and help the old man. But he knew that would be an insult, so he let the man struggle to prove his usefulness. We all need that from time to time.

"What is that flag?"

The little man cocked an eyebrow. His face was still plump, somewhat round, his skin faintly olive-toned underneath all the wrinkles. His whiskers stuck out of his face, sharp and white. The top of his head was exposed, thin strands of white hair, drifting across a liver-spotted scalp. "That is the flag of the Romani."

"Romani?" Lil' D asked. "Are you Italian?"

The elderly man smiled then, a pained thing Lil' D would feel sorry about later when he learned the truth and realized his ignorant ways must have harmed him.

"No, no. *Romani*. Not Roman. A common mistake."

"What's the difference?"

The odd man smiled at him. "I will tell you, but first we must make introductions. My name is Robert."

"Is that a common Romani name?"

Robert shrugged. "Common enough."

"I'm Daniel, but everyone calls me Lil' D… well, they did."

"I know," said the strange man nodding.

From there, there was a small moment of awkward silence. Lil' D leaned forward and gripped the small teacup. It was delicate, fancy, the type of thing he would imagine finding in the houses of the rich people on the other side of town, far away from drunk Indians who pissed on their own fences.

"Where were you going tonight?" Robert asked.

To kill. "Nowhere."

"Going nowhere with a gun. Never a good proposition." The elderly man smiled at him then, and Lil' D couldn't help but feeling like a small child caught scribbling on the walls with crayons by his father. He didn't like the feeling. "I know where you were going."

Lil' D sipped his tea. It was bitter and hot, and he didn't understand how anyone would choose to drink it. Give him a Dr. Pepper any day. "We are not so different, you and I," Robert said.

At this, Lil' D put his tea back on the table. Its warmth worked his way through his body, and he began to worry the elderly man had drugged him. Maybe he was a pervert. Either way, he doubted he had anything in common with this old man. "What could we possibly have in common?"

"Pain."

"I'm not in pain," Lil' D said. Talking about feelings and emotions was not a thing done in his family. If you were hurt, you put a smile on your face and pretended you weren't. If you were really hurt, you put a beer in your belly and kept doing it until you were so drunk you wouldn't remember when your emotions had topped the dykes of your heart and came spilling from your chest and your eyes in screams and wails. It was better that way.

"It's hard, isn't it?" Robert asked.

"What?"

"Changing your reality, admitting your world has been irrevocably changed. This was something your brother understood, why he would go away sometimes."

"What do you know about it?" Lil' D spat.

"I know your brother loved you, wanted to make life better for you in the only way he could, by going out there, into the uncaring world, and trying to find something that would help you. Something that would allow you and him to escape the fate of your father."

"What are you?" Lil' D asked. "Some sort of fortune teller?"

At this, a beautiful smile broke over the man's face, his tea-stained teeth glinting in the gloom of his trailer. Behind Robert, the Romani wheel on the flag began to spin. "Fortunes don't need to be told. They need to be interpreted. My people were known as fortune tellers at times. Though we had no such gifts, our culture, our people, lived outside the rules of European society. We could see the way the world worked because we were denied a part in it. Observers we were, and when the Germans or the French or the Polish came to us and begged us for their fortunes, we only told the things we observed… and sometimes they didn't like this, and so they accused us of witchcraft and thievery. When Hitler rose up, he didn't just kill Jews. He killed my people too, brought death and ruin down upon us, shipped my people off to concentration camps. This you can understand. Your people are much the same, yes? Dwayne understood this."

"Understood what?"

"That the world hates the other. The world can't stand someone or something that refuses to fit in, and so they concoct lies to make them different, to transform them into enemies. We had our concentration camps. Your people had your reservations, your forced removals from lands that had been home for thousands of years. My people were gassed and shot and stabbed, after they had their fun with us. Yours were harassed, shot, and forced to pretend to be white. Sometimes, at night, I wonder which is worse. But all pain is pain, and when we experience loss, we experience a shift in reality. The strong adjust. The weak run off in the night with a gun in their hands, never to be seen by their loved ones again. Which one are you, Daniel? The weak or the strong?"

The room was getting hot. "What did you put in that tea?"

"Something your brother gave me to help with my arthritis, something useful to your people."

"I don't understand," Lil' D said.

"You will."

Sieg Hair

Chapter 5
Robert's Tale

Sweat oozed from Lil' D's pores. The wheel behind Robert spun faster and faster, when he didn't look directly at it, but when he concentrated on it, it stopped spinning altogether and hung there, pulsing and swelling with a heartbeat of its own. In Lil' D's ears, he heard the rush of the old man's breath.

"Peyote?" Lil' D asked.

"Mescaline, but the same thing."

"Why would you do that?"

"Your brother talked a lot about you, told me of his hopes and dreams for you. Your brother was a good kid, just like you are. He would hate to see you throw your life away, especially on his account. So would I."

"You don't even know me."

"I don't need to know you to know your pain, to know the peril you are in. I've seen it before."

The man leaned forward and pulled the tea from Lil' D's grasp. As he did so, he noted a series of numbers tattooed on the man's forearm. "I am going to tell you a story. Focus and learn, and maybe we can both have what we want."

"I don't understand."

"You want revenge. I want you to fulfill your brother's wishes."

It sounded nice, like having your cake and eating it too, but Lil' D was not a cake man. He was a pie guy.

Robert leaned forward and tapped Lil' D between the eyes with a thick, twisted finger, swollen at the knuckles like a bursting sausage. "Focus."

And Lil' D did.

Robert Holomek was seventeen years old when his life was changed. With their caravans circled in the forest, the villagers from the nearby town, people they had not necessarily considered friends, but who they had considered kind, came for them, led the jackboots against them. With rifles in their hands, they came, their faces pale and smooth, their cheeks shorn of mustaches and beards. They came baby-faced, and somehow this made it worse.

Their hands poked out of stiff looking clothing. Red armbands with a black symbol in white strangled their upper arms, like the hands of a father pulling a child back from the path of a rushing horse so he wouldn't be crushed underneath its hooves. They came for them, his family, his people, like parents rounding up the children from the woods before the sun went down.

As they left, Robert cast a look over his shoulder, fixing the sight of the only home he'd ever known in his mind. The caravans sat still and forlorn. Their horses were removed from their traces and plodded along with them, their hooves clipping and clomping on rocks. He didn't know then what it all meant. They had kept free of the troubles so far, assumed the people in town didn't hate them that much. They were wrong.

When they were marched through town, Robert saw many familiar faces. Some cursed and spat at them, making gestures to ward off the evil eye. Some couldn't look at them at all. These were somehow worse.

His sister, Anya, called to the children she had played with, because she often came to town with father when he came to cut hair. These children looked sad, and when they went to call to Anya, their parents shushed them and pulled them close to their bodies.

"Father, what is happening?"

"The same thing that's always happening. Hate upon hate. But we have each other, and this is enough."

"But what about our things?"

"Things are replaceable."

A man in a jaunty cap smacked his father in the shoulder with a rifle butt, breaking his shoulder blade. Father screamed in pain and gritted his teeth. From then on, no one talked at all, until they were ushered to the trains. They were shoved inside, forced to stand, their arms around each other. Only when the doors closed completely did they speak, quietly, lest the soldiers open the doors once more. Anya cried while Robert tried to tend to his father's shoulder. Robert's tears were silent, but all around the train car, underneath the stink of anxious sweat, he could smell the salted tears of his people. There were so many of them. He imagined the train car filling with tears and drowning them all in the darkness.

"When we get to where we are going. Stick together," his mother said.

The train ride was long, and whenever they stopped, more people were added to the car, shoved in on top of each other. His father hissed in pain as people pressed against him and his broken shoulder. Every stop, more and more people. Different voices, different accents, same fear.

When they got to the final stop, they were relieved to climb from the train car, but not for long. The baby-faced soldiers separated them, sent Anya and Mama in one direction, Father and Robert in another. They cried and called for each other. But they shut their mouths fast when one of the soldiers smashed in a woman's face with the butt of his rifle, splattering her nose. From then on, they walked with their heads down, their eyes on their shoes, wondering when this nightmare was going to be over.

It would be a long time.

Robert thought he had turned eighteen a few days ago, but he couldn't be sure. There was no one there to keep time with him. Father had… disappeared… a few weeks ago.

A man, smart-looking in his evil clothes, sat with a heavy sigh in a chair.

"Shave," the man commanded as he pulled his black leather gloves from his hand.

Robert reached for his razor, pulled a leather strap tight and began dragging the blade across it. The razor had to be sharp. If he cut one of these men with a dull razor, he could wind up like Peppi. He didn't want that. Didn't want anyone to see his brains, ever.

"I need to look sharp before the next load comes in."

Robert knew better than to talk back to the man. They were not equals. He was not here for conversation. Better to keep quiet than to raise the man's ire. The man was not the one in charge, but he was higher up than most of the baby-faced boys who pointed rifles at him and dragged his people off to die.

"People feel better when they see a clean man, yes?"

Daniel nodded his head, just in case the man was looking for some sort of confirmation.

With the razor's edge gleaming, he leaned the man back in the chair, exposing the soft skin of his throat. One sharp slice would be all it would take to kill the man. He could watch his skin part, watch the red stuff begin pouring out. It would be his last act, but it would be a fine last act. A tragedy, like the stories his father had used to tell around the campfires. But in those stories, no one was ever happy. Revenge was a child's emotion. His father, who had been beaten and harassed in town, never sought revenge. Perhaps he should have. Then they would have thought twice about turning in his people.

Robert set the edge of the razor blade on the man's throat, dragged it, listened as it scraped away the stubble of the previous evening. Robert had shaved many a neck since he had been put here, shaved many a head as well, both the soldiers… and the new arrivals.

He lost himself in the process as the man blathered on and on. He thought himself important, superior, and he talked like it. Robert nodded in all the right places and concentrated on making the white shaving cream disappear from the man's skin.

After some time, the man finally said something that caught Robert's attention. "You have been a great worker. I wish to reward you for this." The man's arm raised and pointed to a box sitting on the bench where the new arrivals waited to have their heads shaved. It was important that their heads be shaved. It was another method of control, another way of demeaning the people and letting them know they were nothing more than animals in the eyes of the Nazis. Treat them like animals, strip them of their hair like they were sheep, and as a group, they would act like sheep. Is that not what Robert did every day? For the past few months, he had had the opportunity to strike, to kill a person who was as evil as evil could be, and yet he had stayed his hand at every turn.

Dutifully, he walked over to the box and picked it up. It was a cheap cardboard box, the type of thing one would receive in the mail. Had the soldier received a care package from his family, gifts and chocolates, sweet reminders of home, a home that would still be there when this was all over? Just in case that was the case, he carefully opened the box, making sure to keep it intact. Inside the box, he discovered something strange. He pulled out this odd item, heavy and metal, with a rubber cord snaking from one end. Sharp teeth, dangerous and deadly and gleaming, sat inert. He found a container of clear oil and a set of instructions written in German in the box as well.

"What is it?" Robert asked.

"Electric hair clippers."

"What?"

"Electric hair clippers. You plug them into the wall, and it cuts the hair for you, quick and easy, like in Berlin. Should make processing significantly more efficient. Also, it'll keep your gypsy hands from touching my head nearly as much. I swear every time I get a haircut from you, I need another shower."

So, not so much a gift as much as it was a representation of this man's disgust at being touched by someone he considered less than human.

The man smiled as he looked into Robert's face, waiting for his shave to be finished. "Gypsy, listen. Take good care of those clippers. When they break, your life is over. Can you read the instructions?" the soldier asked.

Robert shook his head.

"Better find someone who can. Your life depends on it."

Even though a slight tremor wormed its way into his hand, Robert managed to finish the soldier's shave. For a moment, the soldier sat examining his pale face in the mirror. Satisfied, he nodded, stood up, and placed his hat upon his head.

"Read the manual. Learn it," the soldier said. Then he left.

After he had shorn a new batch of bedraggled survivors of their hair, a soldier escorted him back to the prisoner's quarters. It was cold that night, and his breath plumed in front of his face as he pulled the manual from the box. An old Jewish man sat next to him, and Robert explained his situation.

"Can you read?" Robert asked.

The man nodded his head. "It seems reading was the only thing I was meant to be good at in this life."

From there, the man read the directions, reading them over and over into Robert's ear, until he was able to recite the instructions word for word. Oil was key. Forget to clean and oil the teeth of the clippers, and they could seize up, and then his life would be over. Robert fell asleep whispering the instructions to himself in the middle of the night. No one said anything or asked him to be quiet. If he could prolong his life by inconveniencing those around him, then so much the better in their minds. The next morning, the old man who had read the instructions was taken away, and Robert never saw him again. Two months after that, the Americans came. Several years later, he finally discovered the fate of his mother and sister, along with cousins and uncles, and aunts. He was the only survivor, though he felt dead for a long time after. He moved to America, making his way as a barber.

In America, he was still the lowest of the low, a forgotten person from a forgotten culture. While the news detailed the horrors of the holocaust and the genocide of the Jews, for his people there was no outrage, no homeland for the Romani, which was fine. They wouldn't have wanted it anyway.

Over the years, Robert learned to read and became obsessed with it in fact. He needed to read, needed to hunt and find the men who had killed his family. It was not a glamorous hobby, and in time he would come to regret all the time spent poring over records and old photographs and listening to testimonies. But one day, he found the man who had given him the clippers, living in Morocco.

But before he visited the man, there was one stop he had to make.

The Romani community in America was small and insular, relatively speaking. Once the Romani had traveled to the land of promise, most of them had set about screwing like jackrabbits and trying to repopulate the earth with their people. But he knew of one man who was like himself, a man so consumed by revenge he had eschewed the trappings of family. Pavel Gerhart was his name. His accent still spoke of his Russian upbringing, and his eyes, despite the thick eyeglasses perched on his nose, still smoldered with a life-affirming hate.

"You are going to see this man?"

Robert nodded.

"I know we've talked of this, joked about it over drinks, but are you sure this is a good idea?"

"I must do it."

"He is the same man. You're sure?"

"I have done the research. He is the same."

"How is it that he has escaped notice all these years?"

"Money, charm, these things can get even the Devil a seat at the table of God."

Pavel grunted. "This is not untrue." Pavel leaned forward then, pushing his gin and tonic to the side. "What is that you want then?"

"What we talked about."

In addition to being a friend, Pavel was a bit of a mystic, a man who believed in the stories of his childhood, when demons walked the world, before it had been made safe by the ever-present burn of electric lights. He could do things no other man could do, and when he was gone, he would take his ways and his stories with him, leaving the world a poorer place. But for now, there was time… time for him to leave his mark.

"I want you to do it. Do what we talked about."

Pavel swallowed, then snatched his gin and tonic off the table, the ice cubes clinking in the glass. He drained the tumbler in one go and set it upon the table. "Can you believe it? Ice on demand, gin whenever I want it, but life still comes down to one thing. Who hurt us? And did they pay in kind? You know, we could sit here all night, drinking and laughing, and everything would be fine. We would live as we have for decades, hurt but alive. It doesn't have to be done."

"For me it does," Robert said.

"The thing… the thing I said I could do… I am afraid."

"I am, too. Every night, when I go to sleep, I see this man's face, I imagine him coming for me, making me take the humanity of people who are going to die, whole families at this man's hands. If this is what it takes to be unafraid, then I am ready."

That night, Pavel kicked Robert out of his apartment, and he had to stumble through the streets of New York until the sun came up. It snowed all night, and when he returned, he was frozen, his fingers stiff with early signs of arthritis. Pavel had done his work, and then hung himself. Robert packed up the clippers, hating himself for what he had done. Pavel's death was on his hands.

Robert, overcome with emotion, stopped his story then, stood up, and hobbled back into the kitchen.

Lil' D, trapped in his mind, and trying as hard as he could to focus, sat on the loveseat, watching the wheel on the flag spin. From the kitchen, the sound of rushing water, the clank of a metal teapot on the small, electric stove.

When the old man trundled back into the room, Lil' D's head was still spinning. It seemed they had been talking for hours. From deep inside, he clawed his way up from the hole he had been resting in, forced himself to make words happen. "What happened when you met the man?"

"I got my revenge."

"Was it worth it?"

Robert shrugged his shoulders. "Worth it; not worth it. I had to do it."

"How did it work?"

"It needs hair."

"Hair?"

Robert nodded, and from there, he told the rest of his story. When he was done, Lil' D rose from his chair and headed to his trailer to check on his father. He took the rifle inside, unloaded it, checked that his father still breathing, and then went to his room. On his bed, he stared at the ceiling for hours, recalling Robert's tale as if remembering a dream he'd had months ago. The ceiling above quaked and trembled, the cracks between the cheap ceiling tiles glowing with an angry, orange light.

In the morning, he walked over to Robert's trailer, and Robert handed him a box, ancient and faded. Inside, he found the clippers, older than his father even. Next to the clippers was a small, bedraggled paper manual, yellowed with time, written in a language Lil' D couldn't understand.

"Be safe," Robert said.

Sᴵᴱᴳ Hᴬᴵᴿ

Chapter 6
In The Club

The last few locks of Carl Trotter's hair fell on the floor, fluttering to the ground like a butterfly whose heart had burst in mid-flight. He stepped to the side, not wanting the hair to touch his boots. He handed Trotter the mirror, spun him around in the chair so he could see.

"Top notch," Trotter said. "You got a real talent, Daniel. Maybe one day, I'll let all these boys grow their hair out. Then we'll really get some work out of you." Daniel smiled, though he didn't mean it, and he pulled the cape from around Trotter's neck with a flourish, like a matador side-stepping a bull.

"You given any thought to that job opening?" Trotter asked. Earlier that month, Trotter had asked him if he wanted to drive to Portland, to attend a rally, shake up the liberal fucks in the big city. If there was one thing Trotter hated, it was the liberals in Portland.

"Why not?" Daniel said.

"Why not indeed?" Trotter said.

Something in the man's tone put him on alert, but when he looked at Trotter, he was just the same old man, ruddy cheeks, and eyes swimming in alcohol tears. The moment passed as quickly as it had come, and he didn't think twice about it.

The parking lot filled with shaved-headed goons dressed in bomber jackets and camouflage pants as if they were going to war. These pants were held up with skinny suspenders, and underneath the suspenders, they wore simple polo shirts, tight-fitting to show off the muscles of their arms. Their wrists were decked out in bracelets studded with metal, and every one of them wore boots, leather and heavy, tied up with laces that climbed up to the shin.

Daniel wore the same clothing he had been wearing for months. The first time he'd seen someone dressed that way had been the night his brother died, at the American Circus concert.

Lil' D wasn't a huge fan of punk rock. He found it simplistic and childish. Like, it was mostly stuff he would have found cool in middle school. Back then, he'd been angry at everything: his mother, his father, hell, sometimes himself. Eventually, he'd grown out of it, but his brother loved the shit. Seldom did a band deign to stop on their way to Portland from California, but when they did, you could bet that Big D would be in the audience. You could also bet he'd be three sheets to the wind, and that's why Lil' D was there even though he didn't care for punk rock. Big D needed a driver.

Packed inside, the first band came on. Even if they weren't drunk as shit, he doubted they could have played their instruments very well. The sound system in the Eaden Lounge was garbage, the venue itself even more so. It was the type of place that seemed held up by graffiti and band stickers. At one point, Lil' D had to take a piss, and he stepped into a dark bathroom with no lights. The smell of urine was strong, and the soles of his shoes splashed as he walked. Fighting the urge to throw up, he aimed his pecker at what he thought was a urinal and let loose. He didn't even bother washing his hands when he was done, and he vowed not to return to the bathroom, even if he had to hold his piss all night long.

When he came back, he found his brother engaged in a circle pit, running counterclockwise, his arms pinwheeling, his body spinning in circles as he bounced off people, a huge toothy smile on his face. Grants Pass didn't have a huge punk rock community, and there were many people out of place in their cowboy hats and boots. So seldom did something new come to Grants Pass, that when a band did show up, you'd find all sorts of people there.

Lil' D stood to the back, smoking cigarettes and ashing on the concrete floor. A haze of smoke filled the hall, most of it from cigarettes, but some of it from stinky, cheap weed. The floor grew slick, and the bar at the side of the room did steady business. He would have bought a beer for himself, something to pass the time, but he wasn't yet old enough to drink. A couple more years, and he and Big D would have to find someone else to drive them to shows.

He was eyeing the bar longingly, trying to imagine his future with alcohol, when a commotion arose at the entrance to the dancehall. The crowd parted for a group of newcomers, repelling each other like the similar poles of a magnet. The newcomers were big, mean-looking, their heads shaved, and their arms encircled in red bands. Nazis. Lil' D's anxiety flared, and his first instinct was to go into the pit and grab his brother, tell him he wasn't feeling good and needed to go home. But he knew what Big D would say. "Then go wait in the car." He couldn't leave his brother alone while those Nazi fucks were around.

The Nazis strode to the pit, and a space cleared around them despite the packed nature of the venue. They walked with a drunken sway, a brash cockiness people only had when they knew they could start shit and get away with it because they had backup. In the middle of the pit, they pushed and shoved each other, their faces split with dumb grins. The largest of them, also the stupidest looking of the bunch, jumped in the air, spinning, lashing his leg out like a martial artist, his Doc Martin flying through the air with dangerous momentum, a fascist Bruce Lee. The foot didn't connect with anyone or anything, but if it had, it would have done some damage. Then they were all doing it, spazzing around, striking the air with their fists and their feet. They reeked of barely contained violence, and the crowd pressed further against the sides of the venue to escape their furor.

Big D, still in the throes of punk rock, didn't notice the group until he was already in the midst of them, spinning and swinging. The skinheads pushed and moved him along, and Lil' D breathed a sigh of relief. It didn't last long however, as his brother finally noticed who he was among. He spun away one last time, and then came to a halt at the edge of the pit, eyeing the bald bastards.

Lil' D saw the look on his face, that obstinate look he got when he decided the world wasn't going to tell him what to do, a frown as of a three-year-old thinking. His brow furrowed; his fists clenched. Lil' D tried to push through the crowd to calm him, but whereas they had been packed tight before, they were now virtually plastered together in a seething, stinking ball of humanity. There was no room unless you were in the pit. The band played on, loud and distorted, Lil' D's pleas and cries unheeded by the crowd around him.

Then he saw Big D pointing at the skinheads, yelling and shouting, his words lost in the grind of electric guitars and the bang of drums. The Nazis fanned out. "Help him!" Lil' D yelled. But these were Grants Pass folk. A fight was a fight, and no one would step in. The rules of the fight dictated such.

Big D charged in, one fist connecting with the tall man's jaw, and the other shoving one of the smaller Nazis to the side. He swung and pummeled, looking not so different than from when he was dancing to the music. Then the skinheads closed in on him, surrounding him. As Lil' D tried to push through the last line of people separating himself from his brother, he saw the glint of something among the shadows, something metallic, something shiny. Then the man raised his fist and approached his brother from behind. His arm swung, hard and fast. Big D had no idea it was coming. He couldn't brace himself, couldn't dodge it. As the large skinhead's brass-knuckled fist plowed into the side of Big D's face, his head snapped to the side. He fell like a G.I. Joe action figure, his legs stiff, his arms locked into position, and his fists clenched. He rocked like a banana on the ground, and then the Nazis stomped him with their boots. The crowd, shocked by the violence, stood stunned for a moment and let the skinheads do what they were gonna do. Then he saw people stepping in, people who couldn't stand by and watch a man be killed.

The skinheads cursed and shoved, daring anyone to take a swing at them. But no one did, and when the man with the brass knuckles still gripped in his fist saw the blood, saw Big D wasn't getting up, he rounded up his crew and dragged them away. Finally, Lil' D was able to break through the edge of the crowd and reach his brother. By then, his legs were drumming against the filthy floor. The skinheads were gone, and Lil' D's life was changed forever.

Daniel watched as Carl Trotter exited the barber shop, greeting the animals in the parking lot with his Nazi salute. It was returned by young men looking for a good time, looking for a place to belong, looking for the

American Dream that had been promised to them. But all they'd found so far was hate and a world that, quite honestly, didn't give a shit about them.

Before the other guys would come in to get their hair taken care of, Daniel carefully swept up Carl Trotter's hair and placed it gingerly among the other bits of hair in the plastic bucket by the back door. When he was done, there was already a crowd of five people looking to get shined up. They smiled and laughed and joked, like anyone else, not a racist word spilling from their mouths. But they didn't need to say the words to show their hate; they embodied it, oozed it with their outfits and their barely contained aggression.

The afternoon was long, and by the time the sun went down, and the first strings of electric noise assaulted the cool night air, Daniel had shaved three dozen heads. It would be the last time he ever cut someone's hair.

Sieg Hair

Chapter 7
Burn the Hair

When the music started, the last of his customers left the small barber shop, exiting through the front door. Daniel turned out the lights and moved through the barber shop in the darkness so no one would see him. In the back of the shop, he picked up the small bucket containing all the shorn tufts of hair he'd collected that day.

He carried this bucket out the back door, into a wild area, dusty and quiet, the way backsides of buildings naturally are, nature patiently waiting to take back the land. The clippers were safely stowed in the ancient box under his arm, and for the first time since he had met Robert, he began to question if maybe the man was crazy. He was old, for sure, had seen much in his life, but maybe he wasn't all there. Maybe, what Daniel was about to do wouldn't make a lick of difference at all. He decided he would be ok with that. If it didn't work, he would just walk away, no muss no fuss. He'd given it a shot.

From his pocket, he pulled a pack of matches, struck one, and dropped it into the bucket. The hair caught fast, and the plastic bucket began to melt, the stench of burning hair mingling with the reek of melting plastic. He stood watching it, making sure it didn't go out. That was his biggest mistake.

"What are you doing?" a voice asked.

He turned to find Sage standing in the corner.

"Nothing," Daniel said, nervously clutching the box holding the clippers. *Why is she here? Why her? Why now? Dammit.*

"Doesn't look like nothing."

Daniel was at a loss to explain his actions. He'd figured that with the concert going on, no one would care about someone lighting a small fire behind the barber shop. "Come on," he said, "let's go to the concert."

"Well, aren't you going to put it out?" Sage asked.

No. "I can't."

Sage was confused, and he felt something snap between them, whatever tenuous relationship he had built with her switched, and she became… something else.

"And why is that, Daniel?" another voice called from the darkness. The voice sounded like a twenty-dollar cigar.

No. He knew the voice, had been scared of it for months now. Ever since he had made friends with Clint and Aidan at a local dive bar, and they had introduced him to the compound, that voice had haunted his dreams. Carl Trotter stepped out of the shadows. Behind him lumbered a handful of shaved heads, glinting in the moonlight.

"What are you doing, Daniel? Some sort of Injun ritual, some sort of savage magic?"

Daniel said nothing. There was nothing he could say.

Carl came up to him then, put a meaty hand on his shoulder, squeezed his meat painfully. "I saw a man today. He was looking for his son. He stank of alcohol, had skin the color of shit. And would ya believe it? When he showed me the picture, it was you, a little tanner, but I'd recognize your face anywhere."

Oh, fuck.

"Daniel Greene, brother of Dwayne Greene. Am I right?"

Daniel nodded his head. His legs were frozen in place, Carl Trotter's big hand acting like some sort of fleshy taser, freezing his feet in the dirt. Behind Carl, he saw Clint, large, stupid, the man who had killed his brother, and he was cracking his knuckles now. Aidan stood to his side, just as furious, just as full of hate.

"You come for revenge, didn't you, boy?"

A lone tear fell from Daniel's eye, and he regretted everything that had led up to this moment in an instant.

"How were you gonna do it? Huh, kid? Were you gonna go squeal to the cops?" Carl stepped away, and the skinheads moved in, surrounding him, grabbing him by the arms, squeezing him painfully. The box of hair clippers fell from his hand and to the ground, and Clint kicked them to the side. The stench of melting plastic and burning hair stung Daniel's nose, but he couldn't make himself talk, couldn't make himself fight, even though it would be quicker that way, quicker than whatever they had in mind for him.

"You should know the cops are in my pocket. Me and the police in this town are real tight. They would have told me, Daniel. This would have ended the same. You should have left well enough alone, kid. Now we have to kill you."

"You can't!" Sage yelled.

"He's not even one of us," Trotter yelled, cowing Sage. "This piece of shit lied to us, pretended to be someone he wasn't. You understand?"

Sage nodded her head, the tuft of green hair on her forehead bobbing up and down.

"Good." Trotter stepped up to Daniel, his arms held tight by Aidan and Clint. He punched Daniel in the ribs, and the air exploded from his lungs. He sagged, but the Nazis held him up so Trotter could continue his beating. Five punches later, with his ribs destroyed, Trotter said, "Let's get back to the show."

As the skinheads led Daniel away from the barber shop, Sage stood off to the side. There was nothing she could do. He didn't blame her.

SIEG HAIR

CHAPTER 8
IT COLLECTS

Daniel Greene had the best seat in the house. It wasn't the most comfortable, but damn if it wasn't the best. Suspended from a large, white, wooden cross, his wrists and ankles bound by rope, a group of men moved below him, piling up dry branches. Daniel wasn't surprised by any of this. Carl Trotter had been a member of the Klan since he was a little boy, and while the Klan's power had waned in many places, in the rural areas of Oregon, it was still very much active. While Trotter had changed with the times, adopted a newer, sleeker, less "white hoods" and more "punk rock" approach to the spread of hate, he still clung to some traditions. The burning of a cross was always the highlight of any music concert on Trotter's compound.

On a makeshift stage constructed from wooden pallets draped in a blood-red carpet, Torque Wrench blasted away at their guitars and bass and drums, wailing the words to *Fourth Reich Rising*, their neo-Nazi anthem. Drunken skinheads swirled in circles, their arms slung over each other's shoulders as they pumped their fists in the air.

The smell of burning plastic still clung to Daniel's olfactory senses, almost drowned out by the stink of gasoline rising from his feet, but not quite. *They're going to burn me alive.*

Daniel's head sagged, and he resisted the urge to cry, though he felt the sadness for his father. *Will they ever find my body? Will my father ever have rest? Is he going to have to go to the morgue and identify my charred corpse?* It wasn't his life he cried for, but the lives of his brother and his father.

Carl Trotter sat on a set of metal risers, a cigar clamped between his teeth, puffing occasionally, and sending up a cloud of acrid smoke. He hadn't stopped staring at Daniel since he'd been put up on the cross. Behind his thick glasses, shining with firelight, the man studied him.

Clint and Aidan, arm in arm, danced by, shooting him the bird, and then laughing. They spun away into the crowd. Burning a man alive was nothing to them. Why should it be? They had already killed one man and gotten away with it. There were maybe a hundred people here, and not one would lift a finger to save his life.

A rowdy group of broads, their Chelsea haircuts glowing with all the colors of the rainbow, strutted by him, mocking him with rude gestures and unpleasant faces.

The worst part about the whole thing, other than his own impending death, of course, was that he didn't want to be here when it happened… when it came to take what was promised. He almost wished he hadn't completed the ritual. At least then, he'd only have to take part in his own death. Daniel knew he was cowardly. He had been fine with performing the ritual and then disappearing. It made sense to him. But now… now he was going to have to bear witness to all of it. The dread and the anticipation were too much. He wished they'd just start the fire and get it over with.

Torque Wrench finished performing their latest disaster, leaving a lull in the action as they chugged beers on stage. During this lull, with the music gone, and the world returned to normal, no one looked at Daniel. For that moment, he was invisible. It was like they were afraid of him, as if the music had provided them the courage they'd needed to behave like bloodthirsty animals. Without the music, they weren't nearly as brave. Even their conversations were hushed and secret, as if by speaking too loudly, they would allow Daniel to escape his fate. Raw wrists and ankles from struggling against his bonds let him know it was hopeless to fight. If there was one thing Nazis were good at, it was tying fucking knots in rope.

When Torque Wrench had finished downing all the beers they needed to fuel their affront to every legitimate musician worthy of the title, they headed back onstage, weary like construction workers at the end of their shift. The guitarist pulled the guitar strap over his head, the drummer picked up his drumsticks, and the lead singer spit onto the stage. No one cared what the bass player did.

"One, two, three!" the lead singer yelled, and the drummer kicked into action, followed by the bassist and the guitar player. The singer, Lord Master, screamed into the microphone, shouting rage-filled syllables only the people who had read the liner notes would know. Daniel had never read the liner notes, so to him, this all sounded like abysmal noise. Fitting that it would be the soundtrack to his death. If the fire didn't kill him, the music would. He couldn't decide which way was worse.

With a heavy sigh, Daniel let his head sag. Consequently, he didn't see it enter the scene. Not until the first scream was he alerted to its presence.

"What the fuck?" someone shouted, and Daniel forced himself to blink away his tears and stare incredulously at the monstrosity before him. It presented itself as an amorphous shape, a shadow at the back of the clearing. Like a slug, it undulated across the flattened, beaten grass, but it was no slug. Robert had told him exactly what would happen. The mass, even larger than Robert had expected, made its way to the metal risers, and it rasped up the rough metal edges, flowing upwards against gravity despite the lack of arms and legs.

For the first time that night, Daniel smiled as old Carl Trotter caught an eyeful of his own doom. The shadow moved under the single sodium light hanging above Trotter's strange fairgrounds. The light highlighted the thing's true nature. Shot through with strands of red, brown, blonde, and black, the shadow was in reality a wad of hair, kinky, curly, and straight, all formed into one large mass—a giant, hairy Brillo pad. Carl Trotter threw his cigar at it, and it bounced off the thick hair hide, a shower of sparks blinking and disappearing in the blink of an eye. Standing at the upper edge of the metal risers, Trotter waited until the last minute to dive off the back edge, plummeting to the ground, falling as awkwardly and heavily as you would expect from an old, out of shape man. The blob of hair flowed over the risers, hung down, and then enveloped the screaming Trotter. Within moments, Carl Trotter was gone. The hair beast rolled onward questing for its next meal, as it would until it had completed its task.

As it trundled across the ground, quickly for a thing with no legs or arms, the intertwined hairs spun and weaved. Inside the mass, Carl Trotter's body was turned into spaghetti, the strands crawling across his body like the wire of a cheese slicer, pressing through flesh. The multicolored hairs all turned the same color, different shades of red.

The next victim was Clint. He stood in front of the mass with a rifle in his hand. "Fuck you!" he shouted, aping the action movies he so loved. As he squeezed the trigger of his AR-15, he exhorted everyone else to do the same. "Come on! Kill it!" Only a handful of people joined Clint in his attack. He was no leader, just a violent dumbass. Most people chose to run screaming from the clearing. Torque Wrench had stopped playing altogether and were frantically packing up their gear, one fearful eye over their shoulders. They needn't have worried. The beast only killed those it had been offered. Though, after hearing their set, Daniel sort of wished the members of Torque Wrench had come in for a haircut.

As Clint emptied his rifle into the hair beast, he screamed all sorts of racial epithets at it, even though all the hair in the wad belonged to white men and women. The hair didn't bother to stop. It didn't argue or listen to the insults hurled its way. It didn't care about bullets or screams. Instead, it rolled onward, spinning and grinding like the world's most complex drill bit, excreting bits of Carl Trotter's body as it rolled forward.

Daniel tried to remain invisible on his cross. A small titter of amusement escaped his lips as Aidan fled fully from the field. The hair would get him. It was of one mind, and it wouldn't be stopped. A couple of Clint's friends stood their ground, but they had received haircuts that day, and the hair rolled over a group of three who stabbed at the mound of hair with knives. The hair steamrolled them, driving them to the ground. As it moved across their bodies, it emitted a sound like a buzzsaw cutting through wood.

The sight of his friends dying was quite enough for Clint. As the skinhead tried to escape, a tendril of corded hair shot out and wrapped around the man's ankle. Slowly, the tendril contracted, pulling Clint toward the hair mass. A steady wave of blood and severed flesh escaped from between the million strands of hair. To Daniel, it looked like the top of a fruit punch beverage dispenser down at Dale's convenience store, the liquid always in motion, bubbling and frothing. Underneath the buzzsaw sound of hairs sawing through bone, Clint screamed as he was devoured. *That's for Big D.*

When the hair had finished rolling over Clint's good buddies, Daniel found that one of them had survived, though he looked worse for wear.

Covered in the blood of his friends, he stood up dazed and confused, probably wondering why he survived and no one else did. *Maybe it was God. Maybe it was a message from the Lord above.* Those were the thoughts Daniel imagined were going through the man's head. The real answer was, Clint's buddy hadn't gotten his hair cut that day.

Torque Wrench, fully packed up, swerved around the mass of hair in their van. The hair, buoyed by fresh flesh, moved livelier now. It reared up like a massive, blind worm, sniffing the air and searching for its next victim. It crashed down to the earth with a sound like a thousand crackling branches, and then it was off, chasing after the fleeing skinheads. It wouldn't rest until it had collected everything that had been offered. This according to Robert. When it left the clearing, Daniel found himself all alone, the smell of blood tickling his nose.

As the night went on, the wind kicked up, howling through the stubble on Daniel's head. Still hanging, he bathed in his revenge, laughing quietly at the thought of Aidan running home only to find the hair monstrosity had followed him, tracked him down. It had no nose, but it would sniff out Aidan and the others just the same, take the revenge Daniel could not take himself.

He stretched and wriggled, but still there was no way to let himself down. No way to get free. If no one ever came back to Trotter's compound, he could be stuck on this cross forever, even as his flesh rotted away, he would hang from the cross. He supposed if it came down to that, he could pull hard enough to rip the skin of his hand right off. He might be able to escape that way. He shivered at the thought, even as another cool breeze swept across his body.

From behind—a footstep.

"Who is it?" he called. There was no response, and fearing it was one of the skinheads, back for their own revenge, he fell quiet until he could figure out how much trouble he was in. Trotter had made it no secret why he had strung up Daniel. He was an impostor, a spy, and would be dealt with as such. But in their haste to escape the vengeful hair monster, they had left Daniel behind.

The noise came again. Footsteps. He was sure of it.

His heart hammered in his ears. It pounded so hard some blood managed to make it underneath the choking ropes at his ankles and wrists, forcing life into his abused extremities, just enough to let him feel the pins and needles of still-living flesh.

A shadow appeared on his left—small, female. In the faint light from the clearing's one working sodium lamp, he saw her appear. Sage.

"Wh—what are you still doing here?" he asked.

She didn't smile at him like she normally did. There was no flirting, no sexual chemistry at all. They were simply two people on opposite ends of the spectrum. She held all the cards, and he knew it. And she knew it, and in this way, they knew they could be honest with each other.

"You did it, didn't you?"

"Did what?" Daniel said.

"Don't pretend. We're beyond that."

"I did it."

"Why?" she asked.

"They killed my brother."

"That simple, huh? An eye for an eye."

"That simple."

Sage sat down, cross-legged at the bottom of his pyre. She leaned back, her white neck elongating into something imminently kissable. Her neck spasmed as she swallowed. "It's a lot of stars."

Daniel looked up. Indeed, the sky was full of them. Even with the sodium lamp going, they could make out the glory of the sky above. They were far enough away from the city that its residual light didn't intrude.

"You think there's a star out there, where two people like me and you could have wound up together?" Daniel asked.

There was no response. When he looked down, she was gone. But she'd left him a gift, a small, blooming flame.

"Sage!" he screamed.

The flames were hungry, and he wondered if flame was this world's personal demon, the one they all had to deal with in this dimension. Call it, feed it, and it would spread. Below him, by his feet, it did just that. The flame started small, so small a single puff of wind would have blown it out completely. But Daniel was not so lucky, had never been, not from the moment he was conceived to the moment of his birth to the moment of his death. Some people just weren't lucky, and Daniel was one of those.

The flames spread.

Smoke rose up, stinging his eyes and drawing out more tears, which combined with the tears on his cheeks—the tears he'd already shed for a life wasted. *Like salmon… if they left me like this, I would be like smoked salmon when it was all done*. But it got worse. The flames climbed, licking at his shoes. He felt the heat melting the rubber soles of his boots. The leather cracked, and then burned, the laces going up in flames and burning his ankles and calves. His pants were the next to go, and Daniel bent his head down to watch as his lower half was consumed. He welcomed the smoke and the heat now, taking deep ragged breaths between screams. His lungs filled with the smoke of his own burning flesh, and the smoke prevented oxygen from reaching his lungs. His brain, deprived of oxygen, shut down, and his body burned in the night with no one to see. The small amount of fat on Daniel's body sizzled and popped as the flesh turned black.

Finally, the cross itself caught fire. A piece of Daniel's face escaped as a glowing ember of ash, fluttering into the air. It floated along, taking in the death and destruction, blood puddles and bits of flesh spread throughout the compound. Somewhere, in a house ten miles away, Aidan's parents screamed as a monster made of hair burst down their front door, smashed through the door to the basement, descended a set of stairs, and ground their son into blood and flesh shreds. Aidan was its final meal of the night, and when it had finished, it burst into flames that failed to touch the house and all the junk Aidan's parents stored in their basement. It flared like magician's flash paper and disappeared, leaving behind the smell of burnt hair. Eventually, Aidan's parents had to move when they determined the smell would always be there, the memory of violence burnt into reality.

Back in the compound, Daniel's cheek spark found a place to call home. The roof of the barber shop, made of tin and pitch-soaked tarpaper. It caught fire quickly, and the barber shop burned, followed by the scrub grass of the chaparral and the dwarf trees which had been chopped and pruned to make Daniel's bonfire. Carl Trotter's playground of hate went up in flames. When the fire department arrived, they sprayed everything down, finding only one corpse, a burnt little guy, his head bowed like one of those Native Americans in that picture they put on the windows of their pickups.

SIEGHAIR

EPILOGUE

Robert Holomek stumbled through the charred ruins of the compound with a heavy heart. He'd put the boy up to it. There was no doubt about it. He might as well have lit the match that started the whole thing. He didn't care about the Nazis. Fuck them. Eventually, they would have found a place full of pain and torment, as they deserved. But Daniel was a different story.

When the news broke about the fire, Robert had waited for Daniel to appear. But he'd never shown, and his heart had fallen. He'd held a small hope that maybe the boy was on the lam, but when the news talked about the body they'd found, he'd instinctively known it was Daniel. The monstrosity left no bodies. This he had learned with the German. At gunpoint, he'd shaved the man's head with the clippers, a confused look plastered across his face the whole time.

A quick match and a small fire later, and he'd waited, holding the man at gunpoint. It came from the drain, small at first, rustling in the pipes. As it emerged, it swelled and pulsed, growing with each breath. He'd forced himself to watch as the creature enveloped Herr Kramer. When the blood began to ooze from between the strands of hair, he'd turned and fled, the clippers under his arms.

The guilt of that horror still stayed with him, still made his ears flush when he thought about what he'd done. But it was better that way, only just, but it was.

He'd been able to escape… but poor Daniel. Even now, his father was drinking himself into an early grave next door, another casualty, another victim of humanity's need for revenge.

Robert kicked through the remains of Carl Trotter's compound, combing through building after building. As the sun began to edge downward, and the day began to cool, he kicked over a charred chunk of tarpaper. Underneath he found what he was looking for. He bent down, scooped up the soot-covered box and held it in his arms. He walked like this to the main road, where he hitchhiked home. It was easy. He was too old for anyone to fear. A sad reminder that his own death would be upon him soon.

Back at home, he settled into his chair, sipping tea and staring at the box of cursed clippers. Robert blamed himself for having allowed himself to get too close to someone. This was always the way when he got close to anyone. He began to question whether the clippers were cursed or if it was only him.

"Everyone who knows me goes away at some point."

He leaned forward, his arthritic hand throbbing with pain as he clutched the handle of his cane. He leaned his head on his liver-spotted hand, remembering a time when his skin had been smooth and flawless. Now, tufts of gnarled hair sprouted from the knuckles. His knuckles were cracked and bloody from the dry chaparral air, and his skin resembled a spotted banana peel.

"I guess I'll just have to get to know people who deserve to die."

As the sun went down, and the shadows faded in his trailer, Robert Holomek leaned back, and relived the past for the thousandth time in his life. It never went away. Some things never did.

NOSTALGIA KILLS

Fraggle Jackson hid behind a pile of boxes, rubbing his hands together and dreaming of all the shit he was going to steal.

Underneath his denim jacket, the type one might find a prisoner wearing in Shawshank Redemption, he clutched his tools. Lockpicks, thin gloves, a set of industrial-strength bolt cutters—he had it all. And what he didn't have… well, he could get. It was a shopping mall after all.

The biggest problem he'd had so far was trying to figure out what type of shit he was going to steal.

Jewelry could be good, although, easy to get pinched with that shit. You couldn't just throw it up on eBay or craigslist. The police would be looking for it. But yeah, the weight-to-money ratio was right. Only problem was he'd have to sell it on street corners, chat up shady folks who liked shady things, and then barter them to a spot where he could get paid. But, even then, he wouldn't be making as much as he wished. You could barter all you wanted, but it really came down to how much cash a person had on them in those situations.

He scanned around him, studying the bare-bones storeroom, the walls' white paint scuffed and marred by the hundreds of cardboard boxes that had rubbed against them over the years. He hated it back here. It was weird. Its brown trim, and lighting made him feel like he wasn't seeing everything. Wasn't long now, though.

Only an hour before the mall closed, and then maybe another hour after that before all the workers left. Then it was all about the security guards, however many they had. Fraggle had it in his head that the security guards in the mall would be giant pushovers, lazy fucks who sat in a room watching TVs and walking around the mall a few times an hour. If you were smart, and Fraggle was… mostly, you could get into a store, lower the gate behind you so it looked like nothing was wrong, and then fill your pockets, but if he could pick the locks on the doors behind the scenes, they wouldn't even need to do that.

His buddy Lemon said there were probably alarms on the gates, and maybe there were. But Fraggle thought maybe in here, in these back corridors and passages, maybe there weren't any. Of course, if he heard something, they would have to scoot as fast as they could before the cops got on them. He wasn't worried about security guards. He could deal with them, or his Smitty Wess could. Ain't no security guard gonna die over some rich fucker's merch in a dying shopping mall.

Fraggle remembered the mall in its glory days. Had spent much of his youth cruising up and down the mall's polished hallways, hollerin' at the ladies with his homies. Used to be a place on the first floor where him and his friends would get their hair done right. Wasn't too many places outside of the barber shops on Division where a man could get his hair done in Portland, and not at that cost, and not without that damn chatter, always talking, always getting up in his business.

But that salon had gone out of business a few years ago, when the neighborhood had started to change. The white folk moved in, the brown-skinned people moved away, or were priced out of their neighborhoods as their rents rose or their property taxes increased. Now, there weren't no classic barber shops on Division. Now, if you wanted to get your hair cut, you had someone in your family do it. They knew how to cut your hair better than some bitch at Great Clips. Ever since that place went away, he'd grown his hair out into small dreads, and the people on the street had taken to calling him Fraggle, because he looked like a Muppet or some shit in their eyes.

When he'd first told Lemon about his plan, his buddy had scoffed at him, in his usual sour manner. "Whatchu wanna go rob the mall for? Ain't nothin' there but the food court and the movie theater. Shit motherfucker, I'll buy you a movie ticket if you need it. Even sneak in a Big Mac or two."

"Think about it. That mall is a dying place. No one cares about it. You get yourself in one of the backrooms or one of the empty shops, wait a bit, and you'll have the whole place to yourself."

"It's stupid man."

"What's the number one problem with pullin' a boost?" Fraggle asked.

"Getting caught. Getting shot. Going to jail," Lemon rattled off.

"Right. Now, think about this. There might not be much to steal in the mall, but there is some stuff. Who you got to worry about? Some fat fucking rent-a-cop who sits on his ass all day pulling his pud in front of some monitors, maybe a custodian or two, and they're making minimum, man. They don't give a shit about you. Lastly, if you don't like how things are going, there's like a hundred doors you can leave through, and outside, a hundred different directions to go. And on the streets, with all the tweakers and the homeless, we're just faces in the crowd man."

Lemon had thrown a few more curveballs Fraggle's way, but he knocked them all out of the park, and in the end, Lemon had no more arguments to hit back with, so here they were.

They'd scoped the mall out a few times a month ago, knew the police would likely scan the security footage back a week or so for any suspicious activity, and they'd fucking find it. While the neighborhood around Lloyd Center had never been particularly great, it was fast sinking into oblivion. The homeless lay in clusters all around the mall, holding out their hands to beg for money no one could spare, because they were all hand-to-mouth now, ever since the white folk moved in, started building modern apartment buildings with locked gates and locked garages, modern-day castles to keep out the dying masses. Fuck, you couldn't even rob the fuckers as they made you poor. If you could, that would have been something, at least.

Lemon had wanted to hide in one of the clothing racks, get behind some clothes or some shit like that, said he'd seen something like it in a movie called *Bad Santa*, which he also said Fraggle should watch. But Fraggle didn't like Lemon's plan. Too easy to get caught, too easy to get pinned in. Then Lemon suggested the vents, and Fraggle had to break it to Lemon that that's not how vents worked.

From there, they decided they needed to get in the back parts of the mall, find somewhere where a person could hole up, away from the cameras. In order to keep from arousing suspicion, they'd sent a friend of theirs into Lloyd Center. This "friend" had a problem, needed money to keep the problem going, and they were only too happy to oblige.

They told Tracks what to do, sent him in with a cell phone to take pictures. The security guards had caught him, but not before he'd snapped several pictures of a cool storage room, piled high with seasonal décor. Tracks had also remembered to take pictures of the ceilings and the hallways, and they were able to plot out where the cameras were in this particular section of the mall.

When the security guards had kicked Tracks out of the mall, it had been no big deal. Just another junkie wandering where they shouldn't. Tracks had nothing in his pockets but his usual kit, so they'd kicked him to the curb and told him not to come back.

Afterwards, Fraggle handed him a twenty-dollar bill and told him to get lost. When Tracks threatened to go to the cops and rat, Lemon and Fraggle roughed him up a bit and gave him another twenty, told him if he opened his mouth, they'd come back for him.

It was good business to have a guy like Tracks around. He was so desperate for a fix of whatever, he'd do anything to score. Only problem was a junkie has no fear of dying, or else they wouldn't be doing the shit in the first place, so you had to remind them of how pain felt, teach 'em agony again. Tracks was a good dude, just needed reminders about the way the real world worked, not that fucked up drug-fueled world in his mind.

A sudden ripping sound made Fraggle jump. A small giggle erupted from the boxes to his left.

"Yo, man, cut that out. If the sound doesn't give us away, the smell will," Fraggle hissed.

"Sorry," Lemon said.

Fraggle shook his head, his mop of dreadlocks pattering against his skull. I gotta find better friends. *If I score big on this one, maybe I will. Move somewhere cheaper where you don't gotta rob a damn mall just to pay the bills.*

With possible destinations running through his head, he ducked behind a box of Christmas lights and pulled his phone out to check the time. As he did, a message flashed across his phone. *Bring home milk.*

Pshh. It's always somethin'. But that's the way life was, one thing after another. Solve one problem another one pops up. Unless you're rich, unless you got the money to throw at your problems. But he'd never be that guy, a tough realization when you're thirty-five and got a kid at home counting on you.

He filed his girl's text message away in his brain. After he busted this place wide open, he'd have to stop at the store.

As the minutes ticked by, the sounds of the mall faded away. People moved swiftly in the hallways, workers chatting on their way out the door as they headed for the parking lot. A good sign.

A soft snoring angered Fraggle, and he duckwalked behind the boxes to Lemon's hiding spot, placed a hand over his mouth and jabbed him in the shoulder. He awoke with a start, swung half a punch at Fraggle's head, and Fraggle clamped down harder on Lemon's face until he saw the light of recognition twinkling in his eyes.

"Stay the fuck awake," he whispered.

Lemon nodded, and Fraggle released his hold, moved back to his spot, began reminiscing about all the good times he'd had at the mall, all the girls he'd taken to the movies, all the clothes he'd bought, all the time he'd spent sitting in the food court, wasting money, keeping his belly full.

It was a shame what was happening to the place. Would probably be shut down in a year or two. Three stories of glory, that's what it had been. Now the top floor was empty, all the gates pulled down and shuttered. The second floor was mostly the same. The skating rink that dominated the middle of the mall sat empty, walled off by chain-link fences so the people walking on the bottom floor felt like they were circling a prison yard.

Even the stores that were open looked depressing. Walk into the Macy's and you'd find clothes balled up on the floor, hanging half-on, half-off hangers. Only two cash registers operated in a store that used to have twenty working stations, a constant flow of people walking out with shopping bags. But people with money don't go to the mall anymore. People with money buy whatever the fuck they want off the Internet now, and if what they ordered wasn't any good, they balled it up and threw it in the trash.

People like himself and Lemon couldn't do that shit. They had to go to the store, see what they were buying, try it on by waiting fifteen minutes for one of the sporadic employees to come along and let them into the one working dressing room. They had to make sure the fit was right, couldn't afford to be throwing the money away, and returns for a place like Macy's were a hassle, thirty minutes of time down the drain, and there was always the chance the place would go bankrupt, and you'd never get your money back. Then he'd be down at the Goodwill sifting through bins with the other desperate vultures, trying to find the shit the rich folk ordered, never wore, and donated for a fucking tax break.

Fraggle whiled away the hours fantasizing about his score, about living someplace where a guy like him could work a job to pay the bills, to feed the kid, to maybe buy something nice for his girl every now and then. It wasn't here. Not in Portland, that was for sure.

Maybe I'll hit up the jewelry store, see if I can't get Achaia something nice.

Time whispered away in his ears as Lemon tried to stay awake. For Fraggle, he was too pumped up to sleep, though the storeroom was hot, though he baked behind cardboard boxes.

The time finally came, and Fraggle punched Lemon awake. "C'mon. Let's go."

Lemon snorted and stood up, cracking his head on the rack under which they'd been hiding.

Fraggle crept to the door, placed his hand on the handle, and then turned it ever so slow. The weak part of him, the little bitch as his father used to say, expected someone to be waiting on the other side, but when he pulled the door open, all he found was an empty corridor, more white walls and brown trim, the ugliest place he'd ever seen.

Fraggle took his first fateful step into the corridor, and all the moisture seemed to evaporate from his body. His mouth became a desert, and though he knew he should be sweating, his skin remained mummy dry.

Lemon followed close behind him, his marijuana ravaged lungs audible as he breathed, heavy and nervous.

On their left, they passed doorways that led to places Fraggle didn't care about. Here, a hat store, there a clothing store for the well-off white people who dared venture into the mall. Here, a housewares store full of fancy plates and bowls to show off your status to your friends and family. Fraggle didn't have anyone in his life who would have been impressed by fancy bowls and plates, so he continued onward, counting off stores, estimating which one would lead to the jewelry. He'd decided that's where they would go. Some of the other stores might have more cash, but cash was a weak man's game. Better to rob a bank than a mall if you were just going after cash.

When he thought he was lined up with the Harrie Ritchie's Jewelry store, he glanced over his shoulder and nodded at Lemon. Licking his dry lips, Lemon nodded back.

Fraggle reached out for the door handle, tested it, just to see if they even had to break in. It didn't budge, so he pulled out his lockpicks, bought off eBay for twenty-five bucks. The set had come with three sets of transparent locks, so he could understand what he was trying to do with the lockpicks. He wasn't a master, probably wasn't even good, but he had practiced enough to be able to bumble his way through most standard locks, and this place used nothing more than your standard issue Schlage's with a digital keypad. While the employees could use the pad, the managers of most stores still had keys, and that was their first mistake.

Fraggle fiddled with the lock, spinning the mechanism left and right until he discovered which way the lock was supposed to turn. With his tension wrench, he held the lock in place, inserted the probe, and began testing the pins with the end of his pick. He found the most stubborn one, cranked the torque wrench a few more pounds, and pressed up. From there, it was all trial and error.

Behind him Lemon's breathing grew louder and louder. "Come on, come one," he kept repeating, making the task somewhat more tense than Fraggle would have preferred. He ignored his friend's pressure, continued probing and twisting, hoping his delicate tension wrench wouldn't snap in the process. If that happened, they would be shit out of luck, and short of brute force, they would be walking away from this caper with nothing. Less than nothing actually, as they'd already paid forty bucks to Tracks for the information.

A bead of sweat rolled down his face. It tickled his skin, made him feel spastic for a moment. But he couldn't let go now. If he did, the lock would reset, and he'd have to start all over again.

"Come on, Frag. You got it."

Fraggle ignored the words of praise from Lemon. He was in his own world. He'd lost control of his tongue, and it snaked out of his mouth, licked his upper lip, even as his teeth bit down on it. Despite the pain of his unaware body, he continued probing, continued pushing pins and twisting until… *There! I got it!*

He stood back with a smile. The only time he'd ever been prouder was when Achaia had given birth to his son. *Bring the milk. Bring the jewelry. Be a king for a day.*

"Did you get it?" Lemon asked.

"What do you think?" Fraggle asked. He reached out for the door handle, a heavy touch, the type of reach that reeked of cocksure bravado. His hand slapped as it contacted the metal, as loud as weak high-five with a kindergartner. He pressed the door handle down and pushed open the door.

Lemon's first reaction was one of pure joy as the door swung open, and then, his face melted, like… the expression didn't change, the skin of his face just stopped being skin. The hair on his head turned white, and his eyes shriveled in their sockets. A bright, white light suffused his skin, and where it touched, his face ran like melted chocolate, exposing the bones of his skull. Lemon stood that way for a moment as Fraggle tried to make sense of what had just happened. Then Lemon's skeleton dropped to the ground, splashing in the puddle of his being.

Fraggle did what he did best, the only thing that had gotten him through high school… he ran. Though he failed all his classes, though he skipped half the days he was supposed to be at school, he still had a diploma from Jefferson High School, because he was fast as a hiccup, could escape any trouble that came his way. As soon as he saw his best friend Lemon melt to nothing and drop to the ground, surely dead, he turned and ran.

The brown and white hallways slid by him. He ran so fast, it took him a few minutes to realize he must have missed his exit, the door that led to the main part of the mall.

Fuck. Lemon's dead.

But he would be too if he didn't find his way out. He spun around, keeping his eyes low on the concrete floor. Unlike the main part of the mall, they didn't bother with niceties back here. The floor was pure concrete, gray and pockmarked with holes, as if air bubbles had been forced to the surface as the concrete dried. No one cared what the back corridors of the mall looked like. No one cared what went on back here. No one cared if your best friend got a look inside a jewelry store and his face melted. Whatever happened here, he was on his own.

From the corridor where Lemon had breathed his last breath, a high-pitched screech echoed off the plain white walls. The screech made him wince, and he thought his eardrums were going to burst.

Driven to a panic by the scream, presumably coming from the same creature that had melted his brother's face, he rushed for the nearest door, thinking maybe he could get on the other side and barricade himself inside a store. He bounced off the doorway, and another of those hideous screams hit his ears. He heard something pop, and then he only heard half the world.

He turned and ran, continuing down the hallway.

With every door he passed, he reached out and tested the handle. No dice. If he had been a master lockpicker, he would have run as fast as he could until he reached the last door, squatted down, picked the lock and then hidden inside the store until the cops came, jail sentence be damned. Better to go to jail than have his face melted off by… something.

But he wasn't a master locksmith, and so he ran, disjointed and panicked, testing every door he passed. As he ran, he spotted a camera in the corner of the hallway. He waved his hands at the camera, hoping for some security guard to see him, come and capture him and take him away from whatever had killed Lemon.

"Come on! Come on!" he screamed as he did jumping jacks within the camera's field of view.

In a distant part of the mall, a guard sat with his chin on his chest, a thin dribble of spit hanging from his lower lip.

Behind Fraggle came a growl, guttural and otherworldly. He squeezed his eyes shut. *Maybe, if I keep my eyes closed, I won't die, won't wind up on the ground, my skin and muscle turned into a brown puddle.*

He trailed his hand along the wall, still running, not caring if he tripped. His hand fell on another door handle. No luck. He moved onward, until he felt another doorway.

Behind him, heavy footsteps followed him, keeping pace.

Why doesn't it attack? It should have attacked me by now.

A dark laugh came from behind him, a choking, wheezy thing, but deeper than any laugh he'd ever heard. *It's toying with me.*

His panic rose, and he knew he wasn't getting out of the mall alive, would leave behind a woman who maybe could have been his wife, a kid who would grow up without a dad. As he lamented the unfairness of it all, his hand fell on another door handle, and he twisted it out of instinct.

His eyes popped open, and he discovered he was bathed in burning light. He felt his body begin to liquify, and he dove through the open door, stumbling out into a dimly lit hallway, the door swinging shut behind him. He ran, patting his body down with his hands to see if he had turned into runny Jell-O.

With his entire body singing with pain, he slid out into the main part of the mall; his jaw dropped. All around him, people flooded to and fro, their hands clutching bags, an endless tide of consumerism. If you wanted to step out into the middle of that human tide, you had to work up to it, get up to speed, like a car trying to work its way back onto the highway from the emergency lane.

In his shock, Fraggle would have stood there forever were it not for something pounding on the door behind him, something big. His skin still stinging, he ran out into the crowd, pushing people down, noting their out-of-date clothes. One kid he pushed to the ground wore a FUBU sweater. He hadn't seen one of those in fifteen years, maybe twenty.

Onward he ran, heading toward the escalator, shoving people out of the way. They felt real, despite their clothes, despite their hairstyles, despite one man saying, "Watch it, homeslice." Every store stood open, the prison-like shutters invisible, every inch of polished linoleum floor packed with people, fists gripping bag handles from stores like Suncoast and Sam Goody. He split a couple of teenage girls, knocked the Orange Julius cups right out of their hands. He hit the ground floor in a sprint, wondering what the world outside would be like. Then from the corner of his eye, he saw it… the old salon, the woman behind the counter… ringing him up… but not him, the kid he'd been. *Hair looks fucking good.*

Something burst through the door in the back of the salon, and in horror, he watched as it plowed through, sending barber chairs flying, knocking over canisters of blue water and the combs floating within like preserved corpses. Only the heads of the people near the force, bright as the sun, turned to look at it. When they did, they suffered the same fate as Lemon, their skin running from their bodies in rivulets, their fleshless bones tumbling to the ground like marionettes with their strings cut. In a panic, Fraggle took a right, instinctively knowing the force came for him.

He hit a waist-high wall, vaulted it, and found himself on ice, slipping and sliding as some kid, barely old enough to need a bra, did a triple-axel in front of him.

He fell to the ground, scrambling to get his feet on the slippery surface. Behind him, he heard the loud thump of something contacting the ice, followed by a sizzle, the roar of ice melting to water and then steam. He smelled the heat in the air, but still he fought to find his feet, tried to resist the call of the thing behind him, the past... the past was coming to kill him.

It pounced on him, and he felt its hot paws press him to the cold surface for a moment. The ice underneath his chest melted into water, turned boiling hot, and blistered his brown skin. In his mind, the world became simpler, easier, better. He remembered it all, smiled as his body turned to gelatinous nothing. And he understood what held him in place, what weighed him down—the past, nostalgia incarnate. It destroyed him completely, left a stain, and he didn't mind one bit.

"Is it away?" the custodian asked.

The security guard, so rudely awoken by Twitchy Dave's knocking, leaned forward and cycled through all the monitors. "Yeah, it's gone."

"Good," Twitchy said. "Fucking thing gives me the creeps."

"Yeah, well, I don't mind it."

"Any stains to clean up?"

"A couple."

"Cheap bastards," Twitchy said.

"Don't let the management hear you," the security guard said.

"Pssh. Nostalgia can't hurt me. I never look back."

"Guess that's why you're a custodian... at a mall."

"Yeah," Twitchy said, "well, I don't see you goin' nowhere either."

The security guard shrugged, grabbed the handle of his mop, and used it to push the filthy, yellow mop bucket across the pockmarked concrete floor, shaking his head at the boss' new security system. He frowned as he came to the first puddle. It took forever to get a man's juices out of all those little holes in the concrete.

THE NEW GOD

CHAPTER 1
BIRTH

A form, nebulous like a creeping shadow on a wall, materializes from the void. Within this void, something mutable swirls, a moldable mass waiting to become. But there is still much to do. Formed of starlight and need, inexplicably linked to the apes trundling up and down the unsympathetic street, the mass hesitates, delays the decision it must make.

A man, but not a man, waits for it to gain its bearings. The smiling, wrinkled fella wears a hat, old and battered, like something one might see on the head of a cab driver from the fifties. His suit is worn and threadbare, out of place and time among the apes.

"Welcome," he says. "A beautiful day to be born."

But it's not a beautiful day. The sky hangs gray and cracked, carcinogenic pollutants swirling invisible among the frigid wind. Sleet, cold and hard, pelts their bodies. The apes, frozen to the bone, walk with their heads down, their shoulders hunched, unaware of the drama playing out in front of them. Cigarette butts, worshipped for five minutes and then discarded like hookers, line the gutters. Forgotten wrappers, lovingly made in a factory a thousand miles away by people with sore backs, sore feet, sore everything, spin and twirl down the street, while cars spew suffocating exhaust into the air. A man with no traditional home, unless you count the underside of a bridge as traditional, sits huddled in a crumbling military jacket in even worse condition than the man in the cabby hat. Tears stream down his cheeks, but no one sees. He is invisible, just like the man in the cabby hat and the new god.

"You probably have a lot of questions," the cabby says. "Must be shocking to appear out of nothing and all. Happened to me once, but I can't seem to recall those days. Been a long time. But I guess that's all coming to an end now." For a moment, his smile droops as he loses himself in the centuries of memories he has accumulated, stolen from the minds of apes, exploded into his own reality.

"Where is this?" the form asks with a voice emanating from nowhere.

"Pittsburgh."

"Pittsburgh?"

"As good a place as any," the cabby says. "You want it? This city has it."

The form swirls. Upon closer examination, one might see stars and galaxies held within the nebulous shadow of its being. Upon even closer examination, one might find planets, entire civilizations within those galaxies. Upon one of those planets, one might find an exact replica of this entire scene playing on into infinity.

The shadow studies the cabby, recognizes the same swirl of life within it. "Are you me?"

"No," the cabby says, shaking his head. "But we are the same."

"Why am I here?"

The cabby shrugs. "Wish I knew." He looks off in the distance, watches the apes trudging among the idle cars, struggling down the cracked sidewalks, in a hurry to be somewhere, anywhere but on the street. "I'm to show you around, let you get your bearings. Then you can decide."

"Decide what?"

"Who you want to be."

The form swirls, agitated, galaxies destroyed by a contraction somewhere in the head region, the area from whence its voice emanates. The lights flash within its clouded shape, and billions of lives end at a whim. No one cares.

"This what you wanna look like?" the cabby asks. "All them stars and asteroids and galaxies and black holes?"

"What should I look like?"

The cabby shrugs at this. "Maybe we should show you around first. Then you can decide. Come, let's get off the street."

The cabby turns then, pulls open a black glass door set in the side of a building. He holds it open as the form billows and swirls through the door, though it could float through the wall if it wished. Something about the open door seems simpler, and with that, the rules of its life are changed, its capabilities diminished somewhat. Its existence begins to sift through the realms of its own limitations, narrowing down the possibilities.

The cabby follows, circles around the flowing mist, for it has become solid now. "One decision down, a million more to be made," he says.

Inside, the building is old, creaky, held together by time and memory and little else. The ground is covered in carpet like the felt of a pool table. A wooden stairwell leads up into darkness. The hallway ahead bends around the back of the stairwell, blocking off any view, but the form sees it all anyway—people sitting in their apartments, their eyes affixed to distractions, their mouths open, their hands shoving dead life into their faces.

The cabby pulls open another door, and the sound of conversation bubbles out from the other side of the room. It drifts now, drawn to the conversation.

Something warms inside of it at the sight of the room. The cabby moves around the back of a bar. Bottles of liquids gleam and reflect light, their labels intentionally eye-catching, dizzying. The cabby tips his hat at the form, says, "Name's Gazette." With that, he pulls a tumbler from a stack of shining glasses, spins it in his hand like it's made from translucent mercury. He sets it down on the counter with a dull thump, spins around, snatches one of the pretty bottles full of gleaming liquid from the rack, upends it into the glass where the liquid swirls, a miniature brown ocean with a bouquet of sweet poison. With his left hand, he pulls open an unseen cupboard, grips a pair of delicate silver tongs, and plucks out an ice sphere as large as a lemon. When he drops it into the glass, the brown liquid displaces, fills up the entire glass but for a hair's breadth. Gazette pushes the glass in her direction, sliding it across the rich, lacquered wood of the bar. "You drink?" Gazette asks.

The form doesn't know. Doesn't know anything; everything is a decision. At the end of the bar, two apes sit, facing each other, one sliding a brown paw up and down the thigh of the other. Half-drunk drinks drip on the varnished wooden bar, thin napkins disintegrating underneath the tear-like condensation trickling down the sides of the tumblers.

The form admires the way the ape with the longer hair crosses its legs, the heel of one uncomfortable-looking shoe caught on the crossbar of its stool, making the muscles in its leg ripple in a satisfactory matter. It wants to sit like that, but in order to do that, it has to have… legs.

A resolution is made, and the shape models itself after the apes, in a rudimentary way. Its skin takes on the dull gleam of ancient putty, and the galaxies and stars and black holes contained within are hidden by its waxy complexion. Two legs grow, two arms, a vague head shape. With its new body, it settles onto the polished wooden stool, trying to mimic the ape's shape. It succeeds and feels a small sense of satisfaction, a terrific tremor of pleasure. It watches the couple pick up their drinks and mimics their movements. When they open their mouths, the shape rips a jagged slash across the lower part of its head with a dull, gray fingertip and tilts the liquid in the glass into its hole. Tawny liquid floods a planet where a civilization lives, built upon love and respect, before quenching the sun that gave it life, rendering the home of this civilization, perfect in its balance, dead forever.

"Mmmm," the putty-colored form says.

"Thought you might like that," Gazette coos. "I'm supposin' you might be interested in who I am, what I'm doing here."

The shape-nods, not sure where it learned the gesture. The flesh of its skin tears with the movement. It thinks for a moment, and the skin becomes more pliable, less apt to rip at certain movements.

"Nodding's good. You're picking up things fast." Gazette leans on the counter. His arms are covered in hair, fine and gray-red like the pelt of a fox. His face is trustworthy, the type of face an ape might tell its deepest secrets to. "I am the god of veracity," he said. "Used to be a big deal around here. People were always on about the truth. The police used to live on the stuff. The courts, the newspapers, they all worshipped me, bowed down before my altar, prayed to me for facts and proof."

Gazette sighs as the shape dumps another mouthful of civilization destroyer into its mouth. Somewhere in the universe, a planet populated by winged people with phosphorescent asses is wiped out by eleven-year-old Lagavulin Scotch from the planet Earth. They will not be missed.

"But times they are a changin'." Gazette lifts his head, tilts it up to a screen, gaudy and out of place among the natural bar setting. If it wasn't for the TV, the interior of the bar could be set in 1800s Ireland… but the TV, great eyesore that it is, ruins all of that. Gazette sneers at it. "Information is nothing anymore, not worth the breath that spreads it."

The man on the TV pounds his desk, makes his face turn red as he spouts out nonsense. His skin has been turned orange by powders and creams tested on rats in a lab somewhere. The bow tie at his throat is deliberately clownish, a wink and a nod for people to not take him too seriously, but people do.

"They want lies now. Not the truth. They want to be told things that confirm what they believed in the first place. When they are confronted with the truth, they get angry, shout and threaten to kill each other."

Gazette's hand goes to his chest, and his face, so kind and fatherly, scrunches up in pain. He leans on the bar, his hands and lips turning blue.

The shape sits passively on the stool, moving its legs up and down, trying to recreate the physiology of the long-haired ape sitting at the end of the bar.

As Gazette drones on and on about the good old days, the shape listens to the conversation of the humans at the other opposite end of the polished, wooden altar.

"You could do a lot worse than me," the short-haired ape says.

"Could I?" the long-haired one replies, a tease in her voice, not unpleasant.

"You could get one of these cucks out there, one of these metrosexual pantywaists that walk around crying all the time."

"You don't have emotions?"

"Course I do. But I don't go inconveniencing other people with 'em."

"You see emotions as an inconvenience?"

"Real man doesn't let 'em get the better of him."

"Sounds like you live in denial."

"I ain't no pussy."

"No one said you were."

The short-haired ape smiles, tilts his glass back. "You wanna go back to my place and fuck or what?"

"Sure."

"How do you feel about an NDA?"

The shape tunes them out. The words the shape hears aren't the words they say, but rather the meaning behind the words. The apes are fantastic at hiding their true meanings. The short-haired ape's incessant talk about his promotion, about how he is in charge now, are all meant to pump him up, make him seem like a more desirable partner, someone worthy of depositing his seed. The long-haired ape's constant reassurances have nothing to do with his conversation, but are meant to pump up the short-haired ape, let the man know she is interested and not turned off by him. He might be worthy of a DNA donation.

"Hear that?" Gazette asks. "An NDA! They fucking sign contracts now vowing to restrict information! Why, a good bit of slap-'n'-tickle gossip used to be my bread and butter."

As the apes leave, arm in arm, the shape tracks them with its eyes, its putty skin wrinkling at the neck. It watches them exit, their lips and cheeks flushed, to go and do what apes do.

"I suppose you'll be wantin' to see more of the place. Bein' a god's not all it's cracked up to be. Goddin's hard work, so it is. You pick wrong, and you're gone. Why I once had some proto-god fall in love with the steam engine, wouldn't listen to reason, said he wanted to be the god of steam. Couple of decades go by, along comes the combustion engine, and boom, the kid's out. Bye bye, Steamy. Have fun in oblivion with Zeus. You don't want that to happen, do you?"

"I don't know," the shape says.

"Course you don't. Well, come along then. Plenty to see and plenty to do before you decide."

Gazette rounds the bar, holds out his arm for the shape. The shape places one of its hands on his elbow, the cosmos colliding within. Gazette grabs its arm, manipulates it to the right position, and together, the two stroll out into the Pittsburgh night, arm in arm, aping the apes.

THE NEW GOD
CHAPTER 2
COLD FLESH GOD

Gazette leads the way among the blind apes. The two gods climb and hike, though they could have sprouted wings. They try to see the world as apes see the world, stuck on the ground, their feet pressing against the cold concrete. They wend their way through the streets, avoiding cars as they go.

"It's not good to leave behind proof," Gazette says. "Hints is what we're all about. The god who makes their presence known is torn down and buried quicker than you can say Alexcos."

"Who?"

"Exactly."

"Work in the shadows, my friend, and they will see you even when you're not there. And that's power."

The shape nods. Gazette's words make sense. They walk up a hill, indefatigable, the chill air incapable of cooling their cosmic limbs.

Eventually, they stop in front of a man, stooped and hideous. His brown skin gleams underneath the streetlights. So far, the streetlights are the only thing about this world the shape likes. They are so much like the stars within the shape's body.

The man across from them sits with his head down, his scruffy jaw wiggling from side to side. The brim of an ancient and battered baseball cap, pulled down low, hides the upper half of his face. His arms hug himself as if he is trying to keep from being torn apart, a ripped and shredded trench coat flaps in the cutting breeze.

As Gazette and the shape approach, the man stands, growing taller, rising to his full height. His trench coat falls open and exposes his brown chest and stomach. The ribs stick out on the side, but the middle of his stomach is comprised of a mass of scar tissue, pale and knotted.

"Spare a quarter," the man demands.

The shape has no change, has nothing to spare but itself.

"This is Pandle," Gazette says, his face flushing with pleasure as he imparts true information. "He grows in power every day. His purview is those without homes. He's been around for what seems like forever, but only recently has he truly grown in power."

At these words, Pandle lifts his head. The streetlights splash across the sweaty skin under his baseball cap, exposing bloodshot eyes. In the blackness of his pupils, stars swirl and dance. His hand goes to his stomach, and he presses hard, rough digits into the scar tissue there, pulling out a brown bag covered in his own gore.

"Drink with me," Pandle says, "and we shall talk of what will be and won't."

The shape looks to Gazette for confirmation.

"No harm will come to you. Until you've taken your final form, you are unimpeachable."

The shape moves and sits on a berm of concrete separating the road from the sidewalk. Pandle sits next to it, unscrewing the metal cap from a glass bottle. He tilts his head back, drinks from the raw alcohol, squirts a little between his mismatched, rotten teeth and onto the slushy road. He hands the bottle to the shape, and with its unformed, generic hand, it grasps the paper bag, angles the lip of the bottle towards its jagged, unsightly mouth, and tilts back, tasting burning, sweet liquid. It is… not good, and the shape wonders if it has been poisoned. Its head snaps to the side, its cosmic eyes locking on Gazette, questioning. There is danger here; the shape can sense it.

"It's ok," Gazette says. "Tis the drink of his followers, his worshippers, the downtrodden who spend each and every day sitting on corners with their palms in the air, relying on the kindness of others to get them all fucked up."

The shape holds the bottle out to Gazette, but he doesn't need it. Telling facts is his wine, spinning truth his whiskey.

The alcohol makes its way down the shape's gullet and then dumps out into a nebula filled with a dozen planets that had all been colonized by an enterprising race of creatures who most resemble the slugs of earth. Amidst the crushing ocean of Mad Dog 20/20, fortified grape wine, they perish, gripping each other tightly, and wondering why their gods had failed them.

"Used to be I was weak," Pandle says. "Used to be that when people would see my followers pop up, they would chase us out of town, or put us on trains to someplace else. Hard to get a foothold like that. But now," Pandle raises his filthy hands in the air. "I'm everywhere. In Vancouver B.C., I have a whole street to myself. Hastings Street they call it. There you'll find my worshippers lying on the ground, selling the things they've stolen in my name, passed out, communing with me in their drug-laced bliss. I'm an up-and-comer, baby. Not like this dinosaur."

Gazette clears his throat, annoyed by the insult.

"Truth. What good is truth when a lie is so much better?" Pandle mocks.

"What do you want from me?" the shape asks.

Pandle smiles at her, a broken thing filled with shattered teeth, mismatched as if every tooth came from a different mouth. "I don't want nothin'. Just wanted to give my two cents is all. Well, they're not really my two cents. I plucked them out of thin air." The smile falls from Pandle's face. "But that's what I been meaning to talk to you about. You're gonna meet a lot of people, hear a lot of thoughts about what you should and shouldn't do. Such is the world. Everyone has an opinion. But if you're gonna choose to do something around here, this world could use a little more… kindness."

Gazette shrugs his shoulders, and the shape stands listening.

"See, used to be a man down on his luck could hold out his hand, no matter how dirty or maimed, and people would see him, care about his plight. Alms for palms. Now, there's so many of us, no one even sees us. Hold out your hand now, and you become invisible."

"You don't want kindness," Gazette growls. "Tell the truth. You want charity, handouts."

Pandle adjusts his hat on his head, pushes it back so they can see the cosmos in his eyes, the eternal pain of life. "Charity we got. Socks coming out our ass, blankets, tents. What we want, what my followers want, is a way to get out from under the bridge. Oh, people think they're kind. They donate underwear and then wipe their hands of us. But how the fuck does that help anyone?"

The shape speaks in a voice neither male nor female. "Why would you want them to escape?"

Pandle smiles his junkyard smile. "Dead people don't do none of us any good. I need people to make it off the street—to shelter under my wing, and then take flight. There is no one kinder and more charitable than one who has felt the stinging bite of winter while sleeping on the cold concrete. It sucks the life out of you, ya know—the concrete. Sit down on it, and it will literally pull the heat out of you, and people… they just step over you now. While my numbers grow, the turnover—the turnover is no good for anyone."

"You done?" asks Gazette, his voice tinged with irritation, his distaste for Pandle obvious.

The god of the homeless smiles then, is used to being dismissed. He holds out his hand, the creases lined with dirt, his fingernails jagged as if he has been gnawing on them. The flesh on the side of his palms is cracked and worn, faint red lines where the flesh has split. "Can you spare some change? I just spent my last two cents."

Gazette fishes in his pocket, comes up with a shiny quarter. He places it in Pandle's hand, and the dirty god flashes his jagged smile once more. "The boys are up there, waitin' for you." Pandle nods his head at a massive square building, light flooding from its thousand windows.

"Thanks for the info," says Gazette, for old times' sake.

"Any time."

They turn then, trudging away from the ripe man, his rotten scent clinging to them. They leave him squatting on the ground, spinning the quarter as they walk away.

"Why did you pay him?" the shape asks.

"Old habit. Used to be him and me were linked. His people knew everything about the streets, could give you whatever info you needed. Now, they don't care. Nobody asks for the truth of the streets anymore. The link is busted, but for a time we were friends. Call it an old favor for an old friend, I guess."

"Who are the boys?"

"You'll see," Gazette says. "Better you find out without my interference. This is your show, I'm just the ticket-taker. C'mon."

They climb a gentle sloping hill splattered in concrete like gray fudge poured over the ice cream of the earth. Ahead, the slate sky reflects the buzzing streetlights. A bitter wind howls across the sidewalk.

THE NEW GOD

CHAPTER 3
THE BROTHERS AVARICIOUS

A crowd meanders about inside the massive building, apes in brightly colored outfits flitting from one place to the next, walking an eternal circle, pulling bits of paper out of their wallets and trading them for goods—a pressed meat tube in a split piece of bread, fermented corn water, textiles printed with numbers and hanging loose, more textiles to cover their heads, all patterned in black and gold and white.

"What is this place?"

"This is where the Penguins play," Gazette says.

"Penguins… play here?"

Gazette smiles. "It's a very human thing, to take things in nature and turn them into mascots. They love to pretend, love symbols. We're probably to blame for this."

"Are we going to watch the game?"

"Does a human watch ants fight?"

"Sometimes."

"Not the interesting ones."

They slide past the men in suits standing at the front door and waving their wands over the apes. The guards don't see them, don't register them as anything more than a gust of wind. They glide through the crowd, the people parting as they pass, though they don't know why they suddenly shift to the side. Their minds are too small, their worries too mundane to see the world behind the world.

The two gods stand on an escalator, a silver monstrosity of spinning, cycling metallic steps. It feeds them upward into the upper parts of the arena. In the heart of the building, music blasts as people shuffle back and forth with overfilled cups spilling beer on their hands. Gazette leads the shape solemnly to a pair of shining wooden doors. He waves his hand, and the doors swing open for them.

They step through the doors and into a suite piled high with everything a sports fan could need—beers neatly stacked in a small refrigerator and steaming trays of finger foods warming underneath the even heat of Sterno-fueled flames.

Through glass windows, the shape beholds a bowl, thousands of seats packed together for maximum profit, tiered and scaffolded to fit even more patrons. A gleaming sheet of ice glows in the middle of the arena. Tables dot the suite, round, bare, and unattended. Only one of the tables is occupied. Two men, their limbs short, their hands thick and small, sit at a table counting money. Their faces are wide, goblin-esque, but still within the range of human normalcy, despite their overbroad, pink lips and the Bazooka Joe tongues sticking out of their faces as they concentrate on counting their spoils. Sitting next to each other, in their matching black suits, their shoulders pressed together, they look like one creature with two heads.

"I'm pleased to introduce the Avarish Brothers, Joe and Pete." Gazette waves his hand like a museum tour guide. There is no love on his face for these men.

The brothers continue counting, don't look up at all. Their fingers fly across filthy green rectangles of paper. These are important to them in a way the shape doesn't fully understand.

"Hey, how ya doin'?" one of the men asks.

"Likin' the world?" the other one chimes in.

Their accents are thick, brutish, and the shape eliminates a possibility from its future. Whatever voice it chooses, it won't sound like the Avarish Brothers.

"It's ugly," the shape says.

Their fingers fly over their money, and they smile without taking their eyes off their fat stacks. "Ugly can be beautiful, kid," the one on the left says.

"If it wasn't for ugly, wouldn't be any beautiful, ya know what I mean?"

Gazette speaks then. "So far she's only seen Pandle and a bit of downtown."

"Well, no wonder!" the twin on the left says.

"Ya gotta take in the sights, kid! Jeez Louise, Gazette. What are you tryin' to do, scare the poor thing?" the twin on the right asks.

"I thought I'd show the ugliest parts of the world first, move on up from there."

Aware that Gazette considers him a rung on the bottom of the ladder, the left twin's eyes widen at the insult, and he says, "You gotta lotta nerve, Gazette."

"So, you're saying we're just a step above Pandle? That common lump o' shit?" the right twin asks.

"It's no wonder you're on the way out, guy. You got no tact. It's all truth and honesty with you. Maybe if you'd buttered up your truths a little more, people wouldn't be turning away from 'em."

"It's too late for all that now," says Gazette, the matter settled in his mind.

"Yeah, I guess you're correct there," the right twin says with a smile on his face.

The shape, feeling like a fly on the wall, speaks then, making sure its voice is nothing like the Brothers Avarish. "What are you the gods of?"

The twins both smile and reveal perfect square teeth, perfect for nibbling on gold coins to verify their authenticity. "We're not gods," the left twin says, his fingers flying across another stack of dollars. "We're vessels. We are the bank of humanity."

The right twin tosses a block of money on the ground, picks up another, and resumes his endless counting. "The people worship us because we offer them hope, hope they can be something more than shit-shovelers and ditch-diggers. We are the dreams. This"—the twin holds up a stack of cash—"is our gift."

"But you never tell 'em you're not gonna give it to 'em," Gazette admonishes.

The twins stop counting, their heads lifting at the same time. Sitting shoulder to shoulder in suits that cost more than some people make in a year, they look like a mythical, two-headed beast, with bulbous heads and pink tongues flicking out in serpentine fashion. "Whoa, whoa, whoa there," says the left head.

The right head joins in. "You're a fucking guide, Gazette, nothing more. You can do your job, or we can show you to the door right now, send your newspaper-smelling ass off to oblivion. You're already leaving that ink-stink all over our nice suite."

"Say the fucking word," left head says, "just say the fucking word."

The shape is confused, doesn't know what it's supposed to get out of this place. "What exactly are you the gods of?"

Gazette harrumphs and crosses his hands in front of his crotch, his head down, his eyes gleaming a little less than they had before.

Together the twins grin their goblin smiles and say, "We're the stewards of the American dream." Then they giggle.

"Why is that funny?" the shape asks.

Gazette speaks then, as the twins are too busy laughing and smacking each other on the back. "The American dream… there was never such a thing, but enough people came to the country and made it one. These two jokers came into being right about that time, chose pretty damn wisely, too. Thing about the American dream is only a handful ever achieve it. Meanwhile people throw their time and money at it, thinking it's something they can buy. But the American dream is given, by these two jokers, and they only do it often enough to keep the thing alive, keep it on the lips of the people. Here and there, they let someone win the lottery, but for the other hopeless millions of people, they keep 'em down."

The one on the left laughs so hard snot erupts from his nostrils, and he wipes his nose on the back of a hundred-dollar bill. The right head pounds on the table with those short, money-counting hands.

"Taxes, bills, lawsuits, these two chuckleheads have their hand in everything. Think of something holding you back, and you'll find these two holding the leash."

"Oh, that reminds me," the one on the right says. He stands up, runs to a strange machine in the corner, begins pushing and pulling on levers. Steam rises from the machine and the smell of noxious inks sting the shape's nose as polished brass gears, slick with the toil of humanity, begin to turn.

"What are you doing?" the shape asks.

The left head, still blowing snot into hundred-dollar bills, says, "Inflation baby. We're gonna send it up another percentage point. Gotta keep the machine running, you know."

"Inflation?" the shape asks.

"Oh, it's this ingenious thing we made up. Everyone thinks it's real now. Basically, the idea is that the more money you make, the less it's worth. The reality is, it's a way to keep the poor from climbing out of poverty, keeping them right where we want them, buying lottery tickets, betting on sporting events"—the goblin hikes a short, thick thumb over his shoulder—"investing in…"—he started laughing so hard the blood vessels in his eyes burst, jets of green blood injecting into the whites—"stocks. Fucking stocks!"

"It's not even real!" the left head crows.

Gazette shrugs his shoulders, nudges the shape in the ribs. "I tried to tell everyone, but the draw of the dream is too much. They'll believe anything if they think it's going to make them rich and powerful."

"And that's where you come in!" the right head says.

"We've got a plan for you, buddy!" the left head adds.

They chuckle at each other—two jokers in on the punchline when everyone else waits with less-than-bated breath. "You see, there's a new gig in town. Real juicy, junior. We'd take it on ourselves, but as you can see, we only have four hands between us. Unless uhh, you wanna make us triplets?" The twins' eyebrows jig up and down suggestively.

The shape shakes its head.

"Didn't think so," the right head snorts.

The left head fans itself with its snotty money. "Anyways, there's a new trend coming down the pipe, and we thought maybe you'd like to be the god of that. What's good for you is good for us. That's why we'd cut you in on the pie."

The right head speaks then, "You see, there's this new fad out there of people just sort of making up their own money. Cryptocurrency, NFTs, and now EVTs—the next phase. You put your hand into that pile, and it's gonna come away worshipped and glittering. You see, the system they got now, it's weak, ain't no one running it but the damn apes. Soon as they get enough money, they cut and run, getting their cut of the American Dream."

"And that's no good for our business," the left head says. "Every time one of these jagoff tech bros scoots outta town with everyone else's money in their pockets, the dream gets a little weaker. Soon it becomes a myth, then a legend, then a fucking fairy tale, and we wind up floating around this place like the goddamn Tooth Fairy. Now there's a sad sack o' shit, still clinging to godhood thanks to the lies of parents. Pathetic fucker doesn't know what's comin' when money goes away, when people stop having cash to give kids, he'll wind up Gazette over here."

"Thought you was gonna live forever, eh, Gazette?" the left twin mocks.

"Nothing lives forever," Gazette intones.

"Tell that to Apps."

"Her day will come."

"Apps?" the shape asks.

"You'll see soon enough." Gazette turns to the brothers. By now, the room is filled with piles of crisp, clean, hundred-dollar bills, the funky smell of new ink wafting up their noses. "Is that all you had?" Gazette asks.

"What else is there?" the brothers ask together.

Gazette tips his hat at the twins and turns to leave.

"Think about it!" the brothers call as the shape exits the room.

Outside, people bustle about, unaware of how their lives are being planned out for them, how every decision they make is influenced by the machines running behind closed doors, the money machine, the lying machine, the goddamn polarization machine. The shape, if it had a stomach, would have felt sick to it.

"Come on," Gazette says. "That's the worst of it. It's all easy street from here on out."

They step on the escalator to leave the building as the cheers from the apes assembled in the arena enwreathe their ears.

THE NEW GOD

CHAPTER 4
KILLER APPS

After exiting the arena, they take a left, then another left, then two more to wind up in a completely different place than where they'd started. The shape doesn't know how the trick works, and when it asks Gazette, all he says is, "When you're in my business, you learn a lot of shortcuts. Shortcuts are truth, ya know."

Together, they stand outside a church in a quiet neighborhood. Up top, underneath the peak of the roof, a cross, white and forlorn, hangs. The church seems old, ancient even. By probing the building with its senses, the shape learns the bricks had been placed a long time ago by a fervent people for whom faith was not something to be parsed and broken up. The people who laid those bricks only had one faith. It lingers in the air like the smell of baking bread.

"A god lives here?" the shape asks.

"In a manner of speaking." Gazette taps the shape on the shoulder, indicates for the shape to follow.

They glide up a clean walkway, surrounded on both sides by dormant mid-winter grass. In the corners of the building's exterior, stubborn puddles of snow cling to existence. The shape feels a kinship with those puddles.

The church doors, ancient wood bound by black steel, open soundlessly onto a surprising scene. Everywhere the shape looks, it sees wooden pews, tainted with the same fervent smell of faith, but it isn't people who sit in the pews, but poorly formed humanoid shapes. When they turn their heads, at angles that would have broken the necks of the apes, the shape hears whirring motors and servos. The eyes of the creatures light up, and the shape takes a step back.

"You have nothing to fear," Gazette says.

On the dais at the far end of the church, a massive monitor fills the pulpit, twice as tall as Gazette. A voice emanates from the screen, and the illuminated eyes of the audience pulse and flash with every syllable. "There's always something to fear, my dear Gazette."

Gazette removes his hat, and the shape senses something in him. Awe perhaps? Fear? Perhaps a combination of the two. "I brought you the new one. You said you had an idea?"

"Step closer," the person on the screen beckons, and Gazette, with his hat still clutched in his hands, beckons the shape onward.

The would-be god glides between the rows of pews, fighting the urge to flee as the heads of the robotic army in the pews track its progress.

"Ah, there you are," the voice says. On the screen, a digitized set of lips speak, and then break apart, kaleidoscoping into shapes no human mind can imagine, into colors no human can see. "My name is Apps." A face appears on the screen, beautiful but twisted in a way that lends it an air of inhumanness, the cheeks too smooth, the features too symmetrical.

"And what are you the god of?" the shape asks, growing familiar with the process.

"I am the god of progress."

"Progress," the shape repeats, rolling the word around in its mouth and mind.

"Yes. You see, without me, the apes would still be sitting around naked and scratching their asses with sticks, sacrificing their children to the rain god or some such shit."

"Is there a rain god?"

The image on the screen vanishes, replaced by that queer mouth again. The lips open wide exposing digital teeth and a pixelated uvula which shakes as Apps laughs. When the laughter dies down, Apps speaks once more. "Kind of. I mean, in some backwater parts of the world where my influence has been ignored, some people still worship the natural elements. But those gods are so weak and so overlooked now that to call them gods is an insult to the true gods."

The shape looks around the church and says, "This doesn't look like progress."

The digital lips quirk on the screen. "Are you going to be the god of rudeness? Plenty of that going around in the world, although you'll have to fight Troll for the title."

"No. I didn't mean anything by it."

"Those machines are the next evolution in life. Why have human followers when you can have something better, something that lives longer, something that once it knows your presence, can no longer deny it?"

Gazette wrings his hands, but keeps his mouth closed.

"You would do away with the humans?"

The mouth smiles. "Not completely. Anyone who knows anything about technology, knows you always keep a backup in case something goes wrong." A few of the heads in the audience turn, and the shape glances at them nervously.

"Do they think?"

"All thought is programming, my dear; the only difference is what the machinery is made out of. Cells and liquid and gooey things or circuits and metal and gold? The humans want to deny this fact, but, well, we know better, don't we? We always know better."

Just then, there is a knock at the door. The lips quirk. The front door pushes open, and a dirty, frozen man enters the room, rubbing his arms, hoping to find a place to warm up. When the shape turns to regard the man, it sees nothing more than a lower evolutionary form.

"Hello?" he calls, his fingers sticking out of his gloves like frozen sausages, the skin cracked and peeling from long exposure to the cold. "Holy smokes, what kind of church is this?" The man steps further inside the church. "Is anybody here? I don't mean to be a bother, but it's awful cold out tonight."

The man shambles past the shape, and underneath the stench of his unwashed body, he is assaulted by the smell of fermented something— grapes? Of the lowest quality.

As the man passes by without so much as a glance, it's clear he cannot see the gods in the room.

The lips on the screen cluck, an oddly human sound coming from a digitized set of lips, the sucking of tongue pulling away from the back of one's teeth to create a perfect "tsk." At this signal, the machines rise, their hands and arms whirring with electric motion. The homeless man turns around.

"No, I forbid it," a voice says. When the shape turns, it sees Pandle standing off to the side.

"You forbid me nothing, Pandle. If you wanted to keep your dog, you should have yanked on the leash when it started sniffing around this particular fire hydrant."

"You gonna work with this one?" Pandle asked. "You gonna do this to all my followers?"

"Oh, come now, Pandle, I'm sure we can make homeless artificial life."

The automatons surround the homeless man. His eyes are big and round as they place their cold hands, not even disguised as human hands, around the man's arms. Then he screams as those metallic digits close, smashing his skin and bones like a mum squeezing a teabag to get the last drop of lovely tea. The sound of his bones breaking is barely audible underneath his screams. A shard of ulna escapes his skin, and his blood paints the floor of the church.

None of the gods react. Even the shape understands this has to happen sometimes.

The automatons squeeze and break the man. When they are done, he falls to the ground, broken and twisted. One of the automatons picks him up, cradles him like a man carrying a sleeping child from the backseat of a car, his limbs lolling in unnatural ways. The automaton carries the broken lump of flesh from the church, and the shape puts the poor creature out of its mind.

"You didn't have to do that," admonishes Pandle, looking from the shape's face to the screen.

Apps clucks again, clearly annoyed by the god of the homeless. "Every time I encounter you, you become more and more human," says Apps, the ultimate insult.

"I'd rather be like them than be like you. I remember when you walked the earth, actually set foot on the ground like the rest of us. Now look at you. You went and digitized yourself and got rid of your body completely."

"Bodies are weak, Pandle. I thought you'd know that by now. This way, I can be everywhere at once. Why soon, I'll have the lag problem all figured out, and nothing will stop me."

Pandle turns and leaves in disgust, only stopping to give the shape a quick bit of advice. "Don't be like that one. There's a fine line between being a god and being… that." He exits through a side door, leaving Gazette, the shape, and Apps alone.

"I'm sorry for the interruption. But he'll pay. Sooner or later, he'll pay with his very being."

"Would you like that?" the shape asks.

"Oh, child, I am not in this world to like things. I'm in this world to improve things, and when Pandle is gone, that will be the very definition of improvement."

Gazette's normally pink face is pale now, and he looks like he wants to be anywhere but in the church of Apps.

The lips on the screen smirk, a wet tongue licking its lips before it speaks once more. "Let us speak of your purview."

"This ought to be good," Gazette says.

Cyclotronic heads turn in his direction, the mechanical eyes in their metal skulls glowing with menace. "What was that, Gazette?"

"Nothing."

"Say nothing. Be nothing. Perhaps there are other dimensions where your talents will be useful."

"My purview?" the shape prompts.

"I have one thought, one suggestion that will usher in the new age, the dawn of the new gods, the cementing of our presence in this world. One word—A.I."

"A.I.?"

"Artificial Intelligence."

"But… I thought gods needed faith. How would I even survive if my flock is not… alive or capable of faith?"

The lips part, emit another laugh. "Simple connection. As the AI rise, there will be those who worship them, those who champion their ways. It's their faith you'll have until the AI become sentient, until they achieve singularity. And then, why, you'll be as powerful as me, and we can put these meat bags to rest, mothball them in a closet somewhere… let's say Cleveland."

"Revolting," Gazette mumbles.

"Think about it," the lips say. Then, without warning, the screen fades, blips away in a flash of light and leaves them alone in the church with the electric hum of robotic believers.

"Is that it?" the shape asks.

"I think so. She has a knack for doing that—disappearing at the wrong time, or maybe the right time in her mind. Come on. Let's get out of here. These things creep me out."

The shape nods, and they turn and stride through the pews lined with electric life, robot necks whirring as they mark the progress of the new god and the old.

THE NEW GOD

CHAPTER 5
PEPPER

"Where are we going?" the shape asks.

"I'm hungry."

"Hungry?"

"Yeah. I have to eat. It's one of the decisions I made when I was a new god, and it's one of the few I don't regret."

They hike through city streets, the heavy sky above pressing down on them, the wind slicing through the streets like a knife, chasing the humans into their homes. Garbage tumbles along the gutters, dancing among the cigarette butts, the broken glass, the discarded Starbucks coffee cups.

"How many gods are we going to see?" the shape asks.

"Only a few more to speak to, and then there will be the ball."

"The ball?"

"Yeah, the God Ball. What? You think a new god is born every day? It's a rarity now. All the good spots have been taken, and humanity has reached the apex of their culture. You seen it with Apps; they're on their way out. You might be the last god who takes humanity as their Source, if that's the way you go. I'm not trying to make you choose or nothing. I'm just here to give you the truth."

"Why did you choose to be the god of veracity?"

They step over one of Pandle's followers, leave him shivering on the cold concrete in the midst of prayer. He tips his sacred bottle to his lips. Communes.

"World used to be different. Used to be dominated by one god, a selfish sort, concerned with making sure no other gods were born. He accomplished this through lies, through witch hunts where his followers would kill in his name. But there were a few among the humans who saw through these tactics, who treasured the things they could see, hear, feel, and touch. If it wasn't for me, none of you would be here. There'd just be the one god, not the many. People would have never grown. They would have sat around on their knees, working the farms, giving their goods to the church, basically toiling like ants."

"Do you think you made the right decision?"

Gazette presses a nostril closed and blows a wad of snot onto the chilled pavement where it begins to freeze. Later, a woman will slip and break her neck on the frozen god wad. "Beats me. I mean, maybe they were happier back then? Maybe?"

Through the streets they wind and turn. Eventually, in a crumbled section of town where the buildings are crowded in on top of each other, low, old buildings with the stink of the ages upon them, they find a glowing source of light. A restaurant, pictures of meats and cheeses plastered on the front of the store, tubes of glass-encased neon glow red, form the word "FOOD." The interior is narrow, impossibly so. You have to turn sideways to pass anyone in the hot dog-shaped building.

Pictures of mortals line the wall. In these photos, they clutch bits of wood, cradle rubber balls in their hands, glide along the ice on metal blades. Some of the photos have autographs on them, unintelligible ink swirls no one pays attention to.

In the back of the restaurant, humans sit alone, bent over, their ever-swelling bodies hunched over as they pile edibles into their mouths, chewing and chewing and chewing. Sweat beads on their shining, greasy foreheads, and they wash down each mouthful with liquids infused with CO_2 and made thick and sweet with the syrup of corn. They swipe at their sweaty brows with the backs of their meaty hands, eating for the pleasure of their god.

One of the sweating men finishes, sits back, looks relieved for a second. Then another plate of food appears out of thin air, steaming hot and irresistible. He sighs and leans forward to feed once more. Another eater's stomach explodes, not in a shower of gore, but silently... inside. He bleeds out internally, his life given to food, to his god.

The deity working the grill waves a hand in the air, and the man's body floats through the air, drops into a shining metallic reservoir, like a massive upside-down bell. A handle on the side turns, and from another end of the machine, out comes the man in pink and gray ribbons. The god grabs a gob of this meat, shapes it with his thick fingers, and plops it on the grill. It sizzles.

"Morning, Peppi," Gazette says.

"Ah, Gazette. You come for your last meal, no?"

"Who's to say?"

"If you say it, it's truth. Yes?"

"I will not say it either way. There's always hope."

"The sands have filed out, my friend. You are but a grain on the precipice of an escarpment, hesitating before falling into the abyss."

"You always have a way of cheering me up," Gazette says.

"And who is your friend? Could this be? The new god?"

"Not yet. Still showing this one the ropes, but my guts got empty on me."

"The usual?" Peppi asks.

Gazette nods.

Peppi, dressed in a meat and grease-stained apron, spins then, turning to a flattop stove. With a gleaming spatula in his hand, he reaches into a bag and pulls out the ingredients he needs, cheese and eggs. He flicks his wrist and flips the sizzling meat. The eggs quicken, turn white. The cheese settles on top of the meat, begins to sag like a Dali painting.

"Is he a god?" the shape asks.

"Ah, yes. Peppi, the god of the gorge. He makes the food for the people, has perfected it, turned it into an art. Every year, he gets them to eat more and more. Hell, every year he gets me to eat more and more. Thank Us for celestial metabolism, or else I'd be as big as a house." Gazette pats his belly. "Sad, really. If humans are on the way out, it's only a matter of time before Peppi's on the way out as well. Robots don't eat food. Unless Peppi can make an electricity sandwich, he's gonna be out of a job."

With his back turned to them, Peppi holds up his spatula. "That's a great idea! I'll get right on it."

Peppi's spatula reaches into his magical bag, pulls out a length of bread as long as a child's forearm. With the spatula, he makes a single, quick slice. He spreads the bread open, exposing its fluffy white innards. In one fell swoop, the man sweeps the ingredients off the flattop with his spatula and places them on the bread. After sprinkling a pile of lettuce on the sandwich, he closes it up and hands it off to Gazette.

"What do I owe ya?"

"What happened to D.B. Cooper?"

"He survived, moved to Brazil, died in an orgy involving a donkey, three women, and a bottle of bathtub whiskey."

"Ah! That's what I thought it would be."

The two gods lock eyes. "You were a good customer."

"Thank you." Gazette turns then, and they leave the restaurant and its walls plastered with pictures of sports figures smiling into cameras while they pose with baseball bats, footballs, and hockey sticks.

Outside, Gazette gasps and leans against the wall. His hand goes to his chest, massaging the skin there.

"What is it?" the shape asks.

"I become… thin." After a few moments, he seems to recover, stands upright. "Better fix my thinness." He unwraps the end of his sandwich and takes a huge bite. The shape thinks he had to use magic to even get his mouth around the thing. No human's jaw could open that wide. He takes his bite, then leans back against the wall, his head staring up at the orange-gray clouds as he chews. "Mmmff-mmmph. So good. I'll miss these. That's for sure."

Gazette holds the sandwich out to the shape. "You want a bite?"

But the shape doesn't know. It regards the strange concoction with some doubt. The flesh of an animal seared, the milk of an animal curdled and congealed, plants beaten to a fine powder and mixed with fungus in the form of yeast, all mixed in with the smashed up embryonic yolk of a bird.

"Oh, go on. It's delish. You haven't lived until you've tried it."

"All that death, so you can eat this one thing. Plants, animals, fungi… for one… what do you call this?"

"The Number Twelve," says Gazette, his teeth sparkling in the winter night.

The shape, unsure of how responsible it is to force itself to eat, holds out a hand and takes the sandwich from Gazette. It brings it up to its face, where a couple of slits open in the broad shelf of its face. The slits open wide, and Gazette hears a small rush of air as the new god takes a deep whiff of the world. Within its internalized cosmos, a planet soon becomes enwreathed in the smell of cooked pork sausage mixed with ground chuck, melted American cheese, and fresh bread. Afterwards, the poor suckers who live on the planet walk around in a permanent state of salivation.

"Go on. Do it," Gazette prods.

The shape opens its mouth, pushes out small, white teeth from somewhere in its body. With these teeth, it leans forward, closes its jaw, and tears off a hunk of warm paradise. It chews and chews until it can chew the food no more. Then it swallows, crushing a galaxy at the beginning of life, where the creatures who roam the planets had just learned to kill each other, to wage war for ideas—the true mark of civilization and superiority. They would be missed. "I like this… eating."

"Just don't let it be a habit," Gazette says, "otherwise you'll end up like the people in Peppi's."

The shape shrugs as its interior adjusts for the sandwich, the cosmos within morphing and twisting to create a reservoir for food, to avoid destroying the universe whenever food is ingested.

"Only problem is, what goes in, has to come out. But that's a problem for a different day."

The shape wonders what Gazette means.

"When you're a god, when you've chosen your purview, you'll know a whole lot more. Might even be able to read minds and take the guesswork out of things."

Gazette's words rock the shape. "Can you read minds?"

"No, no. But I can read people, body language. It's all information, all truth; sometimes more truth than the words coming out of people's mouths or the thoughts in their heads. The body knows it all and never lies."

"Do you like knowing the truth all the time?"

"It is a burden, but that's the nature of being a god, isn't it? We take some of their faith, and we offer solutions. Sometimes those solutions require work. Sometimes they require sacrifice. Give and take, balance, these are the things that allow life to flourish. Without balance, life withers on the vine. If you give a plant too much water, it will die. Too much sunshine and it will shrivel. It's the same with humans."

"What about us?"

"Us as well, I think. That's why you find so many unhappy gods."

Dark streets beckon, and they stride among the lands of men with none the wiser. In forgotten corners, Pandle's worshippers watch them pass, so invisible themselves amongst men that they can behold the intangible because, after all, who would believe a homeless man when he tells of seeing two gods walking down the street sharing a sandwich in the late evening hours?

"Gods can be unhappy?"

"I shouldn't say anything."

"I thought you were the god of truth."

"Just because you know a truth doesn't mean you should say it. I learned that lesson the hard way."

The shape falls silent, spinning the world around in its brain, its neurons nebulae, the spaces between, black holes.

"Come on, there's another who wants to see you."

"I can't wait."

They meander through town, crossing winding yellow bridges that float over cold water churning a hundred feet below. The rivers wind onward, timeless and flowing, carving deep into the earth, leaving scars, unseen but no less painful. On the other side of one of these bridges, the two gods emerge in a more modern part of town. Glass store fronts, shining lights, crisp new finishes, no sign of graffiti at all. Pandle's minions are gone now—disappeared, driven away by luxury and the passing of fresh-minted cash from hand to hand in exchange for goods.

Onward they walk, a giant stadium looming into the sky.

"What is that place?"

"A football stadium. One of the world's biggest altars."

"Who is sacrificed here?"

"You'll see."

A shuttered gate opens for them of its own volition. When they are through, it rattles closed with a metallic bang. The ground is cold on the shape's bare feet, not that it feels it; the shape simply registers the fact. It hopes this will all be over soon. There are many choices to be made, and the hour of decisions is nearly upon it. This the new god can feel in its starry guts.

They stride forward across the concrete and through a gate in the wall.

They emerge into an oval space dotted with thousands of mustard-colored seats all facing a rectangle of perfectly manicured grass. Gazette turns and studies the stands. He spots the god they are looking for, and they head over that way.

They sidle down a row and take their places on the seats next to her, their eyes looking out at the field. The woman sits, her heels up on the back of the chair before her. Her hair is bleached blonde, the make-up on her face thick. Her long fingernails click and clack against the screen of the cell phone gripped in her hands.

"Hey," the woman says.

The shape nods.

"Not much of a talker, huh? You have a phone?"

The shape shakes its head.

"Gazette, what is this? Have you been doing your job or what?"

Gazette clears his throat. "This one is thoughtful, introspective even."

"Oh, yuck. Well, let me get this over with then." A manicured hand extends as far as possible, and the god purses her lips. The cell phone flashes. Her fingernails click and clack as she fires the selfie off into the ether. She sets her phone down just long enough to clap her hands, and from the bowels of the stadium, a long line of uniformed people emerges. They are dressed like warriors, shining plastic helmets upon their heads, pads covering their elbows and knees. In their hands, they hold implements of destruction. In the middle of the field, a black crack appears, widening as the grass slides back. A wall made of cinderblocks as gray and hard as the pavement outside rises upward, two-stories high and as uncaring as the sky above.

The first person in the line—it was hard to tell if it was a man or a woman or something between—lowers its head and runs at the wall. It bounces off, falls to the grass, and then rises again, dusting itself off. The scoreboard lights up, and a video of the proceedings unfolds in near real-time, as one by one the players crash against the wall.

"What is this?" the shape finally asks after the third revolting collision, the sound of plastic hitting concrete ringing throughout the stadium.

"This is my flock," the bleached-haired woman says. "They come to me to pray, to offer up their bodies for glory, for money, for success. In exchange, I take the things they think they won't miss, the things they don't cherish—their brains, their bodies, their hearts. They offer them to me willingly. And I take them gladly if they are ready to sacrifice."

One of the forms turns and raises its hands in the air in homage to the god in the stands. Then he turns and runs, smashing into the wall. The man falls, body stiff, something broken within. A pall of silence descends over the stadium, and then a couple of apes in white coats come out and drag the man off to the side where he lays, his eyes moving in his skull, but his body incapable of carrying out the instructions being given to it.

"This one gave everything."

"And what did you give it?"

"Hope. Hope of getting out from under the thumb of the grind. All I offer is hope, the cheapest of currencies."

"I don't understand. They could die doing this."

"They could. But humans are lazy. They think, oh, it's just a game. If I play this game, I never have to work, and so they are willing to risk it all."

"Quite the Faustian bargain if you ask me," Gazette says.

"No one asked you," the god snaps.

Over the stadium's speakers, upbeat and catchy music blasts them, making their seats shake.

"What is this?" the shape asks.

"Jock jams," the woman says.

"What are jock jams?"

"Fuel for the simple, music meant to inspire a bloodthirst, a willingness to watch and celebrate as people destroy their bodies."

"This song make no sense. Why would people want to jump around?"

The blonde woman shrugs. "Who knows the way of music? Maybe you can ask Lil' Pollo, the god of music, if you meet her. I'm sure Pollo's got some ideas about how it all works; I just know it does." A man crashes into the wall with his bare skull, teeth and blood flowing from his mouth. Woozy, he stumbles a few steps before falling to the ground.

"What happens after this?"

"Tomorrow, they will wake up a little stupider, a little less human, but they will be gifted with great skills, the ability to do things no one else can do. Then they will go out and perform for the masses, entertain them, place the dreams of me inside the heads of their little ones. Then the cycle continues."

"What is your name?"

"It's on the back of my jersey." The woman turns, and on the back of her jersey, she reads the word Ally.

"Ally? Like a friend?"

"No, Ally as in bowling alley. My first name is Pepper."

The shape nods. Makes sense—about as much as everything else in this crazy world.

"I got an opportunity for you here. Been working on this for a while, since we finally got Vegas off the ground, really."

"Here comes the pitch," Gazette mutters.

"And I'm going to knock it out the park," Pepper Ally assures him. "Gambling's getting big, ya know. If there's one thing human's love, it's the idea that you can get rich with little to no effort. We've finally broken the humans down enough that they can't resist the temptation of it. Gambling on sports is now legal, but my friend, Chance, has so many other things in the works that he can't possibly capitalize on the boom. I'm also busy maintaining my faith lines, keeping the team spirit flowing."

Down below, a cloud of blood erupts from the nostrils of a man who drops to his knees and shakes his head. The blood pours from his face as if someone has turned on a faucet hidden in the man's skull.

"Anyway, there's an opportunity there, a chance to be the god of sports gambling. Think about it, over/unders, money lines, odds, teasers, round robins, parlays, sweaty human hands gripping pieces of paper, clinging to the dream of instant riches. The ones who win, praise you; the ones who gamble away their checks and wind up divorced, curse you, which is sometimes better than a prayer."

"How so?"

"A curse has more power behind it, more belief, more faith. I'd rather be cursed than loved, but I didn't think that when I was younger. Thought I wanted people to worship me, worship my body."

The woman stands then, peels off her clothing, reveals arms and legs of pure aesthetically beautiful muscle. Veins worm along her hairless flesh. Every minute movement produces a ripple somewhere else. An anatomy teacher could use her naked body as a teaching model.

"Joke's on me. Love is fleeting. As soon as they lose too much, as soon as they are blithering idiots drooling in a chair, they forget about me, forget I ever gave them their wildest dreams. Occasionally, I get a curse out of it, if the simp is lucid enough to form rational thoughts. But mostly, my worshippers devolve into gibbering piles of flesh with pudding for brains. Just a free piece of advice—love is fleeting, but curses last a lifetime if you really fuck someone over. Right, Gazette?"

The old man nods underneath his hat, stuffs his hands into his jacket as the cold seems to touch him, and for the first time, he seems small, hopeless.

Below, the lines of humanity stop running into the wall, instead lining up across from one another. One man breaks away from the pack, stands in-between the two lines, and they encircle this poor man. With blood streaming down his face, he tries to break out of his imprisonment.

"You want me to be the god of sports gambling?" the shape asks.

"Oh, it's fun. Go ahead and try it," Pepper says.

"How do I do it?"

Pepper rolls her eyes at the new god. "You pick something, any small minutiae that you think is likely, and then you put something of worth upon it. Your house, your life, your love.

"Most people just bet money," Gazette interjects.

"Shhh," Pepper hisses. "That's not a sporting way to think of it." Pepper leans forward, the muscles of her abdomen rippling like ocean waves. "Let's try it. Pick one of those meat bags down there, the one you think is going to win."

The shape studies the apes, really looks at them for the first time. A complex collection of cells all shuffled about by a singular intelligence, not like her own intelligence, not even close, but there is something there spinning in their heads, something vital. They are capable of creation, capable of taking the emptiness of the world and crafting something new and novel out of thin air. But these ones just want to butt their heads against a wall and break each other. What a waste. The biggest of the bunch is a hulking man, towering among the others, but he moves stiffly, as if his limbs aren't meant to be the length they are. Size isn't a way to win this. The shape tries to peer between the layers of cells, get a look at the organs that pump their blood throughout their soft, fragile bodies. But they all look the same. This one jumps faster. That one is stronger. That one is the quickest. In the end, she settles on one who doesn't seem all that impressive. They are right in the middle, well-rounded, shifty, and most of all hungry. The one she chooses is desperate, moves with the ambitious movements of someone who can't afford to lose, of someone who has seen the worst the world has to offer and never wants to see it again.

"That one," the shape says.

"Very good," Pepper replies. "Now, we talk about the stakes. If I win, you will be the god of sports gambling, and we shall call you Bookie. If you win, you walk out of here with my services in your pocket. A favor, no strings attached. You want me to rip Gazette apart? I'll do it. If you need me to climb into a church and rip the man Jayzus apart, I'll do it. Deal?"

The shape listens to the terms. Finds a part of itself that is thrilled by the prospect of losing, of not having the world handed to it on a platter. But another part trembles with fear, doesn't want anything to do with this wager. Pepper's eyes are spinning whorls of green galaxies. She awaits; her palm, soft and smooth, extended.

This is my life I'm gambling. "Deal," the shape says.

Gazette throws his hands in the air. "She hasn't even been to the party yet," he gasps.

Pepper spits a wad of phlegm into her hand, and they press their palms together. Pepper leans back in her chair, a huge smile upon her face. "Turn it up!" she shouts, and someone somewhere cranks up the jock jams until they become an audio assault on the senses.

The shape feels the music vibrating its body. If the nascent god had a heart, it would have synced up with the music.

Pump it! A voice yells over the speakers, and on the billion grass blades below, the group of men and women transform into animals. Fighting to lift each other off the ground, they move like a field of seagrass caught in a shifting underwater current, swaying back and forth, their fists and legs flying as they beat and pummel each other into submission. Blood spills, kissing the ground. Broken teeth come to nestle among the green blades. When a person is lifted off their feet, they scream in disappointment and then join the team of the vanquished. The largest man is the first one to go, as if everyone knows inherently of the man's freakish advantages and resents them completely. He never had a chance.

Pump it!

The shape locks eyes upon its chosen combatant, revels in every narrow escape. Its champion flies through and around the men and women—ducking, sliding, and leaping. He fights as if his life depends on winning, as if he will cease existing should someone lift his feet off the ground. He punches and kicks, even pokes out the eyes of one of his attackers—the tall man again. His face is a snarl, his teeth broken and yellowed by the remains of the blood he swallows. A woman wraps her arms around him, squeezes tight, and the noose begins to close. The man leans forward and bites the nose of the woman. She screams and lets him go. He flutters away like a frightened pigeon, dancing and moving.

Louder!

There are only two combatants left now, and a fever flushes the shape's body as it leans forward and grips the yellow railing in front of it. The two survivors dance among the other men and women, using their numbers against them. The shape's chosen combatant jukes to the left, and two of his assailants tangle legs and ram their heads together with a crack barely muted by the skin of their scalps. They lie on the ground, bleeding from their shattered skulls. The other combatant tries the same move, her eyes wide in her face, her long hair flowing like a horse's mane as her thick legs pump. She leaps in the air, over the tall man who is stooped over, his hands covering his bloody sockets. The top of her shoe clips the man's shoulder, and she tumbles over his body, hitting the ground, wind escaping her lungs. Immediately, the attackers are upon her, lifting her into the air as if they are going to rip her apart, limb by limb.

Louder!

She punches and kicks, making one man's nose point the other way and ripping a chunk of hair and scalp from another woman. But up she goes in the clutches of her competition.

"Fuck," Pepper moans.

A loud buzzer reverberates through the stadium, the jock jams fall silent, and the combatants place the struggling woman gently upon the ground. The game is over. She stands with her head down, her chest heaving. Pepper Ally leaves her seat and begins her stately descent to the stadium floor. The combatants' chests rise and fall, blood pouring from their wounds, sweat setting the exposed nerves on fire. The paralyzed man, still lying on the ground, follows Pepper's descent with eyes gleaming with fervor.

"Come on," Gazette says. "Let's get this dog and pony show over with."

The shape rises and follows the other two gods onto the field.

Pepper walks over to the paralyzed man and stares down at him. She doesn't say a word before she stomps down, flattening his head with a powerful leg. The athletes gaze on with impassive faces. "Better him than me," their faces seem to say. Pepper steps back from the corpse. "A mercy," she whispers. Then she turns and comes to stand in front of the winner, a queen ready to reward faithful and valiant knights.

The shape's chosen champion stands with his shoulders heaving, sweat pouring down his face. He holds his helmet under his arm. Blood drips from his nose, and the skin around his left eye has swelled shut, turning a shade of galactic purple.

"You cost me a lot," Pepper says to him. "But you are the winner. To the victor go the spoils, as it has always been since the dawn of the Olympic games, since the first battles and wars where naked men with sharpened sticks started stabbing each other. You are the victor; your spear is the best."

The man looks at Pepper with fervent eyes, the type of eyes that tell you he'd do anything for his chosen goddess. She leans forward and licks the sweat from his cheek, slurps the blood from his bleeding nose. A glowing nimbus begins to form around the man. The man's passion turns to pain in the blink of an eye, and the people watch as his body is transformed, the muscles bulging and expanding, the bones and tendons in his body thickening to better support the muscles.

The man's uniform rips and shreds, the fabric unable to compete with the muscular expansion of the man. He screams in pain as his body becomes something new, something an ancient Greek sculptor would have salivated at having for a model.

His screams echo loudly throughout the stadium, and the other combatants look on with awe and a certain degree of jealousy as Pepper Ally rewards the man with the gift they all coveted. But sportsmanship keeps them from pouting, keeps them from feeling as if they have been robbed. Pepper demands sportsmanship, always has. There is no room for the selfish in Pepper's stadium, no room for the narcissist. Sport has always been about the competition, not the individual, and if any of these combatants dared hope to return, then they must abide by Pepper Ally's tenets.

The man falls to the ground, his body bowing upon itself as he becomes accustomed to his new density, his new thickness. When the pain has subsided, and the glow of Pepper Ally's benevolence fades, the man stands, naked and bulging. Pepper takes his hand and begins to walk away. Over her shoulder, she calls out to the shape, "Think about what I said. And if you ever need a favor, just let me know."

The other combatants wait until Pepper has disappeared into the bowels of the stadium, and then they fall to the ground, groaning and nursing their wounds.

"Always a spectacle with that one," Gazette says.

"Would she have held me to the bargain?" the shape asks.

"Without a doubt. Come on. One more stop and then it's time for the ball."

"What do we do there?" the shape asks.

"It's a party."

"A party?"

"Your birthday party. You're only born once, you know."

They exit the stadium, leaving behind the broken hopefuls. Outside, the wind has picked up. It presses against the shape's body, but it refuses to feel the cold, to acknowledge it as a force. Gazette leads the way, his narrow body untouched by the cold as well. He holds a hand to his hat to keep it from blowing away in the wind.

They enter the valley of the city—tall, cookie-cutter buildings rising up around them. The city slumbers in preparation for the party of the gods, the party to end all parties.

THE NEW GOD

CHAPTER 6
THE OLDEST GOD

They come to a building that seems out of place, like a giant medieval castle plopped down amongst all the perfectly rectangular skyscrapers. The upper reaches of the building pierces the sky like the tines of a fork puncturing the swollen skin of an overcooked bratwurst. The building's windows are mirrored so you can't see inside. To the shape, it resembles a fortress, something pulled from the barbaric past of humanity.

"What is this place?" the shape asks.

"Just another place," Gazette says. "Another hive where the bees make honey and the queen poops out more workers."

"Why are we here?"

"Same as the last few places. Another god, another proposal. It's all rather tiresome, isn't it?"

"That's the truth."

"It should be. That's all I know," Gazette says.

They push through the front doors. The interior of the building is as mystical as the outside. White metal struts crisscross the ceiling, the view dominated by squares of glass that allows them to see out into the darkened world. The floor itself is comprised of tiles of black and white granite shaped like diamonds, as if someone had taken a chess board and warped it by pushing on opposite corners. They stride across the tiles, the shape's bare feet slapping off the material while Gazette's boots click and clomp.

They arrive at a bank of elevators, press a button, and wait patiently.

"Who are we meeting?"

"An old god, been around since man first learned to think."

"Is that good?"

"Eh, means this one's not going away. In fact, he's had something of a renaissance."

The elevator dings, and they step into it. Without touching any buttons, it flies upward, all the way to the top floor.

When the doors slide open, they are greeted by a panoramic view of Pittsburgh through hundreds of panes of glass.

The shape is impressed. Here, finally, is something worthy of a god's attention. The lights of the city hang in the dark air like fireflies underneath the brooding sky. The clouds above swirl like smoke trapped in a bottle, backlit by the specter of a concealed moon.

So impressive is the view that the shape doesn't even notice the man standing across the way. The entire floor is empty but for this one man who stands gazing out at the expanse. He is clad in a suit, custom-tailored to fit his body, his perfectly manicured hands clasped behind his back as he contemplates the world… or some such shit.

Gazette holds out his hand and indicates the shape should walk toward the being. The shape does so and comes to stand next to the man. His hair is perfect; his features, based upon the image of his reflection in the window, are as well. He is of a medium height, perfectly proportioned.

"So beautiful," the man says, then he leans forward and kisses the image of himself in the mirror. It is then the shape realizes the man hasn't been looking at the Pittsburgh skyline but at his own reflection.

The man turns to the shape, smiles a toothy, perfect thing. "Do you plan on being beautiful?" he asks the shape.

"I hadn't thought about it."

"Well, do. I'd hate for you to jump into this thing and wind up looking like Pandle of all people, or worse yet, this plain sack of nothing," he says indicating Gazette.

The man turns away from the shape, can't bear to look at the nothingness of the shape's form. "Beauty is on the rise," he says wistfully. "The self is back, big-time." He harrumphs a laugh. "For a while there, I thought it wasn't going to make it, but now we're back like gangbusters." The man holds out one of his perfectly manicured hands, and the shape shakes it. "My name is Self, and there's nothing more important than me in the entirety of the realms of man."

The shape shakes its head. "I don't understand."

"How could you? You haven't even decided who you are. Once you do, you'll see that it's good to be me. You see, there's nothing the modern man loves more than him or her or their self. They love their own opinions. They love them so much in fact that even when presented with indisputable proof, Gazette's pathetic purview by the way, they refuse to believe the facts even if it contradicts what they think about themselves or who they think they are. These are my prayers. Every time someone denies reality for the sake of the self, I grow stronger, more powerful. Why, I think I might be, at this moment, the most powerful god in the world."

"Not if Apps has her way."

"As soon as my followers get wind that they might lose their jobs or be replaced, they'll pull the plug on that stupid god. Imagine, trying to create your own followers. Pathetic."

The shape stands off to the side, listening to the vain banter of the two gods as they discuss the future of man, which it turns out, doesn't seem to be much of a future at all.

The burgeoning deity grows tired of the two gods immediately. Gazette, while he had once been necessary to get her bearings, is wearing thin, the way parents do to children over time. It has outgrown all of the things he knew and thought he knew, realizes he is a relic and on his way out. While the shape is thankful for being introduced to food and drink, what else has Gazette done? Showed the god around town, given it the lay of the land. Gazette is, as they say, now irrelevant. Self is disgusting, his perfection more revolting than the face of an acid-attack victim, his confidence and his smug self-assurance, the stuff of fantasy.

Even as the new god thinks about shoving the man out the window, pushing him through the plate glass and into the cold winter air, Self speaks to the shape. "I have need of you, old chap. You and me, we could rule this place. I have more followers than I can handle on my own. What I need is a counter-part, a yin to my yang, a mirror image who can take some of my burden. It's not easy being the best. Will you join me?"

The shape shakes its head, and the God across from her refuses its rebuttal.

"You don't seem to understand," Self says. "This is the best purview in the land, much better than stupid A.I., feeding the hogs, or waiting for people to drop a nickel in your hand."

"I don't want it."

"So, you want to be a loser?"

"There are more options than that."

"No," says Self, his eyes glowing with a dangerous sheen, flashes of lightning passing across his orbs. "There aren't. You're either with me or against me. You're either a winner, or you're one of the losers. Why would you choose to be a loser?"

The shape feels things shifting inside. The myriad cosmos and stars in its guts swirl, begin taking form. The feeling is painful, though not unpleasant. "Just because you say something is the way it is, doesn't mean it's so."

"The fuck it doesn't."

"You are wrong in so many ways, so wrapped up in your own perceived greatness, your own need to be right at all times that you can't ever be wrong, even when you are wrong."

"I'm never wrong."

"You're wrong this time—about me."

Self's jaw clenches, and he straightens his expensive suit. "You coulda been something. Get the fuck out of here. And, whatever the hell you're going to be, make sure you don't cross paths with me, because, like I said, if you're not with me, you're against me. And I always win."

"You just lost."

Self waves his hands at the shape. "No, I didn't."

"Yes, you did."

"No, I didn't."

"Yes, you did."

Self's cheeks flush, and he screams one last time. "No-I-didn't!

The shape knows they could stand here yelling for an eternity, until the sun blows up and wipes them out of existence, and Self would still never relent. "You keep thinking that," the shape says. "We know reality." The shape winks at Gazette.

"Ain't that the truth," Gazette says. They turn then. Gazette cocks an elbow, old-fashioned gentleman style, and the shape snakes an arm through the opening. Together, they walk to the bank of elevators, refusing to even acknowledge the presence of the fuming god behind them.

"Don't ever let me see you again!" calls Self, so filled with his own importance that he is sure the two gods are listening to him, quaking in their boots even. When the elevator doors slide open and they step through, he puts the old god and the new out of his mind, turns to look at the delicious image in the glass. To most people, it is an ordinary reflection, but if you look carefully, the image is a perfect recreation of Self's face, not the typical inverted image most mortals see. In this image, he sees his true face, perfect in every way imaginable.

Below, in a thousand different rooms throughout Pittsburgh, in a million rooms in the United States, in a billion rooms and hovels throughout the world, people just like him, infatuated with their own bodies, faces, and beliefs, regardless of flaws or illogical incoherency, echo the thoughts of Self. I am the best. Everyone else is beneath me. I'm not wrong. They're wrong. If they don't like me or believe me, they don't matter. I am the best. There is no one more important in the world than me. It is a lonely, sad existence, but what other option is there? Admit that you aren't really much at all, just a collection of DNA, a random chance lottery of alleles? Admit that nothing you do matters in the end? Who could go on living after such an admission? Better to tell yourself the lie, better to pray and deny.

Self, having been denied and rejected, allows himself a brief moment of introspection. He doesn't like what he sees. All throughout the world, people feel their god's doubt as a tremor in their self-confidence. If they are looking in the mirror, they see their flaws, the pores that are too large, that one random eyebrow hair that isn't facing the right direction, the non-bleached whiteness of their teeth, the way that one canine tooth is just a little pointier than the other. They hate themselves, and in bathrooms all around the world, they reached for their razorblades, ready themselves to open their wrists, for their lives, so overwrought by lies and Self-delusions, are empty, marked by constant battles to maintain the web of half-truths and denials they cocoon themselves in.

Then, as Self has done a million times before, he shrugs his shoulders, forgets that a new god has been born. All around the world, the narcissists put down their razorblades and go back to pretending everything is ok. Perfect in fact… well most of them. Those who see through the veil of their lives and can't unsee the truth, can't disbelieve it, go ahead and cut through their arms, spilling their blood on porcelain before settling into a nice warm bathtub to drift away to a place where a person doesn't have to be perfect.

THE NEW GOD

CHAPTER 7
THIS PARTY ROCKS!

The old god and the new stride through the city streets as the sky above grows nine-months gray. Soon it will release its bounty upon them, splash it down upon their heads, but for now, there is only the bitter wind, the slap of the shape's bare feet on the frozen sidewalk, the clip clop of Gazette's polished leather shoes.

"What's the point of this party?" the shape asks, its patience running thin.

"It's traditional. God's born, they do the rounds, people try to get the god to join their cause."

"Do they?"

"Not so often, but occasionally."

"Did people try and recruit you?"

Gazette looks up at the clouds, his mind turning back to the time when he was born, when he had become the champion of what was true and correct, when he had instilled in humans the ability to believe in the truth, to wear it like a badge, a noble trait to be one who told the truth at all times. "Had a few people. This was a long time ago, you see. Had a god who wanted me to be the God of leeching. Said it was going to be all the rage." Gazette chuckles.

"That god's not around anymore though. No one even remembers what the four humours are. Poor Hackrates took the long walk to uncreation after a couple thousand years. Don't know that she ever found anyone to become the god of leeches, but hey, it was worth a shot. Sometimes I wonder if I had become a god of leeching, if it would have taken off, if Hackrates would have stuck around."

"Is that all you remember?" the shape asks.

"Eh, I remember Hackrates lying to me. It was fairly obvious at the time. I asked her if leeching was an effective treatment, and she said, 'Effectiveness is secondary to theatricality.' Wasn't a real answer, but I would have been happier if she had said no. Hell, I might even have gone along with her. I guess I've always hated liars. Like Self, up there in his glass tower, staring at his own reflection. He lies to himself constantly, refuses to tell himself the real truth."

Gazette falls silent, and they walk a block in their own heads.

"You gonna be a liar?" Gazette asks.

"No."

Gazette smiles at the shape. "Do you even know what you're going to be?" he asks.

The shape shakes its head.

"Well, you better figure it out. That's the whole point of the party after all. All the gods come together, they show up bauched, and then get debauched, and at the height of the party, you'll announce your purview, and everyone—well, mostly everyone—will gift you a measure of their faith, send you on your way with a bit of a head start as you carve out your niche. I doubt Self is going to gift you with anything, but that's who he is."

The shape seems crestfallen, as if the prospect of choosing the fate of its entire life is too great a burden to bear. An eternity waits to be chosen. Growing up is hard.

"Cheer up," Gazette says. "There'll be booze, food if you feel like you're going to be an eater. Come. See the sights. Drink them in and decide the rest of your life."

"What if I don't choose?" the shape asks.

"Then it's oblivion for you. Just like all the other gods of nothing. Without a purpose in life, there is no life. You will simply cease to be."

The shape shakes its head. "That isn't fair."

"No. It's not. But nothing in this life is fair. I once saw a new god choose fairness as its purview. Died within five minutes, just shriveled up into nothing right on the stage where it made its announcement. No, nothing's fair in this life. Even among the apes, it's something of a cliché."

They continue walking, winding their way among streets painted with graffiti, names of people who needed to be known so badly they were willing to write their monikers on the wall, even though, the people who see their tags have no idea who they are and care little. The pavement is cracked and broken by the daily funeral procession of a million cars, pallbearers for the dead and dying. The concrete corners of buildings sit cold and angular, bound together by the hands of man. A person can kill themselves by rubbing their necks along these corners for long enough.

"It's just down here," says Gazette, and they turn and walk down a sidewalk composed of red bricks, old Virginia clay, plucked from the soil, stamped in a factory, and baked in an oven at nine-hundred-degrees Celsius. The grout between the bricks is mossy, life fighting to survive, to overtake the blighted touch of humanity.

In front of a pair of glass doors, Gazette stops, places his hand on the handle, and stands to the side as he pulls the door open.

A man sitting on the street corner, underneath a pile of wet cardboard boxes, looks up at them, sees them through malt-liquor-blurred eyes. He holds out his hand, and the shape, having nothing to give the wretched being, steps inside.

Gazette follows, shutting out the carving wind. The shape is pleased to see they are back where they started, and heads for the door that would lead to Gazette's bar.

"Not there," Gazette says.

When the shape turns, he gestures to a stairwell. The gloom of the stairway is chased away by the flicker of celestial lights hanging in the air, tiny globes of multihued light. Green, felt carpet lines the steps, and the wooden banister shines with a life of its own. The shape climbs upward on the staircase, enjoying the feel of the carpet on its bare feet. So soft.

Up and up they climb, the stairs spinning and spiraling on into infinity, only broken by a few landings here and there.

"Here. This one," Gazette says.

They stand on a landing, in front of a door fashioned from lacquered red wood, the doorknob the face of a screaming being with buggy eyes and hair made of waves of brass. Gazette opens this door as well, a true gentleman until the end.

As the door swings outward, the shape steps forward. A wave of noise assaults the new god, and then it realizes the noise is applause and shouting. Some gods hold their fingers up to their lips and make a strange, piercing sound the shape doesn't care for.

Hundreds of them—there are hundreds of gods packed into the space. Among these smiling, sometimes horrific faces, humans cavorted, carrying out barbaric displays of devotion, slicing their flesh open to prove their devoutness. Some fuck like animals, their bodies covered in sweat. Others perform strange feats of acrobatics to try and gain the attention of the magnificent beings around them. But none of the gods pay attention because the guest of honor has finally arrived, and they are after all, only human.

The gods stand in great pockets, various liquids gripped in their hands, some alcoholic, some not, some plucked straight from the veins of the bleeding humans on display. A balcony runs around the room, and eager gods, feathered, naked, monstrous in aspect, lean against the railing, breasts and cocks flailing about. They drip saliva upon the polished wooden floors, so eager for the shape to become like them… so eager for another god to join their ranks.

"This is for me?" the shape asks.

The gods laugh at the shape, stick their fingers in each other's holes, cause their human lackeys to do absurd little dances or to punch and kick each other.

"Yes," Gazette sighs. He sounds weak now, and when the shape turns to look at him, she discovers she can see right through him.

"When I choose, what happens to you?"

"I will vanish completely, never to be seen again."

"Tough way to go," the shape says. "Why don't you just kill me?"

Gazette smiles. "I'd be lying, which I can't do, if I said the thought hadn't occurred to me, but in my weakened form I am no match for you."

A man covered in tattoos with hair like a bird's fanciful plumage screams then. Through the flesh of his face, he has inserted a dozen safety pins. A great angular letter A is carved into his forehead. "Don't do it!" the man screams. "Don't let 'em tell you what to do! Or do! I don't care."

Gazette sneers at the man. "Fuck off, Aeschy, no one wants to hear your anarchy bullshit."

"Or maybe they do!" the mutilated man, the god of punk rock, screams before plowing through another group of gods, bowling them over. These other gods stand up, brush themselves off as if they have seen it a thousand times before. Aeschy spins away into the crowd, flipping off anyone who dares complain.

The gods press forward, their hands reaching out to touch the unformed body of the shape. "Make way! Make way!" Gazette gasps, his voice fading with each breath. "We got a job to do."

From the corner of the shape's eye, it sees a gang of robots with glowing eyes wheeling a TV screen into the ballroom, wires ending in dark black plugs snaking from the back panel. The lips on the screen open, and a flexible tongue emerges, flicking up and down in a suggestive matter. Then the lips part, and Apps' electric laugh echoes throughout the ballroom.

Pandle appears, presses against the shape, the rancid smell of the god climbing up its nose. "Don't forget the kindness," Pandle says. "They need it. There's so much darkness now."

The other gods tear away Pandle, send him spinning into a pile of fucking humans. They stop and piss on him, and he sits there and soaks it in, the other gods laughing at the smelly god, the village idiot of deities.

High up in a corner, on a throne made from the bent backs of his servants, Self peers down at the shape, imperious and demanding.

The shape tears its eyes from the megalomaniac, watches as the Brothers Avarish speed around the room, dropping hundred-dollar-bills on everyone. They spray money in the air with modified machine guns, the bills fluttering down as a dark green graffiti. When they run out of bills, they reach into sacks strapped over their shoulders, pulling out fresh wads of bills, the ink barely dry.

Across a floor soaked in blood, cum, and dollar bills, the hallmarks of humanity, the shape walks naked, unformed, and ready to become.

A troop of naked humans appears, their red boxing gloves peppered with shards of broken glass. They begin to pummel each other, shredding their faces to pieces for the gods' pleasure. After all, what good is a face if it isn't famous? What good is a body if it isn't worshipped?

Pepper Ally appears, two great pom poms gripped in her hands. She dances and hops, exposing the perfection of her nude body, lifting the pom poms into the air and shaking them like a talisman at the shape.

The shape nods at the ebullient god. All throughout the procession, the gods beckon the shape, urge it to become one of them.

"Happy birthday!" a man shrieks before jabbing his tongue in the shape's mouth and swirling it around a bit, wiping out a thousand planets in the process. When he steps back, he puts his hand to his mouth, tries to quench the burn of a thousand suns. "Spicy," he says as he dances away, looking for his next victim.

"Who was that?"

Gazette tsks. "Oh, that's Valentine. Relatively new around these parts. Been walking around sticking his tongue and cock in anything that moves ever since they started making 'love' a thing."

A crowd of fawning lovers, all human, all bleeding from different orifices in their bodies, follows after Valentine, his curly blond hair dancing as he flits from god to god, pinching, squeezing, and groping.

"I hate him," the shape says.

"We all do. Before him, humans used to just sort of get together. Now there's this whole concept of love complicating everything, really putting a damper on our numbers. More numbers, more humans, more power. Now they all look for the perfect one. Some humans make it to the end of their wretched lives having never found the one."

"Ridiculous," the shape says.

As they stroll onward, the shape glides past an empty table set with several reserved placards.

"Who sits there?" the shape asks.

"Oh, those are the heavy hitters. God, Buddha, Allah, who is really just God but pretending to be different? Jesus shows up every now and then, but these ones are all too big to waste their time with something like the birth of a new god. Until you have wars fought in your name, they won't even acknowledge you. Hell, they never cared for me at all, saw no need for truth one way or another."

They continue past a man licking another man, the inner workings of his tongue not fleshy, but mechanical in an organic sort of way. If a person could mix machinery and organic flesh, this is what would be protruding from the man's mouth. With his buzzing robo-tongue, the man slides down a naked woman's body, his tongue puncturing her at a thousand-needles-per-second, leaving behind stains of ink that will never come off.

The woman underneath him groans, and on they walk past Modifico, the god of tattoos.

Finally, they arrive at the stage. The shape climbs up the steep black stairs, polished to a shine so it could see its generic nothingness in the reflection below. On the stage, a cavorting crowd of humans, locked in the throes of some god's worship, breaks apart, spilling across the stage, rushing in their need to escape, to not offend whatever this new god will become. They are like pets brought to a party, expected to be kept out of the way lest they wind up with a kick in the ribs and exiled to the car to wait for the end of the evening.

The shape stands on the stage, peering out over the assembled mass of celestial royalty. The god of agriculture looks up at the unformed god, his beard a collection of hanging grapes, his eyes two pearl onions gleaming in the light. The goddess of music beams up at the shape, shakes her head once, her hair tinkling like chimes in a tune no human could ever hope to replicate. The table of the established gods sits untouched, but respected. All about the gods mill, their worshippers ceasing their revolting activities, cowed to silence by their chosen idols.

The shape leans forward and speaks then, no longer bound by its ignorance. It has all the proof it needs to be able to make its decision, to be able to pick the work of its lifetime. But it needs one more thing, needs to check off one last box before its decision can be confirmed.

"You there," it says, pointing at an innocuous looking human. Covered in bites and white fluid, it stands naked, the hair shorn from its body, blood dripping from its orifices. "Come to me."

The human, standing upon greatness it never knew existed, flushes all over from its head to its toes, and it begins to climb the stairs, its head down, its embarrassment total and complete. The shape holds out an arm, the limb flexing in an unnatural way, as its insides are not bones and tendons like the humans, but cosmos and nebulae. The shape encompasses this naked human in its arm, draws it forward.

"What kind of god do you want?" the shape asks.

The human brings its arms inward. There are so many eyes upon it, that it seeks to protect view of its privates and its secondary sex characteristics from the gods, despite the fact it has been engaging in deeds of glorious depravity for most of the evening. But now, here, on-stage, under the focus of all the assembled gods in her world, minus the big ones of course, it grows shy.

"Speak up," the shape commands, no sympathy in its voice.

"I suppose…" the human begins, its voice meek as a dust mite. A being, a god, swoops down from the ceiling, a monstrous collection of cartilage twisted and bent into the semblance of a giant ear, it holds an arm out to the pathetic human. Its hand ends in phallic rods, and these it holds up to the mouth of the human.

"Do you want me to suck them?" the human asks, confusion on its face. The gods laugh, and someone sends a thought across the ballroom, slips it in the human's ear, and it understands that Lobeulus, this giant moving ear, is the god of sound.

"Answer the question," the shape prods. "What kind of god do you want?"

The human, dying to get off the stage and resume its deplorable orifice excavation, speaks with more surety now. "I suppose we want someone to hear us, to actually hear our needs and help us out. We want to love and be loved, to be valued, even if we aren't of value. We want to be safe and not judged for the mistakes we make. We're not perfect. I'm not. I know that. I guess we just want someone to be there for us?"

The slit of the shape's mouth curls up at the end. It is as it had expected. The shape steps forward, brushes the human off to the side. The woman recoils at the touch of the new god. The shape, having no need of Lobeulus, kicks the hideous god off the stage, its microphone fingers and toes twitch as it lays upon the ballroom floor, and a spill of waxy filth drips from its ear canal.

The shape doesn't care, has been bled of anything that might be construed for compassion by the night's events. "It's all clear to me now. They don't want gods; they want slaves to come running at their beck and call. And all you fools signed up for it!"

A murmur runs around the room. *Who is this new god to tell them anything? Why, it has only been walking the earth for little more than an evening!*

"You signed up to be their lackeys, to make things better or worse for them, to constantly meddle in their lives, but what good is that? Are you happy?" the shape asks the human.

It shakes its head.

"Are you happy?" the god asks the assembled pantheon of Earth… minus the really important ones.

Many in the crowd shake their heads, but most remain still, unwilling to admit this whelp of a deity has stumbled onto something they refuse to admit to themselves, something they had all discovered soon after they selected their own purview and chose the path of their own eternity, their own hell.

"You sit here, hosting me, begging to me to choose this purview or that. Really, all you want is for someone to share in your misery, to watch another god bear the yoke of humanity, to toil alongside you so you can pretend as if you're better than me. That's all any of you want, and them… "—the shape points at the bloody, cummy, shitty humans—"all they want is more. Give 'em what they want, and they come back for more. Give them all the athletic gifts in the world, and they'll come back the next night demanding more. Give them all the money in the world, and they want more. Give them a night of blissful happiness and ecstasy, unmatched and unrivaled by anything in the natural world, and they'll want what?" The shape takes in the crowd, notices the diminished twinkle in their eyes, the dull knife of truth butchering its way through their self-delusions.

From behind, the ghost of Gazette speaks softly, so soft only the shape, the filthy human on stage, and the giant ear puking wax onto the floor could hear. "You coulda been the god of truth, kid. Coulda been."

"They want more. It never ends!" the shape declares.

"Enough of this! What are you going to be?" the imperious Self calls from his perch in the balcony, though he refuses to look at the shape, to acknowledge it with a glance. His time is important, you know.

"Be? What am I going to be?"

The crowd waits, leaning forward, anxious to hear the new god's answer.

"I am going to be the god of nothing."

"Ooh!" that's a good one Pepper Ally says. "Why didn't I think of that one?"

"Because you're a fucking vain idiot," Pandle calls from his spot on the floor, conspicuously free of other gods, whether that is because of the smell or his status is unclear—but probably the smell.

"At least I'm not a stank ass bum. You stink like a microwaved diaper," Pepper Ally spits.

Pandle reaches into his pants, as if he is going to pull out a diaper, but all he brings out is a wad of fetid shit, crawling with maggots and brimming with silver coins. He tosses it once in the air like a pitcher on the pitcher's mound tossing a bag of rosin, and then he chucks this wad of god filth at the chipper Pepper Ally. It splatters across her face, and then the action kicks into high gear. The gods, unhappy with their lot in life, bogged down by the tedium of having to do the same thing every fucking day of their semi-immortal existence, let loose their frustration upon each other. Valentine sails through the air, his shoulders pumping blood from where his arms used to be. "Make love, not war!" he screams.

Pandle and Pepper Ally fight in hand-to-hand combat scratching, clawing, and pummeling each other. The poor humans who had come to sup at the table with gods are used as bludgeoning items and suppositories, shoved into celestial holes as punishment for the frustration the gods feel.

The human the shape had singled out is snatched up by a massive hulk of a man covered in hair and an overhanging brow ridge. With the screaming human clutched in its hand, it straddles the ear on the ground. Despite fighting back with its microphone-fingered hands, the haired, masculine monstrosity forcefully shoves the human into the ear canal of Lobeulus.

The poor human is shoved into the expanse of the great universe with breath in its lungs, which it promptly loses as the void sucks the breath from the hapless creature, leaving it only a moment to marvel at the magnitude of reality. A comet flies by, crashes into the human's head, and obliterates its skull. Machismo, the god of manliness, pulls the human free. All that's left of its head is a bloody neck cauterized and frozen. In disgust, the god flings the corpse to the side and picks up another human to insert into something. He doesn't care where he puts the human as long as he puts it somewhere. Classic Machismo.

All around the ballroom, the gods scream, fight, violate each other, tear each other limb from limb, knuckle from knuckle. From their wounds, the cosmos spill like glitter floating in the blank ink of creation. Still, they pummel each other as millions of trillions of sentient lifeforms bellow their pain, filling the ballroom with a hungry roar.

The shape strides among them, its body growing intangible. With nebulous steps, the shape, never male, female, or even other, strides among the dead and dying gods as they tear a hole in creation itself, ripping it to shreds out of sheer frustration. But, if you stop those gods, ask them how they felt about it, they would say, "Well, goddamn, I'm having myself a good ol' time." All except for Lobeulus, who kept having things stuck in him by Machismo.

At the threshold of the degenerating ballroom, the shape turns and watches as Pandle climbs a column and hangs from the balcony railing. The god of the homeless pulls himself up and over, places his shit-covered hands upon Self, and throws him down to the ground. The other gods pounce upon Self, who can't believe what is happening. They beat and pummel him, marring his beautiful face, tearing his perfect eyes from their sockets.

The god of nothing catches the eye of a fading Gazette, nods at him. Gazette waves, gives a wink, and then disappears completely, as if he had never been.

Then the new god turns and leaves.

THE NEW GOD

CHAPTER 8
SO IT GOES

The bitter cold of the world could not match the cold within the seething mass of stars in the shape's chest. Wherever it walks, the concrete cracks, snapping like bones. Around the god of nothing, the world shakes, vibrations sending spiderwebbing fissures up the sides of the buildings nearest. On cold, bare feet, the shape strides through downtown Pittsburgh, walking in a direction it only understands as an instinct, leaving behind pockets of delicious anti-matter.

Onward it strides as people begin fleeing from the breaking buildings around them. Broken bricks and shards of busted windows pelt the pavement as they stand in the streets, looking upward, waiting for the buildings to come tumbling down completely, wondering what is going on. Their heads are tilted back as the world punches them in the face with the first dusting of snow. The sky, full all night, finally breaks open, and what starts as a slow, tranquil flurry, quickly turns into a howling blizzard of bitter blinding white.

Clad in their pajamas, the regular folk of Pittsburgh stand on the streets, watching as their homes bend and quake from the ripples of the god who never was. They shiver, not because of the cold, but because of the realization of how insignificant they are. When a planet revolts, when the fabric of time and space stops following rules, it tends to do that.

In the streets, they avoid speaking their thoughts, keep these newfound realizations to themselves lest someone confirms their fears—they are nothing. To speak it is to make it real. Better to be silent. The god of nothing strides among them, placing its rubbery, formless hand upon their shoulders. They wilt underneath its touch, shiver uncontrollably until tears well in their eyes. The hopelessness, the meaninglessness of their existence, hits them like a semi-truck to the heart. They don't have to say it now. They know it with every cell of their dying bodies. When the quaking stops, they pull their robes tight, finish their panic-fueled cigarettes, and stride back into their buildings. In their beds, they wait for the towers to collapse, to bring them crashing down to the ground and send them off where they belong—nothing returning to nothing, a drop of water in an ocean.

The shape marches onward, winding through the city, delivering truth, stone-cold sobering truth that kicks the poor, weak apes into action.

As the shape strides among the blocks, a child, too young to know gods don't exist, notices it moving among the street. With a teddy bear clutched in its arms, it approaches the shape, its unformed, unspackled mind allowing it to see the shape for what it is.

"Aren't you cold?" the child asks in a high-pitched voice. The voice is like the sound of breaking glass… or maybe the shape just confuses it with the sound of the first building's collapse.

"We're all cold at one point or another," the god of nothing says.

A human might have looked at the child standing in the cold, curiosity on its face, and taken pity. But the god of nothing feels its purview completely, and when it reaches out with a chilling finger and taps the child on the shoulder, all it does is drop its teddy bear on the ground and turn to head inside the trembling building with its family. Some gods might see the potential in the child, see the hope of the future, but not the god of nothing. The god of nothing knows hope is an illusion, a logic-twisting mirror capable of warping reality. The reality is this hopeful creature will be warped and twisted by the forces around it. It will be chewed and mangled until it is just another meaningless blob of cells and flesh spouting off the things it is told and replicating those lies and half-truths and bigotries for the next generation. Better to die while fresh.

When the child disappears, the god of nothing continues its trek through town, undoing the fabric of reality with each press of its heel into the ground. The earth sighs with pleasure, the snow swirling in a blinding blizzard as the scab of the city is slowly peeled back by the new god's progress. Like a surgeon sawing off corrupted flesh, the god brings the city to a swift death. When it is done, it stands at a point of land where two rivers combined to form one. The snow zips around it, buzzing like white bees, and it turns its head up to the sky, lets the flakes brush against its cold cheeks.

Its business done, its message delivered, it walks along the riverbank, passing a small building where homeless men huddle in the dark, fearing the dark god who walks among them. From the middle of the city, the light of uncreation bursts upward, a blackness that rips through the clouds, shreds them like cotton balls, and sends them tumbling to the ground as the law of gravity itself is eaten up, a shattered and broken chain, never to be forged again.

With no gravity, the homeless men on the ground float upward, the earth spinning under them so fast that soon they are tossed around at a brisk 1,000 miles per hour, their clothes ripped from their bodies. They collide in mid-air somewhere over Madagascar, their bodies bursting into clouds of blood. These clouds are ejected into space.

The new god walks on, climbs a set of rickety metal stairs, up and up, toward a bridge, long and double-deckered. The bridge spans a river, cold and filthy. It trudges onward, the wind kissing its skin. The rules do not apply to the god, neither does the absence of rules. Nothing applies to nothing.

The road continues onward. The sky fills with bits of flotsam and jetsam as the world turns into a massive, whirring blender. Onward the shape processes, down the center of the bridge. On the far bank of the bridge, a path leads off to nowhere. Amid the swirling slurry of snow, blood, and broken bones, the new god chooses this path. It veers to the right, a path ending in mid-air, the yellow railing vibrating in the chaos of the undone world. The god of nothing steps into the air and disappears, becoming exactly what it was always meant to be.

URL'OOZR'S JANITOR

It was nice to have job security. Finally. When U took over, no one knew it would be like this. Even though Patrick Carlson couldn't pronounce the name of Url'Oozr—he just referred to him as U—his life had been changed for the better. There'd he'd been, at home, in his fifteen-hundred-dollar-a-month studio apartment, slurping down a cold can of Van Kamp's Pork and Beans, when the situation had played out over the TV.

A dark shape had emerged off the New England coast, some 3,000 miles away in a town called Fantucket. Helicopters had swirled around the dark mass crawling from the gray-green waters of the Atlantic; news choppers and military aircraft whirled around the mass like flies around a horse's ass. The sky had been gray, but you could excuse people for thinking it was night, as the great hulk of U's body blocked out the sun.

Midnight black, and with more tentacles than a Japanese porn site, he'd watched in sick fascination as the military bombarded the dark mass with bomb after bomb, bullet after bullet. With tentacles as thick as school buses, it swatted them out of the sky as if they were nothing.

The camera angle had switched, and he'd watched, drinking the last of the sweet bean juice from his can of Van Kamp's, as the camera focused on a man standing on a rocky, windswept promontory, an ancient, flesh-bound book clutched in one hand, a strange crystal wand held in the other.

On the scrawl at the bottom of the TV, a super read: "Humanity's last hope."

It was good TV. You know… up until the dude dropped his glowing wand into the roaring ocean by accident, and the tide swept it away. From there, the many tentacled behemoth that they would come to know and love as U, emerged from the ocean, and ripped the man's body in half on national TV. It was to be the first of many.

It was funny now how scared he'd been.

Patrick dipped his mop into the bucket, yellow and plastic and permanently filthy, the fate of all mop buckets in the world. He dipped the mop in the squeezer, pressed down on the handle as hard as he could, reveling in the small joy of liquid being squeezed out of the mop's hair.

He pulled the mop free, plunked it down on the cold concrete surface, and began smearing away the coppery liquid. His job kept him busy all day, but he wouldn't have it any other way.

He laughed silently as he thought about those days, about how he had thought he was losing everything. Oh, he'd been a custodian before, in a middle school where the kids pissed all over everything and threw their garbage on the floor without even thinking about the fact someone had to come along and clean up after them. He'd hated the job, hated the way those people looked down at him every day for making a living. Like they were gonna be anything better than him.

Well, most of 'em were dead now. No real loss.

In reality, the rise of their benevolent overlord was something of an improvement over the way things used to be. For one thing, he didn't need money anymore. Plenty of cool stuff just sitting around for the taking these days, the owners dead and gone.

U had given everyone the choice within a few days after wiping out the entire United States army. Join him in servitude or perish as meat for the beast. Well, old Patrick knew a good deal when he saw one, and he signed right up.

As he swirled the mop around, he caught sight of the tentacle sticking out of his back. U liked to be connected to his followers. All around the country, everyone who was anyone had one of those thin tentacles gripping their back, right between the shoulder blades. A million tentacles all guiding and comforting those who had chosen correctly. Everyone else? Well... they shoulda been a little more understanding.

You see, people hate change. This Patrick knew inherently. Doesn't matter how good that change would be for them, they don't want to hear it, won't even consider it. Why, he was better off now under the sway of U than he had ever been during the time before the Coming.

U didn't care what you did as long as you showed up. Social classes didn't exist anymore, because all humans were inferior to their great lord, and U could remove the tentacle whenever he pleased, marking you as food. This had happened to some of the earlier chancellors and bureaucrats who'd thought to raise themselves in U's eyes.

Marvin Tell was the name of the first chancellor, and he'd gone over fast, as soon as he saw the power of U. He'd thought to make himself indispensable… but what does a god want with a man? Nothing. And when he'd thought to take liberties with U's tenets, began making a harem out of prospective food to keep them from being fed to U, he'd been devoured on live TV.

But most feedings were group things, a simple stuffing of the bodies into a tank, and U rising out of the ocean and chomping down on them.

Sure, one day the Earth would become a lifeless chunk of rock floating through space thanks to U's insatiable appetite, but you know what? That was going to be long after Patrick was dead and gone. And in the meantime, he got to listen to his tunes. U didn't give a shit about if you listened to your music on the job. Didn't give a fuck if you didn't wear a stupid uniform while you mopped up blood. Yeah, he was a good boss, better than some he'd had, those self-important principals who only talked to him when they needed something. "Hey, can you do me a favor, big guy? Can you move all those desks from that room upstairs to room 204 by the end of the day? Thanks, you're the best," and then not a peep until they needed something else. "Lil' Jonah puked in the hallway. Can you take care of that for me?"

Yeah, at least U appreciated cleanliness.

At first, he had been disappointed by the way things shook out. He'd appeared before the job assignment board a day after pledging his allegiance to U, applied to be one of the men in the breeding pens, making food for the beast. But, the job-giver guy, whatever the fuck he was called, inhuman resources? Yeah, well, that son of a bitch had taken one look at him, dipped a tentacle in Patrick's ear, read his past, and said, "We have need of you in the feeding tank."

At first, he'd panicked. I mean, one day he was going to wind up food for U, but he'd hoped that day wouldn't come until long into the distant future.

"Oh, no, not as food," the inhuman resources officer said, "but as a sanitation technician."

He'd smiled at that, at being given such a technical, cool name. It was a sign of respect. Sanitation technician. Much better than custodian.

As the last bars of AC/DC's Let There Be Rock faded away, the first haunting melodies of Queensrÿche's Silent Lucidity began to play. He moved to the rhythm, swirled to the beat. Though his hands blistered, and his hips ached from the repetitive motion of mopping and inching backward, he wouldn't change a damn thing.

He lifted his mop, dunked it in the filthy, red water. He plopped it in the squeezer and wrung it out real good as he sang along with the song. There's another thing that doesn't get enough respect, just like U... motherfuckin' Queensrÿche.

The sanitation technician bopped along to the music as he twisted his torso back and forth across the feeding tank, mopping up the refuse of the last batch of U's food. When the bucket's water grew too filthy, he wheeled it along to a drain, dumped the bucket out, bits of hair and shards of bone swirling around the drain as the crimson liquid slowly leaked into the sewers.

U might be a world-eating god, but man was he picky when it came to food. A tremor tickled his back, and he tried to rephrase his thought. *Not picky... particular. And why not? A god should have what a god wants? Am I right or am I right?*

The tremor disappeared.

Break time?

"You will break in due time. I will suck the marrow from your bones, crunch you in my bowels, turn you and a billion others into a multi-legged, multi-armed, multi-headed, steaming interplanetary dump. But yes, a break, my faithful servant."

Patrick dug in his pocket, searching for his cigarettes. Before U, he'd had to pay an arm and a leg for the things, not even the name brand shit either. Now, he could have whatever he wanted, just walk into a store, say what he wanted, and they handed it over. Outside, he stood in the darkness, staring up at the black tentacle lines as they snaked across the sky. Another truck pulled up, the people inside sobbing and whining and moaning. They shoulda known better, shoulda taken U's deal when they had the chance.

Oh sure, eventually he was going to die. Eventually U would drain the entire life force from the planet, and then move onto the next life-filled place in the cosmos, but that would be a long time from now. It was no different than toiling away with the world dying from climate change. Hell, it might even last longer now. Certainly, the air in Portland was better these days. He took a deep breath, coughed up a wad of lung butter, and spat it on the ground as U's lunch was led into the loading pen.

He only had a few hours now. All the people had to be shorn of hair. U didn't like hair, wasn't any life in it. Once they were cleaned, and shorn, they would be loaded into the hopper. U would swim up out of the depths and they'd dump the food in his mouth, and he'd swim away until the next feeding time.

"Better get to it," Patrick said when break time was over. He stomped the cigarette out on the ground and stretched out his back and shoulders.

Then he walked back inside, rinsed out his bloody mop bucket, and continued his work, sweeping and mopping. "Oh, yeah, Rancid!" he crowed as his favorite punk rock song played on his phone.

He mopped with a feverish frenzy, loving his job, loving his place in life, loving U.

When the red light blinked on in the feeding tank, he'd just finished swabbing off the last few feet of the deck. He wheeled his bucket out fast, lest he be confused for part of U's lunch. At the blood-dump drain, Patrick left his mop bucket sitting there to clean up later. He didn't want to miss his favorite part of the day.

Rushing to the viewing platform, he stood amongst a hundred other of U's caretakers, their tentacle threads twitching and swirling as the great mass of their benevolent overlord neared. Smiles graced their faces as U's lunch was led into the hopper, their bare bodies hairless. They salted their meat with their own tears, and Patrick smiled down at them.

In the distance, the Columbia River boiled as a great bulk, swallowed up the light, darkening everything around it. U rose up, eyeless and black. It pressed itself forward, and a wave of water knocked the dark god's lunch off their many feet. It leaned upon the edge of the hopper, tipping it upward like a great slide, and a hundred bodies slid into U's mouth. All around the world, similar scenes were taking place in hundreds of coastal towns. U was punctual, always showed up on time. You had to respect him for that.

His lunch screamed as it squeaked down the feeding deck and slid into the blackness of U. Its great bulk compressed, and a sloppy spray of blood washed over everyone standing on the observation deck, bones shards and teeth bits ejecting from the body of his god along with blood.

The crowd oohed and aahed, and through the tentacles attached to their spines, a feeling of gratitude and satisfaction infused them. They patted each other on the shoulders, congratulated each other, and took pride in a job well done.

But Patrick didn't stay for long. He had to get the place ready for dinner, then he could go home and watch some TV, eat some caviar out of a tin he'd requested. He wondered what was on tonight? Maybe he'd watch a rerun of Friends. He always liked to think about feeding those soulless chuckleheads to U. He'd love to see that Ross piece of shit dumped in the hopper.

With a spring in his step, Patrick emptied his mop bucket and reached for his mop, a severed leg and torso with a woman's head still attached. He rinsed this off as well. It was getting a little gamey. He wondered if he would get a new mop when this one wore out. He dunked the dead woman's head in the water. The water remained clean, and he knew he was ready to do his job once more… for U.

DUDE LARUDE SINGS THE BLACK AND BLUES

CHAPTER 1
A JOKE

Dude LaRude wasn't supposed to play halftime at the National Bouncy-Ball Association's All-Star halftime show. Hell, Dude LaRude couldn't play anywhere in California thanks to his ridiculous antics. Ask Dude about it, and he'd just laugh. Getting banned from places was a point of pride with him. He wore his bannings on his sleeve, a line of black slashes tattooed upon his forearm the way a gunslinger might put a notch on the grip of his pistol for every man he gunned down. *See that one there? That's from when I took a shit on the stage.*

But as with most things these days, someone had to go and ruin it. The National Bouncy-Ball Association, constantly starved for social media representation and a way to get at those untapped youth dollars, needed something to get the kids interested. Most of the youths were into cool shit like dancing in front of their phones or calling the cops on people who needed to be canceled—real, upstanding citizen shit like that. They didn't want anything to do with the caveman worship of professional sports players, superhuman genetic freaks whose lives revolved around balls, babes, and generally treating the entire world as second-class citizens… all because they had won the genetic lottery.

Today's youth wanted nothing more than to see the world burn, and the people who held onto the joys of the past burning right along with it while they clutched their beloved symbols of a broken system in their arms—their flags, their debit cards, their precious sports paraphernalia.

In the past, religion was referred to as the opiate of the masses, a calming, insidious ritual meant to keep people from questioning their lot in life. But now the chosen opiate had become sports. Where can you find the average day laborer at the end of the week? Sitting around the TV watching millionaires in stupid pants golf, watching cars race around a track for lap after mindless lap, watching monstrous creeps thudding into each other like angry rams but without the protective thickness of skulls that would prevent brain damage. On a Saturday afternoon, you could find whole hordes of round-bellied, stressed-out simpletons festooned in expensive jerseys made for pennies in a third-world country throwing down brain-cell murdering swill on their sagging, ass-smelling couches. The amount of capital put into the research and design of those jerseys cost more than the average worker would earn in their entire life. Despite this injustice, the masses paid for it! They paid for it all, tithing as blindly as a mid-second-millennium sinner eager to secure an indulgence from a philandering, fork-tongued priest. Jerseys, hats, G-strings for the missus, coats, and coasters, a neon clock to hang above the mantelpiece—it was only a matter of time before they branded food with the faces of the hometown hero, so good at throwing a ball, but so bad at hearing the word "no" and understanding what it meant.

Into this world, one of these youths, not better or worse than the people she hated, mind you—just different, confident in a way only Americans can be in their own righteousness, their own cleverness, a youth named Khalisee Sanchez-Aguilar, thus named after a popular television show because, after all, who doesn't name their child after their favorite fictional character on a television show that cost more to produce than Paraguay's entire GNP—and you know those illiterate savants didn't read the damn books because otherwise, they might have spelled her name right.

But, that's neither here nor there. The Bouncy-Ball Association, a magnificent and mighty organization propelled by constant greed, exploitation, and an incessant need to overlook the revolting behavior of its athletes was in sore need of people like Khalisee. Maybe, just maybe, if they held a contest, took advantage of social media, a different type of opiate—but let's not get into that—they could pull Khalisees and Tearyons from all around the country out of their dens, out of their dark rooms and their ironic clothing, out of their disdain for belonging and their need to do their own things, and maybe… just maybe, they'd become fans. So what did the Bouncy-Ball Association do? They held a contest to pick the performer of the halftime show.

Not a bad idea. Sports leagues had been doing that type of shit for some time, in fact. When interest started to wane in their products and All-Star games, once big business became less-big business, they would allow the uncultured swine a voice in the game. The consequence of course was a trivializing of the game. When some benchwarmer named Meat Latigo was selected as a sort of ironic middle finger to the commissioner of the Bouncy-Ball Association, did that deter them? Why no, it just emboldened Donald Mint even more. With a last name like Mint, everything the commissioner touched had to become money, so the Association put together a documentary crew, followed around this no-talent journeyman as he goofed around at the All-Star game, generally having a good time. And when he managed to jam the ball straight in the hole, why the audience even voted the poor sucker MVP… and Donald Mint and the Bouncy-Ball Association raked in the dollars and the ratings and the human-interest collateral. Suddenly, everyone wanted a Meat Latigo jersey, everyone wanted his autograph. His newfound celebrity landed him on the talk show circuits, where he joked and was generally amicable. Of course, Bouncy-Ball purists complained about the integrity of the game, and all all-star games became a huge joke, even less likely to rake in the youth dollars Donald Mint and the Bouncy-Ball owners desired.

Khalisee Sanchez-Aguilar hated sports with a passion. She hated the boys at her school who reeked of sweat and walked around in their sweatpants, bouncy-balls tucked under their arms. She hated how important they thought they were, hated that they thought they were going to be the next big thing and thus acted like spoiled celebrities, though for every thousand boys like them, only one would make it to the big show. Khalisee set about ruining the one thing these boys liked… the Bouncy-Ball All-Star Game Halftime Show, brought to you by Tastitos—which despite their name had absolutely no taste to them.

Even though Khalisee's intentions were pure and based in glorious hate, she wasn't bright enough to see the hypocrisy of her world as she stuffed another Tastito in her mouth, her greasy, salty fingertips flying across the keyboard, her fingers plucking out letters, numbers, and symbols from thin air.

Her jaws crunching bland, flavorless, salty corn between her teeth, she scanned the Bouncy-Ball association's website, not the site everyone else saw, but the behind-the-scenes shit, the code. Maybe not bright enough to understand how buying the products associated with her least favorite endeavor perpetuated the very thing she hated, Khalisee was definitely bright enough to bring down a million-dollar website designed by people who were really not worth the money they were paid. Such was the way of the world. While it took a team of twenty college-educated individuals to design and implement the Bouncy-Ball website, it only took one sixteen-year-old woman with greasy fingers a few clicks and twenty hours of coding to undo it all. Not that anyone would notice. Khalisee was that good.

A simple piggyback, and she had it all set up. For every three votes someone put into the website, one vote for her chosen target would be registered, and no one would be the wiser. Dude LaRude... a despicable shell of a human being, seemingly intent on tearing down everything normal and acceptable in the world, was her chosen champion. His on-stage antics included cutting himself, bashing himself over the head with beer bottles, taking a dump on stage, and even, if you were lucky and he was feeling limber, a bout of auto-fellatio conducted in time to a punk rock version of Tchaikovsky's *1812 Overture*. To the casual observer Dude LaRude might seem like a hack, one of those standard-issue attention whores with no talent who would do anything for a little attention, but lo and behold, upon further investigation, one would find a man with no social media presence, no digital footprint whatsoever. He didn't care about fame.

Despite this self-imposed handicap to success, Dude LaRude had built quite a name for himself. His lyrics were the type of potty mouth punk that would make a nun blush. Songs like *Eat My Fart*, *I Lit Your Cat on Fire*, *Punch Me Till I Cum* were some of the lighter fare on his albums, which only came on seven-inch vinyl and seemed to be limited to runs of a thousand. But it was the stage show that set him apart.

If Guinness was keeping records for the band banned from the most venues, the record would belong to Dude LaRude and his motley crew of punk rock musicians—scabby junkies who could barely play their instruments. At least they were ugly. None of them wanted to be compared to that other famous junkie who could barely play his instrument and seemed to have been chosen simply for his looks. A heroin overdose was the best thing that could have happened to that bastard.

The Orpheum in Bakersfield had banned Dude LaRude after he lit his hair on fire on stage, causing the sprinkler system to go off. The Podium in Sacramento had banned him after he busted a beer bottle over the head of a man who had spit at him. When T.S. Rooker, noted punk rock documentarian and e-zine author had asked Dude LaRude why he hit the guy with a bottle, his answer was, "He missed." Dude had wanted to be spit upon, and that was the strange paradox of Dude LaRude. For every action he took to seemingly destroy his career, he only became more popular, and this only drove him more and more insane. According to Rooker's groundbreaking exposé on Dude LaRude, "*PsychoGenius: the Many Scars of a Punk Rock Pariah*," LaRude's sole motivation was to open the eyes of the world to the realm of possibilities, to break them free of their sleepwalking lives, bound by rules and laws, tortured every day by a society that tells them its normal to feel miserable, to be miserable. In LaRude's mind, the only way to break people out of their meaningless existence was to show them things they couldn't fathom doing. Not things they wouldn't do, but things they had never thought of in their life. The unthinkable. Dude LaRude was the master of the unthinkable.

It was only a matter of time before the world would learn to think in a different way. As Khalisee Sanchez-Aguilar watched the voting totals rise and rise, she smiled, not aware of what she had done in the name of kicking the establishment nest. But man—those Tastitos were good.

DUDE LARUDE SINGS THE BLACK AND BLUES

CHAPTER 2
THE COMMISH

Donald Mint didn't know one thing about what the kids were into, not just kids at large, but even his own children. Hell, he didn't know what his wife was into. Money and power had separated Donald out from the rest of the sheep, made him something more than a man, but less in many ways. He need not concern himself with the everyday concerns of regular people, those without money or power. All he needed to know was how to keep the machine running, how to keep the cogs of the magic money machine spinning, chewing through lives and spitting out hard-earned cash at the other end.

So, when one of his many faceless employees and advisors came to tell him there was a problem, he didn't think much of it. There wasn't a problem in the world money couldn't fix, and thanks to the owners of the National Bouncy-Ball Association, Donald Mint was rolling in money.

"Yeah, yeah, what is it?"

Donald was in a rush. He had many meetings and meaningless soundbites to deliver to the flock of reporters who surrounded him like fleas on a dog's ass. Life as the commissioner was a never-ending job. The machine was always chugging away, needed his constant presence. Putting his face in front of cameras and reporters was the grease keeping the cogs spinning and crushing and chewing.

"There's a problem with the All-Star Game Halftime Show, brought to you by Tastitos."

Donald, always moving, never stopping, strode down the hallway, his five-figure suit conforming to every inch of his rail-thin body, emaciated from long hours of toil which didn't leave him the time to take care of himself. It looked good though. It was the type of suit that would make a corpse fashionable. "Spit it out," he said.

"It seems the fans have selected someone rather unsavory to play the halftime show."

"Unsavory?" Donald laughed. "Name me a celebrity who isn't unsavory."

"No, sir. I mean really unsavory."

"Spell it out, Ethan. I don't have time for your vagaries."

"This man, this Dude LaRude—"

"Dude LaRude? Never heard of him."

"—well, he's somewhat of a degenerate."

"Aren't we all?"

"No, I mean this guy took a… a… number two on stage."

This brought Donald Mint up short. "You're talking about a shit?"

Ethan, whose name might actually be Mike, nodded.

"That's what the kids are into?" It didn't surprise Donald one bit. "Anything else?"

Ethan, who might actually be Scott, blushed red. "I can't even say." Instead, the man handed him a sheet of paper with a trembling hand. On that paper, a list of degeneracies the Marquis De Sade would applaud.

"This is what the kids are into?"

"He is winning by a considerable margin."

"Well, can't we, you know, fudge the numbers."

"I fear it's too late for that."

Donald Mint didn't like to hear the word no when he asked a question, and what Ethan/Mike/Scott—maybe Joseph—was saying definitely sounded like a no. "It's never too late. This guy is clearly unfit to be at the half-time show. I don't even know what auto-coprophilia is, but I'm certainly not about to have it broadcast in two-hundred nations to mothers, sons, and daughters."

"I'm afraid that this thing has gotten out of control, sir."

"How so?"

"Well…" The fumbling, sniveling nobody reached into his ill-fitting three-figure suit and pulled out his cell phone. After a few taps, he held the screen up to Donald's face.

Though the screen showed Donald Mint spectacle after spectacle, there was one thing he couldn't deny. All the people sharing and resharing and liking and skweeting and hearting and whatever the else you could fucking do on social media, were of the appropriate age, all talking about Dude LaRude. So many likes, so many skweets. So many dollar signs. Donald Mint's eyes didn't see scenes of a brown man slicing himself up. They didn't see the shit onstage. They didn't hear the lyrics to Fist Me Please. The only thing Donald Mint saw was those dollar signs, green and glittering. The only thing he heard was the clink of coins and the ka-ching of a cash register.

"What are we going to do?" the no one asked.

"We're going to become snake charmers. Get your turban and whatever horn they use to charm snakes. We're going to meet with this… Dude LaRude, and make sure he understands how this is all going to go."

"Yes, sir."

A social media firestorm. Dude LaRude had gone viral. Donald Mint wasn't going to let this situation get out of control, not like that goddamn Meat Latigo incident. Sometimes, when a fire started, you just had to get out in front of it, chop down trees, burn the underbrush, remove all the fuel to stop the fire in its tracks.

DUDE LARUDE SINGS THE BLACK AND BLUES

Chapter 3
A Sit Down

Dude LaRude, real name Henry Twofeathers, Hank to his family, sat in his squat, blitzed out of his mind. No one had called him Hank in years, and he was fine with that. Let them rot in their hovels and their holes, slaving away, trying to make ends meet, giving their money to the same church that had killed Indian children, committed genocide through both deliberate action and strategic funding. Let them do that, but they would do it without Hank.

Now he explicitly went by the name Dude LaRude. On his family's hardscrabble farm, wearing third-generation clothes, he had a dream once, a God dream, his mind touched by an otherworldly presence, reaching across space, time, and entire dimensions to dip its wick in his brain and stir it around a bit. Or maybe he was just crazy. Maybe all his parents' religious austerity and puritanism had finally gotten to him. Or maybe he just wanted to do whatever the fuck he wanted. But the fact remained that on his fifteenth birthday, something reached into his head and gave him a new name.

When he awoke, his eyes snapping open, Henry Twofeathers was dead. Dude LaRude had taken his place. His pilgrimage from Oklahoma took him west. On trains where he let bums bugger him in exchange for food, he rode west, heading for the land of promise. California, a lie, a façade, every bit as fake as his old name.

In the land of California, he sat and watched people move to and fro, walking from point A to point B, a plan in their heads, order weighing them down, sitting heavy on their shoulders, and he vowed not to live that life. Later that night, he met the first of his band members, Felcher, in an alley. A blowjob and some meth later, they were fast friends, eager to corrupt their bodies in as many ways as humanly possible. Everything from there was a blur. Awash in drugs, pleasure, and pain, every day Dude LaRude woke up was an unplanned gift, and that's how he lived life. Knowing death came for him, he did whatever he felt like.

Sometimes, people in his band booked him at a place, and having nothing else better to do, he would climb up on stage and sing the songs Felcher sung into his ears when he was high. None of it was planned, and none of it mattered. There were times when he didn't perform, when someone had booked him to appear somewhere, and he didn't show up. He didn't feel bad about it, didn't care if anyone was disappointed Dude LaRude didn't show up. He didn't live his life for the happiness of others. That was a fool's errand.

One time, someone had tried to introduce him to a talent manager, one of those suited fucks from the dying decrepit music industry, as out of place in a punk venue as a '50s mobster in contemporary Chicago.

"I love what you're doing. It's unlike anything I've ever heard before. I think I can make you big, the next Sid Vicious."

Dude LaRude's response had been two fingers down his own throat. In an instant, the talent manager's suit had been turned into a violent tapestry of vomit laced with beer and hot dog chunks, as it had been a good day, and Dude had actually remembered to eat. The talent manager had screamed and shouted, getting in Dude LaRude's face, his fists all balled up and his face an angry pinkish red like the hot dog chunks stuck to his lapel. But Dude never said a word, just held his middle finger up to the man's face and pressed it against his cheek while making a sizzling noise.

What the manager didn't understand was that Dude LaRude wasn't putting on a show. He wasn't pretending to be punk rock. Money and fame were nothing to him, in fact, they weren't real things at all. They were social constructions designed to keep people down, lock them into a way of thinking that kept them docile and safe. A manager? For what? For money? Dude LaRude didn't need money. He barely wore clothes, could sleep anywhere from under an overpass to in a dumpster. Food? Hell, he only ate a few days a week, and when he did, people, in love with the idea of him, would give him whatever he asked for. Drugs? People loved him on drugs, and to be honest, he'd never bought a drug in his life, only taken what the world offered him.

Everything he needed, punk provided. Everything drug-laced cell of his body served the force of anarchy. So, when Donald Mint showed up in his five-figure suit, an entourage of yes-men at his elbow, Dude LaRude's associates, every bit as free and abhorrent of society's mores as Dude himself, smirked with anticipation. This, might be the day, they whispered. The day Dude kills someone.

Dude, clad only in a pair of cum-stained briefs, sat on a couch, scratching at his face. He had become itchy lately. Didn't know if it was something he'd pick up with his dick or with a needle, and didn't really care. Life was gonna go how it was gonna go, and no doctor was going to fix what was wrong with him because there was nothing wrong with him.

"Good evening, Dude," Donald Mint said.

Dude didn't bother with a response, just kept scratching red furrows into his forearm.

"By now I'm sure you've heard the news."

Dude shook his head. To be honest, he didn't know why he was talking to this slave-wager, with his fancy suit, his manicured nails. Those nails couldn't even do the scratching a good man needed to stay sane. "Don't know why you're here. Don't know what you want."

"Oh, uh, did your people not tell you why I'm here?"

"Don't got no people. Just me."

"Do you know who I am?"

Digging a jagged brown fingernail under a scab, Dude shook his head.

"I'm Donald Mint, Commissioner Donald Mint."

Dude shook his head. He had no clue who the guy was.

"Of the National Bouncy-Ball Association."

At this, Dude stood up, pulled his filthy underwear to the side, and let his balls hang while thrusting his hips back and forth. "Pleased to meet ya. I'm CEO of the National Swingin-Ball Association."

"Yes, well, that's sort of what I wanted to talk to you about today. You see. I find myself in a bit of a pickle."

"Best thing to do when that happens, turn around and put the pickle in you."

The commissioner motored on. "Well, good advice." Behind him, his aides and yes-men tried to avoid looking anywhere but at Dude LaRude and his swinging nutsack. "We held a competition to see who would play the halftime show of our All-Star Game, and can you believe it? You won."

At this, Dude stopped swinging his nuts around and let his underwear slide back into place. He sat on the couch and crossed his legs, taking on an almost effeminate demeanor. "Wow. I never won anything before."

"Well, due to the nature of your show, I wanted to meet with you and see if we could come to an agreement of sorts. You see, the National Bouncy-Ball Association is a family company. Lots of children and families consume our product."

"Your product is sweaty men, bumping and grinding against each other while trying to shove things in holes? Yeah? Doesn't sound any different than porn to me."

"Yes, well. Our consumers don't think that."

"Your consumers don't think, you mean to say."

At this, the commissioner's face grew red, and Dude could tell the man was losing patience. He liked it, loved to see this man in his five-figure suit squirm, enjoyed it so much in fact, that he stopped enjoying it. Pleasure was fine in small doses, but it in big doses, it was a crime. Life was about toil and struggle and suffering. Pleasure had its place, but languish too long in the pleasant pool of endorphins, and you'd find yourself enslaved just like the man with his paycheck, or the dude with his hard cock and his girlfriend. Shackles came in all shapes and sizes, some made of flesh, some made of struggle, and some made of bliss. Some people liked their shackles, but not Dude.

In his brain, he felt something happening, something magical. His eyes went up and to the left, as he felt something there, a presence, dipping its cold, metal-studded fingers into his mind and swirling them around like a kid trying to pull a fingerful of frosting from the side of the bowl. The finger stirred and stirred, and the five-figure suit man droned on and on while Dude LaRude paid attention to the finger in his mind, scratching at the inside of his skull, poking bits of his brain until stars appeared.

The commissioner finished his spiel, which he had practiced in the mirror for hours upon hours, his yes-men at his side trying to throw him curveball after curveball to mimic the unpredictable nature of Dude LaRude. All that practice, all that time he would never get back, had been a waste, because much to Donald Mint's surprise, Dude LaRude agreed to all his stipulations.

He wouldn't swear on national TV. He would wear appropriate clothing. He wouldn't make any obscene hand gestures or reference anything of a sexual nature. In return, the commissioner would make sure Dude and his associates were well-compensated.

All these stipulations were put in place, chains on the unchainable. Dude's associates, when the commissioner left after handshakes all around, gathered around him and asked him if he had meant it all.

"Yes. Yes, I did."

Some of Dude's associates, never friends, called him a sell-out. His drummer, Fuck Sticks, walked out right then and there. But his guitarist, Felcher, smiled knowingly, prepared a lovely spike of heroin and plunged it deep within Dude's forearm, all while their bassist Rawdog tinkered with three-chord, discordant riffs drowning in distortion. In this way, Dude LaRude communed with his god. With his eyes closed, Dude LaRude sowed the ultimate seeds of Chaos, a Trojan horse of destruction that would be delivered on a national stage.

The commissioner would never know what hit him.

DUDE LARUDE SINGS THE BLACK AND BLUES

CHAPTER 4
THE LEAD UP

Though many of Dude's "friends" abandoned him at the news of his willingness to accept a corporate dick up his ass, his new friends were ever so accommodating. Upon news of Fuck Sticks' departure from the band, the folks in the Bouncy-Ball Association's P.R. Department found Dude a suitable replacement. Celebrity drummer and all-around fuck-up Pete Harker. Pete Harker was as famous and as talented as any drummer could be, though he was fickle as the wind, as swayable as one of those dancing, nylon air-monstrosities you find out in front of a car dealership. Covered in tattoos, his hair always fashionable, he was more of a celebrity than a musician, and on the first day Dude met him, he wanted to punch his face in.

The entourage Pete Harker brought in included several reality TV stars, people famous for their plastic good looks and the size of their asses. Donald Mint loved it. Dude didn't give two fucks.

In addition to a new drummer, Dude was given a variety of new songs to learn. They had catchy Hot-Topic-punk titles like *Down with the System*, *Vote Against Voting*, and *I Don't Belong*, real scintillating shit.

For weeks, Dude sat in a studio, watching the chaos play out as Felcher, Rawdog, and Pete Harker tried to put together the songs the N.B.B.A. had written for them. Rawdog, often high as a kite, would take his bass for a walk while Felcher would start wailing nonsense on his guitar, shredding eardrums and causing the people in the production room to turn off the feeds. Meanwhile, Pete Harker, known for jumping ship from one band to the next, would sit at his drums, trying to figure out what the hell was going on.

Between songs, Harker would step outside and smoke copious amounts of weed, leaving massive clouds of marijuana-infused THC, like smoke signals, floating down the streets outside the L.A. recording studio.

This entire time, Dude soaked it in, let the chaos infuse him, seep into his skin like the way alcohol soaked into the fruit of a batch of bathtub party punch. He memorized the songs, not because he planned on singing them, but because he wanted to look the part. He didn't want Donald Mint to have any clue as to his true intensions. Oh, yeah, and he slept with Pete Harker's reality-themed girlfriend, did her everywhere, and when Pete Harker confronted him about it, he fucked that dude, too.

From then on, the hype wheel kicked into full motion. Dude was spotted with rich people, famous people, beautiful people, and his picture went out to millions of children and teenagers, rabid consumers of pop culture. His name grew, and his marquee, once soiled with burnt out bulbs and faded neon was replenished with bright LEDs. Word of this mysterious punk rock genius spread, and YouTube views of his random, poorly recorded performances gained views by the millions. Despite the fact he had done nothing of consequence, his fame grew like a wildfire in August, consuming and charring the world, preparing the way for regrowth, rebirth.

Suddenly, an online industry cropped up, pictures of Dude in mid-debauchery silk-screened on T-shirts and sold all over the world. And no one, not a one of the entrepreneurs profiting off his likeness had ever seen him play or heard his real music. He was Che Guevara, Kurt Cobain, a Bob Marley T-shirt sold in the edgy store at the mall to kids who had no fucking clue who Bob Marley was—he was a face, an idea, but not the one they wanted him to be. He was fine with this, as it was only a matter of time.

The Bouncy-Ball Association sent out a crew of people to do promos of Dude LaRude and his wacky band. Most of the promo footage, which aired between episodes of cop-procedurals glorifying rape and murder, showed Pete Harker, but for the first time, Dude LaRude's ugly mug appeared on national TV. He wasn't a handsome man, didn't look tough. In fact, if it wasn't for the constant droop of his face from being wasted, the bags under his eyes from lack of sleep, or the emaciated structure of his face, he would look like any old Native American.

On the day they shot the promos, Dude couldn't stop laughing. Without a need for sound, Dude spent the day fake screaming into a microphone, having his body posed and positioned by people who thought they knew what punk rock was.

"I saw Good Charlotte before they were big. Blink-182 as well," one of the men in a Descendents T-shirt said. Dude just smiled and nodded, though in his head, he knew those bands were about as punk rock as the two motherfuckers who sang that Macarena song. The band, with the exception of Pete Harker, laughed nonstop, their rubbery, drug-fueled bodies quaking as they watched each other play "punk rock star" on a sound stage. When one of the P.R. people tried to get Rawdog to play his bass dorkister style, high up on his chest, geeking his neck back and forth, Dude and Felcher couldn't help but cackle their asses off, to the chagrin of many of the P.R. people—nameless, faceless fucks whose job was to know what would sell and what wouldn't. Never did they stop to consider the fact of whether or not something should be sold.

When it was Felcher's turn, they threw him in tight leather pants and a billowy shirt that made him look like some butt rocker from the '90s. They put make-up on his face to make him look like an emo bitch and then had him pinwheel his arms around like one of the slow "hard" rockers from the seventies. When Pete Harker's turn came, he did it like a pro, one of the reasons he was so sought after by bands who wanted to be popular, who wanted to push themselves over the edge and into the stinking miasma of the pop culture zeitgeist. He drummed feverishly, his hands a whirlwind of activity as his drumsticks twirled between his knobby, delicate fingers. His head and shoulders bobbed along, while his feet thundered on the kick drum. His mohawk, a three-hour production by the hair department stayed in place through all of this, a feat of engineering unrivaled since the building of the Golden Gate Bridge.

When they were all done, Dude was dragged away from his band members, with tears in his eyes from laughing so much. They dragged him into a room piled high with more food than Dude could eat in a month. You name it, it was there. Sandwiches, candies, a taco bar. To wash it all down, there were a variety of beverages, from the hoppiest of microbrewed

IPAs to the hard stuff to bottles of champagne that cost more money than Dude had made in his entire life. He grabbed one, shook it up, popped the top and sprayed it all over the wage-slave who asked him to sit in a chair. She screamed and pouted, and in the end, Dude apologized and offered to sleep with her. She said okay, and they were all good.

Sitting in the chair, a ring light blasting his face and blinding him, a parade of stylists came and went. He felt like a car on a car lot, sitting there in the hot sun while potential buyers and the salesman discussed what features they wanted added to the ride. Dude was nothing more than a consumer good to be modified and tricked out for display. The whole process lacked soul and heart; he didn't regret spraying the stylist with champagne. His only regret—how perilously close he'd come to blowing the whole ruse, showing his hand too soon. It was hard to play the game for him, went against everything he stood for, everything he was, which was absolutely nothing.

When they'd decided what to do with his hair and done several make-up tests, a new man appeared. Skinny and toting what looked like a tacklebox, he sat in front of Dude, a latex-gloved hand snaking out and turning his head from side to side.

"You got good brows, my man."

Dude sneered, but the man didn't seem to notice. Instead, he sat down on a wheeled stool and pulled himself closer.

"Who the fuck are you?"

"I'm your tattooist."

Dude laughed then. Tattoos. He wasn't against them—had the generic slashes on his arm—and there had been many a shadowy-faced person who had offered to ink him up in his days. But drug-fueled tattoos were not the type of thing that floated his boat. Dude didn't care how he looked, thought dressing up or caring too much about your appearance was a sign of vanity. Who cared how you looked? It was what was inside that counted, and all that was inside him was blood and shit.

"I don't need any tattoos."

"Well, it's gonna be weird when I start stabbing your face over and over again with a needle."

"The only needles I like go in my arms."

It was then that one of the faceless, Bouncy-Ball P.R. automatons stepped in. "Dude, this is standard in the industry. It's not enough to simply have the edge in your lyrics or your attitude. You gotta have it so every time someone sees your face, they stop and take a look. Look at some of the no-talents we have in the industry today. Pre-Malone, Nerf-Gun Kelly, Tiny Wayne. They all have the face tattoos."

"I don't know who any of those people are," Dude LaRude said.

"Hsst." An amused hiss from the tattoo man before he said, "You're lucky."

"Shut it," the automaton said. "Listen, we know you have the talent."

Dude laughed a bit. He had no such thing.

"Now you need the look. You let us do this, and you'll skyrocket, you'll book your ticket into outer-space, baby."

When Dude studied the automaton, he thought he saw his real face—the true visage—buried under a layer of slime, caramel-like sewer liquid clinging to his skin. It was the stink of money, the filth of greed obscuring the robot's face. The poor bastard thought he was alive, but he wasn't. Dude was looking at a walking corpse who would never take a free breath in his life.

"What could one little tattoo hurt?" the automaton prodded.

Dude smiled. Hurt. He was going to hurt a lot. It didn't matter if his skin was unspoiled.

"Wanna see some samples?" the tattoo man asked.

"Sure," said Dude, scratching at the scabs on his forearms.

Tattoo man opened his tacklebox, and inside, Dude caught sight of plenty of little bottles of ink, bandages, and other equipment. Off to the side of the tackle box sat an o-ringed collection of laminated pictures. The man pulled this free, and together they studied faces—tattooed, generic faces. On those faces, he saw a variety of things, words in flowing script, flowers, shapes, stars… just really, lame-ass, basic shit. One dude looked like the personification of a middle schooler's notebook, ridiculous and amateurish, his tattoos drawn in thick lines, the images laughable.

"See anything you like?" the tattoo man asked.

"No."

"See anything you could live with?"

He wasn't planning on being around for very long, so technically, he could live with it all. "You know about dragonflies?" Dude asked.

"Sure. I know about 'em. I can do one up for you."

"No, motherfucker—" It never crossed Dude's mind that maybe he shouldn't be rude to the man who was going to give him a tattoo. Like so much in his life, if something went wrong, he simply rolled with it. The future was for the masses, the unthinking zombified multitudes toiling away in their hated lives. "—I didn't ask if you could draw one. I asked if you knew about them."

The tattoo man, so intent on beginning his work, on making his wages for the day, leaned back in his stool. He didn't like Dude LaRude. The emptiness in his eyes belied a strange way of thinking, and he was uncomfortable with people like this. He encountered them every day in his shop in L.A., the broken and the weird, the artistic, the masochistic. They all came to him for their work, sometimes ridiculous, sometimes perverse, but he tried not to let it rub off on him. Though, many were the times when he would have a conversation like this. Sometimes, you just had to let a motherfucker ramble before they'd settle into permanency. It came with the job. Plus, he was on the clock, so it didn't bother him one bit. More money. "No," he sighed. "Can't say as I've ever really thought about them."

"A dragonfly begins life in an egg, a hard-shelled-protective incubator underwater. Eventually, it runs out of food and emerges, small, defenseless, and on its own. Other larvae, if they're hungry enough, will eat the other dragonflies. It's like school that way. Sometimes the weak don't make it. But they don't make a big deal out of it, the dragonflies don't, because they don't have TV. They don't write. They don't whine and moan when a member of the species is lost. It's not special. It never was. Anyway, a dragonfly might spend years living underwater, feeding of its brethren and sisterthren. Keeping the others down. And then something happens, something magical. They wake up!" Dude LaRude snapped his fingers suddenly, and the tattoo man jumped.

"At some point in their miserable life, they stop worrying about other people. They stop trying to keep each other down, and they say fuck it. There's a whole new world out there. Then they sprout wings, they break the surface, and suddenly, they're in the air. It's hard to do this. Underwater, they can live for years, but once they break that surface, once they're free of the water and their small, dragonfly-eat-dragonfly world, they might live for a day or a couple of weeks tops, flying around the world, living life to the fullest."

The tattoo man nodded and Dude knew he was only half-listening. But Dude didn't care. The words were mostly for himself. "And that what's amazing about a dragonfly. So many of them never get to see the world, but every dragonfly you see said, 'Fuck it. I'm going to live. Fuck this place.' And though they burn out, they die fast, better to have lived for a few weeks than to have grinded away your life, only to get eaten by something bigger and badder than you are."

The tattoo man nodded his head, as if he had attained deep, transcendental meaning. Then he looked over to the P.R. man. "So, a dragonfly? Yes?"

The P.R. man shrugged, and Dude said, "Fuck that. I want a pile of dog shit tattooed on my face."

At this, the P.R. man exploded. "No, no, no, no, no. No way, Dude."

"What? You want me to be like those motherfuckers in that binder? It's the same stuff, just dog shit." Dude leaned down and picked up the binder, snatching it off the tattoo man's lap. He jumped at Dude's touch, and he knew he'd gotten under tattoo man's skin. Good. Fuck him. "Look at this shit. It's just a bunch of scribbles."

"The market research shows that…"

"I'm not a product, motherfucker." Dude threw the binder at the mirror. It broke. Seven-years bad luck came his way, charging from the mirror dimension and into the back pocket of Dude's ripped, mangled jeans. "I'm a punk rocker. If everyone else is doing it, you know what I say?"

"What?"

"Fuck 'em."

"Everyone else eats."

"Fuck 'em."

"Everyone else breathes."

"I fucking know. That's why dying is the most punk rock thing you can do."

Dude inched closer to the P.R. man, invading that most bougie of concepts, his personal bubble. Go to a punk rock show and see how quickly your bubble was fucked into submission, drooling apes bouncing off each other while spinning in circles, while dancing and singing and sweating.

The P.R. man suddenly looked like he was going to be devoured by his four-figure suit, the tie spilling down his white dress shirt looking like a noose as he craned his neck backward, away from the pointed brown nose of Dude. "You know what I want? I want a copy of your face on my cheek, with a big, old, veiny dick squirting cum right into your mouth. Cuz that's all you are, man, a corporate dick sucker. Might as well immortalize you forever."

"Oh, c'mon, Dude."

"I can do that," the tattoo man said, then he set about getting his equipment ready.

Dude left the P.R. man sweating and returned to his seat. "Do me up," he told the tattoo man. In the mirror, he smiled at himself as behind him he watched the automaton swipe a hand across his sweaty brow, his cell phone to his ear as he talked to someone more important than himself. "Gimme a dragonfly tattoo," he whispered to the tattoo man.

The tattoo man smiled as he taped protective sheets of paper across his thighs, plugged in the tattoo gun, and switched it on. It clicked on with a buzz, like the hum of dragonfly wings.

DUDE LARUDE SINGS THE BLACK AND BLUES

CHAPTER 5
THE HANDLER

Sequestered. That was the word for what they were doing to Dude LaRude. But for visits to the studio where he earnestly tried to learn the songs handed to him, Dude spent most of his time locked up in a hotel room. Doc Hilliard had handled people like him before. They called him Doc because he had a PhD in psychiatry and had helped many a self-destructive star in his lifetime. Of course, his work was always private, and when people asked him about his clientele, he refused to talk about them, though he had stories up the yin-yang. He'd written some of them down as well. When he died, it was his idea that maybe his kids could publish it, give the world a peek behind the curtain at the depravity and narcissism of the celebrities he'd dealt with. It'd be a nice paycheck for his kids.

When Doc Hilliard stepped into the Hotel Bon-Aire, he thought he was prepared. He'd seen it all—drug addiction, sex addiction, crippling depression, delusional narcissism. All treatable, though often frustrating to deal with. Doc Hilliard's patience knew no bounds. And from what he'd been told about Dude, this would be a walk in the park—comparatively speaking. It was hard to help people help themselves if they were comfortable with who they were. He'd just have to wait and see on that account.

In the hotel, he passed many elites lounging around, sipping cappuccinos, their cell phones glued to their heads. At over a thousand bucks a night, not many casual folk came to stay at the hotel. This was where the cream of the crop stayed. It was also a great place to put a mess, the type of mess who might fuck up a hotel room or die of an overdose at any minute. The staff, long-timers who were paid extremely well compared to your average hotel staff, had seen it all. He was familiar with them, greeted the concierge who had a mind like a steel trap and remembered every single person who came through the front doors.

"Hi, Doc," Charlie Stafford said.

"Hey, Chuck. Good to see you again."

"And you."

"Is our boy here?"

Old Chuck would never talk bad about a guest, but Doc could sense the faint tinge of distaste oozing over the counter between them. "Oh, he's here."

"And?"

"Well, you'll see."

Doc nodded. He had expected no less. Leave an untrained dog in your house for too long, and it would chew up your couch, your slippers, get into the garbage, you name it. But the National Bouncy-Ball Association had a checkbook, and they were willing to open it up. Doc would train this dog.

"Is it true this guy is going to perform at the halftime show of the All-Star Game?"

Doc nodded.

"How?" Chuck whispered.

Doc shrugged his shoulders. It wasn't his problem. His problem was he had to keep the bastard from overdosing or killing someone, which his handlers insisted wasn't off the table for Dude LaRude.

"He had any guests?"

Chuck, uncomfortable with speaking about a guest in the open, pulled Doc back to his office. Only when the door was closed, did he turn and speak. "It's been a constant parade. It's like another planet around here. The people who come in, well, I don't think I've ever had such a parade of characters come through that door. And the smell!"

Doc nodded. "Don't worry. Should slow down around here now that I'm on the scene."

"That would be great," Chuck said, straightening his jacket, as if merely talking about Dude LaRude's entourage had rumpled his suit. Chuck was an orderly man. His fastidious office, simple and clean, everything arranged symmetrically on his desk, told Doc all he needed to know. Not that he didn't know it already based upon the attention to detail Chuck presented with regards to his appearance. A pencil thin mustache spread across his upper lip, not a hair longer than another. He must spend a good twenty minutes every morning making sure his mustache was neat and orderly. Why, the mere thought of someone like Dude LaRude messing up one of his hotel rooms must be driving him crazy.

Chuck handed him a key, his fingernails perfectly manicured and shellacked. Even when Chuck retired, which would probably be sooner rather than later, Doc suspected Chuck would maintain his fastidious ways, and the odd superstitions he probably had.

"Well, off to work," Doc said.

Chuck wished him well.

Doc turned and crossed the pristine lobby, his heels clicking and clacking as he walked across the polished marble floors. He opened a door and stepped outside, the smell of chlorine stinging his nose. As he strolled around the pool, Doc wondered how long it would be until Chuck found his way from behind the counter to wipe the fingerprint smear off the door handle. A terrible way to live. Doc could help him if he was allowed, but not for free, and even though the Hotel Bon-Aire paid well, he doubted Chuck could afford his services. Besides, he doubted Chuck was even cognizant of his condition. People like him seldom were. Hell, most people had a thing or two they could fix if they but gave themselves the chance, but mental health and the stigma attached prevented those who needed help from getting it most times.

That's why he liked his job. He wasn't sitting around listening to young starlets bitch and moan about their looks or their fears of growing old. He was helping the hopeless, the ones who had all the talent in the world, but who just couldn't seem to keep it together. Dude LaRude was a special case, of course. On the other side of the pool, he stepped inside the main part of the hotel. Here, the floors were carpeted, each door lining the corridor opening to an opulent suite that had been the temporary home of movie stars, dignitaries of state, and the occasional religious icon. History oozed out of its walls. A special place, one only one-percent of the world could afford.

To have someone like Dude LaRude stay there seemed like an affront, but word from Donald Mint was they wanted him out of his element. If he should escape and get on the streets, he would have a hard time finding heroin or whatever the hell it was LaRude was into. From the dossier the P.R. department gave him, it seemed he was into whatever he could get his hands on. Booze, pills, flesh.

At the door to room 154, Doc straightened his suit, took a deep breath, and prepared to do battle with the beast. He knocked. From inside the room, he could hear the sound of loud music, raucous voices yelling loudly. Doc would bet that the two rooms on either side had been left purposely empty so as not to disturb the other residents of the Hotel Bon-Aire. Chuck was smart like that.

When no answer was forthcoming, he knocked on the door a little louder, looking up and down the hallway, waiting for the familiar face of a celebrity to come peek at who was making all the noise in the hall.

No one came.

"Jesus Christ," he muttered under his breath. He took the key Chuck had provided him and slid it into the lock. None of those fancy shmancy card reader locks for the Hotel Bon-Aire. Just good old-fashioned locks made of shining steel. He turned the key and pushed the door open.

A smell wafted out, hit him in the nose like a punch. It was the smell of stale body odor, of people who cared not one iota what other people thought about them. It was the smell of the unwashed, the smell of those looking for a way out of this world—the smell of dependence on chemicals and flesh. He'd smelled it before. It was nothing new, but it always took his breath away at first.

He stepped inside, the loud, blaring music assaulting him. It was discordant—jangling guitars, pounding drums—and he hated it. Doc was a classical man who sometimes dabbled in jazz every now and then. He listened to music to relax, not… whatever the hell effect this shit was supposed to have.

"Good afternoon!" he called. "Doc Hilliard here. They sent me to come help you out."

Two half-naked people, both vaguely familiar to Doc, ran by holding hands. They bounced into a bathroom and slammed the door shut. They were not who he was here for though. He stepped deeper into the suite. On the floor, a shattered vase had given up its watery goods and dried, leaving a faintly brownish stain on the white carpet. Among the pottery shards, a selection of flowers, already dead as soon as they were clipped, continued their hasty, wilting demise. The flat-screen TV lay on the floor, its wires ripped from the wall. Dirty boot marks soiled the leather couches. Mostly empty bottles littered the coffee table, extinguished cigarette butts floating like bog bodies in the dregs.

Doc stepped over the shattered glass of the vase and headed deeper into the suite. He ignored the pile of brown—let's say it's mud—on the floor, ignored the thumping music pounding his brain. In the master suite, he found a monster cavorting among half a dozen men and women of various ages. His first sight of Dude LaRude was almost enough to send him away. Completely naked, fully erect, Dude stood covered in sweat, blood leaking down his chest from a dozen razorblade slashes. His face was one of both ecstasy and anger, hidden barely by the swirling nightmare of a dragonfly on his face. With a razor held in his skinny fingers, dude slid his hand down to his erect penis, and that's when Doc turned and closed the door. Hours of groaning, shouts, and screams of either ecstasy or agony, it was hard to tell which, assaulted Doc through the walls of the Hotel Bon-Aire suite. No one seemed concerned that some stranger was in their apartment and had seen them naked. No one cared that the same man heard their filth and fury from the living room.

As the sun went down, Dude emerged, still naked, his penis flopping from side to side, blood still trickling from a dozen wounds.

"Hey, fella. You been waiting for your turn?"

Doc, taken aback, shook his head.

"Then whatchu want? And why are you dressed like that?"

"I'm here from the National Bouncy-Ball—

Dude cut him off with a curt wave of his hand. "Don't need a handler. Just stay out of my way."

With that, he walked to the kitchen, poured himself a glass of water and gulped it down. After a loud burp, he strutted back into the bedroom, his rear-end red with bites and lash marks. The man closed the door, and the oversexed group within snored for the rest of the evening.

Doc fell asleep on the couch in the living room.

In the morning, Doc woke up staring at a couple of raw butt cheeks. A puff of rancid air came out and hit him in the face.

"That's anarchy, baby." This from Dude who danced away, a wry smile on his face. He sat across from Doc, who was trying not to throw up.

"You like doing things to people?" Doc said. "You like getting under their skin?"

Dude sat on the couch and riffled through the contents on the table. Finding a spoon, a baggy, and an unused belt, he set about cooking his breakfast. "Don't like anything. But I will say I find it interesting."

"Interesting how?"

"Under the skin is the real, you know what I mean? Peel the skin away and you find out who a person is."

"Can't you just talk to them, get to know them?"

"Do that, and all you know is a lie. For instance, you."

"Me?"

"Yup. You're lying right now. Your clothes are a lie. You're trying to look professional, you're trying to send the message that you are an authority, whether you meant to or not. It doesn't matter the intent behind a lie. A lie is a lie is a lie. And you're swathed in them."

"So, you think everyone walking around in a suit is a liar?"

"I don't think it. I know it. So why don't you take the suit off, let me cut on you a bit? Then we can really get to know each other."

Doc had no interest in being cut up by a punk's filthy razor. But, having broken the ice, he plowed ahead. "I'm interested in keeping my skin the way it is. My wife likes it that way."

"I bet she does."

"What does that mean?"

Dude squirted some water onto the powder on the spoon. Meanwhile, a woman, naked as the day she was born, walked behind the couch. She was cut up as well. Bad news in Doc's opinion. If Dude ever got a chunk of money, she looked like the type of girl who would come after him down the road. Though everything he had heard in the room had been consensual, you never knew how desperate people would get once money was involved. Some of his more unsavory clients kept piles of NDAs sitting next to their bed for just such a thing. An NDA was sort of a buzzkill, but if it kept you safe, kept your name out of the news, there wasn't any harm in it.

With the tip of the needle, Dude mixed the powder around in the spoon. "It means, you're married, so again, another layer of lies."

Doc smiled. He was getting a handle on the guy. "Everything's a lie, huh?"

Dude shrugged. "Believe it, or don't. Makes no difference to me. I just tell it how I see it. You wanna be blind, be blind. I don't even want you here. You're boring."

Doc laughed at this. "Because I don't do drugs and cut up on myself, I'm boring?"

The skinny man smirked as his brown hands placed a cotton ball in the concoction and then sucked the poison up the needle. "You're boring because you do what everyone else tells you to. Because you dress like an asshole. Because you're married like an asshole. Because you're doing this for money."

"Let me guess. Like an asshole?"

"Like a brainwashed son of a bitch I was about to say."

"You like to keep people on their toes. That's good."

Dude didn't even seem to hear Doc. He wrapped a belt around his arm, pulled it tight with his teeth. With the needle dangling between two fingers, he tapped on his forearm, his fist opening and closing until a vein popped out. Surrounded by bruises and missed injections, Dude drove the needle home, and then he disappeared.

When Dude leaned back on the couch and let his eyes close, Doc stood up, pulling the needle from Dude's arm. He stepped into the backroom, kicked the wastrels awake, and told them to pack up their shit. Despite the promises of blowjobs and other things, Doc made them all leave, which they did. Dude might believe all the bullshit he spewed, but his followers weren't on that level. They were run-of-the-mill scumbags and dead ends. Dude was as well, but at least he believed his own bullshit. Doc was sure of that.

When the last man had scurried out, Doc called room service, ordered a big pot of coffee and some food. Dude needed to eat. The Association didn't want him looking like a skeleton onstage. He searched the suite for more drugs, pocketed them all. Dude would be an unhappy man for a while, but that's part of breaking the cycle. It takes some pain to get off the shit. Doc knew. He'd developed a pretty severe addiction to morphine some years ago. Dude could talk all he wanted about liars and frauds, but

Doc had been there, been in the gutter, and he knew no one wanted to live that way.

Now, the trick was getting Dude sober enough and miserable enough to see he needed to quit. Otherwise, as soon as Doc was gone, he'd start back up again. Which wouldn't bother him so much, but it was bad for his reputation. The Junkie Whisperer they called him in high society. Got a movie star with a monkey on his back? Doc could chase it away with a banana. Dude was nothing. Just a sad man who didn't even know he was sad. Doc's job would be to sober him up enough to deal with his demons.

While Dude slept it off, Doc called his wife. He did this every day. She worried sometimes, didn't like how his job took him away for long periods of time. He smiled as he spoke to her, assured her everything was fine. It wasn't a lie if you didn't know the truth.

DUDE LARUDE SINGS THE BLACK AND BLUES

CHAPTER 6
GETTING CLEAN

A couple of thick men sat in the other room watching football on the TV they'd reattached to the wall. While they waited, they had put most of the hotel room back together. But Chuck was going to have a fucking embolism when he saw the state of the master suite. Doc kept the door to that room closed.

Sunlight streamed through the French double doors leading to the back patio, and Dude, a hundred and thirty pounds of broken man, lay snoring softly on the couch. When he woke up, he would be pissed. Might even try to fight. That's why Jamichael and Jalen were here.

He'd seen it before.

Doc wondered when Dude had last had an actual good night's sleep. From the dossier, it was understood that he always had people around him, kept odd hours. His friends were leeches. When you spread your arms wide and said, "Come. Feed off me," that's what people did—sucked you dry, gave you things that kept you giving whether you wanted to or not. Getting his friends away was key. In his pocket, Dude's cell phone buzzed nonstop. His band members, unimportant in the grand scheme of things, texted, wanted to know where he was, if he wanted to party. Then the messages changed, and they asked if he was ok. To avoid police interference, Doc jotted down their phone numbers on hotel stationary and called the authorities, filling them in on the situation.

Such silly names—Rawdog and Felcher. He could have helped them as well, but the Association didn't care about them. They would be blocked from the All-Star Game altogether. Dude was the ticket. Dude LaRude was the name in the promos. No one skweeted about Felcher and Rawdog. As part of his due diligence, he had listened to the recordings they had put together in the studio. Utter garbage. Hell, Doc was doing this kid a favor. Maybe with some real musicians, he could actually make something of himself. He doubted it. You had to want to be helped after all.

As Dude slumbered, a voice screamed in his head. A high-pitched, angry voice, lilting and bizarre. It spoke sweet nightmares to him, and he envisioned them in his damaged brain. Then he felt that sensation again, of someone thumbing through his mind, and he knew he was in for some pain. Not from the voice. The voice didn't care enough to hurt him. When it was done screaming about chaos, it spoke whispers to him, whispers of suffering to come, of pain and secrets, events that would come to pass whether Dude wanted them to or not.

The voice gagged and wretched, spewing its ether into Dude's mind, lending him the strength he would need to survive his ordeal, if survive was what he wanted.

Not really, Dude answered back.

I have a plan for that too, the voice screeched, a cross between a young Johnny Rotten and early Jello Biafra. Dude liked the voice, thought he could copy it, bring it to his music, make it unique.

Good, the voice screeched.

And then Dude awoke, his mouth dry, his head pounding, the sun assaulting his eyes. He sat up like a hungover drunk, but ten times worse. This was the pain; this was the promise.

"Fuck," he said, his tongue sticking to the roof of his dry mouth.

"Here," a voice said, its tone deep and melodious.

Through cracked eyes, he regarded the owner of the voice, remembered something fuzzy and funny about the man. "The liar," he moaned.

"No lies here, friend. Just truths."

Dude flipped him off.

"Another truth. Good," the deep-voiced man said. "Here's yet another truth. Drink some of that coffee. It'll help a bit."

The man slid a cup full of dark liquid in his direction.

"The blacker the better," the man said.

Dude sat up, his skinny arms groaning, his veins screaming to be fed. "Fuck coffee. Where's my gear?"

"No lies, right?" the man asked. His curly hair was cut close to his head, his hairline clean. His dark brown skin fairly glowed in the sunlight, so bright, Dude had to turn his eyes away. Perched on his nose were skinny eyeglasses with silver frames. His face was kind, and Dude hated it immediately. "I'm holding your stuff for you."

"Where's my phone?"

"I'm holding that, too."

Dude stood up then, swaying on meatless legs. "This is kidnapping."

Doc laughed. "You gonna call the police?"

Dude scoffed at the words. Never. He'd never gone begging to the police in his life. Wouldn't do it. Couldn't do it. If you couldn't handle your own problems, you might as well kill yourself.

"That's what I thought," Doc said.

Dude flipped Doc off once more, then headed for the front door.

"Boys," Doc called.

In the front room, two burly fellas stood. Dude could almost hear the air shrinking away from them they were so large. The one on the left, a face like an orc, cracked his knuckles. The one on the right looked at him in disbelief, as if saying, "Really? You're gonna try me?"

Dude knew when he was bested. He wasn't an idiot. Those two men could beat him to a pulp or twist him into a pretzel if they wished. Didn't mean he wasn't gonna try, but expectations were dampened.

Releasing a snarling scream like the ones he frequently bellowed on stage, Dude made a dash for the door. The man on the left reached out with one thick arm and stopped him in mid-flight. It wasn't even hard for him, and his feet and body didn't even shift in the slightest. Dude swung at his face, though the man towered over him. His fist connected with the man's smooth, brown cheek, and then Dude was flying, literally flying, through the air as the man threw him on the couch. He landed with a thud and thought of all those times he'd wrestled with his father back home, back in the days when he'd still idolized the man because he could do things Dude could not. That's how he felt now.

"You can't do this!" Dude yelled.

Doc, standing at the edge of the room smiled and said, "Watch me."

From there, Dude's life became a crucible of pain.

The first clue Dude was in for some pain came in the form of muscle aches. All over his body, he felt as if he'd been beaten to a pulp. He hammered on his legs with his fists to try and get the pain to go away.

Meanwhile, Doc watched over him, a small smirk on his lips. "It's gonna get a whole lot worse before it gets better."

Doc was right. An hour after the muscle pains came, he began to start feeling ill. His nose began to run, and his body shook with chills even though he was covered in a layer of sweat. When he started throwing up, he cursed Doc between gags, calling him all sorts of names. Doc leaned against the sink, unwilling to leave him alone.

"This what you bargained for when you started shootin' up? This how you envisioned it'd go?"

Dude didn't bother to answer. He simply filed the words away in his brain, etching each letter of each word in rage. Doc would pay for this. They all would. He tried to act like he was doing his job, but Dude knew he enjoyed it, got off on it the same way cops got off on beating people up.

"It sucks now," Doc continued, "but on the other side of this, you're going to find a whole new you. Of course, it's up to you if you're going to stay that way."

Another heave contracted Dude's innards, and he retched bile into the toilet, his throat stinging and his teeth rough from stomach acid.

"Don't know why anyone would start using like this in the first place. Maybe you wanted to die?"

"We all die."

"Yeah, but most of us don't dance with death. Sooner or later, the big guy is gonna step on your foot, and then what? Then you're gone."

"If I'm lucky."

Doc shook his head at this.

Dude let him lapse into silence. The few sentences he had managed to utter had taken all the energy out of him. He slumped down between the toilet and the sink, enjoying the cool of the tiles. Then another feeling came over him, and his guts began to churn painfully. Something was going to come out the other end.

Dude tried to get himself off the floor, but he was too weak.

"You need help?"

"I gotta shit."

Doc helped him up, pulled his pants down like a father with a toddler. The ailing junkie released the contents of his colon in a watery spray. Goosebumps broke out on his arms, and Doc, despite the stench and the fury, didn't back away. Dude had to give him credit for that at least.

"You like this," Dude said. "You get off on it."

"Don't feel any particular way about it, truth be told. It's a paycheck and a job, and I'm getting all the room service I want thanks to Uncle Donald."

"That fucking piece of shit. I'm gonna kill him when I see him, kill all of 'em, you included."

"That's just the pain talking, but if it helps you feel better, keep it up."

The suffering junkie was about to do just that when another painful bubble rocked his guts. Out came more filth, and his death threats were all but forgotten. Dude put his head in his hands and groaned. The voice in his dreams was right. This was about the worst he'd ever felt in his life. Thoughts of suicide flit across his mind. He groaned in frustration. "How long is this going to take?"

Doc pulled a can of air freshener off the sink, shook it, and sprayed it into the air. "Oh, give it a week. Should start feeling a little better after that."

"A week of this?"

"Wipe your ass," Doc said. "And don't worry. We got plenty of time. I'll help you keep your mind off it, if I can. It's the first three days that are the bitch. You get through that, and you'll be alright."

Under the watchful eye of Doc, he dutifully wiped his ass. He stood up to head into the living room, to the comfort of the cool leather couch. Doc said, "Wash your hands, you filthy animal. Don't be walking around this place with diarrhea mitts. What the hell is wrong with you?"

With a groan and a shiver, Dude turned around and did as he was told. After drying his hands, he turned around and said, "There. You happy?"

Doc nodded and Dude headed to the safety of the couch, flopping on it and pulling bloodstained covers over his body.

His tormenter sat across from him and studied his face.

"Would you stop looking at me?" Dude asked.

The man looked away, and Dude closed his eyes. A few seconds later, he could feel the man's eyes on him once more.

Dude retreated into his mind, searching for the solace of sleep, but it was slow to come. The echoey cheers of some type of sporting event in the front room distracted him, as did the chills and the aches. Eventually, he forced himself out of the mortal world and into the realm of sleep. There, the voice waited for him.

The voice reached out to him, wrapping him in comfort. It spoke of glory, of life attained and spent. Dude lapped it up. To some, they might think the voice a figment of their imagination, but not Dude. He'd heard the voice before, knew it had greater plans for him. And he was near the end now, only had to get through the hard part, and then everyone would see. They'd see the world for what it was.

Snuggled in his dreams, he was able to ignore the stare of Doc, the sound of sports droning on and on in the other room.

Meanwhile, in the real world, the world outside his mind and outside his hotel room, a rescue was being mounted.

DUDE LARUDE SINGS THE BLACK AND BLUES

CHAPTER 7
THE RESCUE

Say what you will about junkies, but when they set their mind to something, they fixate on it until the job is done, as long as drugs were in a steady supply. When Rawdog and Felcher found out their good buddy was being held hostage, they came together, put some stuff in their veins, and concocted a plan. The number of unfamiliar faces around their squat had grown considerably. As Dude's flickering flame grew brighter, more and more people flocked to it. Posers and weirdoes, human moths, the people Felcher loved the best.

They didn't have much in the way of weapons, but what they lacked in firepower, they more than made up in ferocity. Felcher in particular had a knack of turning random things into weapons. It was a side gig of his. Rebar could do wonders, as could the broken handles of household items.

From the time he left home, Felcher had always been something of a lowlife. He'd boosted cars, sold drugs, even been a male prostitute for a while. There wasn't anything he wouldn't do in the bedroom, hence the name. Most of the people in Dude's inner circle were addicts, addicted to all manner of recreational drugs, but not Felcher. Oh, he'd partake as much as the next person, but he was gifted, could quit whenever he wanted to. But that didn't mean that Felcher wasn't an addict himself, only, his drug of choice was Dude.

The man fascinated him, had from the first day they'd met. Skinny and fiery, Dude was something to behold. The shit he came up with, the raw energy and creativity drove him crazy. Watching Dude onstage was tantamount to watching God build the world. And they'd taken it away from Felcher.

He'd spent that first day on the couch with Rawdog, trying to call Dude on the cell phone he'd purchased for him the day before. Money was tight, but whatever little scratch they managed to pull together went into Felcher's pocket, including Dude's cut. For all his genius, Dude was shit with money and would fritter it away on whatever the hell popped into his mind.

Text after text, phone call after phone call, and no one responded. On his own cell phone, Felcher had located Dude's phone using an app he'd installed for just such an occasion. He was chilling in the fucking Hotel Bon-Aire of all places. A quick visit to the Hotel had left him fuming.

The manager, some pristine prick in a clown suit, had rushed at him as soon as he'd entered the door.

"What is your business here, sir?"

"I'm here to see Dude LaRude," he'd said.

"Oh, Mr. LaRude is not receiving visitors at the moment. If you leave me your phone number, I'll have him call you when he gets the opportunity."

"Listen, you fucking clown," Felcher had begun. "I want to see Dude, and I want to see him now!" He'd intended to go in all smooth and James Bond-like, but something about the officious little man and his stupid suit caused something in Felcher to snap. The speed he'd taken in the car probably hadn't helped either.

"I'm afraid I'm going to have to ask you to leave," the little man said, his creepy little molestache bobbing up and down as he spoke.

"I ain't leavin' till I see Dude," Felcher growled.

"Then I'm afraid I'm going to have to call the authorities." The little man turned from him then and headed behind a burnished oak desk. When he picked up the phone and began dialing numbers, Felcher turned and left the building, screaming and swearing at the top of his lungs as the people in the lobby, just as fancy and fake as the man behind the desk, watched him and shook their heads. They looked at him like he was scum, which he guessed he was, but you didn't just openly glare at people like that.

He'd stalked back to his car. Slammed the door and hammered on the steering wheel for a good ten minutes. When he saw flashing police lights in the rearview mirror, he started the car up and drove back to the squat, an old paper warehouse filled with punk rockers and junkies.

Back at the squat, with Rawdog, who was not the brightest of individuals, they concocted a plan. The first thing they did was to get Dude's newfound social media following mobilized. Despite the fact that Dude had never posted anything on social media, and indeed had no need or desire to, Felcher had created accounts for him on all the major platforms. Dude might not be interested in social media now, but he'd want them and need them in the future, especially once people saw how righteous he was. As the Bouncy-Ball Association's promos had taken over the airways, building up hype, Felcher had taken on the task of impersonating Dude, and he was good at it, too. All he had to do was say something ridiculous, of which he had a thousand such drug-fueled Dude-isms catalogued in his brain from long nights and days of partying. People ate it up, and Dude's follower count skyrocketed.

In order to facilitate their plan, Felcher put out the call for help, let people know someone was holding Dude hostage in the Hotel Bon-Aire. A dozen people showed up, a dozen wild, tattooed, pierced people, fueled by their own special concoctions of drugs. In their hands, they held weapons; in their hearts, they held chaos.

Before Dude, Felcher had been a drifter, a troublemaker. But the man had opened his eyes to the true meaning of the world, to just live, to fight for what you believed in, even if what you believed in was absolutely nothing. You had to fight for that. You had to prevent people from taking away your ability to not give a shit. They tried to do it all the time, with taxes, with rent, with jobs, with health-care. Find yourself wanting that stuff, giving in to the demands of society, and you were gone, evaporated into thin air, leaving only a shell behind. That's what Dude taught him.

They were dangerous thoughts, a philosophy and a lifestyle the regular world, the blind, would not accept. So, they had come for Dude, locked him up and tried to make him bland. First, the music, then the tattoo, now they wouldn't even let him hang out with his friends. That couldn't happen. There was only one perfect, pure thing in the world, and that thing was Dude.

Felcher's co-conspirators gathered around him, homemade weapons in their hands, waiting for some sort of speech, some sort of Braveheart monologue like this was some sort of swords and sandals epic. Though it reeked of cliché, he gave them one anyway.

"I wanna thank you all for bein' here. What we do here tonight is important. We're not just saving Dude. We're saving ourselves; we're striking a blow for freedom, freedom to be a piece of shit. Freedom to be a homeless junkie who lives outside the law. Some motherfuckers might look down on that, might ask why one would want to be a homeless junkie. Dude would say, 'Because I can. Because I chose it. Because I choose my own destiny, not you—with your expectations about what is acceptable and normal.' These are the lessons Dude has taught me over the years, and right now, they got him trapped in a room in some fancy ass hotel. They got him on the ropes, and we're gonna slice those ropes, wrap 'em around their throats, and hang 'em up high with 'em."

A raucous cry went up from Dude's supporters.

"When we go into the hotel, don't let anyone stand between you and Dude. Someone gets in your way... well, that's what we got weapons for, right?"

A murmur of assent greeted his question.

"Right?" he screamed.

This time the chorus was louder, more enthusiastic.

"Tonight, we strike for freedom! For chaos! Tonight, we strike fear into the hearts of every man woman and child sleeping secure in their bed. Because they shouldn't be. They should be scared out of their minds that they're wasting their lives away! They should be walking away from their school, their jobs, their mortgages. Tonight, we open the world's eyes."

Felcher stared around the room, looking into the dark-ringed eyes of these people. He didn't know them from his own asshole, didn't rely on them in any way. They were here now, but when the shit hit the fan, they could very well turn and run. The only one he was sure of was Rawdog, standing with the broken neck of a guitar in his hand. He'd sharpened the end, and could swing it with some strength despite his wiry arms.

"For Dude!" Felcher finished.

"For Dude!" the crowd echoed.

Charlie Stafford had seen many things in his days as the concierge of The Hotel Bon-Aire. It seemed people with money were capable of anything and everything. Charlie Stafford was not what one would consider a good person. He'd taken money to turn a blind eye. He knew a stable of fixers like old Doc Hilliard upstairs. Knew even more security guards like the two Black men with him. Despite the rich, opulent interior of Hotel Bon-Aire, he was not a naïve man. Though he spent his days working in splendor, he knew there was a crust of unsavoriness splattered over every item in the Hotel. But that was his job, to hide that unsavoriness from the average guest, to uphold the glamour of the hotel, whether it was earned or not.

Though Charlie Stafford had seen everything, he was unprepared for the newest threat to the Hotel's reputation. At nine in the evening, a group of—he hesitated to call them men—humanoids pulled up in shitty vehicles that rattled and spat clouds of dark exhaust into the air. It ought to be a crime for them to even drive those wretched things on the street.

The people who climbed out of the vehicles were dirty, subhuman. In their hands, they gripped weapons. Charlie's first instinct was perhaps the incorrect one.

At the door, Shane Watson, the doorman, stepped in front of the group of people with a hand outheld. His lips moved, and he spoke in a calm manner, though Charlie couldn't hear his words. He did hear the reaction though, and soon after the yelling and the shouting began, Charlie reached for the phone, dialed the number for the security office.

"Barbarians," he said into the phone. Then he hung up, straightened his suit, moved his stationary pad to the correct position, one millimeter to the left, and prepared himself for the invasion.

The doorman held up for a little while, until one of the men clonked old Shane Watson on the head with what looked like the neck of a guitar. Charlie swallowed, lifted his chin. I could leave right now, let these freaks have whatever they want. "But that's why they pay you the big bucks, Chuck, my boy."

The residents hanging out in the lobby, having seen the violence, picked up their cell phones, started making calls, and moved down the hallway to their rooms. They scattered like leaves in the wind, none of them wishing to confront the dirty mob. Charlie couldn't blame them. They were important people with eight-digit bank accounts, but what good was money when some angry cretin stove in your head with a guitar neck.

The mob pushed through the front doors, screaming and shouting. Their violence was not contained to people, and the decorations in the lobby were unceremoniously knocked to the floor or shattered by lengths of rebar and sharpened spears made from the handles of mops and shovels.

The lead goon, skinny and older than the others, his arms peeking out through a tattered jean jacket with the sleeves missing, approached him. His face was long. "Old World" was the phrase that came to mind. Underneath a jaunty paperboy cap, gray hair escaped, tied into a filthy ponytail. "What room is Dude LaRude in?" the man asked.

"I believe you meant to ask, 'In which room is Dude LaRude?' Sadly, I am not at liberty to divulge such information." Where the fuck is security?

"Liberty's got nothing to do with it."

Even as the gray man spoke, the filth began climbing over his lovely desk, leaving dusty boot prints on its polished wood. Hands, ending in grimy, jagged fingernails, grasped him by his suit. He could feel the germs crawling over him. Who knew what sorts of sicknesses these people bred in their flophouses? Hepatitis? A, B, and C? Hell, even Z? His body shriveled underneath his clothes. They leaned in smiling, their teeth broken, the smells coming from their mouths unbearable. They stank of uncleanliness, and for the first time in his life, Charlie Stafford considered giving in and abandoning the Hotel Bon-Aire.

Just then, security burst through a door, nightsticks in their hands. The filthy people, didn't care though. They turned and swarmed over the security guards beating them and bashing them to the ground. For their part, the security guards gave as good as they got for the first few moments. One of the filthy people fell to the ground, unconscious, blood dripping onto the polished marble floors. That's going to stain.

Then the security guards were down, and the filthy mass rained down boots and shoes on them, leaving twisted piles of bleeding flesh upon the ground. More blood. Great. "The police will be here any minute," Charlie said as his captors held him in place.

"Then we better be quick," the gray man said. He climbed over the desk and began pummeling the concierge. Then, with his dirty hand, he began clawing at Charlie Stafford's eye. Pained screams escaped his throat, so sharp and intense he could hardly believe they came from his own mouth.

"If you value your eye, you might want to tell me which room he's in."

Fingers scrabbled and dug at his eye—intense pain shooting into his brain. The gray man's questing fingers dug deeper into his eye socket. Fear of losing an eye, of having to wear an eye patch the rest of his life, took hold of old Charlie Stafford, and he couldn't resist. He gave up the information. Immediately, the gray man stopped his tortures. When they asked for the room key, Charlie didn't argue. He simply handed it over, his head hanging. The gray man accepted it with his filthy hand. With a swollen eye, scratched and battered, Charlie watched as the man turned and left. Two of the filthy people stuck around, and they began wailing on Charlie with their fists. Each hit brought Charlie a question. "Is this the one that'll knock me out?" He almost wanted it, pleaded for it. When the blackness finally came, a deep sigh escaped his body as he collapsed to the polished floor behind the desk, his blood seeping into the marble floors.

Doc Hilliard heard them first. Down the hallways they came, hooting and hollering, bashing the walls with whatever weapons they had at their disposal.

"Duuuuuuuuuude?" they called in sing-song voices.

Doc was under no delusion Charlie Stafford had held up to whatever mob had been assembled to rescue Dude. The man himself, knee-deep in his own sweat and suffering, sat up, like a dog hearing its master returning home.

"Jamichael, Jaylen, the door."

The two big men stood; Jamichael cracking his knuckles once more. They took positions on either side of the door. Doc wasn't scared… yet.

At the door, they heard the rattle of a key sliding home in the lock, and Doc knew Charlie had rolled over, meaning the force outside would be large and dangerous. The hotel's security would have taken care of anything less. The door burst open, and Jamichael and Jaylen began pummeling attackers, keeping them blocked in the doorway. The shouting echoed in the room, and Doc caught sight of the faces through the rectangular opening. Frenzied. That's the word to describe them.

"Just let me go," Dude said.

"I've been paid for a job, and I intend on doing that job." Doc tried to sound confident, but he didn't know if it was working.

"Then you're dumber than I thought."

"You're the one about to die because you can't handle reality."

"Your reality," Dude said. "I can handle my own reality. The first mistake Donald Mint made was thinking he was right. The second mistake he made was thinking I was wrong."

"You're speaking nonsense."

In the doorway, a sharpened guitar neck stabbed Jamichael in the face, and he fell backward, his hands covering his wound, blood seeping between his fingers. He didn't even scream. Tough bastard.

Now that he was left on his own as Jamichael spun around the room, his face hidden in his hands, Jaylen fell back swinging a dark black truncheon at his attackers, cracking their jaws, their teeth, their eye sockets. Blood fell from both the attackers and Jaylen, but he lost ground. Dude's entourage surrounded the hapless bodyguard, and it wasn't long before he hit the ground.

Doc Hilliard, confident in his own abilities, had one demand when he took the job. No guns. You never knew what a junkie would do if they got their hands on a gun. But right now, he began to regret that decision. When Dude's friends had finished stomping Jaylen into unconsciousness, they stood facing Doc Hilliard. Wounds purpled their faces, blood dripped from busted lips, scalps, and noses. They smiled at Doc with broken teeth, and he did the only thing he could do—he stepped to the side.

Dude stepped past him, small and visibly shrunken. His body shook with chills and the blanket wrapped around his shoulders showed the dampness of his sweat. The old man with the gray ponytail, dressed like a gypsy king, stepped up to Doc, and Junkie Whisperer saw the violence in his eyes.

"Don't," Dude said.

"Why?" the gypsy king asked.

"Cuz it's funny."

The gypsy king shrugged, and they all laughed at Doc as he stood facing down twelve junkies, knowing there was nothing he could do.

"You sure you wanna go?" Doc asked Dude.

"You sure you wanna stay?" Dude asked.

Doc didn't want to stay. He wanted to get home to his wife and his children, but he allowed himself a moment to imagine what it would be like to go dwell in the wake of Dude's chaos? His world was different.

Doc could see that now. Where most people might be bound by laws and fears of winding up in jail, Dude LaRude's fans had no concept of fear, no concept of destroying their own lives. They had nothing but each other, occasionally some drugs, and in this they were free. Doc meanwhile… well, he had a lot to lose, had spent his life collecting things. First, he'd collected grades, mostly A's. Then he'd collected knowledge and diplomas and degrees. Later, he'd collected the trappings of contemporary life. The job, the mortgage, the wife, the two kids, the cars. And was he better off? Was he really better off than Dude?

"Later," said Dude, and a couple of people with multicolored hair leaned up under Dude's shoulders and helped carry him from the hotel room. In their wake, they left busted light fixtures, dents in the doors, and holes in the walls.

When he was sure they were gone, Doc called Donald Mint personally, told him he'd failed—that Dude couldn't be tamed.

Doc didn't enjoy the words tumbling from Mint's mouth, and for a brief second, he considered maybe he had made the wrong choice, maybe life in Dude's wake was how life was meant to be. Then he went home.

DUDE LARUDE SINGS THE BLACK AND BLUES

CHAPTER 8
THE SECOND SIT DOWN

Dude was at home with smiling, sweaty faces all around him. Rawdog tinkered on the bass guitar in the corner, strumming ominous tunes. A whirlwind of new people came and went, people who wanted to bask in his presence. Though he had nothing to offer but himself, for many of them, that seemed enough. They sat at his feet, listening to his words, his ramblings as he recounted his miserable time under lock and key.

The police came, knocked at the door of their squat, but they were told to fuck off, and eventually, with no warrant or no probable cause, they left. It was treated as a victory, but Dude knew they would be back. The cops didn't like to be showed up. It shook their whole understanding of the world, and they would do anything to maintain their delusions. Make fun of a cop, and you made fun of the law, and the law was their sole reason for existence. Social control was the reason for their being, and when people acted out of control, didn't treat them with the respect they imagined they deserved, well, that couldn't stand.

Dude told his fans this, and though he didn't care about them, his words made them think he did. He toyed with the idea of beating one of them up, but that was small-time. Smashing delusions was the ultimate duty of a punk rocker, but sometimes you had to let those delusions hang out like shower mold, because you had bigger things on tap, like washing your nuts. Cleaning the mold out of corners was best done with clean nuts.

In his mind, that voice stirred, whirring around, making plans, offering scenario after scenario of how Dude could achieve the goals of the voice. Some people might think themselves crazy if they listened to a voice in their head. But not Dude. He took the voice at face value, knew it was something greater than himself, which wasn't hard. Every real punk knew they were nothing more than meat on sticks all wrapped in skin, living, breathing corn dogs, always looking to dip themselves in mustard and ketchup before they dove willingly into the world's mouth. Punks knew that. Of course, they did. All except for the posers.

When the next knock came at the door of their squat, the delusional sycophants grabbed their weapons, sure the police were back with their riot shields and their protective helmets, looking like life-sized cockroaches in their tough exoskeletons. Kill a cop and five more would pop up in their place.

But surprisingly, only one man stood on their doorstep when they opened the door—Donald Mint in his five-figure suit. Rough, dirty hands grabbed him by the jacket and pulled him inside. In the street, among knee-high weeds sprouted through the cracks in the sidewalk, Mint's security detail broke into action, but their overlord waved a hand. The security guards relaxed, their hands falling from the weapons holstered inside their suit jackets.

Dude's sycophants pulled Donald inside, handling him rough, getting their rocks off on treating the big bad corporate man like a prisoner in a third-world country. They were wrong for doing it, hypocritical. Hurting people wasn't punk rock, about as far from it as Avril Lavigne. It was fascism, plain and simple. It was amazing how quickly these "free-thinkers" began to act like the oppressors as soon as they attained a little bit of power. All the more reason to ditch power, to ditch ego and desire. The true punk rocker was a Zen affair, as close to a Buddhist monk as he was to the grave. These people manhandling Donald Mint didn't get it. Not one bit. It reminded him of the motherfucker who showed up to his January Sixth Insurrection hearing wearing a Descendents T-Shirt. The son of a bitch just didn't get it. And that was the hardest thing about being a punk, about worshipping at the church of chaos and rebellion.

Everyone thought they knew what punk was. It was music, a particular sound. It was giving everyone the middle finger for the smallest of things. It was pretending you were better than others. It was the mohawks, the tattoos, the clothes.

All these people were wrong. Punk was not about anybody else but one's self. It was about standing up and saying this is what I believe and why I do it. You don't have to like it, and you can shit on it all you want, I'm still going to do it. If you try and stop me, there will be trouble. If you don't try and stop me, I'm going to say things that will open your mind, challenge your misconceptions.

No, wait. That was entirely wrong. It was uhh… it was like. Dude's eyes rolled into the back of his head as the voice from the other world dipped its entire hand into his gray matter, squeezing his sponge-like brain and massaging it.

Donald Mint came to him then, and one of Dude's sycophants spraypainted a red anarchy symbol on the back of his expensive jacket. Donald smiled a pitying smile at the man. "True art. You just made this jacket a one of a kind. Thank you."

This pissed the man off. Dude didn't know his name, but as soon as he cocked back the arm with the paint can in it, Dude told him to stop.

"Why?" the artist asked.

"You hit him, you use your power to cause pain, and you're just as bad as he is. An eye for an eye, the mantra of a simple man, a thoughtless neanderthal. That's a dog talking. Not a human."

These words hurt the man, and for a moment, Dude wondered if he was a hypocrite as well. The artist's paint can tumbled from his hand, and he backed away.

"Have a seat, Mr. Mint."

Donald nodded. He was a thin man, about to disappear from the world. His shoulders were narrow and he carried himself with a straight back, so straight that Dude imagined when he got home, he doubled up into a ball on his bed, like one of those slap-bracelets broken against the wrist. His hands were thick, manicured so they wouldn't look like an ape's hands, but Dude knew that's who Donald was. His spirit animal was an ape, capable of grand tricks, but still likely to fling his own shit if things didn't go his way.

Dude kicked a passed-out man off a couch. He rolled to the floor, looked around for a brief second, and then went blissfully back to sleep. Donald came to sit on the couch, the soles of his expensive shoes resting on the back of the man. It was a perfect image, and Dude took in every color and curve, committed it to memory.

"First off, Dude, I want to offer my heartfelt apologies about what happened at the Hotel Bon-Aire."

Halfway through his apology, the sycophants started razzing the man. Dude did not offer Donald Mint any relief. It was good for people like him to experience the truth of humanity, to realize not everyone bought their bullshit. While his apology might be good enough for a press release, everyone in the squat knew he was full of shit.

"I sincerely hope we can move on from the past."

"I don't even remember it," Dude said. He did, but it didn't matter. The past was another thing people clung to too much. Oh, it was good for future predictions, but to dwell on the past and remain angry about it… might as well wear around a pair of shackles. That's what many of the people in his family couldn't understand. Yeah, it sucked what the white people had done to their tribe. It sucked; it was bad, but it was also the past. Wearing that pain around, that hurt, all it did was drag you down. The saddest Indians he'd ever seen were those who clung tight to the past, let the hurts of their ancestors scar them even though they'd suffered nothing physically. It was okay to be aware of it. Being aware of the past prevented you from doing things like becoming part of the problem. While Dude knew the history of his people, he didn't let it control him. But he also didn't forgive it. So, when his family had become religious, had sidled right up to the bar of Christianity and drank the wine of the man Jayzus, he'd left. Fools, all fools, every single one of them. He'd rather burn in hell with people who looked like him than live in a heaven where everyone was white.

"Water under the bridge," Dude whispered, and his sycophants fell silent. They didn't understand. They wanted to rip this man apart, tear him to pieces, send him scuttling from their squat, ashamed and changed. But they couldn't do it. This man was no more capable of understanding his role in the world than a shit-flinging ape in a zoo.

"Good, good. So, we're still on for the All-Star game."

"I wouldn't miss it for the world."

"Very well." Donald Mint was all smiles now. "Is there anything you need for the performance? We're only a week or so away now."

Dude nodded. They were friends, or at least, people pretending to be friends. "Just need to practice is all, get our fingers live and the vocals right."

Donald nodded.

"We also need the police off our backs."

At this Donald hitched.

Dude stood up then. His body still covered in the sweat of withdrawal. He hadn't dosed yet, didn't know if he was going to. Somewhere in his mind, he understood he'd become a slave to feelings, to emotions, to endorphin releases, and he knew this needed to change. Maybe kicking his habit in a squat full of users wasn't the best idea, but he could do it.

"I don't know what you think I can do with the police," Mint began.

"Police are like anything else in America. A little money, and they go away. You have money. I'd hate for my band to be arrested. If something should happen to Rawdog or Felcher, why, I think I'd be so broken up that I couldn't perform at all. And then you'd just have a drummer out there. Us Native Americans like drums, but I'm not sure Native Americans are the audience you're going for, right?"

Donald Mint nodded. "Anything else," he asked, voice clipped, short. One way to ruin a rich guy's day was to tell him he was going to have to sink some more money into something.

"Could use a ride to the show. Odds are, none of us are going to be able to drive."

At this, Donald Mint's head cocked to the side. "Just don't overdo it," he spat. "I need you to perform. You go out there all red savage wasted, and I'll scalp your ass."

"Donald," Dude began, comically offended, "I thought we were friends."

"You shit in my backyard, and I'll bury you under it."

"Understood."

Donald stood up then and held out his hand. "I'll send my best limo for you three."

Dude looked at the man's hand and left it hanging. Donald straightened his now ruined suit. It had gone from five-figure to one-figure in a matter of moments. He turned and departed to the jeering of the sycophants. When he was gone, they all laughed, and Dude sat among them, wondering if this was how Jayzus felt.

DUDE LARUDE SINGS THE BLACK AND BLUES

CHAPTER 9
THE BIG DAY

The limo pulled up to their squat at 10 a.m. No one noticed it until eleven. The driver inside was too freaked out to go up and knock on the door which was spraypainted in anarchy symbols and swear words and didn't even close all the way. It looked like the type of place where a murder had happened; the type of place people would leave abandoned because no one wanted to deal with the bad karma inside.

After taking a piss in the hallway and spying the limo outside through one of the boarded-up windows, Rawdog kicked Dude awake. Dude yawned as Rawdog and Felcher spiked up before they went. The halftime show was at five-thirty or thereabouts, so they loaded up some extra doses and hid them about their persons. They wore whatever they'd been wearing the night before. Hair and makeup were not their specialty, and they knew they would be spending some time in a chair before they ever got near the stage.

Smelling like human morning breath, they piled into the limousine. The driver immediately put up the partition between them.

"You guys ready to rock the world?" Felcher asked.

Dude smiled. "Oh, we're going to do a lot more than that."

Out the back window, Dude watched the long line of police cars following them. Looked like Donald Mint had kept his word, but it also looked like when the show was over, the pigs were going to slap cuffs on all of them. Dude wasn't surprised, had expected it even. But he knew it wouldn't matter. Nothing did and nothing would.

The limousine dragged them through the innards of the city, right through its concrete intestines covered in shit. Impatient people sat inside thousands of cars, rushing off to do something that didn't matter—all sitting and looking at each other's asses, human centipedes locked in lanes and lines. Revolting. The limousine inched forward as Felcher dug through the complementary contents within. Snacks and food, but it looked like someone had expeditiously removed all the alcohol. Dude tore into a bag of pretzels and washed it down with a can of Coca-Cola that made his teeth sting. It was a good pain; let you know you'd eaten food and kept yourself alive… to some degree.

As they munched on snackables, they discussed their plans for the day in hushed tones lest the limousine driver turned out to be a spy, which, at this point, none of them would put past Donald Mint. Their plans were glorious things, the type of things children, unfettered by rule or the fear of consequences, might come up with in their treehouse. The only difference was they were going to pull their plans off. They spoke with smiles, their hands striking the air like prizefighters sparring in preparation for the big moment.

Behind them, their pig tail rolled on, forgettable faces and forgettable minds, tools of a country and a society that quite simply didn't want you rocking the boat. When they pulled up to the arena, a giant archeological monstrosity placed upon what was once sacred land for the tribes who had lived there before, the three band members tumbled from the limousine, falling over each other. A handler stood looking down at them like a man in an SUV watching a corner panhandler from the safety of ten car-lengths.

The police, eager to make sure—to make fucking sure—that Dude and the others saw them, stepped from their vehicles as one, pulled their batons from their belts, and stood holding them like big-dicked men in a porno movie, stroking and looking to fuck someone. Their handler eyed the police warily, and then hustled the band members inside.

Once inside, they were hustled past the craft services table. Before they could get very far, one of the Bouncy-Ball players, clad in the most ridiculous of outfits, somewhere between a 1920's Southern gentleman and a Venetian gondola operator called Dude's name. Dude didn't know him from a dick in a gloryhole, but the man insisted on getting a picture with Dude anyway. He stood next to the man as he draped the longest arm Dude had ever personally seen over his shoulder. With his other hand, the bouncy-ball player held his cell phone a mile away, smiled, and took a picture. This man, this athlete, had more followers than the president, more followers than the smartest man alive, more followers than the Jayzus, more than all of them combined, and Dude's picture shot around the world like a celebrity's mugshot. In the days to come, people would pore over the picture, wonder what was going on behind those glassy eyes, if he had any inkling of what he was about to do. Was that middle finger meant for everyone? Was it a message to the world? A warning? No one would ever know.

The make-up chair was the worst. Dude never liked to sit still. He liked to move when he felt like it. Sitting in the chair was torture. An over-made collection of fake human beings painted and dyed and trimmed him, taking his nature away, making him as fake as they were. Looks… overrated and another tool of societal control. It didn't matter what you looked like. What mattered what was in your heart, the freedom of spirit and the ability to walk the world knowing you were true to yourself. Focus on your looks, and you lost that. It was easy to see why people did it. They were slaves to their genitals, absorbed message after message that you had to look a certain way to be fuckable. And then, when you got laid, you just kept the cycle going out of habit, never realizing you'd lost yourself in the quest for sex. The people around him were war criminals, totalitarian masterminds tapped into society's desires and whims.

But the end result of their ministrations looked pretty cool. If it wasn't all bullshit, he might have even thought himself handsome. The sides of his head had been shaved—his long, brown hair bleached to death and dyed a sweet vermillion, the color of blood. His skin, shorn of its filth and the dust of the squat, shined, the fresh tattoo on his face gleaming against his brown skin.

The clothes he wore were loaner things, leather with studs and buckles, strategic rips to show the brown skin of his belly and chest. He was a clown, the picture of what a punk rocker should be.

"Sell out," Felcher called him when he rose from his own chair and got his first look at Dude.

"You should talk," Dude laughed.

They'd cleaned Felcher up to the point where he was almost unrecognizable, a stranger's skin and hair. His gray ponytail gleamed with cleanliness, and his yellow teeth smiled behind a freshly manicured beard. On any given day, Felcher looked like a homeless man who had slept rough. Today, he looked like a wizened movie star. His skinny arms, muscular and gnarled with age, poked out of a vest bedazzled with metal chains and straps. War paint covered his face in a broad stripe across his eyes and the bridge of his nose.

Rawdog looked much the same, and Dude could see how uncomfortable he was. "Anyone seen my big red nose?" he asked.

Rawdog did indeed look clownish. Never what someone would call an attractive man, the make-up artists, rather than polish a turd, had completely redone Rawdog's face, slapping a coat of ridiculous white paint over his face and darkening the area around his eyes, painting lines over his lips so when he held his mouth closed, he gave the impression of a skeleton. A black, mesh T-shirt and some leather pants completed the ensemble.

"Ain't we a trio," Dude said.

From there, they were ushered to a green room. Inside, Pete Harker waited for them, a cloud of marijuana smoke escaping the room when they opened the door.

"Boys! Boys! Boys! You ready to rock?" he asked, a cloud of smoke escaping his lungs.

"We're ready," Rawdog said. "You just keep up."

"How long until the show?" Felcher asked.

"Game just started," Pete said. "Here, you can watch it over here."

Pete turned on a TV in the corner, and the game popped on. The massive man Dude had taken a picture with ran up and down the court, the ball sticking to his hand like a large yo-yo. Down and then up, everywhere he went, the ball followed as if he were some sort of banal magician. Dude kicked a hole in the TV, and Pete laughed marijuana smoke through his nose, coughing and sputtering.

"Too real," he kept muttering.

On the table, an ice bucket filled with alcoholic beverages sat. Funny. For as much as Donald Mint had frowned upon his drug use, his connections to alcohol companies made him as much of a drug dealer as the man who sold Dude smack. Alcohol killed more people every year than weed, heroin, and cocaine combined, if you took the gangsters and dealers out of the equation. But here it was, ready and available, as it had been to his father when he was a youth. Most people growing up like he did might have eschewed alcohol. Most people, taking a beating here and there from a drunken father or drunken brothers or drunken mothers, would say "no" to the cause of their pain. But not Dude. Again—that was the past, and holding on to the past was like trying to wrestle the wind, a losing thing, pitiful and sad to see.

The three musicians rushed at the beers, Pete smiling in the corner as he rolled up another joint. Dude popped the top of the can and drank it down as fast as he could. He hated the taste of beer, didn't see how others could drink it to enjoy it. He figured that was a lie as well. Rawdog and Felcher sat on the couch with big, shit-eating grins on their faces.

"Can you believe this? Can you fucking believe we're actually going to perform the halftime show?"

Dude couldn't believe it. As he popped the top of his second beer, he closed his eyes, and listened to the voices in his head. A slow smile spread across his face. It seemed like they hung out that way for hours, filling the room with smoke and laughter. It was a good time, the last of Dude's good times.

A funny little woman, mousy and out of place, came and retrieved them from the room and escorted them through the bowels of the stadium, named after some stupid insurance company… millions of dollars wasted on naming a building while the company that wrote the check skimped on benefits and laid people off based upon declining market share, replacing them with cheap, benefit-less contract workers. Their name was known though. That's what's important, right?

When they had first climbed out of the limousine, the arena had been a dead thing, a concrete skeleton with its flesh stripped away, but now it had come to life. The people had filed in, and the place thrummed with life. The crowds in the main part of the arena gave the stadium a soft breath. The people walked up and down the stairs, purchasing beers, acceptable drugs, at twenty dollars a pop. As one, they queued up in lines longer than a cat's stretched out intestines to buy mass-produced, subpar-quality food, again at twenty dollars a pop. Up above, in the luxury boxes, in fancy suites, fat cats reclined, dollar signs in their eyes as the people below moved through the arena's innards, shuffled along like fecal matter through bowels. This arena, dead upon arrival, had resurrected, and on the arena floor among hot-waxed, wooden boards shining like a baby's glistening forehead upon birth, its heart beat as men with giraffe legs loped up and down to the crowd's delight. Soon, Dude would replace that heart, step onto the shining court, and deliver himself, sharp and sudden like a heart attack, to the entire world.

In the tunnel, Rawdog, Felcher, and Dude LaRude waited like an inert torpedo in a submarine's torpedo tube. Rawdog cracked his knuckles and chewed the inside of his lip until blood came out of his mouth. Felcher stood with his head down, burping stale beer burps. In the green room, they'd left a wake of dead soldiers scattered all about, and a puddle of urine in the corner. Someone would have to clean it up, but at least they'd have a story to tell.

A roar went up from the crowd, and a gaggle of towering men walked by, dripping sweat by the bucket. "Man, I can't wait to get my dick sucked tonight," one of the men said as the lights on the court dimmed. A sad man, Dude decided, driven by his penis. Cut his cock off and what did he have? Nothing. He would die. Maybe that's what they should do when men were born, remove their penises, keep 'em tucked away in cold storage until they learned to find something in life with more meaning than the thing that dangled between their legs. Once they found that, then they could apply and have it sewn back on.

The funny little gal, perhaps she was an elf hiding in plain sight, waved them onto the court, and Dude and his conspirators stumbled in the dim light to their spots on court. A quick soundcheck that morning had been all the practice they'd really received, but the cool thing about punk rock was if you fucked up, you could just pretend that's what you'd meant to do in the first place.

As Pete Harker walked by, Dude grabbed him by the arm. Shirtless, covered in sweat, and with his eyes glazed like a donut, Harker looked at Dude in confusion.

"When we go off-script, see if you can keep up."

Pete nodded his head as Rawdog and Felcher pulled the straps of their weapons over their head. Was it any coincidence that a guitar had as many strings a classic revolver? Dude thought not.

Over the P.A. system, a deep, manly voice pumped up the crowd. "And now, put your hands together for L.A.'s own Dude LaRude and the Lords of Chaos!"

All about, flashes of light swirled. The stadium rocked with strobing lights from the scoreboard to the LED displays encircling the upper bowl. Above, in the rafters, stood people who didn't make enough money to be anyone important, headsets in their ears as they swirled lights around, splashing expectant happy faces with blinding doses of light. If God came down from the heavens, this is what it would look like.

The funny, mousy, elf girl's hand counted down. 5… 4… 3… 2… 1… fist. Felcher hit his guitar like it had flushed his gear down the toilet, and the entire auditorium rang with distortion. Dude, with the microphone gripped in his fist, smiled as several children in the audience placed their hands over their ears. There were few moments in a person's lifetime they were bound to remember—their first ass-whupping, their first love, and the first time a guitarist hit you with a full blast of distortion like a sledgehammer to the brain.

The drums kicked in, the bass picked up, and Dude did as he was told. He sang the first song, *I Don't Belong*. Its mellow, driving rhythm lulled the crowd into a false sense of security. The song's catchy gang chorus was simple enough that people could sing along, and some of them did. It was revolting.

All around the world, in a hundred and ninety-nine countries, the sneering image of Dude LaRude belting out a modern version of a fifties pop song played on TVs, on phones, on laptops. In the crowd, a legion of lights reflected back at him as people recorded and livestreamed their experience, hoping to gain likes and followers, things with all the real-world cachet of a thumbs up from a stranger. What was it all for? At that moment, Dude became one with the song because it was true, he didn't belong.

Here, among the temporary heart of capitalism and the American dream, a brown boy from a broken home, from a broken race, sang about not belonging, and the people around him, mostly white faces who could afford the five-hundred-dollar tickets, soaked it up, living through him temporarily. But once the song ended and the lights came up, and the strobe lights and graphics stopped flickering, they would cross the fucking street to get away from him. Moms would clutch their purses. Children would hide their faces in their moms' skirts, and the men would reach for one of the many weapons strapped to their bodies. Perhaps one particular bitch, seeing him walk down the street, would pick up her phone and call the cops because he clearly didn't belong in her neighborhood, so he must be up to something— probably the theft of a catalytic converter or searching for a home for some proper, clandestine peeper masturbation. The cops would show up and tell him to get down on the ground, on the hot pavement that had been baking in the sun, and when he hesitated because he didn't want to burn himself, they would fill him full of lead, their body cams recording the whole thing for posterity. At the ensuing trial, the police would go free because the defense attorney would tell people how Dude did drugs, had loose sexual standards, and had needles on him. Probable cause. Plus, his skin was brown, and you know how that is.

Dude let the frustrations of the world flow through him, and for a moment he sold out. He basked in the glory of just giving in. Hell, he'd try anything once. But when the song finished, and Pete's drums fell dead, he found himself standing empty and broken.

The fingers in his mind swirled, and his thoughts shifted. He knew what to do next. Turning, he held up his own hand, as the mousy, elfin woman had done before. Starting at five, he began to count down. 5...4...3...2... middle finger.

Dude's temporary foray into selling out left him raw and angry. From his seat in New York, in a high-rise tower built on the backs of laborers who would die early because of all the wear and tear they put on their bodies, Donald Mint missed it all. Three naked prostitutes and a pile of cocaine, the only acceptable drug in Mint's opinion, tended to distract a man from their job. After the successful first half of song number one, he snorted away, dropped his pants, and went to town.

Meanwhile, in residential Ohio, Khalisee Sanchez-Aguilar had suffered through the first half of the Bouncy-Ball All-Star game, bored out of her mind. On her laptop, she spent the initial time trying to hack into the Department of Defense's confidential records, but when Dude came on, she closed the laptop and smiled, ready to take in the massive in-joke she had perpetrated upon the ridiculous world of sports. And then Dude sang I Don't Belong, and as so many people before her, she experienced letdown in a way only a teenager could feel. As Dude performed something more akin to a Good Charlotte song than actual punk rock, her heart fell. It was the same feeling youths throughout time had felt after their first-time voting, after their first paycheck, after their first child. But then he gave the finger, and Khalisee smiled. It wasn't Prince coming out with a guitar shaped like a giant dick and balls. It wasn't Janet Jackson's bare tit. But it was something, and then Khalisee's smile faded.

From under his leather jacket, Dude LaRude pulled a straight razor as he sang the opening bars of My Blood Made This Country. With a quick flick of the wrist, he sliced a line down his forearm, the skin parting like scored whale blubber. Blood splattered the shining Bouncy-Ball court. Another flick, and the other forearm opened. Through it all, Dude LaRude never missed a beat. Felcher shredded sloppy chords that sounded like nails being pounded into a skull. Rawdog hit them with a bassline that was the equivalent of unprotected sex, and Pete Harker, more a model than a musician, somehow tapped into the anger and frustration of the song, hitting people with machine gun drums that made every eardrum in the auditorium scream in pain.

"Redskin rugs! Burial ground drugs! Backstab hugs!" Dude screamed, his voice shredding as he moved across the court, spreading his blood in a pattern.

He ripped his clothes off, and parents in the stands covered their children's eyes, while being unable to cover their own. The TV cameras cut away, and in the NBC studios, they cut to a confused ex-athlete's face. "What the fuck is that?" he mouthed. But no one knew.

In the old days, that would have been the end of it. Dude LaRude's performance wouldn't have gone anywhere. It would have disappeared never to be seen again, like Fear's SNL performance, buried and hidden because it was a black eye, a reminder that some people couldn't be controlled. But this was today, the day of connection, the day where people seeing a man shooting guns, instead of running and hiding like any sensible person, would stand there and record, dollar signs spinning in their heads. And that's exactly what half the audience of the Bouncy-Ball

All-Star Game did. They livestreamed Dude LaRude as he tore into his flesh and sang his most anti-American song.

On the floor, his blood formed an image as he strutted back and forth, his genitals bouncing between his legs. First, he made one red line, then another at a thirty-degree angle. Around these two lines, he danced in a circle, echoing the dances of his forefathers as they moved around a fire, the feathers on their head and in their regalia flapping up and down as the drummers kept the beat. He repeated this twice.

Security, thinking this was all part of the show, and busy livestreaming the event themselves, stood and watched. They could have stopped it, could have made it all go away. But being a security guard doesn't pay all that much, and hey, if you can pump up the revenue stream of your side hustle, maybe they'd never have to tackle a bloody, naked Indian ever again. Besides, he was only hurting himself, right? America loves a self-starter.

Dude finished his circle, and then danced across the two lines making an inverted-V, bisecting them, and completing the anarchy symbol in the middle of the Bouncy-Ball court.

When the last drop of blood hit the court, and the line was complete, something magical happened—something otherworldly. A light seemed to burn through the anarchy symbol, crimson and bright. The symbol caught fire, flaring a jeweled red. Dude danced in the ruby flames as the second song ended and the band went immediately into Stop Raping Me So Nice, an ode to the American government and its politicians.

The red flames leapt up Dude's body, and suddenly, the people who had been so horrified at seeing a bleeding naked Indian, were happy as a pig in shit. How did they do that? Whoa! Cool! the people said. Dude continued his song, screaming and shouting, excoriating the government and the people who kept them in power. The flames climbed Dude's hairless body, crawling over the scars of religious repentance that crisscrossed his back, crawling up the track marks on his forearms, crawling across the pocked and soiled meat of his cock, singeing away the thick callouses and scar tissue of a heart broken day after day. He was consumed, and when he was gone, and his body was nothing but ashes, after only a few moments, the crowd gasped and oohed and aahed as if they had just seen the greatest magic trick in the world.

And then the ground began to crack and push upward, as if something was climbing out of the earth's depths.

How are they doing that? the crowd asked.

But it wasn't a trick. It wasn't CGI or holograms or any of the other technologies the media and Hollywood used to cover up the truth of the world. It was something else. Rawdog and Felcher knew what came next, had been privy to Dude's strange foresight, but they continued playing anyway. To stop now would be a disservice to Dude. Pete, high as fuck, thought he had smoked some shit laced with angel dust or bath salts or maybe something he'd never even heard of before, and he continued to drum like his life depended on it, not sure what was reality and what wasn't.

The Bouncy-Ball court pushed up, the boards breaking, and all the crowd could think was, Great. How much of a delay is this going to cause? Then the bulging mound disappeared, the boards falling away and plunging into the infinite drop of interdimensional travel. A great, clawed hand, fingernails black as night, gripped the edge of the hole. Rawdog and Felcher backed away, but Pete Harker stood and watched as a massive form emerged from the hole. Skin brown as coffee, body a collection of bruises, bumps, and masses of seething flesh, this being, this something, emerged from the hole, which had once been a Bouncy-Ball court, which had been covered in a blood-forged anarchy symbol by a man who seemed to no longer exist.

Some in the audience, valuing their lives more than new viewers, fled as its hideous head appeared. As it stretched its muscles, new waves of guitar distortion overlayered the music still wailing from Felcher's guitar. As it breathed its horrible breaths, and its heart beat, new thrumming bass sounds drowned out Rawdog's sexual rhythm. The being rose into the air, standing thirty feet in height. One of its great, black-tipped hands reached out and grabbed a security guard around the shins. Dragging the screaming man into the air, the being dangled the guard over its mouth like a gourmand with a penchant for anchovies, dangling a miniature, salty fish over his gullet. When it took a bite, half the security guard's body disappeared. The other half sailed through the air, spraying entrails, blood, and screams across the audience. Screaming, the upper half of the security guard's body flopped around in its mouth. Then, it took a bite. Its thousand-toothed mouth crunched the man to death even as the audience recorded. Every chew created a new rhythm, and when those thick, yellow teeth broke bones, they produced sounds like sticks hitting drums, only a thousand times louder. Together, the being's stretching, breathing, and feeding combined to perform the ultimate punk rock opus.

For every person who fled, three more stayed and recorded as people around them died and sacrificed themselves to the god of punk rock. Every livestream replicated the being's song. For every person who watched one of these livestreams, rapt and taken aback as something from a different dimension came through a portal opened by a Native American junkie who didn't even have a bank account, another portal was opened, another massive being came through, and created more punk rock, each song different, but eerily the same a story as old as The Ramones.

The feeding went on for hours, the livestreaming for even longer, and as word spread from town to town, as children Facetimed their followers, they told each other, "You've got to see this." And all around the world, people died, were consumed by their punk rock overlords.

DUDE LARUDE SINGS THE BLACK AND BLUES

EPILOGUE
NOTHING CHANGES

In the days after the emergence of the dark gods, chaotic beings who roamed the lands feeding off humanity, nothing much changed. The government, seeing an opportunity to thin the population, allowed the gods to roam free. The homeless and the poor didn't have much of a chance of escaping, and the unemployment rate fell drastically. The being in California was named Dude LaRude. Though at first, people had cursed his name, it wasn't long before the roaming demons became just another part of the world, like volcanoes spewing ash or the collection and accumulation of heavy metals in the soil. Thrill seekers walked right up to them, guiding camera drones to harass them like horseflies while they racked up new followers.

Corporations saw an opportunity, and it wasn't long before they sent their own army of drones after the demons, plastering them in advertisements, branding their skin with logos until they were nothing but walking billboards. This soul crunch brought to you by McDonald's.

While Donald Mint didn't last long as commissioner after the All-Star Game, the National Bouncy-Ball Association had finally achieved what it wanted. The major networks once again missed out on a ratings bonanza, but the All-Star Game, as it came to be known, became the most live-streamed event of this century. And when the league, after waiting an appropriate amount of time, finished up the All-Star Game, it was a smashing success, and everyone tuned in.

Every country around the world received a boost to their economy as they geared up for war with the demons and the military-industrial complex kicked into high gear. Tons of new jobs became available. Khalisee Sanchez-Aguilar even landed a job as the new head of tech security for the Bouncy-Ball Association! New weapons were developed to combat these otherworldly beings, and everything fell back into place despite the upheaval. Politicians vowed to rid the world of the demonic menace, and the divided government of the United States came together for a few brief moments. Then, when the Demonic Eradication Bills came up for a vote, they all fell apart as someone included something about abortion in one of them. After that, everything went back to normal. Humans can get along with anything if given a chance. Parasites are infinitely adaptable. This entire story, brought to you by Tastitos, the official tortilla chip of Dude LaRude.

NONE OF THIS IS REAL

Ruth LaRocca's walk turned existential about halfway through. As so often happened when she walked, an idea came to her out of nowhere, as if aliens above had beamed the thought straight down to her brain. From their spaceship to her brain… *None of this is real.*

She stopped on the sidewalk, the summer sun burning up the world. *I'm already dead.*

How else could you explain what was happening to her? What if aging wasn't a thing? What if it was how the dying mind coped with the fact that it was fading away? Ruth didn't really have high blood pressure. She wasn't really wrinkled. Her mind told her these things as the world decayed away to nothing.

Then it hit her. That's why the world is the way it is today. As time stretched on, the world as she knew it fell apart, crumbled in every way. Politics, general decency, the systems that bound the waking world together. In here, in her dying mind, these things would all degrade, because they weren't bound by reality. They were crafted according to her mind solely, and her mind was dying. It only made sense that some chinks would appear in the world she'd conjured.

Somewhere, she had existed, somewhere out there, a perfect copy of her physical body breathed its last breath. Aging didn't make sense. How could one go from young to old in the blink of an eye. One minute, she had been playing tag in her neighbor's backyard, and the next, she was walking down the street, trying to walk fast enough to get a sweat up to keep her heart working and prevent it from seizing up on her at some point.

Ruth stepped into the middle of the road and looked up and down to find she was alone. But of course, she had been alone in this world for so long. And then it clicked. That feeling of lonesomeness, of never being able to connect, was because she was the only real person in this particular universe, which was, in fact, only her mind.

She thought of the people she'd known in her life, starting with family and friends. They'd all died or aged or disappeared. Why would that be? How could that be?

Because her memories were going, fading away as somewhere in the real world, wherever that was, she was dying.

This moment, this unreal world around her, with its rebellions, its every-day murders, was nothing but the crumbling of her consciousness, devolving into alchemical anarchy.

Ruth stood on the sidewalk as the ramifications of her revelation ravaged her insides. It seemed to her the world shook, and though it was hot out and the sun baked down upon her, she couldn't make herself move from her spot in the middle of the road. To do so would be to buy in to this fake world, to turn her back on the truth that had been gifted to her.

Maybe not aliens. That was too bizarre. But maybe someone in the real world was calling to her, trying to bring her back to wherever reality was. Where her body functioned normally, where her tits didn't sag, and no one needed a colonoscopy or blood-pressure medicine.

If this world was all in her mind, then she ought to be able to control it. She peered down at the end of the road, tried to imagine something weird and bizarre, tried to will it into existence with her mind. A car turned down the street, a black SUV, the sun glinting off its windshield. It was too bright for her old eyes, and she tried to dim the world, darken it somehow, but in the end, she gave up and put a hand to her brow.

The SUV stopped, and Ruth tried to peer through the gleaming windshield to see who or what her mind had conjured. The vehicle honked at her, and she jumped, growing pissed at her own mind… if it was even her mind to begin with—but no, she couldn't go there. Not just yet.

She stuck up her middle finger, and the car zoomed around her, the driver in the seat hollering at her. "Get the fuck out of the road!"

Ruth channeled her rage into her fingers, made a gun with her hand, and fired away. Twenty feet down the road, the SUV exploded in a shower of metal, and Ruth fell on the ground. All around, people exited apartment buildings, came out to see what the hell had just happened.

She stood then, feeling guilty, and then it hit her. There's nothing to feel guilty for. She took her finger guns and aimed them at slackjawed figments of her imagination. One by one, she gunned them down with her mind, and they tumbled to the ground, blood gushing from their wounds.

A cheer of pure elation escaped her lips, a guttural thing, wordless because words were unnecessary now.

She began walking again. *Wait. I don't need to walk.*

She closed her eyes, which weren't real. In this darkness, she stood, imagining the crumbling walls of her home. When she opened them once more, her house stood before her, dandelions and other weeds crabbing up through the lawn. How long had she spent in this place trying to take care of the damn lawn? Out in the baking sun, with her back bent, pulling on weed after weed, and yet, they still came back... another sign not all was right in this world.

She bent down, trailing her hands along the stem of a sprouting bunch of crabgrass. Her lips pulled back from her teeth, as she hadn't yet severed her connection to her body, to the needs and habits she had developed in this nowhere place and nowhere time. The weeds caught fire, smoke rising. She choked on the smoldering fog, and then Ruth growled, making the weeds burn without smoke.

Inside the house, she found her family there, her husband, a good guy, but always... empty... because he wasn't real in the first place. Her child was there as well, and they both sat at the table watching her.

"Are you ok, Mom?"

This from her son, Mungo, a dumb name, a nickname given to him when he played sports. She put a hand to her head and groaned, all those moments of time wasted trying to get this thing, this figment, to become a worthwhile adult. But like everything in this dying world, in this piss-poor mental construct, he always went wrong in some way. He was inconsiderate. He never called. He never appreciated all the things she did for him. Why he was even here was beyond her.

But still, somewhere in her past, somewhere in the moments of forgotten and dimming memories, she remembered a joy there, real or imagined or created by her, she couldn't say, so when he talked to her, she didn't light him on fire like a weed.

"I'm fine dear. What are you doing here?"

Her husband, bald on top, his skin red because he refused to use sunscreen, spoke then, and his voice gave her rage. In their mundanity, they threatened to wipe away everything she had realized about the world, all the truths she'd discovered, and this is the curse of family. They twist, they pull, and they beg, and they always want more.

"Seems Mungo's in a bit of trouble," said her husband, his failing, rotting eyes dwindling to brown buttons floating in rheumy whites. It was the thyroid condition… which wasn't real.

Ruth lifted her head to the ceiling. "What is it now?" she growled.

"Seems he's been accused of…" Hs voice trailed off, and the truth in her mind wavered.

"I was drunk," Mungo began. "She's full of lies. I didn't do anything."

Ruth glared at him, and she knew this wasn't her son. How could it be? How could this monster be hers? All the time she'd spent raising him, and here he was, a nothing who continually fucked up his life. Her husband was no better.

"I'm done with you! Away!" she screamed, and they exploded into a shower of mist that couldn't touch Ruth or her skin.

The faint echo of Mungo screaming, "Moooooom!" before his body exploded echoed in her ear as nothing more than an annoyance.

"What have I been doing?" she screamed. "What have I been doing with this life of mine, this pitiful existence in a world that's not real in the first place?" She sat on the floor, wondering how to escape this world. *Where can I go?* Oh, she could remake this place in any image she wanted, but what was the point? What good was a perfect house and a perfect family if none of it was real. The time and effort needed to create such things—why, in the real world, the unseen one, she might now be breathing her last breath. Time was short.

Perhaps out there, she had a husband who was good and nice, who did things without having to be asked, who didn't sit around watching TV every evening, dulling his mind and her own. Then another thought came out of nowhere, slapped her across the jaw, challenging her to a duel of possibilities.

Why did her husband watch so much damn TV? If this world was hers to do with as she wished, why would he do that? No one wants that. No one wants to sit on their ass and watch other people do things. Something was interfering. It must be.

She sat down on the couch in her living room, warped it, shifted its being until it was a plush, cushiony, leather thing instead of the threadbare davenport she'd imagined for years. She picked up the remote, clicked it on.

A sitcom appeared on the screen, young people with simple problems. Mindless tripe, the type of stuff her husband—who wasn't really her husband but some sick joke she'd played on herself—loved.

"Fuck you," she growled at the TV.

The image twisted and swirled, and then came back to rest, as the two girls in the aprons kept scheming up ways to get money to build their cupcake shop. "Fucking cupcakes! No one would write this! No one would create something so banal and meaningless! This isn't what life is about. It can't be!"

Her verbal assault fuzzed the picture, made it roll like an old-timey TV. The picture disintegrated under her furor, and all that remained was the static. She'd read somewhere that static was an echo, a residual result of the big bang. That was another show her husband liked to watch, and fuck that one two, all those science nerds sitting around doing nothing, and people sitting around doing nothing while watching them do nothing, and on and on it went. Nothing to the infinite power.

"Ruth," the TV said. Her jaw fell open, as she was still tied to her body, still used it to show emotions because that's how she had communicated in this fake world with the fake people, with the nutjobs she'd created, who had poured forth from her brain like all the no good children of Kronos. Is this Tartarus? Is this my prison? Am I a god, hidden amongst mundanities?

"Ruth," the TV said.

"Is my name even Ruth?"

"Yes," the static said.

"And who are you?"

"That's unimportant now."

"Fuck you!" she screamed again. She was aware of repeating herself, but repeating herself was the only thing she knew to do. Why waste energy, why waste precious moments on creating new insults?

"Ruth!" the voice cajoled.

"Who the fuck are you?" Ruth screamed. She grabbed the remote control, pounded on the buttons in mystical combinations, as if there was some secret code that would unlock her own personal prison, this Everyday Tartarus.

"You're having an episode."

"An episode? Like that Two Girls, One Cupcake show?"

The TV laughed at her. "I have no idea what you're saying."

Ruth chucked the remote at the TV, watched it fade into the static, sinking like a triceratops into the La Brea Tarpits.

"Get me out of here!" she screamed.

"I can't. You have to get yourself out."

"I want out!"

"Well, that's the first step."

A thought crossed Ruth's mind, a mental butterfly flitting from flower to flower, collecting musings like pollen against its sticky legs. She rose off the plush, leather couch, strode forward to the TV. She pressed her face against it.

"You're not thinking correctly," the voice said.

She pressed against the screen, tried to force herself into the world from whence the voice came. "None of this is real," she murmured.

"If none of this is real, then what is real?" the voice asked.

"Don't play games with me, you cocksucker." For decades of her imagined life, she had never uttered something so crass to anyone, not out loud at least. It felt good; it felt real. Swearing was real, she fucking knew that. "I wanna be where you are."

"Only you can get you from there to here and there again."

Ruth picked up the TV, raised it above her head, and tossed it on the ground.

"Ruuuuuuth," the TV cooed.

She stomped on the thing, breaking it apart to find the insides were made of bits and bobs that made no sense to her, nonsense electronics that could do anything.

"There to here and there again," she said. "What is real?" she cried out in mental anguish.

She sank to the carpet, which she made disappear. Then the foundation of the house, then the pipes underneath, then the dirt, then the rocks, then the underground stream. "Why did I make so many layers?"

She made it all disappear and found herself floating in the core of what had once been the earth. Now it was nothing more than a seed floating in space. Stars and galaxies, and telecommunications satellites, and comets, and meteors. Ruth marveled at her abilities, at the complexity of her creation, and she understood then that the world was what she made it. But goddamn it, she was tired of making things, tired of putting the pieces together, of the crooked lines, of the flaws in her art. If they were perfect, if the colors didn't run, she could have sat there and gazed on her creation forever, enjoyed it for what it was.

She looked down at herself as the stars winked out of existence, studied the layers of her skin, the hairs, the fat, the muscle, the bone, the marrow, the atoms. Perfection eluded her, and she began ceaselessly to remake herself in her own image, for she was her own god and ought to be able to perfect her form. If she could do that, if she could do this one thing, then maybe it would all be worth it.

Her flesh stretched, turned more elastic. She felt her face with her newly smoothed hands, her liver spots obliterated with a thought. She took the loose skin of her neck, ripped it off like Jack Dalton in that *Roadhouse* movie her imperfect husband had loved so much. She smoothed the remaining skin down, reached into her chest and took out her heart, ripping out all the veins and arteries with it. She held it up to her mouth like a conch shell, and after smoothing the wrinkles from her lips with the back of one hand, she blew into it, sprayed the fat clogging her arteries and veins into the void. She replaced her fresh heart in her chest.

She ran her hand through her thinning hair, gone gray and stiff, and she forced life from her brain into the strands, felt them start waving in space. She grabbed her breasts and squeezed and mushed them till they were firm and perky. On and on she continued, changing herself, molding herself into the image she thought she wanted, and when she was done, she made a planet appear, a planet made of water, deep and blue. She tossed a sun into the sky to reflect off her new body, and in the deep, wavy waters of this new planet, she studied her reflection, found a stranger staring back at her. "Arghhh!" she screamed, her voice reverberating throughout the cosmos she'd invented. "I look like one of those cupcake bimbos!"

Ruth dashed away the world, dashed away the sun, and sat formless and floating in nothing.

Her memories, meaningless and faded, paraded through her head, and around her, she crafted little scenes, like when she remembered making a diorama for her second-grade science class. Only these were worse, bare bones cardboard people, cheap backgrounds made from poorly cut construction paper and torn up cotton balls.

There, being born.

There, being taught.

There, being twisted, made to be what she needed to be.

There, dreaming of falling in love.

There, sex. Lots of sex, some of it good.

There, a child, a hope, and a dream.

Here, nothing. It was all worthless.

There, the end.

Ruth understood now, knew the words on the TV had been right, not the ones from those big bang fucks or the cupcake bitches, but the ones from the staticky voice. There, to here, to there. *It's all progression. It's all one thing after another.*

Juggling, moving through life, making this happen, then that happen, then this.

She took a deep breath of void, cleared her throat, and hocked a thick loogie. Contained within were all the expectations, all the needs and wants of others. It blossomed from her as a massive bubble and grew, swirling and brown. It was all the shit she'd been fed, all the crap forced down her throat, and Ruth felt infinitely better with it out of her system.

For the first time in her life, Ruth stood on the edge of infinity, on the edge of understanding the universe. Then she closed her lidless eyes, turned inward, allowed herself to rise above the bubble of filth they had pumped into her mouth, her ears, her nose, her vagina. She came to the ultimate answer, stumbled upon it in the truth of nowhere.

There, here, there. There was the next place. She would break the cycle. Only one way to break it really. She would take her ass to the next world. She pinched her mind shut, made it go away, pulled the electric spark that was her into the void, held it in her hand long enough to realize how beautiful it was at its most basic. Then she let it go, tossed it into the abyss, and became what she was meant to be. Just herself. Just a being, no name, no needs, no nothing. From there to here, to nowhere. Ruth escaped her prison.

ACKNOWLEDGEMENTS

As I mentioned in the foreword, I am impatient. As such, I have never written acknowledgements in any of my other works as I am quite often ready to move onto my next book when one is finished. But I suppose I owe each one of these stories, these poor unloved bastards, a word or two before I put them in the grave and move onto 2024.

ACKNOWLEDGEMENT OF YOUR LAND ACKNOWLEDGEMENT

If you're ever lucky enough to see me read live (maybe unlucky enough?), this will be what I lead off with… it makes me laugh in a sarcastic but serious way. It also drives all the people who don't know what they're in for out of the room. If you can't handle this one, you can't handle any of what's to come after. The story is a response to a time when the school district I work for crafted this horrid land acknowledgement to be read at every staff meeting. We have a lot of staff meetings. Over time, I could see my white colleagues just sort of fade into a daze as they were forced to read the words every single week on Tuesdays at four p.m. This was, of course, quite different from my reaction, as the horror of being talked about like we don't even exist hit me every time. As with most routines not actually believed in, the school district's land acknowledgement fell by the wayside, but the horror remains for me.

WHATEVER DIES, STAYS

This was a story I wrote for a submission call about people who choose to not leave a horrible situation. The anthology is called "Why Didn't You Just Leave?" Must be some good stories in there, because I'm super proud of Whatever Dies, Stays. It made it to the final round of cuts, and the editors were kind enough to send me a personalized rejection. I love the story. Makes me tear up every time I get to the end. My cat's getting older, and sometimes, you just see it happening, and that's where this story comes from.

A CHEMAWA THANKSGIVING

All these next five stories were written for my reading at Rose City Book Pub, entitled, "Not Thankful: A Night of Indigenous Horror." My reading at the book pub was sort of… unplanned. I had gone to see Carson Winter read from his latest book Posthaste Manor. (Highly recommended, by the way. Carson is an awesome writer.) While I was sitting there, drinking beers and enjoying Carson's reading, I couldn't help but think, with the confidence of someone who had just sold a book to a publisher and was a few beers deep, I can do that. Wouldn't that be fun?

So, after the reading, as everyone is hanging out, I approach the owner and ask, "How does one sign up for a reading here?"

Elise, the owner of the pub, pulls out a paper calendar and says, "Oh, it's real easy. You pick a date and sign up."

She begins flipping through the calendar, and I, filled with an over-exuberant confidence I normally lack, go ahead and pick the only date available in the next month… Black Friday. Now, at the time, this seemed like an excellent idea. When I woke up the next day, it seemed less so. It only gave me four weeks to write and practice these stories. Of course, I put it off for a couple of weeks… meaning, all the things I wrote for this reading were written in the span of two weeks.

Chemawa Thanksgiving is a piece I wrote about Thanksgiving, not my favorite holiday, and one filled with bitterness for the Indigenous people I know. My sister sent me a text a couple of weeks before my reading asking why our family celebrated Thanksgiving, and this story came from that idea.

It's based on real deaths from the Chemawa Indian Training School. The circumstances are fictionalized, but some of the names are real ones I found on a list of Indigenous people who died at the school.

Victor Davis, a member of the Confederated Tribes of Siletz, died on December 18, 1918. He was the last of twenty-three children and adults to die in a three-month period due to Spanish flu at the Chemawa Indian Training School, as it was known then. In all, at least 270 Indigenous children have died at the school, some on campus, some sent home to breathe their last breaths. Of course, the true number will never be known, as many of the students sent to the school were orphans, forgotten voices in unmarked graves. The last to die was a girl named Rosie, another Siletz tribal member, who was found intoxicated on campus, and subsequently locked in a detention area. She passed away of alcohol-poisoning on August 8, 2016.

THE PRETENDIANS

If you're like, "real" Indigenous, you'll find that when certain people discover this, they love to tell you about their grandmother or grandfather who was part whatever-tribe. It gets old.

I first heard the phrase Pretendians in a social media post from Shane Hawk. The phrase makes me laugh. As with most groups, there are always those who fit in and those who don't. While traditionally Pretendians has been a phrase aimed at people who aren't Indigenous enough, I sort of played with it and turned it on its head to highlight the phenomenon of white folks who claim Indigenous ancestry, though they know nothing about the culture, or just happen to have some Native Blood on their Ancestry.com report. I never actually read this one at my reading, but I'll read it next time!

THE OMEGA WOMAN

It will happen sooner or later. The last Native American will walk the earth. It will be a sad day, but hopefully, there are worlds after these, and the sadness will become something else. Hopefully, that day will be long in the future.

SEE ME

Murder is the third leading cause of death for Native women (Native Hope website). FBI's National Crime Info Center says that 5,491 Indigenous women are missing. The number is most likely larger than that. The Bureau of Indian Affairs estimates there are currently 4,200 missing and unsolved murders of Indigenous people, mostly women. This story is a call for help, a call for people to do something about the disparity in resources allotted to finding missing Indigenous women as opposed to missing white women. Race shouldn't matter when someone is in danger. All should be seen.

SCUZZPISH

I live in Oregon. In Portland, I have no problems blending in, for the most part. When I go out into the country areas, I am always on guard and looking out for threats, as there are more closed-minded people out in the more rural areas. It's still pretty safe, compared to some places in the country, but that threat is always there if you're a person of color.

Scuzzpish is half-real, half-made up. The first half, at the bar, is all real. It happened when my wife and I popped into a bar in the small town of Oakridge. No kidding, Kip is a real dude. Scuzzpish was real graffiti sprayed on the wall, and this is what my mind came up with to explain the name. So, respect to the real Scuzzpish, whoever or whatever it may be.

hAIck

As AI conversations became big talk among writerly circles, I dug within myself and discovered I hate AI, in all its forms. Turns out, other writers/publishers hate it too, so much so, they were willing to put together a benefit magazine called Thank You For Joining the Algorithm. This story was my submission, and it didn't make the cut, but I like the fuck out of it, so I included it here.

For those wondering why I dislike AI, it's not the whole "shortcuts for the untalented" aspect of it I despise, though that is a factor. Rather, the idea that we, as a society, could possibly get any dumber is what leaves me quaking in my Sambas. Take away the need for people to think, to create, to actually sit down and figure out how to turn their thoughts into reality, and we become simpler. Easier is not better. Struggle makes us human. This is why so many people who have never had to struggle become such monsters. AI will do the same to us if given a chance.

SIEG HAIR

When I was a young lad, I would attend punk rock shows in a place called La Luna, a sweaty, jampacked club in Portland, Oregon. Sometimes, these Nazi pieces of shit would come in and start throwing kung fu kicks and intimidating everyone. Being one of the few people of color in this scene, I didn't understand how these pieces of garbage weren't swarmed and stomped into oblivion, as that was my initial reaction upon seeing swastika armbands around their biceps. I understand now that not everyone has it in them to stand up and confront hate, so it is up to those of us who can, to keep doing it, so that others may follow. Still, the experience was traumatic for me, eye-opening in a scary way. I can still remember keeping my distance from them, while resisting the urge to start something. Youth is dumb. Sieg Hair is what I would have liked to have done… but I feel the results would have been the same for me as for poor Daniel.

NOSTALGIA KILLS

This was my submission for an anthology all about mall horror. I can't remember the name of it, and honestly, I thought the premise was a little… er… lame. But I wrote a submission anyway, as I was in the midst of trying to help out a writing client figure out how to sell short stories, and being a novelist myself, I needed that short story experience. So, I fired up my laptop and wrote this story.

It's inspired by the local mall in Portland, Oregon—Lloyd Center, a three-story monstrosity on the verge of bankruptcy because we all sit on our ass and order whatever we need online. Its days are numbered, which is a shame. Being a child of the '80s and '90s, I grew up in malls, can still remember the smells of it, the sounds of fountains (needlessly wasteful) running nonstop, the gleam of coins in the chlorinated waters, forgotten wishes, always appearing closer than they actually were.

As North Portland has been transformed through the horrors of gentrification, rents have gone up, affordable housing has been torn down to create hideous, high-priced, modern apartment buildings, and the people who need the mall, appreciate the mall, have been forced out of the city. For the poor, sometimes just walking and looking is an activity in and of itself. People with money, people who move into poor neighborhoods to buy up cheap homes and "slum it" while raising the property values of the surrounding land, and consequently the property taxes, don't really need mall crap. Lloyd Center will go the way of the dinosaur any day now. Sad really.

THE NEW GOD

I'm not quite sure where this story came from. I have no recall of ever coming up with the idea. It just sort of appeared, like The New God itself. A love letter to the city of Pittsburgh, which I would totally live in, The New God follows the route I took one snowy day in January 2020 when I was visiting the city to attend some Pittsburgh Penguins games. I love the city, and the characters within are characters I met in real life. The places are actually places I went. Sorry to destroy the city, but you can't control gods. They will do as they please.

URL'OOZR'S JANITOR

This one sort of makes me chuckle. All the Indigenous people I know have this sort of self-destructive streak within, and with this story, mine came out. Someone had put out a submission call for some cosmic anthology. Whatever. It was unoriginal and bland, and I thought it was stupid, so I sent them this story, which took shape as soon as I came up with the name of my dark god. I still giggle about it.

It did not make the anthology's editors laugh, and it was the quickest rejection I've ever received. Amazing really. I don't regret a thing. Sometimes self-destruction is more fun than self-improvement... most times really.

DUDE LARUDE SINGS THE BLACK AND BLUES

Believe it or not, I dreamed this story. I don't mean like in a figurative, symbolic way. I mean, I actually saw Dude LaRude in my head, stripping off his clothes and horrifying a crowd as he destroyed himself. I added the stuff about the interdimensional punk rock gods later, after I had awakened, sometime after I leaned forward with my feet on the floor and my head in my hands, muttering, "What the hell is wrong with your brain?" Nothing! There's nothing wrong with it! Some of us just have weird dreams, ok?

I submitted Dude to a couple of places, which he wouldn't have liked, because he's all DIY and "fuck the system" and honestly, this bizarre slice of interdimensional punk rock terrorism was never going to hit with any publishers… but that's not why I write things. I write them because, well, sometimes you just have to get the poison out.

NONE OF THIS IS REAL

For most of my stories, there's like this big, interesting backstory. This one was simply a "What If?" moment that happened to me while out on a walk. The idea that one could realize that nothing around us is, in fact, real has been done before, but this is my version of it. I submitted it once, and then just filed it away.

Anyway, these stories were my 2023 in writing. These stories were birthed from my brain and shown to the publishing gods, only to be rejected. I love every one, and though they were stillborn, I lay them in the grave with fond memories of the small time we spent together. On top of this mass grave, I lay my keyboard and my heart. Rest in peace, little stories, and may the memory of you live on. Onto 2024!

THE MONOLOGIST
BY AQUINO LOAYZA

What's life without risk?

At least that's what Patrick Gallagher tells himself as he arrives in Las Vegas at the peak of the Cold War with a dream that can't be bought in gold or jewels: To become a standup comedian, a monologist. But nobody can run away from their past, no matter how bright their future may seem. The world isn't as clear as it appears. Will Patrick succeed? Or will he discover that everything has its price and some costs can't be quantified in a dollar bill?

In this queer revolutionary imagining of 1963 Las Vegas, Aquino Loayza, Author of the Queer Cosmic Epic: Deep, explores the seedy underbelly of Sin City in its infancy as Patrick Gallagher embarks on his quest to defy the odds and become The Monologist.

PHOTO © JACY MORRIS 2024

ABOUT THE AUTHOR

Jacy Morris is an Indigenous horror author (a registered member of the Confederated Tribes of Siletz) and a member of the HWA. To date, he has written over twenty novels, including the This Rotten World series, the One Night Stand at the End of the World series, and various other works of horror and weirdness. He is an avid fan of punk rock and horror movies and tries to work this knowledge into his stories. He lives in Portland, Oregon where he works as an English teacher, a writing coach, and an author.